Bar

D1138904

I have something to tell you

Susan Lewis is the internationally bestselling author of over forty books across the genres of family drama, thriller, suspense and crime – including the novel *One Minute Later*, which was a Richard and Judy pick. She is also the author of *Just One More Day* and *One Day at a Time*, the moving memoirs of her childhood in Bristol during the 1960s. Following periods of living in Los Angeles and the South of France, she currently lives in Gloucestershire with her husband James, and mischievous dogs, Coco and Lulu.

To find out more about Susan Lewis:

www.susanlewis.com
www.facebook.com/SusanLewisBooks
@susanlewisbooks

Also by Susan Lewis

SUSAN LEWIS

I have something to tell you

HarperCollins*Publishers*

HarperCollins*Publishers* Ltd
The News Building
1 London Bridge Street
London SE1 9GF

www.harpercollins.co.uk

HarperCollins*Publishers*
1st Floor, Watermarque Building, Ringsend Road
Dublin 4, Ireland

Published by HarperCollins*Publishers* 2021

2

A catalogue record for this book
is available from the British Library

ISBN: 978-0-00-828698-9 (HB)
ISBN: 978-0-00-828699-6 (TPB)
ISBN: 978-0-00-847793-6 (US)
ISBN: 978-0-00-848543-6 (CA)

Typeset in Sabon LT Std by Palimpsest Book Production Ltd,
Falkirk, Stirlingshire

Printed and bound in the UK using
100% Renewable Electricity by CPI Group (UK) Ltd

MIX
Paper from
responsible sources
FSC C007454
www.fsc.org

This book is produced from independently certified FSC™ paper
to ensure responsible forest management.

For more information visit: www.harpercollins.co.uk/green

CHAPTER ONE

'Suspected wife-killer, line two.'

Jay Wells looked up from the papers covering her desk, surprised that Vikki, her trusty and irreverent assistant, had come into the office to announce a call, when she usually buzzed through or even shouted from her desk which was right outside in the senior partner's reception area.

'Detective Inspector Ken Bright,' Vikki elaborated. 'Not that he's offed his Mrs, you understand. He's arrested someone who has, and apparently they're asking for you.'

Jay sank back into her capacious leather chair and shifted her thoughts from intense to receptive. Tall, long-legged, with wavy blonde hair halfway down her back and, according to her husband, Tom, the most indecently come-to-bed blue eyes, she wasn't a typical-looking criminal defence solicitor, but there again, who was? At forty-two she was joint head of the law firm, Bamfield and Forster, that her father, now deceased, had started in these very offices at the heart of Bristol's legal district some thirty years ago. Her partner and life-long close friend, Perry Forster, handled all their family law cases, while she and her team dealt exclusively in crime. Since she'd earned herself an impressive reputation under her father's tuition, it wasn't unusual for a detainee to request her by name.

Vikki, with her plump, cherry cheeks and mauve hair was saying, 'I've taken all the details so I'll log it with the DSCC while you speak to everyone's favourite DI.'

Jay nodded and, draining what was left of her coffee, she reached for the phone. 'Ken, how are you?' she asked cheerily when he answered. She had a lot of time for this detective in spite of all the rings they'd run around one another over the years. He was good at his job, thorough, direct, possessed a very low tolerance for BS and treated her with more respect than many of his colleagues managed to summon for females in general, lawyers in particular.

'I'm good,' he replied. 'I hope you are too. I guess Vikki's told you why I'm calling. Has she given you the lowdown yet?'

'She's allowing you the pleasure.'

'OK. Suspect's name is Edward Blake; thirty-nine; arrested at his home in South Gloucestershire about an hour ago on suspicion of killing his wife. We're holding him at Keynsham custody.'

Opening her calendar, Jay was thinking it was lucky for Mr Blake that she wasn't in court today, or at a prison, or briefing a barrister, or too tied up with one of the hundred or more other demands on her time that would prevent her from going to his aid. 'OK, looking at my schedule,' she said, 'I can probably move a couple of things around and be over there by three, four at the latest. How does that sound?'

'It'll work, if it's the best you can do.'

'Before you go, why not fill me in on the victim, how she died, when it happened, why you think he did it?'

'I've given it all to Vikki, but in brief: Vanessa Blake,

2

aged thirty-eight. Bound to a bed and suffocated with a pillow at her home last night.'

'Any other suspects?'

'None so far.'

'Any in mind?'

'It's ongoing.'

Ringing off, Jay looked up as Vikki returned to the doorway. 'OK, tell me what you've managed to find out about this Edward Blake,' she said, knowing that Vikki would have gone straight to Google the instant she put DI Bright through, only detouring for a moment to call the duty solicitor's call centre to obtain the necessary case reference number.

'Well, he doesn't seem to be your typical slasher, shooter or stabber. Or suffocator, come to that.'

Vikki had a way with words.

'And you've reached that conclusion, because?'

'He's an architect/property developer with nothing suspicious about him that I could find. He's only on Instagram as far as I can tell, none of the others, and his feed comprises mainly before-and-after pics of the old barns and farmhouses that he's renovated or converted. Much the same for the wife, in that their accounts are more professional than personal. She's . . . I guess you'd call her a promoter, or agent, for photographers and artists, and her posts are mainly of her clients' work. A couple of her with hubby and various friends. They both have a hundred or so followers each, and it's been a few weeks since either of them uploaded anything. She has a gallery called Picture This in Chipping Sodbury, same address as her husband's office. Oh, and she's also the daughter of some distant cousin of the Beauforts – as in dukes of. I'll send it all over before you leave.'

'OK,' Jay responded thoughtfully. Then, circling back to where she'd been before Bright's call, said, 'Let me know when Perry's out of his meeting, will you? And can you dig out the toxicology report on the Felix Sanders debacle and send it to my inbox. I don't seem to have it.'

As Vikki saluted and returned to her desk, Jay texted her eighteen-year-old daughter, Livvy, and husband Tom to let them know there was a chance she'd be late home this evening – murder interrogations often went on into the night. And indeed for many days after that. She'd already sent the message before remembering that Tom – a Queen's Counsel and joint head of Brunel Chambers, not a stone's throw from her office – was at Plymouth Crown Court today. This meant he probably wouldn't be back much before seven himself. Still, there was plenty in the fridge for Livvy to snack on when she came in from school, or dance class, or wherever she was today – and with A levels on a close horizon she'd no doubt spend most of the evening revising.

Finally, armed with what she needed for the interview at Keynsham custody, Jay left the office and headed for The Grand Hotel on Broad Street where she, Perry and Tom had use of the secure parking. On the way she passed by Tom's chambers, where she waved out to Ron who manned the street-level reception, and greeted a number of other advocates going to and from the Crown Court on Small Street. It was a dry though dull day, with no random spurts of sunshine to brighten the cobbled alleyways that linked the narrow streets, although the entire district, from the ancient city wall to the landmark Corn Exchange, was as resplendent as ever in its proud and dubious history.

4

Once in the car she took the Bath Road out of town, busying herself on the phone as she went, needing to stay on top of her workload, especially with a Lexcel audit coming up at the end of the week. And if she was about to acquire an alleged murderer as a client, it might not leave her with as much time for other cases as she'd like to give – murders rarely did. Unless Edward Blake was going to plead guilty, of course, but that certainly hadn't been the impression either she or Vikki had got so far. If he didn't, and the case looked as though it might prove time-consuming and complicated, there were two other fully qualified solicitors on her crime team with excellent backup of their own, so it would only be a matter of briefing them to take over her other cases where and when it might prove necessary.

By the time she'd got held up in traffic on Brislington Hill – always to be relied upon – and reached the end of the Keynsham bypass, she was just about ready to give full attention to her new client. A murder of this sort – domestic, landed gentry (according to Vikki), no known history (as yet) of violence – was rare and might make a welcome change to the desperate and often dangerous individuals she usually dealt with.

As she came to a stop at the Police Centre her phone was ringing and, seeing it was Tom, she clicked on.

'Did you finish early?' she asked.

'No, a juror's just chucked up, would you believe? It's a gory case. How come you're going to be late home?'

'Thirty-nine-year-old male accused of killing his wife.'

'Habitual abuser?'

'I don't think so.'

'Drugs?'

'No mention of them yet. Have you heard from Charlie today?' She was referring to their twenty-one-year-old son, who was about to sit his finals at Exeter.

'No. Was I supposed to?'

'Just wondered if he'd finished ribbing you about your spectacular defeat on the rugby field yesterday.'

'OK, I don't need you both rubbing it in,' he groaned, although she knew how much he loved the 'dads and lads' games at the university sports ground, win or lose. 'Do you want me to make you some supper?'

'That would be lovely.' There was a time when she'd have added, *and I'll find a special way to repay you.* And he'd probably say, *Well, we both know how I love your special ways.* Or something equally as corny, and maybe one of these days they'd return to that easy flirtation.

After he'd rung off, she sat for a moment, taking a breath to steady herself past the wretched memories that had suddenly left-sided her; memories that could absolutely not be allowed to distract her over the next few hours. Affairs, she'd learned the hard way, never really went away, any more than trust ever truly came back, and they had a treacherous habit of wrongfooting a person at the worst possible moments.

Two years, he'd been involved with another woman before Jay had found out.

Two years.

That wasn't just cheating, it was sustained betrayal.

He'd given his mistress up as soon as the relationship came to light, but though Jay had worked hard on trying to forgive him, as much for the children's sake as her own, she knew that no amount of time was ever going to allow her to forget.

A further three years had passed since that terrible low in their marriage, and still not a day went by when she didn't think about it and ask herself if she'd done the right thing in allowing him to stay. Worse were the times when she wondered if he regretted his decision to put his family first? He'd sworn he'd never intended to leave them but, even if that were true, Jay felt certain the other woman had expected it, or must surely, at the very least, dreamt of it.

Her name was Ellen Tyler. She was a public relations executive of some sort whom Tom had met during a trial at Southwark Crown Court, and apparently she was married too. Jay had no idea where she lived, although presumed it was London, and nor did she know if Mr Tyler had ever found out about the affair. She only hoped that if he had it hadn't devastated him as much as it had her. Maybe he didn't care enough to have let it bother him, or maybe he'd walked out on the marriage leaving Mrs Tyler to conduct as many affairs as she pleased – or even to try and pick up again with Tom.

Jay had no way of knowing for certain if Tom had been in touch with Ellen Tyler since he'd broken things off, although he swore he hadn't been. Jay had decided to believe him because if she didn't there wouldn't be any point in trying to save their marriage.

Oh Tom, she sighed silently to herself, *it might have been so much easier if I'd only found a way to stop loving you.*

Checking to see who was trying to call her, she quickly connected to DI Ken Bright. 'Hi, I just got here,' she told him, asserting her professionalism front and centre.

'Great,' he responded. 'Lacey Hamble is going to fill you

in. I've had to come back into town, but I'll be with you by five at the latest. I think you'll find your new client . . .' he took a moment to summon the word, 'interesting.'

'In what way?'

'You'll see,' and he was gone.

CHAPTER TWO

Jay was buzzed through to the custody area where she found Detective Sergeant Lacey Hamble waiting for her, all fuzzy curls and blazing green eyes.

'Hi Lacey,' she smiled, giving a brief wave to one of the custody sergeants, 'sorry if I kept you.'

'No problem,' Hamble retorted snappishly. 'DI Bright's had to go back to Bristol . . .'

'It's OK, I've spoken to him. You're going to bring me up to speed.'

Gesturing for Jay to follow, the detective, a surly, over-weight woman in her mid-forties with a famously disastrous love life and mean chip on her shoulder, led her to a consultation room and left the door open as they sat either side of a steel table.

'I take it you have all the basics – name, address, date of birth,' Lacey began, passing over a copy of same.

Responding to Jay's nod she moved swiftly on to the more relevant aspects of why they were there.

As Jay listened with an attentive ear, putting a case scenario together in her mind, albeit from the detective's perspective, it took her next to no time to conclude that Hamble would like the suspect to stop wasting everyone's time and cough to the crime. In fact, she took a moment to say, 'He did it.'

Jay nodded in an interested way. 'And you know that because?' she prompted mildly.

Hamble tapped the side of her nose. 'Trust me. It might not be written all over him, but it's stamped right the way through him.'

Jay wanted to laugh, but managed not to. Nor did she bother reminding Hamble of past instances when that Sherlock nose of hers had followed the wrong scent. She didn't want to belittle the woman, and besides, they'd all misread people in their time.

As the briefing continued, Jay made notes on the pad in front of her, taking in the circumstances of how Vanessa Blake's body had been found – at her home, attached to a bed by wrists and ankles using leather stirrup straps, naked, pillow over face, unmistakable signs of a struggle. She was believed to have died some time yesterday evening – awaiting pathologist's report; husband called it in early this morning. Said he didn't know she was there until then. No other suspects at this time.

Apparently deciding she'd revealed enough for now, Hamble went to inform the custody sergeant that Edward Blake could be brought from the cells.

As she waited, Jay made a quick scan of her notes before putting aside all Hamble's presumptions, judgements and need for a quick result.

Time now to assess events as told by Mr Blake.

Hearing footsteps approaching she rose from her chair and wondered briefly what DI Bright thought she was going to find 'interesting' about her new client.

Her first sight of him didn't exactly answer the question, although he certainly wasn't typical of the type she was more used to championing, those unfortunate enough to have been born into poverty and crime. This man had presence and an air of sophistication that, while striking, didn't, at this point, give off the sense of entitlement or arrogance that she'd half-expected from someone of his background. His clothes – black tracksuit bottoms, a pale blue polo shirt, leather trainers – were clearly of good quality, and his darkly fair hair was a style of its own with the odd wave here and there, and its own way of tumbling onto forehead and collar. His finely sculpted features made him handsome in a conventional way, although not outstandingly so, and his eyes, always an important gateway to someone's character, were arrestingly blue. Right now she could see fear and confusion beyond their natural shrewdness, and the paleness of his complexion spoke to how unsure of himself he was, which would do him no harm considering where he was.

'Mr Blake,' she said, holding out a hand to shake. 'I'm Jessica Bamfield Wells, but please call me Jay.'

Although he was taller than her, and broader, he didn't use his size to assert or intimidate as some in his position did, wanting to show who was the boss in this new relationship.

A good start.

'Thank you for coming,' he said, his voice steady and quiet and his grip firm, although she was getting a better sense now of how shaken he was. He was probably used to hiding his feelings, as so many were from his sort of world – rarely easy clients to deal with, although in truth, few were.

As they sat down across the table from one another she waited for his eyes to come to hers, not wanting to rush him, needing to take things at his pace, at least for now. Sometimes – usually – clients facing such serious charges were agitated, frightened, talking non-stop, declaring their innocence or reasons why the police might think they were guilty when 'no fucking way' were they. They came up with alibis, illnesses, other suspects, cop-persecution. She'd heard it all, but right now she wasn't hearing anything from Edward Blake.

Eventually he looked at her, but seemed distant, distracted, as if not fully engaging with where he was. For a strange moment she felt herself go weak and almost wanted to walk away from this, have no more to do with it, but that made no sense and, even if she did, what excuse would she give?

'OK,' she said, adopting a gently forceful tone to try to bring his attention into focus, 'I'm going to begin by asking you some general questions about what's happened. This is simply for me to get an idea of timeline, circum-stances and what you might have said at the scene prior to being brought here.' She knew already, from Hamble, that they hadn't wasted much time in arresting him, and nor had he spoken since, which meant that he'd at least responded correctly to the caution. She just hoped he hadn't managed to incriminate himself in some way before things had got that far. 'I can't stress strongly enough,' she continued, 'how important it is for you to tell me the truth. We could have a long road ahead of us, and if we're going to travel it together there will be no room for anything but honesty if I'm to help you. Do you under-stand what I'm saying?'

He nodded, clasped his hands together on the table, and stared at them as if they might not even be his. She noticed how strong and elegant they were, but also rugged, as though not unfamiliar with manual work. She was already curious to know what else he was besides an architect, property developer, husband and murder suspect. Was he a father? A son? A brother? A lover?

There was no rush. He hadn't been charged and during the upcoming interrogation she would probably get to know more about him than he might tell her right now.

At last his blue gaze seemed to focus on her, albeit in a way that felt disconcertingly direct, until she realized he might be seeing right through her to something else entirely. 'I'm sorry,' he said, 'I'm having a hard time getting to grips with it all. It's happened so fast . . .' He shook his head.

'It's OK,' she soothed, 'just take your time.' She was used to clients struggling to find words to describe their experiences, especially when shock was preventing the brain from catching up with it all.

His hands tightened their hold on each other as he said, 'It's hard to know where to start, but I guess it should be when I arrived home last night?'

She nodded encouragement. It seemed as good a place as any.

Taking a breath, he said, 'When I got in I thought I was alone in the house. Vanessa, my wife, had gone to London in the morning – I dropped her at the station. We went to Chippenham – she prefers to take the train from there, it makes the journey shorter, she says. Sometimes, when she returns and I pick her up, we stop at a pub on the way home for a bite to eat.' He stared off into the distance, presumably seeing favourite tables and wine lists, friends maybe, log fires, tender, laughing eyes.

Coming back to the moment, he said, 'This time she was – I thought she was – staying overnight with a friend, Melissa Siddall. They've known each other since school. She doesn't always stay the night when she goes to London, but if she does I don't really expect her to call. I think they drink a lot of champagne and maybe meet up with other friends. It's girl time, something that's important to her, and I understand that.'

His eyes closed and Jay noticed he'd started to shake, only slightly, but it suggested that the horror of it all was trying to overwhelm him – and he was doing his best to suppress it.

'I had no idea,' he said, 'that she was in the house when I got home. There was nothing to say she was back – no sounds of any kind. I suppose I didn't look to see if her coat and shoes were . . . I still don't know . . .' He broke off and put a hand to his head, as though to steady himself. 'If I'd known she was upstairs . . . Maybe I could have saved her. Or I'd have called 999, but I-I didn't know, so I carried on as I normally would. I went on into the house, to the kitchen . . . I think I put on the news, I can't be sure, but I usually do. Channel Four repeat at eight o'clock. I made myself an omelette . . . Oh Christ,' he groaned, pressing both hands to his head, apparently finding the thought of being able to eat when his wife was upstairs dead utterly abhorrent.

Jay watched him carefully, knowing from DS Hamble that he was claiming not to have found his wife's body, in a guest room, until this morning. If that was the truth then it meant he'd spent the night with her very close by and in terrible circumstances and having no idea of it. It could also mean that someone else had been in the house prior to his return, had perhaps even still been there after he'd come in, and had somehow managed to leave without being spotted.

It seemed unlikely, but she'd come across far more implausible scenarios that had turned out to be true.

However, she could see why Hamble might be having a problem with this. There again, Hamble wasn't known for her imagination, or readiness to tolerate an anomaly, and presuming DI Bright hadn't been on the scene at the time of arrest – senior investigating officers and their deputies weren't assigned with immediacy – Hamble had apparently gone off like she was at a January sale grabbing the star bargain before anyone else could.

'I texted her around eleven,' Blake said, 'to say good-night. Then I went to bed. I had no idea she was in one of the guest rooms. There was no reason for me to think it, because why would she be? We never use those rooms ourselves. Only friends or family or the cleaner ever go in.'

Jay said, 'Did anything happen in the night to wake you? Such as the sound, maybe, of someone leaving?'

He shook his head. 'I don't think so. I . . . if it did, I don't remember it.' He took a breath, and then another, either calming himself or needing oxygen for the strength to continue.

'What time did you get up this morning?' she asked.

'Uh, it was – my alarm was set for six, so I got up then. I usually go for a run first thing. I was on my way down-stairs . . . I'm not sure what made me notice that one of the guest room doors was partly open . . .'

'You hadn't noticed that at the time you went to bed?'

He looked at her in a way that seemed so bewildered she wasn't sure he'd really heard the question.

15

'Is the guest room door not usually open?' she prompted.

He shook his head. 'No, not usually.'

'So what did you do this morning when you noticed it was?'

He turned his hands over as though they might be able to reveal the answer. 'I went to take a look,' he replied. 'I'm not entirely sure why . . . Maybe I was thinking Nessa had come home and slept there so's not to disturb me, but I can't swear to thinking that.'

'And what happened when you went to check the door?'

He seemed to stop breathing for a moment. 'I-I pushed it wider and that . . . that was when . . .' He clasped his hands to his head, as though to crush the images inside, the images that were probably – guilty or not – going to haunt him for a very long time.

Jay waited.

Eventually he said, 'She was – she was just – lying there. I didn't get it at first. I mean it was all wrong, I could see that . . . This is going to sound crazy, I know – but I thought it was some kind of joke. I mean, I knew it wasn't. How could it be? I can't even believe I thought it now. I ran to grab the pillow. I realize I probably shouldn't have touched it, but all I could think about was getting it off her face . . .' He squeezed his eyes tightly and dashed the tears from his cheeks. 'I shook her, trying to wake her up. I shouted at her in case she could hear me . . . felt for a pulse. I tried to revive her. I was trying not to panic . . . Then I realized I had to get help, so I ran back to the bedroom and rang 999.'

Jay expected him to pause there, to pull together the scattered and crazed memories of those terrible minutes, but he took only a moment to continue.

16

'I wanted to go back to her,' he said, 'but the operator told me not to. I shouldn't have listened . . . Or maybe I should . . . I don't know. I stayed talking on the phone. The person at the other end asked if there was anyone else in the house. I was shocked she'd even ask that. It hadn't occurred to me that there might be. I wanted to look, but she told me to go outside to a neighbour, or to somewhere safe to wait for the emergency services.

'Where we live . . . It's quite remote, just a couple of other houses nearby. I didn't want to disturb anyone. It was still early . . .' His eyes came to Jay's wide, darkly confused, even faintly impatient now. 'I know that doesn't make any sense, but nothing did at the time . . . It still doesn't. How was she there? She should have been in London. I . . .' He dashed a hand through his hair making it stand at angles, and stared blankly at the table in front of him.

With an imagined picture of his surroundings in her head, Jay said, 'How long did it take the emergency services to arrive?'

He gave it some thought, clearly still captured by the moments of discovery. 'I'm not sure. Twenty minutes? Paramedics came first – the police turned up just after. Someone put a blanket around me and sat me on a wall outside. They asked if I'd called anyone, but I didn't know what they were talking about. Then I realized he meant a friend or family member . . . I used someone's phone to ring my sister, Antonia, and she came straight over. By the time she got there they – the police – were asking me if I'd noticed any signs of a break-in, or had I heard anything unusual during the night, were there any messages on my phone from my wife?'

'And were there?' Jay asked.

He shook his head. 'I don't think so. The police have it now.'

'OK. What happened then?'

'More police arrived, there were so many people, they kept arriving . . . The place was taped off, and I could see uniformed officers going into my neighbours' houses. I kept thinking to myself, "I have to go for a run, get to work." It was like I was stuck, couldn't get off the schedule I was supposed to be on. I mean, I knew I wasn't going to work, I didn't even want to, but it was as if a part of me thought everything would go back to normal if I did.' He looked at her with the fraught yet glazed eyes of someone who still hadn't broken out of shock. 'In the end it was my sister who told me I should call a lawyer. I don't know why she understood that before I did. I guess her mind was clearer, she was paying closer attention to the way things were going. I didn't realize they were starting to suspect me. I thought . . .' His head fell back in wretched despair. 'God how naïve I am,' he groaned. 'I thought they believed me. I was telling the truth and I had no reason to think they doubted it. They didn't look like they did, they even seemed to sympathize with me, kept saying what a terrible shock I'd had, and all the time they were thinking I'd actually taken a pillow and . . .' He broke off, unable to make himself utter the words.

Although this wasn't, by any stretch, the most violent murder Jay had ever dealt with, a wrongful death was still a death whether it involved shootings, stabbings, poisonings or pillows, and it was perfectly normal for witnesses to recoil from the horror of it.

Blake was talking again. 'Antonia began taking charge

18

the best she could, but it was hard for her too. She's close to Vanessa . . .' Apparently connecting to his use of the present tense he stiffened and clenched his hands. 'Shit, shit, shit,' he muttered desperately. 'I just can't get my head around any of this. Why would someone want to hurt her? To kill her, for God's sake, and in such a horrible way?'

When his eyes came to Jay's she could see that he hoped she might have an answer to the question, in spite of surely knowing she didn't. In the end he said, 'I'd never hurt her. I swear it. She means everything to me.'

It was his use of the present tense again that went some way to persuading Jay that he could be telling the truth, and the stirring of an instinct was starting to back it up, although unlike Hamble, she knew better than to trust in that yet. This was only the beginning, there was clearly a lot more to unravel, and if experience had taught her anything it was not to draw conclusions this early in a case. She also knew that once Ken Bright began his inter-rogation, all sorts of other pieces were likely to flow to the puzzle and maybe change the picture completely. It was the way it went with this sort of case, and actually what made it intriguing, challenging and sometimes frus-trating, even heartbreaking. Ultimately, though, it was her job to make sure an innocent man didn't go to prison for a crime someone else had committed.

This was presuming someone else had done it and, so far, apart from her client, there hadn't been a single mention, even by him, of anyone who could have.

Jay returned to the interview room a few minutes later with two plastic cups of water generously supplied by the custody sergeant. Refreshments for lawyers and detainees weren't always forthcoming.

As she put one in front of Blake, he said, 'It's because I touched the pillow, isn't it? That's why they think I did it.'

Though he seemed calmer now, or at least slightly less agitated, she could see that he still wasn't quite engaging with her, for he seemed to address most of what he said to a part of himself that might be able to explain or help more than she could.

'Surely it's happened before,' he said, picking up the water but not drinking. 'People act in shock, without thinking. I was trying . . . I thought . . .'

He stopped as she raised a hand, and when she felt she had his full attention, she said, 'There could be a problem with the pillow, but we won't know until the forensic team have carried out their analysis. A bigger issue, for now, is that one of your neighbours told the police he saw you go into the house last night around eight, and some time after he heard raised voices, like someone was arguing.'

Blake looked as stunned as if she'd just punched him.

'The police will ask you about this,' she said, 'so—'

'But it's not true,' he protested. 'I told you, there was no one at home . . . I mean, I didn't know Nessa was upstairs . . .'

'Can you be absolutely sure that she was?'

He looked stupefied, bewildered, as if the possibility that his wife might not have been there had never occurred to him. In the end he said, 'Well, no, I guess I can't be sure . . . I mean, I didn't see her . . . Are you saying she might have come in *after* I got home, with someone who

20

ended up arguing with her and . . .' His incredulity broke into anger as he began shaking his head. 'I'd have heard,' he insisted. 'Of course, I would! How could I not? The house isn't *that* big.'

She gave him a moment to delve further into her suggestion; perhaps there were entry doors he hadn't considered, music or TV had drowned out other sounds.

'The only neighbour it could have been,' he said, 'is Frank Maguire, from the barn. Was it him who said he saw me come home?'

'Let's presume it was. Did you see him?'

He shook his head. 'He was probably inside his house. It's about fifty yards from mine, but I have to pass it as I drive through. He'll have seen my car.'

'How would he have heard an argument, if his house is that far away?'

'He couldn't, not from there, but he couldn't have anyway, because it didn't happen.'

'Maybe he was coming to the house for some reason, heard voices and went away again?'

'I guess it's possible, but the only voices he'd have heard would have been coming from the TV.'

'What sort of relationship do you have with him?'

Seeming slightly startled by the question, he said, 'I don't, as such. He's my tenant. I own all three of the properties that make up Clover Hill Farm.'

'Who lives in the other one?'

'A Dutch couple, the Van der Bergs, but it's for holidays and they haven't been since Easter.'

'So, Frank Maguire. How do you get along with him?'

'Quite well, I'd say, as far as it goes. We're not close, or anything. He and his wife are quite a bit older than us, but Vanessa chats with her sometimes, if they're both outside in the garden.'

'Would Mr Maguire have any reason to say he heard an argument that night if he didn't?'

Blake frowned in confusion.

'Is he the type to make up a story to get himself in on the act?'

His eyebrows arched in surprise.

'Some people do,' she told him.

He shook his head. 'I wouldn't have said that about him, not at all. He's a straight-up, honourable sort of man, the kind it's easy to trust and rely on.'

'And did you, trust or rely on him?'

He shrugged. 'Only to take in parcels or to keep an eye on the place when we were away.'

'So apart from being his landlord, you never had any particular dealings with him?'

'Not socially, no. He fell behind with his rent for a while. He took it hard, and was so ashamed that he tried to pay me back double when it all got sorted.' Apparently dismissing it, he said, 'Have you spoken to my sister, Antonia? Is she here?'

'I don't know, but I need you to stay focused, and tell me who you think could have done this to your wife?'

He stared at her, taking a moment to catch up with the question.

'Friends, family members, colleagues?' she prompted.

He shook his head, appearing to consider it in spite of how abhorrent it was to him. 'No one would,' he said. 'Not anyone we know, or no one close, anyway.'

'Is it possible your wife was having an affair?'

'No! Why do you say that?'

Knowing he must understand that it was a reasonable question, she waited for him to come up with a better answer, but all he said was, 'If it's true, I wasn't aware of it, but I really don't think she was.'

She regarded him closely, registering the lines at the corners of his eyes that could as easily, she thought, have been formed by laughter as stress or grief. It was most likely a combination of all three, as it was for most. From the way he spoke and conducted himself, she could picture him as a kind and considerate man, trustworthy and solid, but even fundamentally good and decent people could reach the end of their tether.

And psychopaths often hid behind very appealing masks.

Since it wasn't her job to decide who or what he was, only to represent him and his version of events, she encouraged him to talk some more about the crucial times, needing to weed out any contradictions, additions or anomalies before Ken Bright came in to take over.

When there turned out to be none that particularly concerned her, she said, 'The police are waiting to interview you. I don't anticipate them taking very long over it at this stage; they'll want to go through what you've already told them for now and to get any further information that seems relevant – names, times, dates that sort of thing. If you want to stop at any time, just say, and if I consider something to be inappropriate or prejudicial I will call things to a halt. I just want you to understand that this first interview will—'

He came in sharply. 'First! Why are you saying that? I didn't do it, for God's sake. I want to go home.'

'I shall do my best to make that happen, but as it stands I'm sure you realize how serious this is. Your wife . . .'

'Where is she? Do you know?' His face had turned white, as if this aspect of the nightmare had only just occurred to him.

'By now she'll be with the pathologist,' she replied.

His eyes closed over the pain. 'Nessa,' he moaned softly, almost as if she could hear him. 'How has this happened? What the hell . . . ?' His voice choked into silence as tears tightened his throat.

Jay waited, giving him some time to collect himself, if that were possible and she doubted it was.

In the end, he said, 'I'm sorry. I . . . You were saying, I could be here for a while.'

She nodded. 'It could be up to thirty-six hours, longer if they need it.'

He looked appalled, and then exhausted, as if the adrenalin of shock and fight/flight had been sucked out of him.

'Before you're interviewed,' she said, 'maybe I can get you something to eat? I don't suppose you've had anything today.'

'No, it's fine. I'm fine. I just . . . I need to get this over with.' After a moment he added, 'But thanks, it's good of you to offer.'

As she stood up he drew a hand over his face and gave a ragged sigh. 'I'm sure you've got better places to be right now,' he said. 'Sorry if I'm ruining your evening.'

Surprised, she said, 'Don't be. This is my job.'

CHAPTER THREE

Detective Inspector Ken Bright was a refined sort of man in his late forties with wavy grey hair, sharp green eyes and a demeanour that wasn't always easy to read or to ruffle. Right now, as he and the far less subtle DS Lacey Hamble went through the process of beginning an interview, he was exuding an air of politeness and quiet efficiency, someone who was keen to get a serious job done in as expedient and friendly a manner as possible.

Jay glanced at Blake's profile and saw how pale he had become since the detectives had taken their places on the opposite side of the table. He was understandably nervous, fearful was a better word – who wouldn't be in his position? – but at the moment she sensed no hostility or edgy defensiveness from him. Thankful for that, since it suggested he was following her advice to keep his answers short and respectful – 'remember they want to find out who did this to your wife as much as you do'. She identified herself for the recording and prepared to make notes as Bright launched into his opening questions.

They were perfectly straightforward and for the most part easy to answer.

'How long have you been married, Edward?' as if they were having a casual chat down the local. 'Do you mind if I call you that?'

'No, of course not,' Blake replied, sounding less relaxed, but not unfriendly. 'We celebrated our eighth anniversary last month.'

'And before that? Did you know each other . . .'

'We were together for three years,' Edward came in readily, although his fingers were locking and loosening, and Jay could feel the heat of tension coming from him. He was at last attuned to where this was going, how badly it could end, so it was only natural his defences were starting to build.

Bright continued. 'How – where did you meet?'

'At a gallery opening in London.'

Knowing Bright was unlikely to request more details on the gallery at this stage, Jay made a note to find out for herself if it had relevance.

'And you started dating from then?' Bright prompted, still matey and even a little smiley.

'That's right.'

'So, it would have been,' Bright made a quick calculation, 'about 2008 when you first got together?'

'Yes. In March of that year.'

'And did you both live in London at the time?'

'No. Vanessa was still at her family home near Cirencester, and I was renting a flat from my brother-in-law in Tetbury.'

'Ah, so you met in London, but as good fortune would have it, you both hailed from Gloucestershire, so presumably dating wasn't difficult?'

'No, it wasn't.'

Bright nodded, seeming taken with the answer, although Jay knew he was unlikely to care one way or another about how easy or not the courtship had been –

unless it turned out to have some consequence, of course. 'So, you married in 2011 and then you . . . Was this when you moved to . . .' He checked his notes, 'Clover Hill Farm?'

'Just before. I bought the properties in 2009 and we did them up together.'

'Ah, that's what you do, I believe. Fix up old properties and sell them on? But you kept these. There are three of them?'

'That's right, and we always meant to keep them. We fell in love with the setting and thought we would enjoy it more if we had some say in who lived at the barn and cottage.'

Bright consulted his notes again. 'And your office, where you work, is based in Chipping Sodbury at the Picture This gallery where your wife exhibits artworks?'

'We both have an office there and at home.'

Apparently satisfied with that, Bright said, 'Do you have children?'

Blake's hands clenched hard and he audibly swallowed as he lowered his head. 'We lost a child,' he said, 'a son, when he was eighteen months old. After that . . . My wife . . . We . . . were afraid to try again.'

Hearing the pain in his voice and understanding how deeply it must be rooted inside him, Jay was moved to put a hand on his arm. He wouldn't lie about this, obviously, no one would – apart from anything else it would be too easy to check.

He didn't seem to notice her touch, simply kept his head down as Bright said, 'I'm sorry to hear that, Edward. I really am. It's tough, losing a child. The worst. Do you mind if I ask how it happened?'

Whether he minded or not, Blake apparently knew he had to answer. 'It – it was an accident,' he said. 'We were in Italy, on holiday . . . He drowned in the pool.'

Feeling her heart catch on the horror of it, Jay glanced at Lacey Hamble and wasn't surprised to see a lack of emotion in the chill woman's eyes – although she felt sorry about it too, for Hamble might just have lost touch with a sense of humanity.

'How long ago did it happen?' Bright asked gently.

Blake lifted his head; his expression was still taut with pain. 'Almost three years. He'd have been five at Christmas if . . . If . . .' His voice stumbled into a whisper and he pressed his fingers to his eyes. 'Sorry. It's . . . Sorry . . .'

'It's OK,' Bright soothed. 'I hope you understand why it's necessary to ask these questions—'

'I don't know that I do,' Blake cut in. 'Lucas's death has nothing to do with what's happened to my wife . . . I didn't realize you were going to ask about it . . .'

'I'm sorry it's distressing, but please try to understand the need to be thorough.'

Bright was nothing if not gracious, Jay reflected, while noting that Hamble still appeared unmoved. For his part Blake looked torn between bewilderment and resentment.

Bright said, 'Let's leave that subject there for now and turn our attention to yesterday morning when you say you dropped your wife at Chippenham Station?'

Blake bristled. 'What do you mean when I *say* I dropped her off? Of course I did. I'm sure it can't be difficult to check. There must be CCTV at the station, or witnesses even.'

'Of course,' Bright conceded, 'but perhaps you can tell us what time you left her.'

Reining himself in, Blake said, 'I guess it was about a quarter to ten. She usually catches the 9.56 when she's going to London.'

'Did you see her get on the train?'

'No. I dropped her in the car park behind the platforms so she could go in over the footbridge.'

'Did you see her cross the footbridge?'

'Yes, I mean . . . She was heading that way when I drove off.'

'So you didn't actually see her go into the station?'

'No, but as I said she was heading for the bridge; actually she was already on the steps as I drove off. I had no reason to hang around. We were on time, as far as we knew the train was too.'

As Bright nodded his understanding, Jay made a note to check that the train had run to schedule. 'And where did *you* go from there?' he asked.

'To the gallery . . . Actually, I called in to one of the projects I have going near Burton.'

'Projects?'

'We're fixing up an old cottage there.'

'We?'

'Me – and the builders.'

'Did anyone see you?'

'Yes, no. Actually, no one was around. It's a small job, workmen aren't always on site.'

'Did you stop off anywhere else on your return journey from the station?'

'No. Not . . . No.'

'Not even for a coffee?'

'No.'

'Did anyone see you arrive at the gallery?'

'I-I'm not sure. Anyone could have noticed me driving up, or getting out of my car. I wasn't making a secret of it.'

'Did you speak to anyone?'

'Not that I recall. Where I park is tucked in behind the shop, so I don't usually see anyone as I go in.'

'Through a back door?'

'Yes. Actually, the postman turned up with a package as I went to unlock the front door.'

'This would be the main door to the gallery?'

'That's right.'

'So the postman wouldn't know how long you'd been inside, only that you were there when he arrived?'

'I guess so.'

'Did you spend all day in the shop . . . gallery?'

'Yes, most of it.'

'Can anyone verify this?'

Blake frowned. 'It's hard to say . . . A few people stopped by to browse the photos and paintings . . . I don't know who they were. We get tourists from time to time . . . When the bell over the door chimes – if my wife's not around, I go through to be on hand if they have any questions, or want to buy something.'

'You said *most* of the day. Did you go somewhere?'

'My sister came to meet me for lunch. We went to the deli on the high street.'

'Your sister, Antonia Debrayne? Who came to the house this morning, after you called her?'

'Yes.'

'Do you have any other brothers or sisters?'

'No.'

'How long were you and Antonia at lunch?'

'About an hour, I guess.'

'Did she return to the gallery with you?'

'No. She had a hair appointment in Tetbury so she left around two.'

After waiting for Hamble to finish her scribbling, Bright said, 'So you were alone in the gallery the entire afternoon, apart from the odd tourist or two?'

'That's right.'

'And what time did you leave?'

'It was later than I normally would. I'm working on plans for an old manor house over at Sherston and time ran away with me. So, it was probably around seven thirty when I finally locked up. Please understand, I wasn't timing myself, or checking my watch . . . I had no reason to . . .'

'Did anyone see you leave?'

'I don't know. I guess people were around, there usually is at that time . . . The pubs are open . . .'

'You didn't speak to anyone?'

'No. My car was right outside the back door so I just got in, drove out to the high street and headed home.'

'How long did the journey take?'

'Around twenty minutes.'

'So you arrived at what time?'

'It would have been around eight, give or take.'

'Was your wife's car outside?'

Blake shook his head and appeared perplexed. 'No. It was in the garage, or I assumed it was. I didn't have any reason to check.'

'You didn't park in the garage yourself?'

'No. There's a workbench in the space I normally use, so I tend to leave my car at the side of the house.'

'And when you parked you were still thinking your wife was in London?'

'Yes.'

'Did you hear from her at all after you'd dropped her at the station?'

'No.'

'So, you weren't aware she was coming home last night?'

'No.'

'And you've no idea why she did?'

'None at all. Maybe, if you talk to Melissa – that's who she was going to see – she'll be able to tell you why the plans changed.'

Lacey Hamble said, 'Melissa's surname is?'

'Siddell, I'm afraid I don't know her number off the top of my head, or her address, but she lives in Elm Park Gardens . . . If you check my phone, or Nessa's . . .'

Bright paused as Hamble left the room, and after announcing her departure for the recording he said, 'How often does your wife go to visit her friend?'

Seeming slightly distracted by Hamble's exit, Blake said, 'She goes to London . . . uh, fairly regularly, on business, not specifically to visit Melissa, although I'm sure that was her only purpose yesterday. At least she didn't mention having any meetings, and she usually does if there are any . . . lined up.' His voice faltered and he swallowed loudly.

'What sort of meetings does your wife have in London?'

He shrugged. 'With artists or photographers, people who want her to show their work. You'll find a record of them in her phone, I'm sure, if you have it?'

'And what do you usually do when your wife is in London?'

Blake shrugged again. 'The same as I did yesterday. I work, watch the gallery, maybe have site meetings with clients or builders.'

'But you didn't meet any clients or builders yesterday?'

'No. Apart from calling in at Burton I was at the gallery all day.'

'But you went to the deli with your sister.'

'Yes, as I said.'

Bright took a moment to check his notes, and said, 'When you got home yesterday evening, around eight, what did you do?'

'I – uh – I let myself in the front door? You mean that sort of thing?'

'Everything.'

'OK, so once inside I guess I put down my briefcase and turned off the alarm.'

Jay's reaction – though silent – was as fast as Bright's. 'The alarm was on?' Bright asked.

Blake stilled as he thought. 'I can't . . . I'm sure it was, but . . . You know, I don't remember setting it when we left in the morning, so maybe I didn't turn it off when I got home.'

'Think hard,' Bright encouraged. 'Did you deactivate the alarm when you went into the house last night?'

Blake blew out air as he shook his head. 'I want to say yes, but it doesn't make sense, does it? If Nessa was already there, it couldn't have been on.'

Unless the killer had reset it on the way out. He or she would have to know the code, so therefore they were a close relative or friend? Jay knew Bright was having the same thoughts, and quite probably Blake had got there himself by now, although if he had he didn't say so.

Good man, she thought, *we need to find out more about this anomaly before we go any further with it.*

33

'OK, let's say the alarm wasn't on,' Bright continued. 'You were in the house, continue from there.'

Blake said, 'I'd have put my keys in the second drawer of the chest just inside the door.' He grimaced. 'Not very security conscious, I know, but we've always kept them there and never had any trouble. It's quiet where we live, it's not a through road . . . Of course you already know that.'

'Did you notice if your wife's keys were there?'

'No, but there are other things in the drawer, torches, gloves, sunglasses, other keys . . .'

'So what did you do next?'

'I went into the kitchen, and probably took a beer from the fridge . . . I might have had a couple through the course of the evening, I'm sure I did. I'd have put on the news, it's like a reflex action when I get home, so I'm sure I did, and then I checked through the mail . . .'

'What mail? Where did you find it?'

Startled, Blake said, 'I collected it from the box outside the gates on my way in.'

'So you got out of the car at the gates?'

'No, I walked back after I parked. It's not far, ten metres or so.'

'Are your gates automatic, or manual?'

'Automatic, but they haven't been working for the past few days. We're waiting for someone to come and fix them. Meantime they're left open.' He looked up as Hamble returned. After handing a sheet of paper to Bright, she sat down, eyes boring ominously into her main suspect.

After reading what was on the page, Bright laid it face down on the table and, once Hamble had announced her return for the recording, he continued. 'OK, Edward, you had a beer, listened to some news, what else?'

Seeming unsettled again by Hamble, Blake took a moment to re-engage. 'Uh – I made myself something to eat. An omelette with cheese and ham, some tomatoes on the side. There was a slice of lemon tart left over from a dinner party we gave on Saturday, so I had that too.'

'We'll need the names of the guests,' Hamble told him abruptly.

As he obliged, and Hamble wrote them down, Jay did the same while thinking of the dinner she and Tom had hosted at the weekend in their Clifton home. She wondered if the Blake's evening had been as relaxed, as liberal with wine and good food, if these names belonged to old friends or clients or family. Had anyone around the table known that Vanessa Blake was in danger of losing her life in the next few days? Had she even? What had been talked about? What was the purpose of the party? A birthday? Anniversary? Celebration of some sort?

Bringing them back on track, Bright said, 'Your neighbour claims he heard the sound of an argument coming from your house at around nine o'clock? Can you explain that?'

Blake shook his head as he turned his hands over in a small gesture of incredulity. 'It has to have been the TV,' he replied. 'It certainly wasn't what he seems to think it was, because I was the only one there.'

'Apart from your wife,' Hamble pointed out bluntly.

Blake tensed, and sounded wretched as he said, 'I didn't know she was there until this morning.'

'But she was there,' Bright said, 'unless she came in later than you, of course.'

Blake regarded him helplessly.

'What did you argue about?' Hamble asked.

'I told you,' Blake replied, 'it didn't happen. I was there alone – or I thought I was alone. If Nessa was upstairs . . .' His breath caught on a sob. 'If she was already . . . Oh Christ, I can't believe this is happening. I love my wife. I'd never hurt her. Please, you need to find out who did this.'

'That's certainly our intention,' Bright assured him, and placed a hand on the page Hamble had brought in. 'We have a small problem here,' he stated. 'Melissa Siddell has told DS Hamble that she wasn't expecting your wife yesterday.'

Blake froze as his jaw dropped and his eyes rounded with shock. 'I don't understand,' he responded. 'I took Nessa to the station . . . Why would Melissa say that?'

'Because it's true?' Hamble suggested.

Blake turned to Jay. 'It's not,' he told her. 'I've no idea why Melissa would lie, but . . .'

'It could have been your wife who was lying?' Bright pointed out.

Blake's eyes were still on Jay and she wondered if he was only now fully comprehending how important she was going to be for him in the coming days, and maybe a lot longer than that. He dropped his head in his hands. 'I don't know what the hell is going on here,' he growled brokenly. 'None of it's making any sense. There was no argument; she went to see Melissa, I'm sure of it . . .'

Suddenly the door opened and a uniformed officer put his head around. 'Sir, can we have a word?' he asked.

Bright signalled for Hamble to deliver the relevant information for the recording and got to his feet.

'I'd like to speak to my client again,' Jay said, before anyone could suggest returning Blake to his cell.

Bright nodded, and with no further glance in Blake's direction, he led Hamble out of the room.

Jay and Blake sat quietly for a moment, listening to the detectives' footsteps retreating into the distant bustle of the custody area. It must feel to Blake, Jay thought, as though he was trapped in a bubble of some sort, a kind of time-lag where real life was going on outside and he was stuck here, in this awful, pivotal moment in his life, helpless to escape it. He wouldn't be wrong to feel that way, for she'd heard nothing yet to persuade her that he'd be released tonight.

'Please tell me you believe me,' he said, not looking at her, clearly fearful of seeing doubt in her eyes. 'I don't know what's going on, but please say that you believe I didn't tie my wife to the bed, that I didn't kill my wife.'

'I do believe you,' Jay reassured him. There was still a long way to go, but the principle of innocent until proven guilty wasn't a difficult one to hold onto when there were still so many questions to answer.

'So what happens now?' he asked, his voice roughened by agitation.

'That'll depend on what's just called them away, but I think you need to prepare yourself to spend the night here.'

His head came up, his eyes sharp with panic. 'Are you serious? I told you, I didn't do it . . .'

'They have the right to hold you without charge for up to twenty-four hours, and because this is a murder case they can apply for an extension of up to thirty-six or even ninety-six hours.' As he blanched, she added, 'I'm sorry, I know it's not what you want to hear, but as things stand there is nothing I can do to make them release you.'

'Then what's the point of you being here?' he cried. 'You say you believe me, but you're just letting this happen.'

Used to the outbursts that came with frustration and fear, Jay simply watched as he slumped forward onto the table and wrapped his arms around his head, letting out a long, low moan of despair. 'Can you imagine what this feels like?' he asked, when finally he sat up again. 'Being accused of killing someone you love, knowing you didn't do it, then finding you have no way of proving it?'

'We'll find a way,' she assured him.

'And how are we going to do that?'

'By listening to what the police are asking you, finding out as much as we can of what they know, who they're talking to, and by mounting an investigation of our own.'

'But what if they're fixating on me just to help their clear-up rate?'

'I know DI Bright quite well; he wouldn't do that. He's thorough and fair, so he won't let this go forward unless he feels there's good reason to. So, what I need to know, Edward, is who you think might have done it.'

He sank back in his chair, eyes closed, expression taut with exhaustion and helplessness. 'If I knew that,' he said, 'don't you think I'd already have told you?'

They both looked up as the door opened and DC Hamble said,

'Mrs Wells, DI Bright would like a word.'

CHAPTER FOUR

It was past seven thirty by the time Jay finally exited the custody area of Keynsham Police Centre, feeling more troubled than informed, although relieved that Ken Bright had decided to call it a day. This, in spite of early testing showing that a fingerprint found on a buckle of one of the leather straps that had bound Vanessa Blake to the bed belonged to her husband. Armed with that knowledge, Bright could have pressed on late into the night, badgering and pushing his main suspect until tiredness and fear got the man so confused and disoriented that he ended up confessing maybe without fully realizing it. Fortunately for Blake, though, Bright had to be somewhere else this evening. Jay hadn't asked where, it was none of her business, but it had to be important for him to have left at this stage of a murder investigation.

Still, it seemed pretty clear to Jay from the brief chat they'd had that Bright was becoming as convinced he had the right man in custody as she was concerned that he did not. Another half an hour with her client before leaving had done even more to worry her on this front, for he remembered trying to undo one of the straps, and failing, before running for the phone. And as far as she knew, no one was saying his prints were on all of the buckles. Also, if it was a premeditated killing – and the circumstances

39

in which Vanessa Blake had been found meant that it could easily fall into that category – then why would Edward Blake have left himself so wide open to being blamed for it? Moreover, his shock and grief were as convincing as any she'd witnessed, and she'd be surprised if they weren't actually giving Bright some pause for thought, in spite of DC Hamble still having him signed up for life.

'Mrs Wells? Mrs Wells? I'm sorry, I hope you don't mind . . . I've been waiting . . .'

Jay turned around to find a dark-haired woman of about her own age attempting to catch up with her.

'I'm Antonia, Toni, Edward Blake's sister,' the woman explained, seeming both anxious and determined as she tried to make herself heard above the squally wind. 'I don't know if this is allowed, but please, can I talk to you?'

Since Jay was keen to talk to her too, she said, 'Of course, but maybe we should get out of the weather? Waitrose is just down the road. It should still be open; shall we meet in the café?'

Seeming almost to sob with relief, Antonia said, 'Thank you. Yes. Just tell me first, is he all right?'

'He's bearing up,' Jay assured her with a kindly smile, while thinking that if he was telling the truth, then this time last night he'd been on his way home from the gallery, certain his wife was in London, probably not even sparing a thought for what she was doing. Tonight he was in a police cell with his entire life in chaos and no idea of what the future might bring.

What a difference twenty-four hours could make.

Ten minutes later, as late shoppers flowed in and out

of the supermarket and a few early diners carried baked potatoes and savoury fajitas to their tables, Jay set a large pot of tea and two cups in front of Antonia and sat down.

'He didn't do it,' Antonia stated as Jay poured. 'I hope you realize that. If you don't, you might not be the right lawyer for us. I have to say that—'

'Stop,' Jay cut in gently. 'Please try to be calm. It's the best way you can help him, and for what it's worth, I want to help him too.'

Seizing the words like a lifeline, Antonia said, 'So you don't think he did it? Oh thank God, thank God. I know the police do, they wouldn't have arrested him otherwise, but if you don't—'

'Even if I did,' Jay cut in, 'it would still be my job to make sure he receives a fair trial – but at the moment no one is convinced he did it or he would have been charged.'

Taking that on board, Antonia tipped a dash of milk into her teacup and stirred in a spoonful of sugar. 'He loves – loved – her, you know? I mean *really* loved her. Everyone knew that, and it was the same for her. He meant everything to her, and he'd never harm her. It isn't in him to harm anyone, but especially not her.'

Replacing her teacup on its saucer, Jay said, 'Have you been interviewed by the police yet?'

Antonia shook her head and flipped her hair over one shoulder. She was an attractive woman, pale-faced, blue-eyed like her brother, and probably a few years older than him. 'Not properly,' she replied, 'I was at the house earlier when they took him away. I told them then they were making a mistake, but no one was listening. It was awful. Terrible. I'm sure they'll tell you I became hysterical . . . I did. I tried to drag them off him so they ended up

41

restraining me, but he's my brother, for God's sake, and I *know* he didn't do this.' Dashing tears from her eyes she checked her phone as a text arrived, and Jay waited to see if she would answer it, but she barely even read it.

'I'm sorry,' she said, looking at Jay again. 'As you can see I'm not handling it very well. I've been asked to go and give a statement tomorrow, for all the good it will do. That detective, the woman, Bramble . . .'

'Hamble.'

'She thinks he's guilty, you can tell just by the look of her.'

Not arguing with that, Jay said, 'Do you have any idea who might have done it? It would help him immeasurably if you do.'

Antonia's face crumpled as she shook her head. 'None,' she said brokenly. 'If I did I'd already have told the police, but Nessa didn't have any enemies, or none that would do something like that.'

'So she did have some?'

Antonia took a breath. 'Not really. I mean, I guess she was as capable as anyone of rubbing someone up the wrong way at times – we all do, whether we mean to or not – but she wasn't the type to hurt anyone intentionally. She was more the other way, she wanted to be liked and she was.' Her eyes flicked to the window beside them, and Jay couldn't help wondering how truthful she was being. Not that she suspected her of lying, exactly, but she seemed uneasy, as if there was more to her description of her sister-in-law's character than she was admitting to.

'Frankly,' Antonia said, 'you're probably going to hear things about her that . . . They'll be from people who

42

didn't really know her, so all I ask is that you keep an open mind.'

'What sort of things?' Jay prompted gently.

'I don't know. I mean, I don't want to put words in anyone's mouths, so it's best I . . .' She glanced away again, and clutched her phone tightly as another text arrived. It was impossible to know what she was wrestling with in her mind, only that there was clearly something . . . Suddenly she said, 'Has Ed told you about Lucas?'

Hiding her surprise, Jay said, 'Yes, he has.'

Antonia's voice was ragged with emotion as she said, 'It was terrible, awful, the kind of tragedy no family could deal with. We all still feel responsible, and I don't think anything will ever change that. Obviously it was a lot worse for Ed and Nessa. We were all there, you know? On holiday in Italy. We weren't paying proper attention. No one noticed him toddling over to the pool, we didn't hear him fall in . . .' She clasped her hands to her face as her breath caught on a sob. 'When we realized he wasn't with us we started searching and searching, we were going mad, all of us . . . In the end it was John, my husband, who found him in amongst the inflatables, but by then it was already too late.'

Jay watched as she dabbed her face with a paper napkin, appalled, horrified for them all, unable to imagine how she'd even begin to cope in the same situation. 'I'm so sorry,' she said softly, feeling the inadequacy of the words, but having no others.

Antonia nodded, the nightmare of it right there in her eyes. 'It was three years ago,' she said, 'but none of us will ever get over it. We've never been back to Italy since – that's where we were at the time, at our house in Umbria.

We've sold it now. Needless to say, Edward and Nessa were . . . I don't know how to describe a loss like that? All I can tell you is that neither of them has been the same since. You wouldn't expect them to be, would you?'

Jay shook her head in sympathy.

'Of course, they eventually learned to put a brave face on things, and did their best to put their lives back together – Ness began searching for new clients, Ed returned to his renovation projects, but obviously deep down they were shattered.' She swallowed and pressed her fingers to her lips. 'Sorry,' she said, 'talking about it brings it back and now this has happened . . . Oh God, it's just so awful, so . . . *wrong*. My brother doesn't deserve to go through any more, he's been through enough. That's why I had to talk to you, because I'm absolutely terrified that the police will decide he did it and stop looking for who really did.'

'Don't worry,' Jay said, 'it's still early days and it's possible something will come to light as early as tomorrow to change the course of the investigation.'

Antonia regarded her fiercely, almost desperately. 'I hope so,' she said, 'I really do, because Ed didn't kill her. I know that as surely as I know I'm the mother of my own children. I only wish to God I could tell you who did.'

It was past ten o'clock by the time Jay eventually pulled up alongside Tom's car on the forecourt of their grand, double-fronted Georgian villa at the heart of Clifton's leafy avenues, with the famous suspension bridge, zoo and Downs no more than a short walk away. She was tired, having gone straight to the office from the police station to catch up on the rest of the day's workload – and to leave instructions for Vikki to rearrange her schedule for at least the next three days. She'd have to attend the Pre-Trial and Preparation Hearing for a drugs case in the morning, but at least it was only minutes away in Bristol Crown Court, so she should be free by lunchtime. This meant that Edward Blake would have to wait in his cell until she could get there – the police couldn't interview him without her – and she didn't imagine Ken Bright was going to be too thrilled about that.

It couldn't be helped, and for tonight at least, she was going to try to switch off from the day's events to focus on other things, such as how damned hungry she was.

Letting herself in the front door, she turned on the lights in the spacious entrance hall, glanced up the stairs as she freed her hair from its band and, kicking off her shoes, she dropped her briefcase next to Tom's outside the study they shared. As she went into the open-plan kitchen and sitting room, expecting to find it empty given how quiet the place was, she was surprised to find Tom and Livvy fast asleep on a sofa, her feet resting on his lap and his long legs stretched out in front of him towards the muted TV. Clearly neither of them had heard her come in for they didn't even stir, so she moved quietly past them to the kitchen that occupied the whole of the back of the house, the delicious smell of whatever they'd had to eat already making her stomach growl.

Thrilled to see it was one of Tom's specialities – a smoky aubergine shakshuka with cherry tomatoes – and that there was some left, she popped a couple of slices of sourdough into the toaster and went to the fridge for some wine.

'Hey you,' Livvy whispered, coming to sit on a bar stool, wavy hair flattened to her head on one side, bleary eyes ringed with smudged mascara. She was as beautiful as she was willowy, as full of attitude as she was spilling over with insecurities.

'Hey you,' Jay whispered back. 'Everything OK?'

'Yeah, just tired. How about you?'

'I'm fine. Long day, so glad to be home.'

'That's kind of what Dad said when he came in. I think it was a bad one for him, because he was really grumpy, you know how he gets. He bit my head off when I tried talking to him about something really important.'

Used to Tom having difficult days and snapping at them when he got home, Jay held up the bottle, offering a glass, but Livvy shook her head.

'Actually, I will have one,' she said, eyes on her phone, 'but don't give me too much.'

Half-filling two glasses, Jay pushed one across the island and drank from the other as she took out a plate and cutlery for herself. In no time at all Livvy was offloading about her day and her growing interest in Nat Truman, her brother's best friend, also the son of Tom's partner in chambers.

As she listened, Jay took the bread from the toaster, and piling every morsel of shakshuka that was left onto her plate, carried it to the breakfast table and gestured for Livvy to join her. They didn't have enough heart-to-hearts these days, and usually Jay loved to hear her daughter chat, even when she was reliving the one occasion she and Nat had got together at a party last winter. This crush had been building for a while, and though Jay felt certain Nat was quite keen too, she'd decided not to intervene. If she got it wrong Livvy would never forgive her, and the potential for it was probably far greater than she knew. So, she simply listened, sympathized and gave advice where she could, while Tom got quietly up from the sofa and took himself off to bed. She didn't say anything, for she understood his need for a good night's sleep when he was presumably driving back to Plymouth in the morning.

It was almost two a.m. before she finally slipped under the duvet, hoping not to wake Tom, but at the same time feeling resentful that he appeared to be well into dream-land when she could do with being there too. They both had testing days tomorrow – although no one's job was more important than the other's; they'd never played that game.

She lay quietly, staring into the darkness, with no real hope of falling asleep any time soon. Her mind was full of what might and might not be said during Blake's further questioning tomorrow. She wondered if he was asleep now, locked in a police cell on a hard, plastic mattress with the noise of other detainees a virtual constant throughout the night. There could be as many as forty-eight individuals filling up the cells from all walks of life, some with huge social problems, others with gang affili-ations, or drug addictions; it was even possible that he wasn't the only one there for killing his wife. She'd hazard a guess that he was the only one with his sort of back-ground, whose life before today had been one of privilege and success, whose future had been so firmly set on all the right tracks – until it had suddenly come off.

She tried to picture his home – Clover Hill Farm – its countryside setting, the room in which he and his wife had slept and the one where her body had been found.

She imagined it as an idyllic, characterful place now transformed into a crime scene with tape all around it, police outside and the detritus of a forensic search littering and dusting the rooms.

'Are you awake?' Tom mumbled next to her.

'Mm,' she replied.

'Is Livvy OK?'

'She's sad, but she'll be fine. Are you?'

When he didn't answer she presumed he'd fallen back to sleep, but his arm went around her and he pulled her in close, spooning her into the masculine curve of him. She was taken unawares by the heat that suddenly flared inside her, and as she nestled herself more tightly she felt him responding. He slipped inside her easily, fully, and as they made love, hardly moving and yet feeling intensely, she thought about how much he meant to her – and how deeply Edward Blake and his wife had loved one another too – and how terrifyingly easy it was for trust and dreams to be shattered.

CHAPTER FIVE

Jay made it to the police station by two the following day after spending most of the morning in court, and the hours through lunch at her desk briefing Ash Baqri and Sallyanne Jones, the crime team's senior solicitors, on where and when she needed cover for the rest of the week. This would enable her to focus on Edward Blake's interrogation, which could easily go on until Friday, by which time a decision would have to be made on whether or not to charge him.

Ken Bright was waiting for her in the custody area as she came through, his expression worryingly grim. There was no sign of Hamble as he led Jay into a consultation room where he related what had come to light overnight and this morning, and to her dismay none of it was good for her client.

'I'll need to take further instructions,' she informed him, knowing this wouldn't come as a surprise, although it was undoubtedly an annoyance given the time constraints. However, he was well aware that throwing grenades into an interview without providing any warning would simply force her to bring proceedings to a halt.

As she waited for Blake to be brought from his cell, she quickly jotted down the issues they were facing, wanting to be sure they were all covered before Bright resumed his interrogation. To her surprise she realized she was feeling nervous, although much more for Blake than for herself. She didn't want to be wrong about him, she really didn't, but if he had killed his wife it was best that she knew.

She looked up as he came into the room. Though his face was strained by angst and tiredness, he'd apparently attempted a shave and was wearing fresh clothes – white polo shirt and jeans – presumably brought in by his sister.

'Hi, how are you?' she asked, getting to her feet and stretching a hand across the table to shake.

He almost smiled, but there was too much angst and sadness in it to make it real. 'As I'm sure you don't want the real answer,' he said, taking her hand, 'I'll tell you I'm fine so I don't use up any more of your time than I have to.'

'I know this isn't easy,' she responded, gesturing for him to sit down, 'but you're entitled to as much of my time as you need, and I'm happy to give it.'

He regarded her gratefully and took a breath as though steadying himself.

Coming to the point, she said, 'I need to ask you more detailed questions than I did yesterday, and once again I'm going to urge you to be truthful so we can avoid any contradictions or misunderstandings.'

'It's OK,' he said softly. 'I have no problem with answering, or with the truth, as painful as it is.'

Although certain he was referring to his wife's death rather than his own situation, she offered no words of sympathy in spite of feeling it. It wouldn't help him to dwell on his grief now, he needed to put himself first and it was her job to help him focus on how best he could do that. 'As you know,' she began carefully, 'initial tests have shown that your prints are on the buckle of at least one of the stirrup straps, and we also know that Melissa Siddell has told the police that she wasn't expecting to see your wife on Monday.'

His eyes seemed to lose focus as he shook his head in bewilderment. 'I guess she knows whether or not she and Nessa had an arrangement,' he said, 'all I can tell you is what Nessa told me.'

Having expected the answer, Jay braced herself to deliver the next piece of news. 'The pathologist has put the time of death between six o'clock and ten o'clock on Monday evening.'

As he registered the times he went very still, as if the words were slowly turning him to stone. It was a moment before he looked at her and there was no mistaking the devastation and disbelief in his eyes. 'So just before I got home?' he said shakily.

She didn't say, *Or while you were there*. He'd get to it in his own time, and when he did she saw the realization reverberate through him in shockwaves of horror.

'Jesus Christ,' he muttered, putting his hands to his head. 'This can't be happening. I feel like I'm going out of my mind.' He looked at her again, his eyes blue and wretched and raw with fear. 'Someone was there before I got home,' he told her. 'They had to have been.'

'OK, but who?'

He seemed to deflate as he shook his head in frustration.

'You must surely have some idea.'

'If I did, do you really think I'd keep it to myself?'

Accepting that he probably wouldn't, she made a note to find out if the neighbour, Maguire, had seen anyone else coming or going from the house before Blake had returned home. If he had it should have come up by now, but there was no harm in checking.

'Are they going to charge me?' Blake asked, his voice unsteadied by dread.

Deciding to avoid the question for now, she said, 'In light of the pathologist's report I need to know how you want to proceed. If you're—'

'I didn't do it,' he cried fiercely, 'that's how I want to proceed. I don't know what the hell is going on, but if you're expecting me to own up to something I didn't do . . .'

'I'm not *expecting* you to do anything, but you can see what a difficult position this puts you in. That's not to say their case is watertight; if they thought it was, they'd have charged you already. So, I need to know if anyone can attest to you being in the shop until seven thirty on Monday evening when you say you left. There should be CCTV footage of the high street that will hopefully show you getting into your car, or driving it away. Will it?'

'I've no idea where the cameras are, so I can't answer that, but if they cover the main road then the answer is yes.'

'Will it show you coming or going any earlier than that?'

'Only when I arrived in the morning, and went out to lunch with Toni.'

'Are you sure there's no one who can confirm you were in the shop until seven thirty?'

'I don't see how. I was there alone for most of the day, apart from a couple of browsers, and I've no idea who they were.'

'OK. What about when you got home? Go over it in your mind again. Did anything seem unusual, or look out of place when you drove up?'

He shook his head slowly as he thought. 'Nothing,' he replied.

'There's a lane leading to your house, yes? Did you pass anyone going in the opposite direction as you came along it? Someone on foot, another car, or delivery van?'

Once again he shook his head.

'What about when you got inside? Was anything different, out of place, not as it should be?'

'As far as I remember it was just as we'd left it in the morning, but I wasn't checking.'

'OK, keep thinking it over and we'll come back to it. Now let's get to the burglar alarm. It'll have recorded the last time it was turned off, so have you remembered yet if it was you as you let yourself in after work? We have to hope you did, because if it was set it *could* provide a small window between six and eight when you weren't in the house. Otherwise we could be asking them to accept that you were there when the murder happened and heard nothing.'

He paled and even seemed nauseated by the suggestion.

'Believe me, Edward,' she said, 'their questioning over this part of the evening is going to be much tougher than you experienced yesterday, so is there anything I need to know before we start?'

With no hesitation he said, 'I'm not hiding anything, I swear it. I've told you the truth as far as I remember it. Now you tell me if you can recall every single detail of what you did when you got home last night. If you were put to the test, could you recount the precise time you arrived, what you did as you walked in the door; where you put your coat or your keys? When you went to bed, where were your thoughts? Did you read? What was the book about? Check emails? I can see you're married, so have you ever thought for a single minute when your husband's away that he might in fact be lying dead in another room in the house while you're drifting off to sleep? Has that thought ever entered your head?'

Though Jay was sure he didn't know there were tears on his cheeks, or that the tone of his voice was broken, desperate, she could tell how focused he was on trying to make her believe him. And she did, in spite of knowing how often she'd been lied to in the past, and how even her finely honed instincts weren't entirely failsafe. However, for the moment at least, she was more concerned about him being charged with a crime he hadn't committed than she was about him trying to deceive her.

'OK, one last thing before I let them know we're ready,' she said. 'It might be advisable from hereon to answer all questions with no comment to avoid incriminating your-self—'

'No!' he cut in sharply. 'I've already told you I have nothing to hide. I didn't do it, so how can it be possible to incriminate myself?'

'In more ways than you might imagine,' she cautioned, 'and if you'll just listen to the questions without leading yourself into a minefield, it'll give me a clearer picture of what they do and don't know.'

He was unmoved. 'I'm sorry. I understand why you want me to do it, and I get that I should be taking your advice, but I need them to stop doubting me, and that won't happen if I refuse to cooperate.'

54

CHAPTER SIX

Bright and Hamble were already in the interview room when Jay and Blake were taken through and Hamble wasted no time in setting up the recording. Though she wasn't obliged to reveal who was on the other end of the electronic monitoring, only that someone was, Jay strongly suspected it would be Detective Chief Superintendent Todd Menosa, the senior investigating officer – Ken Bright being his deputy. If she was right it meant they were close to making a charge and, though this dismayed her, it at least told her that if they were sure of their case right now they wouldn't be holding back.

It didn't surprise her when Hamble kicked things off – Bright would be as keen to observe as Mendosa was at this stage, and she, Jay, was poised to bring things to a halt the instant Blake looked to be in trouble.

Instead of going straight to the pathologist's four-hour time-frame, as Jay had expected, Hamble kicked off with a new revelation. 'We've heard from the alarm company,' she stated in her broad Bristolian bark, 'and it turns out the system at Clover Hill Farm was last deactivated on Monday 29 April at three p.m.'

Jay turned to Blake. She could see he was frowning, trying to work out exactly what this might mean, as was she.

'Did you go home at three p.m.?' Hamble asked.

'No,' he replied.

'Are you sure?'

'Perfectly sure.'

'What if I told you someone saw you entering the house . . .'

'They'd be lying. I wasn't there at three p.m. I was in the shop.'

'Is there anyone who can attest to that?'

'I don't – I don't think so.'

'Did you receive any phone calls on the landline that could place you there?'

'No, I always use my mobile. I would have made and received several calls. Isn't there a way of telling where I was at the time?'

Ignoring the question Hamble said, 'If it wasn't you who deactivated the alarm in your home at three p.m., who do you think it could have been?'

'I don't know.'

'Your wife?'

'I-I suppose so.'

'Who else knows the code?'

'The cleaner, my sister and brother-in-law, the handyman . . . I can't think of anyone else.'

'When does the cleaner go in?'

'On Tuesdays and Fridays.'

Hamble passed over a sheet of paper. 'Please write down the names of the cleaner and handyman.'

After doing so in a way that enabled Jay to make note of them too, Blake passed the sheet back and returned his attention to Hamble. There was nothing hostile, or in the least bit antagonistic in his manner, but Jay could sense his tension, his eagerness to get things right, and fear of saying something that could be misconstrued or used against him in some way.

'Is it possible the cleaner went in a day earlier than usual?' Hamble asked, staring at the name on the page as if it might answer for itself. 'Maybe she deactivated the alarm and forgot to set it again when she left?'

'If she enters the house outside of her scheduled hours,' Blake replied, 'maybe to return or pick up ironing, she rings us first to make sure it's all right. The same goes for the handyman, and neither of them called me that day. I guess they could have called Nessa. If they did I imagine there would be a record of it on her phone. Or, of course, you could speak to them.'

With a long blink Hamble said, 'What about your sister and brother-in-law? Could they have gone into the house at three p.m. on Monday?'

'My sister was having lunch at the deli with me until two, or thereabouts, and from there she was going to her hairdresser in Tetbury. I'm sure that can be verified. John, my brother-in-law, would have been in London where he works three or four days a week.'

Hamble's eyes were flinty as she regarded him, and Jay knew exactly where her mind had gone. *Was there something between the brother-in-law and Vanessa Blake? Had* he *been at the station waiting to pick her up as soon as Edward had dropped her off?* Since she'd risk making herself look foolish if she pursued this line right now, Hamble scrolled through the tablet she was holding and said, 'The alarm's computer at the shop tells us it was deactivated at 11.34 on Monday morning, presumably when you arrived, and was activated again at 19.36 in the evening when you say you left. So you didn't set it while you went out for lunch?'

Sounding unfazed, he said, 'Apparently not, but I would have locked up and we were very close by, able to see the place from where we were sitting in the window of the deli.'

'Mm.' Hamble clearly wasn't particularly satisfied with that. Looking up from her tablet she said, 'OK, here's the problem we're having with the timings, Edward. On the one hand, the activation of the shop's alarm at 19.36 could indeed confirm that was when you left to go home. On the other, you didn't set the alarm while you were out in the middle of the day, so after lunch with your sister you could have gone home . . .'

'I did not go home after lunch with my sister. I went to the gallery. There must be plenty of CCTV cameras around the high street. Surely you're checking them. They'll show when I came and went.'

The way Hamble stared so fixedly at her screen told Jay that the footage was either still being scrutinized or was possibly compromised in some way. Not unusual, and very inconvenient for the police if that turned out to be the case. On the other hand, it wouldn't be great for Blake either.

'What we know for certain,' Hamble continued, 'is that someone went into your house at three p.m., and if it wasn't you, then who was it?'

Swallowing audibly, Blake simply shook his head. 'I want to say my wife, but I . . . I thought she was in London . . .'

'Yes, but we only have your word for it that she was going to London. Her friend wasn't expecting her, we've found no evidence of her buying a ticket, or of her boarding the train, or of her getting out of your car in the car park.'

As Jay's insides tightened, Blake cried, 'She'll have had an e-ticket, it'll be on her phone . . .'

'But it isn't.'

He stopped, stunned. 'I dropped her off,' he persisted. 'We went to the station. There must be CCTV to show that.'

Hamble said, 'It picked you up driving in and out, but I'm afraid it's not possible to determine if anyone's in the car with you. And as there are a number of blind spots in the car park, we either have to assume she got out in one of them, or that she wasn't there at all.'

Jay said, 'This is bordering on the absurd, detective. As there's CCTV to show that my client drove in and out of the car park, I have to wonder why we're wasting our time on this.'

Bristling, Hamble said, 'Once again, there is not any *clear* evidence to show that Mrs Blake was in the car. At the moment we only have your client's word for it that she was. And if you're wondering why he would drive to the station without her, and then leave again, it is a question we'd also like an answer to.' Her eyes fired into Blake.

'I didn't go there without her,' he said tightly. 'She was with me. She got out near the bottom of the steps to the footbridge and I drove away. If the cameras don't cover that area then I'm sorry, but it wasn't on either of our minds to make sure we were seen by station surveillance.'

Wincing at the sarcasm, Jay said, 'It sounds to me as though your technical experts need to study the CCTV again, DS Hamble. Perhaps they'll find Mrs Blake leaving the station *after* her husband drove away.'

Clearly irritated by the suggestion, Hamble breezed past it and said, 'OK, let's agree you took your wife to the station. We know she didn't buy a ticket there, nor is there any footage showing her getting on a train. So, where do *you* think she went after you dropped her?'

Looking and sounding defeated, Blake said, 'I have no idea.'

'Could she have been meeting someone?'

'If she was I knew nothing about it.'

Jay said, 'If your examination of CCTV footage and search for witnesses at the station are still ongoing, can I suggest we return to this when you've got something meaningful to ask us?'

Though Hamble shot her a withering look, letting it be known that she didn't appreciate being told how to handle an interview, she ended up moving on anyway – and her next question almost made Jay wish they'd continued on the same path.

'Did you and your wife often engage in extreme sex acts?' she asked bluntly.

As Blake stiffened beside her, Jay cast a quick glance at Bright, but the detective's eyes were fixed on Blake, showing nothing but an interrogator's interest.

'No,' Blake said quietly, 'we didn't.'

Hamble said, 'Was it you who introduced bondage into your bedroom activities? Or was it her?'

'I told you, we didn't . . .'

Hamble clicked a mouse and the computer screen beside her filled with the graphic image of a naked Vanessa Blake bound by her wrists and ankles to four corners of a wooden bedstead. Her eyes were closed, her mouth slightly agape, her lips were bloodied and blue and her long hair was tangled over her face and the pillows. The angle explicitly revealed her open vagina, and as Blake sobbed in anguish Jay also looked away, wanting to ask if this was necessary, while knowing it was.

'Why the guest room?' Hamble asked. 'Why not your own bedroom?'

Blake simply shook his bowed head.

'Can you speak up please?'

'I don't know why she was there . . . We've never . . .'

'Is it because there are no posts on the bed in your room?'

Blake's voice was torn with anguish as he said, 'This isn't the kind of thing we . . . I don't know why she was there.'

'We can see the injuries to her wrists and ankles, so she clearly put up a fight once she was in the bonds, but no other bruises or abrasions on her body. There doesn't appear to be any evidence of a struggle anywhere else in the room either. So presumably she didn't object when you took her in there.'

Gulping on a sob, he said, 'I didn't take her there. I've never seen her like that before . . .'

'Do the stirrup straps belong to you or to her?' Hamble asked.

'I-I don't own any, but she does. Maybe they're hers. I can't tell from this.'

'Did you have sex with her before you killed her?'

'Please stop this,' he implored, pushing back from the table.

'Is that a yes or a no?'

'It's a no!' he cried. 'I did not tie her up, and I did not have sex with her. Oh God,' he moaned clasping his hands to his head. 'Why won't you believe me?'

'Was she having an affair?' Hamble pressed.

'What? I-I don't know.'

'Maybe *you* were?'

He shook his head.

'Louder, Edward. We're very interested to hear what you have to say.'

'I have – have no more to say,' he choked. 'Only that I was not having an affair, and I didn't kill her.'

'So who did?'

'If I knew that, don't you think I'd be telling you?'

'What I think,' Hamble said, 'is that you found her at home when you returned from work, the two of you became amorous and decided to play a little game. She was willing for you to tie her up because it was something you did regularly; you had sex and while she was still unable to defend herself you smothered her to death.'

'But why?' he shouted helplessly. 'Why the hell would I do that?'

'Please tell us.'

'I can't, because I didn't do it!'

'But your prints are on the buckle . . .'

'Because I tried to untie her . . .' He looked baffled, afraid and exhausted.

'It happened between six and ten in the evening. You admit to being there for at least half of that time.'

'I don't know what you want me to say.'

'Simply that you did it and—'

'*I didn't!*'

'Edward, please look at the screen and tell us why you left her like that for so long before calling the police. What were you waiting for?'

'I've already told you, I found her that way in the

morning. If I'd had anything to do with it, I'd hardly have left her like that would I? Apart from anything else it would have guaranteed me ending up where I am now.'

Suspecting he might be about to throw up, Jay quickly grabbed a plastic bin and shoved it onto his lap. 'My client's answered your questions,' she told the detectives tersely. 'If you don't have any others, I'm calling this to a halt.'

After Blake had been given some water and returned to his cell, badly shaken and terrified of how ominous things were looking for him, Bright signalled to Jay to join him in a consultation room.

'You know things aren't going well for your client,' he said, closing the door behind them. 'But we've known one another a long time, and I have a lot of respect for you. So, here's what I have to say: I'm pretty sure he did it, and you must know that we've already got enough to charge him.'

'So why don't you?' Her eyes glittered the challenge.

'Two reasons,' he replied, 'I think there is more to this than we currently know, and because I get the sense that you believe him. So, I'm prepared to allow more time, but not much, for you, or your client, to come up with more than you have now. Give us something else to work with – another suspect would be a good start.'

Which meant, she realized, that they were afraid there was one who they hadn't yet been able to find and no one wanted to be responsible for sending an innocent man to prison, least of all Ken Bright, who knew first-hand how it felt to find out he'd done just that. No one held it against him, not even the Force; in the circumstances he couldn't have known he was being gaslit by a London gang. However, having been there once meant he was doubly determined never to go there again. 'I'm working on it,' she assured him, already intending to call Antonia as soon as she got out of here. 'Have you spoken to his sister?'

'We have, but if you're hoping I'm about to divulge what was said . . .'

She shook her head. Since it couldn't have incriminated Blake or it would have come up in the interview, she said, 'Let me ask you this, do you believe he dropped his wife at the station?'

'We know his car was there.'

'OK, let's presume he was driving it and he did drop her; you don't know yet if she met someone after he left?'

'Your point being that if she did, I wouldn't be asking you to come up with another suspect.'

'Exactly, and you're the one with the access to CCTV. So, what's the problem?'

With a sigh, he said, 'The usual, faulty cameras, or simply not covering the area of interest. You know as well as I do that's a far more common story than the public are led to believe. But we do know she didn't get on a train, either to London or anywhere else, around the times we've been given.'

'What about the front of the station? Have you checked that footage?'

'Of course, but so far no sign of her.'

Knowing that by now officers would be asking questions all over the platforms, car parks and taxi ranks, she said, 'So, let's get this straight: you think she did meet someone, and that someone quite possibly went back to the house with her and . . . what? Tied her up, had sex with her, Blake came in, caught them together and murdered her?'

Although he didn't respond, she knew that in essence she'd just outlined at least one of his theories, and put that way it wasn't holding up at all.

Turning on her phone as she got into the car Jay paused to read the slew of messages that came through, and felt the frown relax between her eyes as she read the first.

Hey Mum, just wanted to say thanks for last night. Love you. You are totally lit.

Replying straight away, Jay said, *Everything's going to work out. Love you too xxx*

The next four messages were work related and could be dealt with on the phone as she drove. The fifth was from Antonia Debrayne asking her to call, and the sixth from Tom letting her know he was going to the gym when he got back from Plymouth and did she want to join him there? *We could pop into The Ashton or Cote for a bite after. Tx*

Leaving that until she'd spoken to Antonia, she quickly called up the number and pressed to connect.

Blake's sister answered on the third ring. 'Hello Mrs Wells,' she said, sounding both relieved and stressed. 'Thanks for ringing me back.'

'Please call me Jay. I hear you've spoken to the police.'

'Yes, this morning. I don't think I was able to tell them anything that'll be of much help to Edward, I'm not sure. Have they discussed it with you?'

'No, they wouldn't, but nothing was said during the last interview to suggest that you did, except they're worried they're not getting a full picture – quite literally – on what happened after he dropped Vanessa at the station on Monday. Is it possible we can meet?'

'Yes, of course. Any time.'

'Great. I'm just about to leave Keynsham. Where are you?'

'At home with John and the family. The children arrived back from uni yesterday. This has shaken them badly. We've always been a close family and none of us quite knows how to handle things.'

Understanding that, Jay said, 'Would you like me to come there? It's still not quite rush hour so it shouldn't take much more than forty minutes.'

'If you're sure you don't mind. I'm happy to come to you . . .'

'It's fine, honestly. I have a lot of calls to get through, so I can make good use of the journey. Just text me your address and any special directions I might need.'

'Will do. Call when you get to the gates and we'll open them from the house. The press have found us and it's possible some are still there.'

'Have you spoken to any of them?'

'No. None of us has.'

'That's good. We don't need to make any comments at this stage.'

After ringing off, Jay was in the process of sending a quick message to Tom letting him know she couldn't join him when Livvy texted again.

Did you remember I'm seeing Caitlin tonight?

Jay messaged back, *thanks for reminding me. Be good. Love you. Xxx*

To Tom she said, *Have to go to a meeting. Will see you at the house later. Sorry. Xx*

It was strange how she experienced a perverse sort of pleasure at turning him down, all laced through with dread that it would somehow backfire.

CHAPTER SEVEN

As Jay entered the black, wrought-iron gates to Highview Hall, in the heart of the countryside about halfway between Tetbury and Chipping Sodbury, she was relieved to spot no signs of anyone from the press. It was possible another, bigger story had broken somewhere else in the country, or they'd simply given up hassling the Debraynes for today.

After following a sun-dappled curve in the estate's tree-lined drive, she spotted Antonia on the front steps of an extremely grand house, clearly waiting for her to arrive. The place, characterful and sprawling, seemed to have as many outbuildings as it did chimneys and windows, and copious amounts of wisteria (no longer in flower) were climbing the grey stone walls. Spread out as far as the eye could see was an undulating patchwork of fields bordered by hedgerows and sunken lanes, while closer to the house was a tennis court, a manège, and what looked to be a bank of cricket nets.

Coming to a stop between an overflowing flowerbed and an old black Range Rover, she turned off her phone and stepped out into the breezy warmth of the late afternoon. Though she'd never lived in the countryside, it was on days such as this, with the glorious scent of fresh air awakening her senses, and tranquil views spreading in every direction, that she could seriously consider it.

'You found it all right,' Antonia said, coming to greet her. 'Is there any more news? No, don't tell me yet. Let's go inside. The others are waiting.'

'It'll be good to meet them,' Jay responded, interested to know more about her client's family, and to find out if the fact that Mr Debrayne worked in London might connect him to a relationship – or a meeting even – with Vanessa Blake on Monday 29 April.

Antonia led the way into an impressive entrance hall, full of paintings and statues and the kind of furniture that probably comprised a whole collection of cherished heirlooms, although given how scuffed and laden with family bric-a-brac most of it was, it was hard to tell for certain. 'Through here,' she said, opening a door beside an imposing inglenook fireplace topped by enormous antlers and some kind of medieval crest.

Jay followed her along a short corridor into what turned out to be a spacious but cluttered kitchen with dried herbs and copper pans hanging from overhead beams and wooden frames, a large dining table to one side and a beautiful orangery opening from its entire back wall.

John Debrayne and his children were already getting to their feet as she approached. All three looked worried, even dazed, but as relieved to see her as Antonia had been.

'Hi, I'm John,' Debrayne said, coming to shake her hand and meeting her gaze with shrewd grey eyes. He wasn't as tall as his wife, Jay noticed, and was probably a good ten years older; however he was a distinguished-looking man with an air of authority about him that wasn't surprising if all this was his – and she had no reason to suspect it wasn't.

'I'm sorry to meet you in these circumstances,' Jay told

him. 'I understand what a difficult time it is for your family.'

'We're very close,' he responded, 'so you're right, it's hard. This is Guy and Camille,' he added, turning to the children.

Camille came forward first, dark-haired and fresh-faced in spite of her bloodshot eyes and tear-streaked cheeks. She was probably a year or two older than Livvy, Jay guessed, which would make her nineteen or twenty. 'Edward didn't do it,' the girl said softly. 'If you knew him, you'd understand that it couldn't be possible.'

Jay gave her a reassuring smile and took Guy's hand as, blushing, he reached out his own. He was clearly sporty, given his physique, and good-looking in spite of his troubled complexion. She softened towards him right away simply for reminding her of Charlie, although they were hardly similar, so maybe it had more to do with how edgy and close to tears the lad seemed than any real resemblance to her son.

'I don't know who'd hurt her like that,' he said hoarsely, his young man's awkwardness making it hard for him to meet her eyes, 'but Cam's right, it wouldn't have been Ed.'

Antonia said, 'Can I get you a drink of some sort? John and I usually have a G&T around this time.'

'I'll take the tonic, thanks,' Jay replied, going to the chair in the orangery that John was directing her to.

'I'll get it,' Guy said. 'Cam, you do the other bits.'

As the youngsters busied themselves in the kitchen, Antonia and John sat side by side on a sofa and joined hands as they faced Jay, apparently gaining comfort and support from one another. Antonia said, 'How was he today? I took some clothes in. I don't know if they got to him.'

70

'They did,' Jay assured her, 'and he's holding up the best he can under the circumstances. But I have to be honest with you, unless we can give the police a good reason not to charge him, I'm pretty sure it'll happen tomorrow. Friday at the latest?'

'No!' Guy protested from behind them as Antonia put a hand to her mouth to cover a gasp.

John said, 'This is absurd. I don't understand any of it. Why didn't she get on that train? Where did she go after Ed left her?'

'It's what we'd all like to know,' Jay replied, looking at him frankly. 'With four hours at least not accounted for – I'm talking about between the time Edward dropped her off and when the alarm was deactivated at their home at three—'

'It was?' Antonia broke in confusedly. 'At three?'

'Apparently so, and the police aren't ruling out the possibility it was your brother who did it. At the moment he has no alibis for that time. Do you know anyone who might be able to provide him with one?'

Antonia regarded her helplessly, as Debrayne glanced at the children, who apparently had nothing to say.

'We'll keep thinking about it,' Debrayne promised, 'but right now . . . I'm sorry, none of us was around that day, apart from Toni and—'

'I was at the hair salon,' she said miserably. 'There might be someone else though. As John said, we'll keep thinking.'

Jay nodded her thanks. 'Would any of you have a suggestion for where Vanessa might have been instead of in London?'

Antonia shook her head again, clearly still at a loss. 'She comes here to ride sometimes,' she said, glancing at her husband, 'but she wasn't . . . The farrier was here on Monday, so she wouldn't have been able to take a horse out then.'

'Do you know if you're missing any stirrup straps?'

Antonia frowned. 'I-I'm not aware of it if we are.'

'Would Vanessa have had her own?'

'I'm not sure. She had all sorts of riding gear. Some of it she kept here, some at home. Why are you asking about the straps?'

Jay met her eyes with a meaningful stare, and a moment later Antonia's face flooded with colour as understanding dawned.

'Does your brother ride?' Jay asked.

'Not so much,' Antonia replied. 'When he does, he tends to use whatever's available in the stables – saddle, pads, bridle, girth; sometimes he even uses John's boots.'

'So no equipment of his own?'

Antonia shook her head.

Deciding to leave ownership of the stirrup straps to the police for now, Jay returned them to the alarm being turned off at three p.m. 'At the moment there are no witnesses to anyone going in or out of the house at that time,' she said, 'or later in the day. There's only the neighbour who claims to have seen your brother arrive home around eight and then to hearing raised voices around nine.'

'That'll be Frank Maguire who lives at the Long Barn,' John replied. 'He's an ex-army chap – long time ago – Scottish, a regular churchgoer. A decent enough sort of chap.'

'Nessa had a soft spot for Maddie Maguire, the wife,' Antonia put in. 'She's a sweet woman. Very keen on gardening.'

'Did you know that Mr Maguire fell behind with the rent?' Jay asked.

John nodded and sighed. 'Yes, an unfortunate business. Poor bloke got scammed – you know how these shysters prey on the old, although Maguire's probably not much more than mid-sixties. Still, never too young, or too old, to fall for a con. It all got sorted out in the end and he paid Ed everything he owed.'

Knowing her next question was probably going to cause an uncomfortable, even spirited reaction, Jay watched them carefully as she said, 'The police asked Edward today if Vanessa was having an affair. Do you think she was?'

While Antonia blanched, John seemed almost offended. 'As far as we're aware she wasn't,' he retorted, 'but given what's happened, I guess the possibility has to be considered. What did Ed say?'

'That if she was he knew nothing about it.' Then she added, 'Is it possible Edward was seeing someone?'

Antonia blinked in shock as Camille shouted, 'No! He wouldn't.'

'Nor would she,' Guy cried, his cheeks reddening with anger.

Jay turned back to Debrayne as he said, 'Do you think he was? Has he said so?'

'No. He says he wasn't.'

'He's telling the truth,' Antonia declared with alacrity. 'We don't have secrets, Ed and I. We never have.'

'Have any names come up in either regard?' John asked.

Intrigued by his interest, Jay said, 'Not that I know of, and I have no reason to suppose that the police have one either. However, they're not ready to dismiss the possibility that a lover, or a third party of some sort, might exist and was there that night – and at the moment it's all that's saving Edward from being charged.'

'Mum,' Camille interrupted shrilly, 'you've got to tell Jay what you—'

'Cam, stop,' her father barked, silencing her.

There was a stunned moment, before Guy muttered furiously. 'I'm not hanging around for any more of this. It's all fucked up and—'

'Go to your room,' John snapped. 'Now! You too, Camille. We'll sort out the drinks.'

'They're done,' she shot back, slamming a tray of ice cubes into the sink. 'God, this house makes me sick – but you need to know, Jay, that my uncle *did not do it*.'

Watching them storm off, Jay waited for the door to close before turning back to the parents, fascinated to hear what they were going to say next.

Holding his wife's hand between both of his, John said, 'I'm afraid that little scene is causing you to think we're hiding something, and so I suppose I have to admit that we are . . .'

'John,' Antonia cautioned.

'It doesn't have anything to do . . .' he began, speaking over her. 'Well, I'm not sure *what* has anything to do with Nessa's death, but I'm afraid, if you haven't already heard things about our sister-in-law, you're going to. We're trying to stop it, but I don't know if it'll be possible.'

'Whatever it is,' Jay told him, 'this is a murder inquiry, so I can guarantee the police will find out sooner or later. So it's best I hear it from you than from them.'

Debrayne nodded agreement, and tightened the grip on his wife's hand as he said, 'People can be as cruel as they can kind, I'm sure you know that, and ever since Ness and Edward lost their son . . . Things have been said, not by our friends, you understand, none of them would ever believe Ness and Ed capable of harming their boy.' He swallowed, seeming to find it hard to go on for a moment. 'We were all there,' he continued, 'as a family. We know what happened and we all bear the guilt and the shame of it. We weren't watching Lucas when we should have been . . .'

Antonia added, brokenly, 'We were interviewed by the police in Italy, and again when we got back by detectives here. There was an inquest and it was found to be an accidental death. I don't believe anyone in authority ever thought otherwise. They were very sympathetic and sensitive, but you know how it is . . . People gossip and turn things around . . . I'm not sure how much of it ever reached Edward and Nessa, but I know they heard some of it and I'm convinced, we both are,' she said, glancing at her husband, 'that it was what made Nessa . . .' She stopped and lowered her eyes.

John said, 'Lucas's death broke all our hearts and no one's really been the same since. I mean, we get on with our lives, you have to, but for Nessa, his mother . . .'

'John,' Antonia cautioned again.

'It has to be said,' he told her. 'And if it helps Ed . . .'

'It *won't.*'

'Why don't you let me be the judge?' Jay suggested gently.

John nodded. 'I don't think it will help him,' he admitted, 'but ever since Lucas died, with all the rumours and gossip . . . Ness became . . . You have to understand how hard it was for her. Every day was a struggle, she wasn't coping at all well and she became . . . Well, let's say, difficult to live with at times, especially when she started blaming Ed, as if she believed the gossip even though she was there when Lucas went into the pool, so she knew it wasn't his fault.'

Antonia said quickly. 'She didn't blame him all the time, and I don't think she ever believed what she was saying, but you can imagine how hard it was for my brother. He loved her, and I know that in her heart she loved him, but a tragedy like that . . . It does things to people, and puts such a strain on a marriage. Sometimes it seemed to bring them closer together, then suddenly she'd flare up and start accusing him of being glad Lucas was dead. Or she'd say she asked him to keep an eye on him that day and he hadn't bothered. After, when she calmed down, she'd beg Ed to forgive her, and he always did, but it took a toll on him. How could it not? He was grieving himself and in some ways it was as though he was losing his wife as well as his son.'

Jay was rapidly processing this new insight into the marriage and what it could do to Edward's case – none of it good – but before she could ask any more she heard a dog bark and turned to see two women, one quite old, the other in her forties coming through the knot garden outside.

Antonia got to her feet. 'My mother-in-law, Elizabeth,' she told Jay. 'And Melissa, Nessa's friend – the one she was going to see on Monday . . . except she didn't. She's being interviewed by the police tomorrow, so we invited her to come and stay with us for the night.'

As Jay stood too, the dear old Labrador with silvery grey eyebrows and matching muzzle came to look up at her with curious and cloudy brown eyes.

'This is Max, Edward's dog,' John told her. 'We've been taking care of him.'

'Hello Max,' she said, fondly ruffling the dog's head.

'He can't see too well,' John smiled, 'but he always manages to bring Mum back when they go for a walk.'

'She has Alzheimer's,' Antonia said in a whisper, and turning to the doors she greeted her mother-in-law with a hug while saying to Melissa, 'This is Jay Bamfield Wells, Edward's lawyer.'

Melissa's close-set eyes came to Jay. She was round faced, attractive in her own way, and slightly overweight. 'It's good to meet you,' she said with cool politeness. 'How's Ed?'

Jay shook her hand. 'Holding up as best he can. I'm sorry for your loss. I believe you and Vanessa were good friends?'

Melissa nodded and stood aside as Antonia said to her mother-in-law, 'Betty, this is Jay. She's helping Ed.'

The older woman fixed Jay with pale green eyes and a gentle smile. 'Hello dear,' she said. 'Do you build houses too?'

'Not that sort of help,' John corrected. 'She's his lawyer.'

Betty continued to smile.

'It's nice to meet you,' Jay said gently.

'Yes, dear, yes,' Betty responded, and looked past her towards the kitchen.

'Drinks!' Antonia announced. 'We forgot about them. I'm sorry, Jay, you must think us terribly rude.'

'Not at all,' Jay assured her, and might have excused herself at this point were it not a perfect opportunity to speak to Melissa.

After refreshments had been brought to the round table

at the centre of the summer room, and everyone was seated glass in hand, Antonia said to Melissa, 'We were just telling Jay about some of Nessa's . . . difficulties.'

Melissa's expression showed surprise, quickly followed by wariness. 'What about them?' she asked, focusing on the stranger in their midst.

'Just that she had them,' Antonia replied. 'Max, sweetie, you're on my foot.'

The dog didn't move, perhaps didn't hear.

'Did anyone tell you,' Melissa said to Jay, 'that Nessa believed Ed loved his dog more than his son?'

Antonia gave a gasp. 'That's absolutely not true,' she cried angrily. 'She never believed any such thing.'

Melissa didn't disagree. 'Maybe not, but she used to say it, and it was cruel, irrational, and very hard for Ed to argue her out of once she got started. She used to say it to me, and I found it difficult not to get angry with her, because I knew that in her heart she didn't believe it. She just didn't seem able to stop herself from saying it.'

'Ed adores his dog,' Betty stated to no one in particular as she whirled an olive around her virgin martini.

Wondering, in the back of her mind, why Blake hadn't yet mentioned the dog, Jay said to Melissa, 'I know you're seeing the police tomorrow, but would you mind telling me why you think Vanessa said she was coming to see you on Monday if she wasn't?'

With no hesitation, Melissa said, 'I've no idea.'

'So you don't normally cover for her?'

'Not in the way you're thinking. In fact, no. As far as I was aware Nessa either came to London to see me and a couple of friends; or to meet with various gallery owners, artists or photographers. I honestly didn't have control of her calendar, so I never questioned anything.'

'But if she needed to stay the night, she'd be in touch with you no matter who she was seeing?' Jay prompted.

'Not necessarily. There's Sheri, who lives in Shad Thames. Sometimes Nessa would stay at her place. Sheri's in the finance world so she's regularly out of town. She gave Nessa a key way back when so she could use the flat if she needed to.'

'Did she use it often?'

'I don't think so. I can't say for certain.' As her eyes shifted and a faint colour seeped into her cheeks, Jay felt sure she was lying – or at least not telling a full truth.

'Do you know if she went there on Monday?' Jay asked.

'Not according to Sheri. Usually if Nessa was intending to use the place she'd call in advance to make sure it was OK. When I spoke to Sheri yesterday to tell her what had happened, she said she hadn't heard from Nessa for a couple of weeks.'

So, as things stood, Jay was thinking, it didn't look as though Vanessa had been intending to go to London at all.

With half an eye on John Debrayne, she asked Melissa bluntly, 'Do you think Vanessa was having an affair?'

While both Debraynes seemed to flinch, Melissa appeared more defensive than fazed. 'Not an affair, no. I mean, if she was, she never told me.'

'Might she have told Sheri?'

'You'd have to ask Sheri.'

'Can you let me have her number?'

Taking out her phone Melissa said, 'If you give me yours, I'll text it over. She's back now. She got the red-eye from New York last night.'

After making sure she'd received the text, Jay was about to continue when the kitchen door opened and Camille came in.

'It's on TV,' the girl announced loftily, and picking up a remote control she turned on the set in the summer room.

DI Bright was saying, 'So if anyone saw Vanessa Blake in or around Chippenham Station on Monday morning could you please contact your local police, or call the number at the bottom of the screen.' The screen split to include a shot of an extremely lovely Vanessa, one Jay recognized from her Instagram page.

The gathered press began calling out questions, mostly about Edward Blake, until someone asked, 'Is it true Vanessa was seen getting into a taxi outside the station?'

Jay's interest piqued as Bright said, 'We've interviewed the station's regular taxi drivers, and so far no one has been able to provide any information to help further our inquiries. However, she could have used a taxi firm from elsewhere in the area.'

'So, you're saying someone *did* see her getting into a taxi?'

Bright spoke quietly to an officer standing next to him, and turned back to the microphones. 'At the moment we have no evidence to say that she did, but we're still exploring the possibility. Any help from the public would be greatly appreciated.'

Someone spoke in his ear, and after nodding that he'd heard he wrapped up the conference.

As the broadcast returned to the studio John said to Camille, 'Turn it off.'

The silence was abrupt, seeming to plunge them into another kind of reality for a moment or two.

Jay was the first to speak, saying to the Debraynes, 'Had you heard anything about a taxi before?'

They both shook their heads. 'Had you?' Antonia ventured.

No, Jay hadn't, but it was clearly a relatively recent development or they'd have asked Edward about it while interrogating him earlier. 'The gossip about Edward and Vanessa,' she said, bringing the subject back to what they'd been discussing before, 'do you know who was spreading it, where it might have come from?'

Antonia sighed as she said, 'Not really. No one ever says anything like that to your face, do they?'

'So how do you know about it?'

Antonia glanced at Camille. 'It was in the papers for a while,' she replied. 'You know what they're like, how they love to speculate and try to come up with a scandal of some sort to sell their rags. They stopped after the inquest, but I guess the seeds were sown, so things carried on being said from time to time.'

'We mostly get to hear about it,' Camille continued, 'from people who work for us. Or from well-meaning,' she drew quotes around the words, 'friends.'

'Actually, we haven't heard any rumours for a while,' Antonia said, 'or I haven't. Have you?' she asked her daughter and husband.

Both shook their heads.

'So, there's no one you can pinpoint,' Jay said, 'who might have had a grudge against Edward or Vanessa? Someone who could have had a falling out with one or other of them and got heated enough to do this?'

Antonia looked baffled and helpless as she said, 'Even if they had fallen out with someone, and I don't know if they did, would it really end like this?'

81

Jay had to admit that on the face of it, today, it seemed unlikely; however something had clearly happened or they wouldn't be sitting here now.

'From what we've heard,' John said, 'Nessa wasn't forced into the . . . position they found her in, so I'm not really following this line of questioning – unless you're saying she was having an affair with someone who wanted her dead?'

'Oh God,' Camille sobbed, 'so you think she *was* having an affair?'

Reaching out a hand for her daughter, Antonia said, 'The circumstances are such, my darling, that we have to accept that something was going on, but I've no idea,' she said to Jay, 'who it might have been.'

Jay looked at Camille.

'Don't ask me,' Camille sniffed, dabbing her eyes. 'I just can't believe she would.'

Jay's eyes moved to Melissa.

'I swear,' Melissa said, putting a hand to her heart, 'that she never said anything to me about an *affair*.'

Why emphasize the word, Jay wondered.

Melissa was still speaking. 'And I'd be amazed if Sheri knows more than I do. We three pretty much tell one another everything.'

Which wasn't exactly what she'd said just now, Jay noted.

Wondering if they understood that the failure to come up with a possible lover for Vanessa was making everything look pretty bad for Edward, Jay put her glass on the table and stood up. 'I should be going now,' she said, glancing down at the dog as he groaned and snuffled in his sleep. 'You know how to get hold of me if you need to,' she said, picking up her bag. 'Please call any time.' To her relief John was already getting to his feet, so she didn't have to ask him to walk out with her.

'Thanks for coming to see us,' he said, as they went through the front hall. 'I know we haven't been of much help – or I don't feel that we have, anyway.'

Aware of the lavish surroundings, Jay said, 'Can I ask what you do for a living, Mr Debrayne?'

'John, please. I'm a lawyer, same as you, but in the commercial and corporate world. My firm's in the City, which is why I'm there for part of the week. Semi-retired, actually.'

Coming to a stop beside her car, Jay said, 'Did you ever meet up with Vanessa when she was in town?'

He seemed startled by the question, and, she noticed, vaguely uneasy. 'I did once,' he replied, 'about a year ago. She was supposed to be meeting a client somewhere near my office. Whoever it was let her down, so she gave me a call to ask if I was free for lunch.'

'And were you?'

'I was. We met at a bistro near the cathedral, but I couldn't stay long.'

'And that's the only time you met her in London?'

'When it was just the two of us, yes. There were other occasions with Toni and Edward to go to the theatre, or a concert.'

'Did you ever get the train to or from London with her?'

'No. I don't tend to use Chippenham Station. I either go from Bristol Parkway or Kemble.'

Jay glanced up at the house as she opened her car door. To her surprise she saw someone watching them from an upstairs window.

Following the direction of her gaze John sighed sadly. 'Guy,' he said, as if gently scolding the lad. 'He's always been close to Ed so this is particularly hard for him.'

Imagining the gap uncle and nephew might fill in each other's lives, with Guy's father older and often in London, and Edward having no children of his own, Jay said, 'Where's he at uni?'

'Bath Spa, first year business and management. I'm afraid he's not overly ambitious or academic, like his sister – she's in her second year at Oxford – but he works hard and Ed was kind of . . . I guess you'd say, his mentor.'

Interested to hear that, Jay said, 'So your son is keen on architecture?'

'Property development. He's been working with Ed for the past few years during term breaks and most weekends. He's pretty hands on, I believe . . . I'm not sure what's going to happen if Ed doesn't . . .' He stopped, stumbling over the words. 'Do you really think there's a chance . . .?' He stopped again, and said, 'Shit, I can't believe I'm even asking the question.'

Registering his distress and confusion, Jay said, 'Have the police called you in for interview yet?'

He nodded and took a breath. 'Tomorrow, same as Melissa.'

'Do you have legal representation?'

He balked at that. 'Do you think I need it?'

'What I think is that you'll be asked if you were having an affair with your sister-in-law.'

A flush of colour rushed around his collar. 'Have I given you some reason to think that?' he protested tightly.

'Not exactly, but were you?'

'I was not.'

84

'So, you've no idea how she came to be tied to a bed?'

'I have to say I resent the implication—'

'You need to understand,' she cut in briskly, 'that if you've ever stayed in that guest room, and I'm presuming you have?' She waited for him to answer.

He nodded.

'Then it's highly likely your DNA will be found there. And if it is, you'll be asked when you were last in the room and what happened while you were there.'

His face was losing colour by the second. 'I can answer that now,' he growled angrily. 'Toni and I stayed over last Saturday night following a dinner party. So, you're right, my DNA very probably will be found, but a lot of friends have stayed over who might also have left traces of themselves behind. My mother and my children stay now and again – presumably not in the same sheets – but I hope you're not suggesting that either of them committed this horrible crime.'

'I'm not suggesting you did either,' Jay assured him calmly. 'I'm simply trying to prepare you for what's likely to come up tomorrow.'

Collecting himself, he said, 'OK, thank you, and I'm sorry, this is all . . . It's not something any of us has ever had to deal with before.'

Understanding that better than he probably realized she said, 'To be clear, the police will want to be as certain as they can be that there's no other suspect they should be considering before they charge your brother-in-law.'

He nodded, clearly taking it in.

With a quick smile she got into her car and started back down the drive, aware of him watching her until she disappeared into the trees. She was still picturing him in her mind's eye as she left the estate and began going over all she'd learned during the past hour. There was a lot, more than she'd expected, giving rise to as many questions as answers, suspicions even, and certainly a number of grave concerns. She wished she could speak to Blake right away, put at least some of her concerns to him, but it was late in the day, and this new information was still too fresh in her mind for her to present him with anything before she'd worked through exactly what she wanted to say.

CHAPTER EIGHT

By the time Jay arrived home she was tired, hungry and slightly bad tempered, although unsure which of the many issues on her plate was causing the irritation. Certainly, the upcoming Lexcel audit at the office was a pressure – she'd just spent the best part of the journey discussing it with Jilly, the practice manager – but so were the many other demands of her workload. And finding the house empty and a mess wasn't improving matters. She'd been hoping to discuss Blake's case with Tom over a glass of wine and bite to eat, but he'd already texted to say he'd run into Perry and Gretchen at the gym and accepted their offer to go to their place for supper.

In spite of her partner and his wife being only a ten-minute walk away, it was too late for Jay to join them now; besides, she had far too much to write up following her chat with the Debraynes even to think about kicking back and socializing. So perhaps, instead of feeling tetchy with Tom for not being here, she should focus more on being thankful that Livvy wasn't lying in wait for another heart to heart.

Where was Livvy?

Quickly firing off a text, she discarded her bag and shoes in the hall, released her hair and went straight to the fridge to take out a bottle of Pouilly-Fuissé. Her mind was so full of Blake, or more accurately his family, that she forgot about finding something to eat and took her drink through to the study to start work.

Most of the notes she made over the following two hours, interrupted only by Livvy reminding her she was upstairs in her room revising with Caitlin, were in preparation for the meeting she'd organized for tomorrow morning with the rest of the crime team. She needed to brainstorm this case before returning to Keynsham custody, try to get some clarity going while the clock ticked fast towards the deadline of charge or release. Right now she was becoming increasingly concerned that her client wasn't going home any time soon.

And that, she realized, as she sat back in her chair and rubbed her tired eyes, was the real reason for her irritation – Edward Blake's presumed innocence was getting to her in a way she wished it wouldn't. Not that she thought he was guilty, she actually didn't, but there was a lot more to his marriage than anyone was admitting to, and while his family had been more forthcoming, it had been only up to a point. They were clearly holding something back, as was Melissa, and Jay couldn't imagine why any of them thought it was going to help Edward's case to keep things from his lawyer.

Unless they didn't want to help him, but that seemed to make no sense at all.

'Why are you so sure he didn't do it?' Ash Baqri – apart from Jay the most senior solicitor of the crime team – asked the followed morning when they were gathered in the conference room. He was a slight man in his late forties with a mop of inky-black curls, red-rimmed specs and an intensely serious face – until he smiled, when he seemed to morph into a ray of pure sunshine.

Jay considered the question, in spite of having asked herself the same one several times these past couple of days. 'Actually, I'm not sure,' she admitted. 'But when can we ever be a hundred per cent certain someone's telling us the truth?'

'We can't,' he conceded.

'I just don't think he's lying to me.'

'Not lying isn't the same as being completely honest,' Sallyanne Jones, another valued solicitor in the crime team, put in. She was in her mid-thirties, always sparkly eyed and attentive, a serial internet dater and sworn singleton. 'As we know,' she continued, 'it's possible to tell part of a story and sound utterly convincing for the simple reason that it's the truthful part. What else goes to making up the full picture is anyone's guess, and until someone's questioned beyond their comfort zone . . . Well, you know what I'm saying.' Reading from her laptop she said, 'You've said here that you got the impression the family was holding back about something, and that Melissa Siddell might also know more than she's telling. Can you give us any more than that?'

Jay cast her mind back to yesterday's gathering in the summer room, conjuring the faces and words and how her instincts – her truth radar – had reacted at the time. 'I couldn't work out who they were covering for,' she said. 'Edward or Vanessa, or even themselves, but their behaviour was . . .' She shook her head, unable to find the right word. 'They were guarded,' she said, 'in spite of putting on a good show of being eager to help – and they couldn't have spoken about Edward more lovingly.'

'Even Melissa?'

'Less so in her case, but she didn't give the impression of not liking him.'

'So lovingly,' Ash prompted, 'that it began to sound insincere? That often happens when someone's overdoing it. Always leads me to think they actually secretly hate the person in question.'

Jay smiled. 'I know what you mean, but I don't think that's happening here. They seem genuinely to care about him, and on the few occasions I've met him he comes over as a decent man under all the crap he's dealing with now; someone who's easy to like. Or in his family's case, to love.'

'And you've never been wrong about a client before?' Ash commented wryly.

She laughed and said, 'Never,' while they all knew that she had, as indeed had they all. It was one of the dreaded hazards of their world, being gaslit by clients with cunning intellect, likeable personalities and plausible stories.

Sallyanne said, 'Tell us more about the brother-in-law, John Debrayne. You didn't seem to believe him when he denied having an affair with Vanessa?'

Jay's eyes narrowed as she thought. 'I didn't, completely,' she admitted. 'It made him uncomfortable to be asked, although not overly so . . . It made me wonder if perhaps there was something once and now it's history?'

'Or it's still happening,' Sallyanne suggested, 'and she threatened to tell all to make him leave his wife?'

'So he did away with her to shut her up,' Ash put in. 'Do we know where he was on Monday?'

'In London, apparently. I'm sure the police will be checking it out.'

'What's the wife like?'

Jay gave it some thought. 'Same as her brother in that she comes over as easy to like. Quite county, you know, plummy, but friendly. I'd say she's an older sister – Blake's thirty-nine, so I'd put her at early to mid-forties. Lovely to look at in a Kate Middleton sort of way, but as we know, beauty's never stopped a man playing away before.'

'OK, my money's on the brother-in-law,' Ash declared, reflexively checking his watch as the nearby guild churches began chiming the hour. 'If he wasn't in London on Monday, he could find himself with a lot of explaining to do – depending, of course, on where next he claims to have been, and if anyone can corroborate it.'

They all looked up as the door opened and Terry Josephs, known to all as Joe, a bullish, weathered man in his mid-fifties came into the room. Though his appearance was more prize-fighter than part-time investigator, he was one of the most valued members of the team, given his many years as a detective with the Wiltshire constabulary.

'Sorry I'm late,' he said gruffly, pulling out a chair to sit down. 'But I've read it all, so here to serve.'

Jay smiled. She was extremely fond of this man, possibly because he reminded her of her father even though there was no physical resemblance between the two at all. What created the bond was that her dad had had all the time in the world for Joe, and she would never forget the moving words the ex-detective had delivered at his old friend's funeral. 'Thanks for coming,' she said. 'We've been throwing out a couple of theories – in that everyone's hiding something, not sure what yet; the brother-in-law did it, and now I'm interested to hear what stands out for you.'

Josephs scratched his jaw as he took his time to say, 'I'm on board with the brother-in-law as a possible, but tell me more about the neighbour who says he heard raised voices. Blake owns all the properties in the close vicinity, right?' he asked.

'As far as I'm aware there are only three,' she replied. 'The Blake residence, aka the crime scene, the Long Barn rented by Maguire and wife, and a cottage that is some sort of weekend/holiday retreat for a Dutch couple. The Van der Bergs. Do you know something?' she asked, for the simple reason that Joe was often ahead of the game.

'In your notes,' Joe replied, 'you say Maguire fell behind with his rent. What was that all about?'

'Apparently he was the victim of a scam, lost a lot of money, but it all got sorted out – or at least our client got paid. No reason to think there's anything suspicious there, but I would like to talk to the man at some point.'

'If he had anything worthwhile to add to what he saw or heard that day, wouldn't Ken Bright know by now?' Sallyanne put in.

'Probably, possibly, but for all we know Bright and his team are holding something back.'

'I agree, Maguire's worth talking to,' Josephs declared, 'so I'll search him out.'

Nodding her thanks, Jay checked her phone for emails as she said, 'Ah, great, confirmation from Matt Kowalski, our favourite defence scientist. He'll be on board as soon as we need him. So good news there.'

Giving a thumbs up, Josephs said, 'With the lack of any other suspects or witnesses, they should have enough to charge our guy by now. I don't get why they haven't.'

'DI Ken Bright,' Sallyanne reminded him. 'We know the last thing he wants is to risk sending someone down for a crime they didn't commit, which tells us he's not a hundred per cent on board with it being our client.'

Jay said, 'He'll take it right up to the wire before he's forced to charge or release – but my guess is, unless something changes today, he'll charge.'

'And the something that could change,' Ash murmured, focusing on his screen, 'is a witness to her getting into a taxi at the station.'

Jay nodded agreement. 'If the taxi actually exists?' she countered.

Everyone regarded her with interest.

Josephs said, 'You think someone might have rung it in to try and misdirect the investigation?' His scepticism deepened. 'Like who?'

Jay shrugged. 'A family member? One of the anonymous gossips you'll have read about in my notes? Which reminds me, I'd like you to take a stroll around Chipping Sodbury, see what you can find out from the locals, how popular – or not – our client was, what they know about him and his wife. I don't have to tell you your job.'

Josephs saluted.

'When are you next seeing Blake?' Sallyanne asked.

Jay glanced at the time. 'I should probably start heading out to Keynsham in the next half-hour. Even if the police aren't ready for us, I want to have a chat with him before they get going again.'

Ash said, 'OK, I'm still stuck on the taxi. Let's say it does exist. Do we know where it's supposed to have picked her up?'

'We need to check that,' Jay replied, making a note.

'Has anyone come forward yet to say he or she was the driver?'

'Not that's been reported on the news. I should know more when I get to Keynsham. If Bright's not forthcoming, I've made a note to ask Edward if he can throw any light on it. Is there a company he and Vanessa regularly use, for instance. I'm also curious to know why he hasn't mentioned his dog. I got the impression from his family that it's a precious pet, dear old soul that it is, so it either wasn't there when he went into the house at eight o'clock on Monday, or it was and he . . . forgot about it?' Her scepticism was evident.

Sallyanne wrinkled her nose too. 'Most dogs are all over you the minute you go through the door, so I can't see how he'd forget it was there.'

Stepping in as devil's advocate, Jay said, 'Maybe it was already with him and came in at the same time.'

Ash said, 'OK, consider this if you haven't already. Vanessa changed her mind about going to London, so he brought her back from the station, strapped her to the bedposts and left her there to contemplate her fate until he finally got around to doing the deed.'

Everyone groaned and booed. 'There are so many holes in that,' Joe snorted, 'I can already feel myself drowning.'

'We need to take another look at the timeline,' Jay stated, calling up the one she'd created. 'We have him dropping her at the station just before ten in the morning. She apparently vanishes into thin air – putting mysterious taxi on hold for the moment – while our guy returns to the gallery in Chipping Sodbury via a build site where no one was at work. The address is in the notes,' she told Joe, 'so talk to the builders and see what they have to say

94

about their employer. Same goes for any other projects he has on the go.'

'Will do,' he replied, jotting it down.

Moving on she said, 'The alarm at the gallery was deactivated at 11.34 and, unless you tell me differently, Joe, given you know the area, that fits for the journey time between locations?'

He nodded. 'But that's presuming it was him who turned off the alarm,' he countered. 'According to your notes there are no witnesses to him coming or going from the gallery, apart from his sister when she turned up to take him to lunch at the deli. Good place, by the way. Recommend it.'

'Thanks,' Jay responded, not making a note. 'It's quite possible witnesses will come forward,' she pointed out, 'it's still early days. But going with what we've been told, Edward was with Antonia in a public place – plenty of witnesses – until two o'clock-ish. We can presume the police have already verified this, but no harm in checking it out, Joe.'

'On it,' he assured her.

'Then Blake and his sister part company when she goes to a hair salon in Tetbury.'

'I'll find out which one,' Joe assured her.

Continuing, Jay said, 'So Antonia ceased being an alibi for her brother during the early afternoon and someone deactivated the alarm at Clover Hill at three.'

'It could have been *her* on her way to get her roots done,' Joe suggested.

'If it was, why wouldn't she have said so?' Jay countered.

As no one had an answer for that, Ash said, 'If it was

Vanessa who turned off the alarm at the house, it still doesn't give us any insight into where she was between being dropped at the station and arriving home.'

'It's a big gap that needs to be filled,' Jay agreed, 'and right now we don't have a single theory – never mind suspicion – to run with.'

Sallyanne said, 'I don't suppose there's any way of knowing if someone was with her when she turned off the alarm at three – presuming it was her?'

Jay shook her head. 'Not unless someone saw them, and so far we don't have anyone.'

'And we've no idea how long she was tied to the bed before she was suffocated?'

'Not yet, but apparently there are no indications of a struggle to get her there, so it seems reasonable to suppose she was a willing participant to the bondage part at least.'

'Do we know if she had sex?' Ash prompted, searching for the early scientific reports.

'Apparently there was slight bruising around the vaginal area,' Jay answered, 'but no semen has been found.'

Sallyanne said, 'If a condom was used there's not likely to be, unless they've picked up someone else's blood, or saliva? Any mention of that?'

'Not so far.'

'Of course,' Sallyanne continued, 'she could have been with a woman and they used a device of some sort. Slight bruising, no semen.'

As several eyebrows rose, Ash said, 'Antonia?'

Though doubtful, Jay said, 'Right now, anything's possible. Once Matt Kowalski's talked to the pathologist and forensic team we should know more.' Turning to Joe she said, 'If you can get any inside knowledge from your old colleagues on the Force about who's being interviewed, what new witnesses are coming forward . . .'

'I've already put in some calls,' he assured her, 'but you know it'll be easier the other side of a charge. Right now, the pressure's on everyone: you, cops, family, suspect . . . Only one resting in peace is the victim.'

With an unwelcome image of Vanessa in her head, spread out lifeless on the bed in such an undignified way, Jay said, 'I need to be going. We should meet again later or tomorrow morning about this and *the audit*. Is everyone OK with it so far?'

'Our trusty Jilly is on top of it,' Ash assured her. 'I think she's still chasing Perry's team for a couple of things, but we should be in good shape for when the inspection begins.'

Sallyanne said, 'We didn't discuss Melissa Siddell. You said you think she might know something.'

Glad to be reminded, Jay said, 'The police will have interviewed her by now. If she said anything interesting, it could come up when they talk to Blake. If nothing does I'll contact her later.'

'And what about the other friend, Sheri? Do we know her surname?'

'Razak. I left a message for her to call, but she hasn't got back to me yet. I'll try again on my way to Keynsham. Now, before I go, who, at this stage, thinks our client is guilty?'

All hands rose.

Dismayed, she said, 'OK, so who thinks he's not guilty?'

All hands rose again.

She laughed and Ash said, 'I think we can all agree he

had means and opportunity – even he's not contending that . . . If there was an affair it could provide motive and that won't be good.'

'I'm not convinced he did it,' Sallyanne stated, 'but it's definitely not going his way right now.'

'My mind's still open,' Josephs put in, 'in spite of everything being against him.'

'OK,' Jay responded, pleased they were more or less on the same page, which might actually not be a page at all. 'Let's just hope nothing's come up this morning to make them charge him before I get there.'

Twenty minutes later, Jay had barely left the Grand Hotel car park when her phone started to ring. Seeing it was Tom she clicked on with the handsfree. 'Hi, what's up?' she asked, indicating to turn down towards Bristol Bridge. 'And how come you slept in the guest room last night?'

'I didn't want to wake you when I came in.' He sounded gruff, distracted, irritable even.

'Were you that late?' she asked.

'Late enough for you to be asleep. Perry and I tied one on, I'm afraid. Have you seen him today?'

'No, but I think he was around the office. What were you putting to rights?'

Instead of answering, he said, 'Where are you?'

'On my way to Keynsham. Where are you?'

'In chambers. Listen, I'm going to be in London next week for this rape trial.'

Unease closed in on her the way it always did when she knew he was going to be in London; for London, to her, meant a closer proximity to Ellen Tyler. 'What rape trial?' she asked mildly.

'I'm sure I told you about it, but you've had other things on your mind.'

He was right, she had, and now she felt bad for apparently not listening to him properly.

'We need to talk,' he said.

Hooting the horn as someone cut her up, she said, 'That sounds ominous. What about?'

'Not on the phone.' He paused. 'I have something to tell you . . .'

Turning cold at the words, hearing the echo of the last time he'd said them, she blurted, 'If it concerns your mistress—'

'For God's sake,' he snapped. 'She's not my mistress and why do you always assume the worst?'

'Maybe because you've given me good reason to. So, what do you have to tell me?' She was shaking, stupidly. What an overreaction!

'I think we should make some time at the weekend. Is there anything in the diary I don't know about?'

'I'll have to check. Shall I presume you've already discussed whatever it is with Perry and that's why you were up so late?'

With a sigh, he said, 'Are you going to be around this evening?'

'I'm not sure yet. Why?'

'Freddy and Carina have invited us for drinks at the Clifton Club and I'd like to go.'

She liked their friends Freddy and Carina, a lot. 'What about Livvy?' she said.

'What about her?'

'Have you forgotten she's up to her eyes with revision? She might want help, or food, or just to know that someone cares.'

'Why are you laying this on me, when you know perfectly well she's capable of feeding herself or asking for help—'

'OK, OK, I'm sorry, I didn't mean to . . . Yes, let's meet up with Freddy and Carina, but you might have to be prepared to go on your own if this interrogation runs on, and there's every chance it will.'

'How's it going?'

'Much like any murder at this stage – more questions than answers, lots of economy with the truth and part of me is afraid that my client's family is holding out on me – or him.'

'Charming. Does he know that, or suspect it?'

'I'm not sure, but I don't think so. In fact, I think he believes they're doing everything they can to help clear him, but it's not exactly happening like that.'

'Poor guy, lucky he's got you onside.'

She smiled and felt her defences lowering. 'I'll tell him that,' she said, knowing she wouldn't. 'I should go now. I need to make some calls before I get to Keynsham.'

'OK, text to let me know what's happening later.'

As she rang off she quickly turned left to follow the Feeder – the dull, muddy canal that linked Netham Lock to the Floating Harbour – and was just passing CID headquarters when she spotted Ken Bright getting into his car. She didn't bother attracting his attention, although she was glad to see him, for if he was here and not at Keynsham custody, she could safely presume no one, other than Blake, was waiting for her.

Aware of how fast time was running out, she quickly detached from the unease Tom had left her with and voice-activated her phone to call Sheri Razak. After three rings the woman answered; she sounded harassed and impatient, but at least it wasn't her messaging service again.

'Oh, Mrs Wells,' she said after Jay announced herself. 'Yes, sorry I haven't got back to you. Things are pretty crazy here, and I'm afraid I can't talk now. I'm about to go into a meeting and I'm catching a flight to Singapore tonight. Would you mind waiting until I'm there? I should have some time to myself over the weekend. We can Skype if you like.'

Making her frustration audible, Jay said, 'Edward Blake is very close to being charged. So, if there's anything you can tell me that might help to avoid this, I'd appreciate knowing it now.'

There was a lengthy silence, during which the sound of background voices and ringing phones assured Jay that the line hadn't gone dead. Finally Sheri Razak said, 'There are things I can tell you, Mrs Wells, but I'm afraid I don't think any of them will help in the way you'd like them to.'

CHAPTER NINE

By the time Jay arrived at the police station, irked and worried by Sheri Razak's refusal to say more until the next time they spoke, she'd talked further with Terry Josephs, urging him to do his best while in Chipping Sodbury and the surrounding area. They needed, if at all possible, to find a witness to someone coming or going from Clover Hill Farm around three p.m. or after. The neighbour Maguire was, of course, their best bet, but if he'd already told the police who, or what he'd seen, it would surely have come up in interview.

'I'm just parking up in the town now,' Josephs had assured her only minutes ago, 'but according to the map, Clover Hill Farm is a pretty isolated spot, so finding the kind of witnesses you're looking for . . .'

'I know, but there might be a dog walker, a hiker, someone who drives those country lanes with deliveries, or taking a scenic route home. Just look around, check the nearby properties . . . The police will already have carried out a door-to-door, such as it is in rural areas, but if you explain who you are you might get somewhere. Most of all we need to focus on those two crucial hours between six and eight before Blake arrived home.'

'Jay.'

She turned to find Ken Bright coming into the custody

area behind her. Quickly she ended the call with Joe, and said, 'Ken. Do you have anything for me?'

He regarded her curiously, as though thinking it might be the other way around, that she had something to share with him. She didn't, so she simply cocked her head, waiting for him to speak first.

Sighing he said, 'It's been a busy morning, and it seems no one has a bad word to say about your client – and I don't know about you, Jay , but I find that . . . Unusual?'

She almost laughed. 'If you're having a problem with him being a regular guy . . .'

'Not a problem, just a . . . concern. It's like someone's spinning a web of some sort around him so we can only see Mr Nice Guy, best brother, uncle, friend, no enemies.'

She flashed on Sheri Razak, but said, 'Have you caught up with the other neighbours yet, the Dutch people?'

'By Skype. They weren't around on Monday, in fact not at all since Easter, and Maguire in Long Barn confirms this.'

'What about Mrs Maguire? Have you spoken to her? Did *she* hear raised voices around nine o'clock?'

'She's in Sunderland, moving her mother into a care home. Left last Friday and not due back until this coming weekend.'

'I see.' Jay was thinking about John Debrayne now, who'd presumably given a statement this morning, but had it raised any red flags for Bright? Instead of asking, she said, 'Has anyone come forward yet about the taxi?'

He glanced over his shoulder as he shook his head. Lacey Hamble had arrived in a flurry of laughter and banter clearly reserved for her colleagues, certainly not for criminal solicitors.

Bright said, 'It was an anonymous tip-off that so far hasn't led to anything.'

'But you're still following up on it?'

'As far as we can. The caller said it was a car that might have been a taxi, they weren't sure.'

So not even definitely a taxi. 'Did they say whether it was at the front of the station?'

'The back, apparently.'

'Kind of car? Did they see a driver?'

'Negative to both.'

Glad to have that clarified, she regarded him closely as she said, 'If you don't mind me saying, Ken, you're looking worried.'

His frown deepened as he replied. 'Edward Blake was in the house at the time of the murder . . .'

'Hang on,' she jumped in, 'you're forgetting the little matter of the two hours before he . . .'

'. . . got home, OK, but he could have come back earlier than eight and the neighbour just didn't spot him.'

'So he came home, went out, came back again, at which point he had a row with his wife and killed her?' Her tone made it sound as implausible as it was.

Bright's shoulders slumped.

'How are you getting on with the CCTV?' she asked.

Wryly he said, 'Still a lot to get through.'

Jay glanced at Hamble as the now poker-faced detective came to join them.

'I'm guessing,' Hamble said, 'that you want to consult with your client before we continue?' She made it sound such an unreasonable exercise that Jay felt tempted to make her chat with Blake stretch all the way into the evening, just to keep this irritating woman waiting.

However, that would only use up valuable time as they drew closer to the wire.

To Bright, she said, 'If you can arrange for my client to be brought through, I'll send someone to let you know when we're ready.'

Although less than twenty-four hours had passed since Jay had last seen Blake, she understood how long it would have felt for him, being locked up in a cell with nothing like the comforts he was used to, and easy prey to the torment of his grief and fears. So, it wasn't a surprise to see how drawn and even, to a degree, reduced he seemed – a dignified, but bewildered man who was clearly struggling to come to terms with what was happening to him. He would know without being told that friends, family and even strangers were being called upon to give statements about him and his wife, to attest to his character and their marriage, their sex life, the loss of their child, even to offer opinions on what he would or wouldn't be capable of. For him it must feel as though he'd lost all control of his life, and to a great extent he had.

'Hi,' she said softly as a custody officer closed the door.

It touched her to realize how pleased he was to see her. She wasn't only his lawyer at this time, she was his main contact with the outside world, his ally, his defender, although in spite of wanting to trust her, he must be terrified she wouldn't be able to help him.

'How are you?' he asked before she could.

With a smile she said, 'I'm fine. How about you?'

He nodded, then closed his eyes and shook his head. 'Scared,' he admitted. He tried to laugh, as if to mock himself. 'Do you think they're going to charge me?' He met her eyes with the magnetic blue of his own, and she could see his courage, but also his dread.

'Not yet,' she replied, 'but now is a good time to give you this piece of advice: if they do and I'm not here, you must tell them you're not guilty. As soon as they finish reading the charge, you say, "I'm not guilty."'

After echoing the words, almost as if they were losing meaning, he said, 'Why wouldn't you be there?'

'I hope to be, if it comes to it, and we still don't know if it will, but there's no rule to say I have to be.'

Swallowing he said, 'I keep telling myself it's not possible to be sent to prison for killing someone I loved so much, who I'd never do anything to hurt, but I . . . I know that it is. People go to prison all the time for something they didn't do.'

Unable to deny it, she said, 'I've been talking to your family – the police have too, obviously – so I know Vanessa had . . . problems.'

As his head went down, his hands closed into loosely bunched fists, almost as if he wanted to fight, but could hardly summon the will. 'What have they told you?' he asked gruffly. 'What did they say?'

'That she had difficulties coming to terms with the loss of your son and that sometimes she took it out on you, even blamed you.'

Keeping his head down he nodded and continued to nod. 'She blamed herself too. She never stopped blaming herself, and it's the same for me. I should have been watching him. He was my son, my responsibility.' He forced himself to look up at her. 'You know, something like that . . . You never get over it. If you have children . . .'

'I do have children,' she said softly, 'so I understand.'

She wished there was more she could add to give him comfort, but what else was there? The tragedy would always be a tragedy, the heartbreak would never fully heal, because it couldn't.

But she wasn't here to deal with his grief, only his current nightmare, so bringing them back on track, she said, 'I'm concerned that the police will put Vanessa's unpredictability forward as a motive for killing her.'

He seemed to flinch at that. 'Is that what they think,' he said, incredulously, 'that because I couldn't stand her pain, that she made me do something so horrible, so . . . *perverted?*' He stopped, clearly realizing he wasn't helping himself by losing control. 'What happened to her,' he said, keeping his voice steady, 'couldn't have been in the heat of the moment. It was planned. It has to have been, but *not by me*. She was tied to the bed, for God's sake, and apparently there was no struggle to get her there. That's not something we ever did, or even talked about doing.'

'So who was it likely to have been?' she pressed. 'It was clearly a sexual . . .'

'Do you know if she had sex?' he broke in forcefully. 'Have they established that yet? There could be DNA . . .'

'You're right, there could and it's possible we'll know more when you're questioned after this.'

Taking a breath, as if to centre himself, or at least to accept that this conversation was really happening and he needed to take part, he said, 'This was either some random killing – and I don't think any of us believe that, why would she allow a stranger to tie her to the bed? Or it has to have been someone she knew. But why would anyone *do* that to her? I don't understand it.'

'What about when she goes to London?' Jay asked.

'Could she have been meeting someone there? Someone who got off a train at Chippenham after you dropped her and spent the day with her?'

He threw out his hands in exasperated despair. 'What do you want me to say? Of course it's possible, but did I ever suspect it? No. OK, the last few years have been difficult, but we were always close . . .' He stopped and closed his eyes. 'Sorry,' he said in a strangled voice. 'Sorry, it's really starting to get to me.'

'There's nothing to apologize for,' she assured him. 'Would you like some water?'

He shook his head. 'I'm fine. Let's carry on.'

'OK. How well do you know her friends, Melissa and Sheri?'

He shrugged. 'Fairly well, I guess. She knew them before we met, the three of them were at uni together – Manchester – so they go back a way. She and Melissa might even have been at school together.'

She nodded encouragement for him to continue.

'They were at our wedding, and they come to stay at the house, weekends, bank holidays, you know, Melissa more than Sheri – Sheri's away a lot. She's got a job that pays a fortune, but never allows her the time to spend it, is what Nessa always says.'

Picking up on his use of the present tense again, as if his wife were somewhere just out of reach, simply waiting for this to be over, Jay was about to speak when he said, 'She gave Vanessa a key to her flat so she could use it if she wanted to stay in London.'

'Did she use it?'

'No. I . . . I'm not sure. She wasn't in London that often. When she was, I always assumed she was with Melissa.'

'Who else did she see when she was there? Apart from her friends.'

He drew an arc as if to encompass them all, 'Artists, photographers, *galleristes.*'

'Did you know any of these people?'

'Some, but none of them ever came to the house.'

'Or not that you're aware of?'

His colour deepened as he shook his head, an unspoken, angry and embarrassed acceptance that he could have been more than a little blind as far as his wife was concerned.

Moving on, she said, 'Someone rang in to say they saw her getting into a taxi in the rear car park of Chippenham Station.'

His eyes sharpened with interest, and confusion. 'Why . . . How? Who called, do you know?'

'It was anonymous, apparently. Do you have any idea who it might have been?'

He seemed slightly bemused by the question. 'It was obviously the person who saw it, but as for knowing who that might be . . .'

'I meant, do you know who might have picked her up?'

He frowned. 'You said it was a taxi . . .'

'They weren't specific about that. No description of the car, or driver, just that it might have been a taxi. So I need to be sure you didn't go back for her. Did she ring to say she'd forgotten something, or changed her mind—'

'If she had we wouldn't be sitting here, would we?' he interrupted harshly. Then seeming less sure about that he said, 'The police will have our phones. They'll know she didn't call or text to ask me to go back and I'd hardly have done so when I thought she was on the train.'

'OK. Is there a taxi company you regularly use?'

'No. We rarely get them, unless we're in London. Why did this person do it anonymously? What's wrong with saying you saw someone get into a car?'

'Some people want to help, but aren't keen to get involved. Or it could have been an attention seeker, in which case it would probably be a hoax.'

Seeming as sickened by that as anyone would, he simply turned away.

Jay said, 'I had a short phone conversation with Sheri Razak on the way here. She implied that there were things she could tell me, but nothing that would help you to avoid being charged.'

As his face paled she saw him swallow dryly.

'What did she mean by that?' she prompted carefully.

He shook his head and continued to shake it. 'Did you ask her what she meant?'

'Of course, but she didn't have time to speak to me. We're going to Skype over the weekend.'

He took a while to think about this, to realize, she thought, that he had no idea yet where he would be by then. More likely in a prison cell than back in the comfort of his home.

In the end, almost as if talking to himself he said, 'Even if they don't charge me, this isn't going away, is it? It can't until they find out who did it, so even if I'm not stuck in here they'll be hounding me . . .' He fixed her with his intense blue eyes. 'But that's OK,' he said firmly, 'as long as it leads to the right answers, I can bear it. I just don't want them to keep focusing on me, because if they do it'll mean whoever tied her to that bed and put the pillow over her face will end up getting away with it.'

No mention was made of the taxi during the detectives' interrogation, which didn't surprise Jay – it was looking increasingly like a hoax and, as Edward himself had pointed out, they had Vanessa's phone, so they would in fact know if she'd called one. The question of whether he'd gone back to the station didn't arise.

The only new evidence, which turned out to be no evidence at all, was that a DPD driver had come forward to say he'd been in the vicinity of Clover Hill around five thirty p.m. on Monday and had passed two cars on Mapletree Lane. A red Audi, or similar, and a black Range Rover.

'You own a black Range Rover,' Bright stated, looking at Edward.

'I do,' Edward confirmed, sounding less shaken than he probably felt.

'Could it have been you that the delivery driver saw?'

'No, because I wasn't there at that time. A lot of people drive those cars in the countryside, including a few of our neighbours.'

Jay said, 'Can you tell us the registration number of the vehicle that was sighted?'

Bright couldn't, and since there was no CCTV coverage of the area, there was nothing to be gained from going any further with that for now.

So, Jay reflected as they continued, they were still lacking a witness either to Edward coming and going from the gallery, or to someone, anyone, entering or leaving the house during the afternoon.

Was it at all possible that Terry Josephs would come up with one in time to save Edward from being charged? Maybe he'd get some new information out of Maguire, the neighbour, although that seemed unlikely given how closely the police must have questioned the man. Presumably official CCTV from the high street wasn't helping or they'd be having a different conversation right now, so they must be trying to locate a passing dash-cam, or a private security device from a nearby property, or simply someone who didn't watch the news and so was not yet aware of how helpful they could be.

In spite of his mounting anxiety, Edward handled himself well through the next few minutes, though Jay could see the shake in his hands as they asked him again about finding Vanessa, and what he'd done while he'd waited for the police to arrive.

She could tell how hard it was for him to keep his voice steady, how harrowing it was for him to relive those moments, especially when Hamble waded in with, 'When you stifled her . . .'

'I didn't . . .'

'How long did it take her to die?'

'Oh Christ,' Blake choked, dropping his head in his hands.

'Did you keep checking to see if she was still breathing? Lifting the pillow up and down?'

Jay said, 'My client has already told you that he wasn't there.'

Hamble shot her a poisonous look as Bright said, 'Talk us through what happened when you found her, Edward. I'd like to hear it again.'

Blake took a breath, and another, and began to repeat what he'd already told them.

Jay listened carefully, sensing how hard it was for him to keep his thoughts straight. They were wearing him down, stressing him, tiring him to the point of exhaustion, and bombarding him with questions he'd answered a dozen times in the hope he'd slip up, crack, or break down and confess. She stepped in several times, reminding the detectives that they were going around in circles, and to ask Edward if he'd like to take a break. He shook his head. He wanted to go on with this, to do whatever it took to convince them that – in spite of the evidence – they had the wrong man.

'Let me ask you this, detective,' Jay said. 'Why would Mr Blake have stayed in the house if he'd wanted to distance himself from the crime? And why hasn't he even tried to find himself an alibi?'

She received no reply to her questions, however the points had been made, which was what really mattered.

In the end it was past seven o'clock by the time Bright called things to a halt and had Edward returned to his cell. As Jay watched him go her heart ached for him – this was a truly hellish time for him, a nightmare scenario for anyone who had no way of proving their innocence. Not the way the law should work, but so often did.

'You know it's still not looking good,' Bright told her as they met up in the custody area. 'We've given it as long as we can, but with the way things stand . . .'

'Are you going to do it now?' she interrupted.

Bright turned to Hamble as she said, 'The CPS has been kept informed throughout, as you'd expect. We should be in a position to charge him tonight or tomorrow morning.'

Bright looked at Jay. 'The lack of witnesses is causing

113

a real problem. I'm not saying none will be found as our inquiries continue, but right now, with the clock ticking . . . You can't accuse us of not giving him the benefit of the doubt, and there was always a lot of doubt here, Jay.'

Understanding that, she said, 'Will you call me when you're ready to do it?'

'Of course,' and with a vague salute of his hand that seemed more regretful than triumphant he turned and walked away.

CHAPTER TEN

'You know what's really getting to me about this case,' Jay complained over drinks later with Tom, Freddy and Carina, 'is that Ken Bright's no closer to being certain my client did it than I am, but he's under pressure from the top. With the lack of another suspect, he'll go ahead and charge.'

'So, tell me why you don't think he did it?' Freddy prompted, ever the author as his crime fiction antennae alerted and his dark eyes sparkled excitedly behind his glasses.

Jay shook her head and sipped her wine. They were in the main salon of the Clifton Club, an exclusive meeting place on The Mall, originally set up at the beginning of the nineteenth century for the city's prosperous merchants. Today it remained a members-only venue for Bristol's business elite. 'It's just,' she said, trying to assemble her thoughts, 'actually, it's hard to put into words that don't include instinct, gut feeling, sixth sense and all those corny, clichéd reasons your dedicated readers no doubt adore. Which isn't to say I'm not getting them, of course I am, but it's more than that. If you met Edward Blake, spoke to him, I know you'd find him as convincing as I do, as Ken Bright does, in spite of the evidence being so stacked up against him.'

'Sounds a must for one of my books,' Freddy enthused. 'So who else would you put in the frame if you could?'

'That's just it, there isn't anyone. If there were, you can bet Bright would be onto them by now.'

'So doesn't that make the case cut and dried?'

Jay slanted him a look. 'For you that's a very surprising question,' she commented wryly.

He laughed. 'You know I had to ask it, but actually having no other suspects makes it more intriguing.'

'It seems that way to me too,' Carina piped up loyally, 'but now you're going to tell me that almost nothing ever is cut and dried when it comes to murder.'

Jay glanced at Tom, who didn't appear to be engaging with the conversation, as Carina continued with, 'What was Blake's marriage like? Have either of them had affairs? Did they ever break up and get back together for some reason? Hang on, I saw on the news there was a baby that died – a drowning accident.'

Jay nodded as she leaned forward to pick up her drink. 'That's right, when they were on holiday in Italy three years ago,' she confirmed, taking a sip. 'It was an accident, and as yet I've no reason to doubt that. Obviously it had a pretty devastating effect on them both. The family say she's been suffering from emotional issues since, and who wouldn't in her shoes?'

'Such a horrible thing to happen,' Carina commented sadly.

Starting to become irritated by Tom's apparent distraction, Jay said, 'Sorry, I'm hogging the conversation, why don't we change the subject?'

'No, no,' Carina protested. 'I'm fascinated by this one.'

'Tom, my friend,' Freddy called across the table,

evidently more sensitive to the moment, 'are you with us or has something come up?'

Quickly tucking away his phone, Tom said, 'Sorry, just updates on this trial next week.' He glanced fleetingly at Jay and she just knew he wasn't being truthful. Her heart churned with the dread that it might be happening again. Another woman, or the same one? Or was she just imagining it? *What the hell was going on with him?* 'So, where were we?' he asked, cheerfully. 'Can I get more drinks?'

'I expect we can sink another bottle between us,' Freddy agreed. 'Are you guys up for dinner later?'

Before Jay could respond her phone vibrated and, seeing it was Antonia Debrayne, she excused herself to take the call. She went to an empty window seat where it was unlikely she'd be overheard. 'Antonia,' she said, 'thanks for getting back to me. How's everything there?'

'Tense,' came the reply. 'We're hoping he might be released tomorrow. They have to let him go if they can't prove he did it, don't they?'

'I'm afraid it's less about proof than probability at this stage, and right now we're no closer to finding another suspect.' She paused, needing to phrase her next question carefully, or at least in a way that didn't carry a *j'accuse* subtext. 'I need to ask you,' she said, glancing out at the grassy, gated gardens of Caledonia Place opposite, 'if it's possible Vanessa might have been involved with a woman?'

Silence. It went on for so long that Jay ended up saying, 'Are you still there?'

'Yes, yes, I'm sorry. I'm just so . . . What on earth makes you ask that?'

'It's something that came up as a possibility.'

'But I don't understand. Is that what Edward thinks? Did he say that?'

'No, but there was no semen found—'

'John and I were there on Saturday,' Antonia broke in hastily. 'We slept in that room, so our DNA will surely be found. Edward and Vanessa have a lot of friends who stay over, theirs will be there too.'

'I realize that and I'm sure the forensic team have everyone's samples by now. It takes time to process them, I'm afraid, but meanwhile I wanted to run the idea past you that she might have been involved with a woman.'

Still sounding upset, Antonia said, 'But why would you even think it? What have they found to suggest it?'

Deciding to be frank, Jay said, 'The pathology shows slight bruising around the vaginal area caused by ante-mortem penetration. There was no semen collected or any other secretions, so either a condom was used, or a sexual aid, which of course doesn't rule out a male partner, but it doesn't rule out a female one either.'

'I see. I see. Well, I have to admit I'm shocked and I'm not sure how to process this. I truly don't think she was involved with a woman, but if you say she was . . .'

'It's not what I'm saying. It's simply what I'm asking, because I have the impression you and Vanessa are – or were – close friends as well as sisters-in-law. She never confided anything like it to you?'

'No, never, but to be honest we didn't discuss our sex lives. Hers is with my brother so it would have been . . . *odd* if we did.'

Having to accept that as reasonable, Jay was about to speak again, when Antonia said,

'Have you spoken to Vanessa's stepmother?'

Surprised, Jay said, 'No, but I'm sure the police will have by now. Why do you ask?'

With a definite spikiness in her tone, Antonia said, 'Let's just say whoever that woman talks to she's likely to paint her stepdaughter in the worst imaginable light. She's not a pleasant person, Mrs Wells, which is why we have so little to do with her.'

Finding that interesting, Jay said, 'How often did Vanessa see her?'

'Hardly at all. They haven't spoken in ages as far as I know.'

'Where's Vanessa's father?'

'He died about ten years ago, and Daphne, the grieving widow, has never forgiven him for leaving just about his entire estate to Nessa, with a condition that she can't inherit until the wicked – my word – stepmother has expired. And said stepmother will get nothing if she moves out of the house alive. So, essentially she's stuck there whether she wants to be or not. It's probably a little more complicated than that, but in essence you have the basics of Nessa's father's will and part of the reason why Ness and her stepmother didn't get along.'

Stunned that no one had mentioned this before, and wondering if Bright knew about it, Jay said, 'Would you mind texting me Daphne's details? Where does she live?'

'Near Cirencester.'

'Do you have any idea what happens to the house now?'

'No, but you could ask Ed, maybe he knows.'

'I will, thanks.'

After ringing off, Jay sat quietly for a few moments watching people come and go from The Ivy restaurant opposite as she thought back over the last few minutes.

She wasn't any closer to believing Antonia had been intimately involved with Vanessa, although she wasn't ready to dismiss it either. And what was to be made of a deceased father, a 'wicked' stepmother, a dead baby and a murdered wife/stepdaughter whose husband was very probably about to be charged with the crime?

It was surely too far-fetched to think that Daphne Whatever-her-name-was could have engineered her stepdaughter's death; however, she would task Joe with finding out as much as he could about the woman and her relationship with Vanessa and Edward.

Hearing an explosion of laughter coming from their table, she looked around to discover that Perry and his wife, Gretchen, had turned up and, always glad to see them, she started back to the table.

It wasn't until she reached it that she realized with a jolt that Tom wasn't there.

'Oh, he just popped to the bathroom,' Freddy told her. 'Another glass?'

'Thanks,' she said, embracing Gretchen before sitting down. 'You didn't stay up late with Tom and Perry last night?' she asked, trying to make it casual, while knowing that Gretchen would probably guess she was fishing.

'I didn't,' Gretchen confirmed, but the slight frown she allowed Jay to see suggested she knew something was afoot.

Not wanting to ask in front of the others, Jay quickly fired off a text asking Gretchen if she knew what had happened.

Gretchen glanced at the message, gave a brief shake of her head and smiled cheerfully as Freddy passed her a generous glass of chardonnay.

'Important call?' Tom asked Jay as he returned to the table.

'Blake's sister,' Jay told him. 'Did you see Livvy before you left the house?'

'I came straight here from chambers,' he replied, pulling up another chair now that Gretchen had taken his, 'but she's fine. Apparently Nat's been in touch.' His eyebrows were raised, showing he was duly impressed that their daughter had received the one call she'd been longing for since God-only-knew when.

Surprised, and curious, Jay said, 'Did she tell you why he rang. Or messaged?'

'Not yet, but it's highly probable one of us will be burning the midnight oil and I'm nominating you.'

With a faintly amused groan, she said, 'I just hope it went well. Actually, it must have done or she'd have called me by now.' She glanced down as her mobile vibrated again.

'Is it her?' Carina wanted to know. 'Oh, I do love a good teenage romance.'

'Not her,' Jay laughed, getting up again, but in spite of appearing light-hearted, her insides were already tightening with nerves. 'Be right back,' she said and, clicking on the line as she returned to the window table, she said to the caller, 'Please don't tell me this is what I think it is.'

'Sorry,' Ken Bright replied, actually sounding it. 'It went over my head. He was charged ten minutes ago.'

Jay sank down in a chair and held the phone in both hands, picturing Blake and how it must have been for him during those terrible minutes of hearing himself charged with his wife's murder. And realizing that he wouldn't be going home tomorrow, or the day after that, or possibly for a very long time. She felt momentarily angry with Ken Bright for not calling sooner so she could have been there – and with herself for not staying when she should have guessed it would happen tonight.

'Are you still at Keynsham?' she asked Bright.

'Just about to leave.'

'Can you tell him . . . Will you explain why I wasn't there, that no one told me it was about to happen, and that I'll see him tomorrow at the magistrates' court?'

'Sure,' he said, 'but you need to know, Jay, that more information's come to light and the nature of it . . .'

'What information?'

'I'll send it to you. When you see it I think you'll agree, we had no choice but to move forward with a charge.'

CHAPTER ELEVEN

As Jay walked quickly down Broad Street the following morning, heading through the arch in the ancient city wall, and across the road towards Bridewell, her head was spinning with so many worries she was struggling to extricate one from the other.

The Lexcel auditors were in today, always a time of stress, although thankfully Jilly, the office manager, and Perry were on top of it, so there was no reason not to put it to the back of her mind. Nowhere near as easy to dismiss were the issues at home, first with Tom acting so strangely last night, and still not saying what he wanted to discuss at the weekend, and then with Livvy. Yes, Nat had rung her, but only because his girlfriend was threatening to break up with him and he'd wanted the best advice he could get on how to win her back.

Such a cruel irony. Livvy, the go-to agony aunt for her small legion of friends and online followers, wasn't taking it well, and God forbid she should make it public, as Jay had mistakenly suggested, in the hope of getting some good advice from her followers.

It had been almost one o'clock by the time Jay had finally been able to spend an hour prepping for Blake's magistrates' hearing this morning, and when she'd finally got to bed she'd taken far too long to fall asleep. She wasn't sure if she'd been more worried about what was brewing with Tom, or how she was going to handle seeing Blake before his court appearance after the information Bright had sent her following the charge.

Oh Edward, she muttered silently to herself as she arrived at the magistrates' court and joined everyone else to go through the necessary security. *Why didn't you tell me about this? You must have known it would come out sooner or later, and holding back on it has made things a hundred times worse.*

Maybe because she was tired, or because she valued the relationship she built up with clients even at this early stage, it was upsetting her to know that he hadn't trusted her enough to confide in her.

After checking the court schedule and talking briefly with the CPS lawyer, she went to the cells to find Blake and, once certain he'd arrived, she set herself up in an interview room to wait for him to be brought to her. When her phone rang she saw it was Antonia and decided to text rather than get involved in a conversation now. She'd have a lot of questions later for Mrs Debrayne, most particularly about why *she* had never mentioned her brother's previous run-in with the law – presuming she knew about it – but now there simply wasn't the time. She texted: *I'm told he's already here; just waiting to see him. Have you arrived yet?*

A text came back quickly: *Yes. John and the children with me. Have you engaged a barrister?*

Jay put her phone aside, deciding to explain later that as a solicitor and Higher Courts Advocate she was fully qualified to represent Edward at this stage of proceedings. However, she would need to instruct a barrister soon and though Tom and his partner in chambers, Ollie, were two of Bristol's finest, they had an unwritten rule not to mix business with pleasure if they could avoid it. If they did, their entire lives could become dominated by a single case and that wouldn't be good for any of them.

Susannah Heel QC had been at the back of Jay's mind from the start. She was London based and one of the best, in Jay's opinion. Moreover she'd always worked well with Cyrus Trott as a junior who was local, highly respected, and even more experienced than she was in murder trials. For that was almost certainly where they were heading now, unless Blake had decided to change his story and admit that he was guilty as charged.

Looking up as the door opened she felt a conflicting mix of emotions to see how unkempt and ashen he was – angry that they were having to have this conversation now and sorry that his world was falling apart.

Would she feel sorry if it turned out he had killed his wife? The answer was more complicated than she was going to think about now.

Gesturing for him to sit down, she was about to speak when he said, 'I did as you said, and told them I was not guilty, but I don't know if anyone was listening. I asked them to contact you, did they?'

'Yes. I asked DI Bright to give you a message?'

He looked baffled for a moment, then said, 'Oh, yes, he did. Sorry, my head's all over the place.'

'It's OK, but we don't have much time. The reason you were charged last night was because some information came to light that I'm afraid could be extremely damaging for your case.'

He regarded her with growing fear and confusion. 'What

information?' he asked, seeming genuinely not to know when surely he must.

'Some photographs were sent through from the Devon and Cornwall Constabulary of injuries you inflicted on your wife a year ago after she reported you for attempting to strangle her.'

He went very still, as if shock was closing him down, until he began slowly to shake his head. He looked as though he might be losing a sense of the hand he was being dealt.

'Why didn't you tell me about it before?' she asked, not even trying to keep the sharpness out of her tone.

'Because it's not real,' he replied, looking at her again and in a way that suggested she should know this already. 'We were at a friend's place in Salcombe . . . They were there too, Tim and Sophie Burns. They can vouch for what happened.'

When he stopped she impatiently urged him to continue.

'Nessa tried . . . She tried to hang herself. Sophie found her and thank God we were in time to get her down.' He took a breath and held it, as though it might save him from going any further into the ghastly memory. 'We drove her to the hospital,' he said. 'They checked her over, obviously, but she was OK, physically, apart from the bruising. They recommended psychiatric help and sent us on our way. A couple of days later, with the bruises still livid on her neck, she went to the police and accused me . . .' He pressed his fingers to his eyes, clearly finding it as hard to speak as to remember. 'It only took one call to the hospital to verify the truth of what I was telling them,' he said, 'so there were no charges, they didn't even arrest me. This all has to be on record, surely.'

Presuming it was, and silently furious with Ken Bright for not forwarding the entire story when he'd surely received more than just photos, she said, 'I'll look into it. As you say, it must be on record, but I'm afraid it's why they charged you last night – and why, after the hearing this morning, you'll be taken to Bristol Prison.'

As his head fell into his hands in despair, she reached out to grip his wrist.

'I'm sorry,' she said, with feeling. 'I understand what you've told me, and we'll make sure the incident is properly told when the time comes.'

'You mean in front of a jury?'

Deciding not to confirm that, she said, 'The process today won't take long and you won't have to speak. You'll be referred to the Crown Court for a bail application but – because today's Friday – your case won't be heard until Monday or Tuesday of next week. Your sister asked me about a barrister, and I'm going to find you the best, but meanwhile I'm able to represent you myself, as long as you're happy for me to do so.'

Though he nodded, it took a moment before he seemed to connect with her words. 'Yes, please,' he said, and the way he looked at her so helplessly and yet trustingly went some way to restoring her confidence in their relationship as lawyer and client.

'You need to understand,' she continued more gently, 'that the seriousness of the charge means it's very unlikely you'll get bail.'

He sat back in his chair, taking this in, and apparently summoning what inner strength he could. In the end he impressed her with the depth of determination in his tone as he said, 'It's going to be all right. I'll get through this and I'm sorry for not telling you what happened in Devon. I didn't think it was important; frankly I'd more or less forgotten it, but I can see how it must look to you, so thanks for staying on my side. Looks like I'm going to need you more than ever going forward.'

Not denying it, she met his eyes, and maybe for the first time she was aware of their sensuousness albeit masked by angst and despair. There was a quality to them, to him, that she felt a disturbingly visceral reaction to, and thrown by it she looked away. Now was not the time for some misplaced attraction to crash in and complicate proceedings, although she knew it wouldn't; she had better control of herself than that. 'I need to know if there are any more incidents like the one in Devon,' she said crisply, making as if ready to write.

'I promise there's nothing else.'

'Spend some time thinking about it,' she cautioned, and glanced up as someone knocked on the door. 'OK, one last thing before we go in, was Vanessa seeing a therapist of any kind?'

With a humourless laugh he said, 'She'd never agree to it, at least not wholeheartedly. If only she had, we probably wouldn't be where we are now.'

Though Jay regarded him sympathetically, she was making a mental note to ensure that he never said anything like this in court, for he clearly didn't realize that all neatly wrapped up in that heartfelt regret could be a motive for ridding himself of a troublesome wife.

As expected, it took no more than a few minutes for Blake's case to be referred to the Crown Court, but to Jay's annoyance, by the time she returned to the cells, he'd already been whisked away.

Remarking to one of the guards that it had to be the fastest prison transfer in court history, she made her way back to the solicitors' room, trying not to begrudge the time she'd spent talking to Antonia and family after the hearing. Actually, she wasn't nearly as resentful of that as she was of the time she'd given to the triumphant Lacey Hamble – no sign of Ken Bright today. Had she known her testy exchange with the detective was costing her a final opportunity to speak to her client that day, she would have abandoned trying to argue against the woman's supercilious insistence that the investigators hadn't been obliged to send her any more than the photographs from Devon, and hurried to do the right thing for Blake.

Now, as she strode back to the office in a shower of rain, she realized her temper was in part due to tiredness, although it was mostly due to how worked up she was becoming over this chat she and Tom were supposed to be having tomorrow or Sunday. Why was it making her nervous? What reason did she have to feel so afraid when he'd given her no reason to suspect that history was about to repeat itself? They were as close as they'd ever been these days, were almost back to the way they'd been before his affair, or in her mind they were, but she couldn't help remembering how well he'd hidden it from her the last time. During the entire two years he'd been with Ellen Tyler, she had never suspected a thing; she'd had no reason to, for nothing had changed between them. It was even possible that, if she hadn't found an incriminating text on his phone, he might still be seeing the woman and she, Jay, would still know nothing about it.

Maybe the relationship hadn't ended after all and now he wanted to make it permanent?

Forcing herself to let it go before she worked herself into a frenzy of imagined crises and doubt, she ran the rest of the way to the office, and was soon throwing off her raincoat and taking a towel from Vikki to dry her hair as she went to her desk. However, before getting down to the calls she needed to make or return, she rerouted back across the cluttered reception where Vikki was now brewing coffee, and went into Perry's office without knocking. He wasn't there, but an auditor was, so she apologized and backed out again.

'He's in a client meeting,' Vikki informed her. 'Due out around three.'

Knowing it had been foolish to think Perry would tell her what Tom wanted to talk about, she returned to her desk, reeling off a list of instructions for Vikki, most important of which was to contact the clerk at Susannah Heel's chambers in Gray's Inn, and Cyrus Trott here in Bristol. Then, asking Vikki to hold all calls for now, she picked up the phone to call Terry Josephs.

'Joe,' she said shortly as the ex-detective answered on the second ring. 'You'll have heard about the charge, so I need you to tell me what you found out in Chipping Sodbury yesterday.'

'I can do that,' he informed her dryly. 'If you give me thirty seconds, I'll be walking through your door.'

A number of guild church clocks were chiming in their steeples as he, in jaunty yellow shirt, tatty blue jeans and his faithful old bomber jacket, kept to his word and strode in. 'Audit not going well?' he asked, plonking himself down in a visitor chair after closing the door.

She looked at him sharply. 'Why do you say that?'

His hands went up as if to defend himself. 'Question,

not statement. Only wondered, because you look like you've been trying to tear your hair out.'

Remembering her rapid towel-dry, she gave him a wry look and waved an arm to indicate the files piled up on her desk. 'Enough to make me do just that,' she informed him, 'but tell me about yesterday. Actually, before you get into it, when this meeting's over I need you to contact Tim and Sophie Burns. They're friends of Edward Blake and wife. We need their version of an incident that took place at their Devonshire home last year. I'll email details of said incident as told by Edward Blake, and get their contact details from Antonia Debrayne, if she has them. Now, back to Chipping Sodbury.'

After noting down his latest instructions, he popped a Tic Tac, and said, 'An interesting selection of the population out that way, that's for sure. Do you know the area?'

She shook her head.

'Well, it's not quite Bristol and not quite Cotswolds, if you get my meaning.'

She didn't, but was less interested in his sociological discoveries than those pertaining to the case.

'It would seem – as we'd expect,' he continued, 'that the police have carried out a door-to-door along the high street, and of those I spoke to most had nothing significant to report, and mainly good things to say about our guy and his wife. A batty old bint a few doors down from the gallery swore they were into the dark arts, but I'm not sure she really cottoned on to who I was, never mind who we were talking about.'

'And the rumours? About the baby. Did anyone mention them?'

'Only to say how sad it was and no wonder Mrs Blake

went "off the rails". They seemed to like that phrase, although one sprightly old bloke preferred "off her rocker". The general consensus was that no blame could be attached to our victim for not being herself after what she'd been through.'

'So they noticed unusual, even irrational behaviour?'

He nodded.

'Which means the police know about it.' Making a note to try and get more out of Bright the next time they spoke, she said, 'Before we go into it, what did they say about Blake?'

'Well, a number of women remarked on his looks – that'd be termed sexist if it happened the other way around, I hope you realize that.'

'I do. Go on.'

'OK, so he's always polite, friendly, helpful if they need referrals to a decent tradesman for their home improvements. Before he lost his son, he played on the local cricket team if they were down a man, and he still donates to local causes including the Chipping Sodbury mop.'

'Do I want to know what that is?'

'It's a kind of annual street fair. Used to take ours when they were young. Anyway, there's a cop shop close to the market cross so naturally I went in. It turns out the chap I spoke to, a PC Granger, was first on the scene after Blake's 999 call, along with his colleague who wasn't on duty yesterday. He said Edward Blake was very agitated when they arrived, pacing up and down outside, shaking, crying . . . One of them got him to sit down, while the other went inside to check the scene. He found the body and got straight on the radio for backup. They sat with Blake outside till CID and the rest of the circus turned up.

'And apparently the sister kicked up a terrible fuss when they took him away.'

'How did Blake react?'

'Apparently he seemed dazed, like he wasn't connecting with it all.'

'Did he say anything?'

'Not that our bobby heard, but the sister made sure he didn't, kept telling him she'd get a lawyer, that he mustn't utter a word until he had one.'

'Good advice. What did she do after they'd taken him away?'

Josephs grimaced. 'You know, I didn't ask that. Does it matter?'

'I'm not sure. I've got to call her anyway, I'll ask then. I want to take a look at Clover Hill Farm, see it for myself, and she seems as good a tour guide as I'm likely to get. Did you go?'

'Only to the outside. A couple of security guys are keeping sightseers and press at bay, but I guess that doesn't include the sister.'

'Forensics will be long finished by now, so there shouldn't be any objection to me going in, but I'll clear it with Bright first. What's the house like?'

He shrugged. 'Big. Setting is quite something, leafy, streams, footbridge, great views.'

'How close are the other houses?'

'I'd say the Long Barn is about fifty yards away, and the Dutch cottage is more or less opposite that, but set back from the track. Bit of an idyll out there, if you ask me. Great if you're into birds or flowers or meditation, that sort of thing. Saw a couple of woodpeckers flitting about—'

She cut him off else they'd be there all day. 'Did you manage to talk to the neighbour, Frank Maguire?'

'Only briefly, he was on his way out, but he raised no objection to a lengthier chat when I suggested it. Apparently, he has to come into Bristol tomorrow, so I took the liberty of inviting him into the office for two o'clock.'

'Excellent. I know it's the weekend, but can I count on you to be here too?' She'd have to postpone her chat with Tom but didn't hesitate; bad news could always wait, especially if it was the kind she was dreading so much.

'Sure. I'll just send him a quick text to confirm it's on.'

'OK. Tell me, did he, or anyone else you spoke to, express a difficulty in believing it might have been Blake?'

'Yes and no. There was a lot of shock, horror, can't be possible, that sort of thing. A couple of neighbours in the high street claimed to have heard her screaming at him a few times, or leaping into her car and driving off at speed.'

'Did they hear what she was screaming?'

'That he was mad. She couldn't take any more. She was going to tell everyone.'

Jay's eyebrows rose. 'Tell everyone what?'

'Not specific.'

'Did they hear his responses?'

'He was more quietly spoken, and apparently used to go around the next day apologizing for the disturbance and thanking everyone for their moral support of his wife.'

Jay sat with that for a moment, knowing it was the classic behaviour of an abuser – also of a man who was struggling with his wife's grief. 'Did he go after her when she drove off?' she asked.

Another grimace. 'Again I didn't ask, but I can if you want me to.'

Feeling momentarily defeated by such a stubborn lack of an alternative suspect, Jay pressed her hands to her cheeks and closed her eyes. In the darkness she saw Edward Blake's face – taut, grey, shaped by grief and fear – looking to her with those mesmerizing eyes for guidance and support. What she'd just heard from Joe suggested that Blake was unused to asking for help, was in fact someone who probably offered it more than he needed it.

Or he was someone she'd never really know, and she only had to think of her own husband to realize how possible that was.

After a while she said, 'We're either missing something – and in that "we" I'm including the police and Blake, given that he can't name anyone who might have done this to his wife. Or, he and his family are holding back some key information.'

Joe didn't disagree. 'I for one am pretty worried about the family,' he told her bluntly. 'And if they are holding back, it's got to be damning, or why not just come out with it?'

Since there was no arguing with that, she said, 'Are you of the view that Bright and his team don't have much more than we do?'

He regarded her wryly. 'You mean apart from a bloody great stack of evidence against our client?'

'Which a crack legal team, such as the one I shall pull together, could tear apart at trial.'

'Maybe, but my guess is they're pretty sure of a conviction at this stage, and however much confidence you have, you can see why they would be.'

135

She could, but said, 'It's not over until it's over. See what you can find out about Vanessa's stepmother – Daphne Drewson-Browne. I might pay her a visit myself, but it'll be good to have some background before I go. We'll schedule another team meeting for after the bail hearing next week. By then I should have spoken to both Frank Maguire and Sheri Razak.'

'Sheri who?'

'The friend who allowed Vanessa Blake to use her London flat while she was out of town. She knows something about Blake that apparently isn't going to help him much. Just what we need.' She checked her calendar. 'I'm due to Skype with her tomorrow evening, so a busy weekend ahead.'

With a wry expression Joe got to his feet and picked up his jacket. 'Looks like the weather's going to be good,' he commented, 'so try to get some time off, won't you?'

As he left, Jay's smile faded at the prospect of what she might be facing with Tom. Whatever it was, she'd have to delay their chat until Sunday, for she wasn't going to allow herself to be thrown off course before talking to two key witnesses. This was presuming whatever he had to tell her wasn't good news, and no matter how hard she tried, she just couldn't bring herself to believe that it was.

CHAPTER TWELVE

Later in the day, after drinks at the office to celebrate a successful Lexcel audit, Jay and Perry wandered over to St Nick's market to join Tom, Gretchen, Ollie and his wife Jenn for a bite at Giuseppe's, one of their regular haunts. Although Jay always enjoyed seeing their friends, and tonight was no exception, her mind was as restless as her nerves. One minute she was wondering about Blake and how he was finding his first night in prison; the next she was worrying about Livvy, and then she was feeling baffled by Tom, who wasn't giving the impression of having anything serious or troubling on his mind at all, although she of all people knew how good he was at putting on a front in public.

As they drove home, neither of them mentioned the chat they were supposed to be having – probably, Jay thought, because neither wanted to spoil the mood of the evening. It was even possible that the issue, whatever it was, had gone away, and she found herself feeling more certain of that when they made love later, for it hadn't been so good in a while. Just as well Tom had no way of knowing that for a few fleeting moments she'd found herself imagining what it might be like to make love with Edward Blake, and equally as good that she couldn't tell whether or not he'd been thinking of

Ellen Tyler. They fell asleep in each other's arms, and rose early the next morning to wander into the village for newspapers and a coffee before driving over to Brackenwood to pick up some bedding plants for the garden.

It was all so normal, and relaxing, as if no mention had ever been made of a need to talk, and since she was happy to believe that whatever it was had simply gone away, she released herself to the pleasure of deciding which new shrubs or herbs or flowers should go where in their border beds. Livvy came outside to join them, setting up laptop and books on the large wooden table in the gazebo, and choosing music she was sure they'd enjoy. So it seemed she was in a good mood too, and when Charlie rang to speak to his father and made him laugh, Jay smiled warmly to herself; Tom looked as though he was exactly where he wanted to be, at the heart of his family.

How could she have thought he might have stopped wanting that?

After lunch, she drove to the office, and was already at her desk by the time Terry Josephs came in with Frank Maguire, who turned out to be nothing like she'd imagined him. He was quite short, sturdy and smartly dressed, in a moss-green tweed jacket and navy cravat, both of which appeared slightly too tight. He was also, she thought, older than the mid-sixties John Debrayne had put him at, probably the wrong side of seventy. In contrast to his sober attire, his round, rosy cheeks, thinning hair and luxuriant silver moustache could have allowed him to pass for a storybook grandpa; however, his demeanour was too solemn, reserved even, to complete that particular picture.

'Mr Maguire, thank you for coming,' she said, reaching out to shake his hand. 'I'm Jay Wells. Joe you already know.'

Maguire nodded, and she noticed as he took her hand that there was a slight tremor in his. It made her wonder if he was nervous, or perhaps he had some sort of medical condition.

'I want to help Edward all I can,' he told her earnestly. 'He's a good man, and I like to think of myself as someone who doesn't rush to judgement, the way the police seem to have in this tragic business.'

Intrigued by that, she waved him to a chair. 'So you think someone else did this to Mr Blake's wife?' she asked, coming straight to the point as she and Joe sat down too.

Maguire coloured slightly. 'If it wasn't him, then it has to have been someone else,' he pointed out, 'but if you're asking me who it could have been . . .' He shook his head, apparently at a loss.

Knowing it had been too much to hope that he'd name an alternative suspect right off the bat, she backtracked a way and said, 'Can I ask how well you know the Blakes?'

With a note of regret he said, 'To be truthful, not as well as we'd like to, given how fond we are of them, but we're a different generation. I'm sure to glamorous young people like them we seem a bit . . . out of touch?' With a small, stilted sort of laugh he added, 'I suppose we are a bit, but best not tell my wife I said that, she probably wouldn't like it.'

Touched by his small show of humour, Jay said, 'I believe your wife is in Sunderland, with her mother. She wasn't a witness to anything that happened at the Blakes' house on the dates in question?'

'I'm glad to say she wasn't. It's upset her enough just hearing about it on the phone. She was very attached to Vanessa, in her way, felt quite motherly towards her. She invited her to join our prayer group when we found out about the baby. We could tell she was struggling, so we felt it our duty to try and reach out to her. She wasn't interested though. Shame that, but we understand our ways aren't for everyone.'

'Did you ever invite Edward to join you?'

'Oh yes, but I'm afraid he wasn't interested either. Although he said he had no objection to us praying for them, said it was a thoughtful thing to do.' He shook his head incredulously. 'We didn't see it coming, you know. I mean what happened to her, it's not the kind of thing you expect to happen right on your doorstep, is it? Shocked me to my core when I heard.'

Still not sure she was really getting the measure of him, she said, 'Can you think of anyone else who might have done it?'

His eyes shot off across the room, restless, searching for answers, or maybe it was a nervous tic, it was hard to tell. 'I really don't like doing this,' he declared stiffly, 'but I understand it's importance, so I will tell you that cars came and went from their house quite regularly, especially at weekends. They were always having people round and sometimes the parties would go on until the wee small hours.' He stopped, tight-lipped, apparently disapproving, and she couldn't help wondering if he felt offended at not being invited to these gatherings.

'Did you know any of their visitors?' she asked.

Several moments passed, making her wonder if he'd heard her, but before she could repeat the question he said, 'Only the family, his sister and her husband. Lovely people. As I said, we didn't mix with their friends so we didn't know any of them.'

'Have you ever been inside the house?'

'Yes, I went in a few times. Mostly to see Edward.'

Mostly. 'Did Vanessa ever invite you in?'

Appearing puzzled, he said, 'Why would she do that? I had no business with her. She invited Maddie in now and again. That's my wife, Maddie.'

Jay nodded, wondering if he thought this was the first time he'd mentioned her.

'I'm going to join her Monday,' he was saying. 'She needs some help anyway with all that's going on up there, and the police have said it's fine for me to go.'

Jay smiled and said, 'I'm sure you'll be glad to get away for a while, given all that's been going on.'

'Yes. And no. Like I said, I want to try and help Edward if I can.'

'That's good,' she said, 'because I expect you know he's been charged and it's likely he'll remain in custody until the trial, unless we can find out who really did this.'

Maguire blinked slowly, as if needing a moment to take this in.

She glanced at Joe to try and gauge his thoughts so far, but as usual the ex-detective was inscrutable. 'I know the police will already have asked you this,' she said to Maguire, 'but did you see anyone coming or going from the Blakes' house on Monday, either during the day, or before Edward returned home in the evening?'

He gave a long shake of his head. 'I keep going over it

in my mind, but all I can tell you is what I told the police. I might have heard a car, but not really registered it.' He glanced away, though whether he was trying to remember, or was momentarily uncomfortable about something wasn't clear. 'You see,' he continued, eyes fixed on the desk now, 'it's only our kitchen and two of the bedrooms that look out on the lane. Our sitting room is at the back and if we're in there we don't tend to see or hear very much, especially if the TV is on. And it usually is. I'm afraid I'm a bit of an addict, especially when Maddie's away.'

'So someone could have come and gone, you just can't be sure?'

He grunted an acknowledgement. 'I don't keep tabs, you understand? I'm not that sort of neighbour.'

She regarded him closely, sensing something was off here, though it was hard to tell if he was obfuscating or . . . *embarrassed* about something? 'Did you notice any cars parked outside the Blake's house during the day?' she prompted.

He shook his head. 'No, but I wasn't looking.' He was perspiring, and the shake she'd noticed in his hand earlier seemed to be affecting his jaw.

'But you did see Edward coming home around eight?' she reminded him.

'That's right. I was getting myself a beer – I occasionally have one in the evenings, after I've eaten – and I spotted his car going past. He didn't see me. He'd have waved if he did, because he always does. He just wasn't looking in my direction.'

'Did you notice if anyone was in the car with him?'

His frown suggested he might not have been asked this

question before. 'No, I don't think so. I'm sure he was on his own.'

'So no sign of Mrs Blake?'

'No.'

'OK, and the next time you saw Edward, or heard him, was when he was arguing with someone inside the house?'

'That's right. I'm pretty sure it was Vanessa. I recognized her voice.'

'But you hadn't seen her coming or going from the house during the day?'

His frown deepened. 'No, I didn't. Well, I saw them go off together in the morning, but I didn't see her . . . I don't know when she came back.'

Flicking another quick glance at Joe, she said, 'Where were you when you heard them arguing?'

He cleared his throat. 'Not far from their gates,' he answered. 'It was a lovely evening, so I was out for a stroll before going to bed. It's very peaceful around there. Maddie and I always say how lucky we are to have found the place.'

'So you often walk along to the Blakes' house?'

'Yes, if the weather's good. Maddie's usually with me, of course, but not on Monday. She was already at her mother's by then.'

'And when you heard raised voices, could you make out what was being said?'

He gave a small sigh. 'I'm afraid not. They just sounded . . . angry. I thought to myself, poor Ed, his wife's obviously really upset about something and it doesn't sound like he's having much luck in calming her down.'

'Are you sure it was them and not the TV that you heard?'

'As sure as I can be.'

'Did you feel alarmed? Worried something might be getting out of hand?'

He gave it some thought, 'I wouldn't say alarmed, exactly, more sorry that it was happening.'

'Did you do anything?'

'Oh no. It's not my place to interfere in other people's business. I went home and said a little prayer for them in the hope it might help to settle things down.'

'Were you aware of anyone else coming or going from the house that night? Before or after the argument?'

He shook his head. 'Everything was quiet after I got home, at least as far as I could tell, but I sleep quite heavily so I might not have heard if there was anything.'

'When did you next see Edward?'

'In the morning. Quite early, when the police arrived. It was a big shock, I can tell you, waking up to blue flashing lights and seeing Edward out by his gates looking distressed and like he . . . Well, like he was crying. Sobbing, I'd say.'

'Did you go out?'

'Of course. I wanted to find out if there was anything I could do, but a policeman told me to go back inside and wait. So that's what I did.'

'Did you watch what was going on?'

Twitching slightly he said, 'I'm afraid I did. I know I shouldn't have, but I couldn't help myself. It would have been impossible to sit down and pretend nothing was happening.'

'Of course. So when you were watching, did you see anyone or anything that seemed unusual, apart from the obvious police activity?'

He looked puzzled. 'I don't think so. I mean . . . Are you thinking someone might have been hiding away in the woods, watching what was going on?'

She raised her eyebrows. His words, not hers.

'I didn't see anyone,' he said, 'but I can't say I was looking.'

'Did the police search the surrounding area?'

'Yes, but not until after they'd taken Edward away. That's when they came to talk to me and I told them what I'd seen and heard the night before.' His face seemed to crumple. 'I'm afraid I've made things worse for Edward, but I couldn't lie to the police, could I? My conscience wouldn't allow it, but anyway, I truly believe they're either not talking to the right people, or they're looking in the wrong places, because I'm sure the man I know would never hurt his wife.'

Jay glanced at Joe again and was treated to an expression that seemed to say, *how much of this are you buying?*

Turning back to Maguire, she tried again. 'Is there anything else you can tell me about the Blakes that you think would be useful for me to know?'

He took a moment, eyes focused on nothing as he considered the question. In the end he said, 'There isn't anything. I mean, sometimes you hear rumours, but I don't put a lot of store by them.'

'What sort of rumours?'

'I don't like to indulge in gossip, especially when it could harm someone who doesn't deserve it.'

'It could be very harmful to Mr Blake if he goes to prison for a crime he didn't commit.'

He flushed. 'Yes, it could, but I have trust in the law. I

145

think you, or the police, will find who really did this and then Edward will be free to come home.'

In the end, after keeping Maguire for over an hour, Jay thanked him for coming and waited for Joe to see him out.

'I have the feeling,' she commented when Joe returned to the office, 'that you weren't very impressed with Mr Maguire. Should we be adding him to our list of suspects?' She was only half-joking, for she wasn't ready to rule anyone out at this stage.

Joe said, 'If I could see her getting her kit off for this guy and letting him tie her to a bed, I'd say maybe we should. After all, there's no accounting for taste, and as things stand he's the only one we know for certain was around the place that night. Other than Blake.'

'But?' Jay prompted.

He grimaced. 'No buts, just a strong feeling there's more than he's telling us, like he's maybe covering for someone? Did you get that?'

Having to admit that she had, she said, 'Any suggestions?'

'One of the family? A friend we might not have heard about yet? Who knows? There's someone though, I'll stake my grandmother's silver on it, and I wouldn't mind finding out if Ken Bright thinks the same.'

'If he does, would he agree to Maguire going off to Sunderland?'

'No reason for him not to at this stage. Blake's already in custody, Maguire's given his statement – which may or may not be the same as the one he just gave us, depending on what he was asked – and they'll know where to get hold of him if they need to speak to him again.

'However, there's something about this case that's not adding up. I can't tell you right now what it is, or if it even involves Maguire, but I'm getting a bad feeling all around about it, that's for sure.'

CHAPTER THIRTEEN

By the time Jay arrived home, Tom was making bellinis for Ollie and Jenn in the garden and apparently Perry and Gretchen were on their way over. She took her cocktail gratefully, feeling buoyed by everyone's good mood and ready to unwind, although she was momentarily worried that Tom might have invited their friends around in order to avoid being alone with her.

Paranoia, Jay. It's not a good look. Let it go.

At six, as everyone started on the second round of drinks, she excused herself to disappear into her study to Skype with Sheri Razak.

The connection was good, enabling her to see how exotic the beautiful Eurasian woman was, with her sleek black hair, captivating sloe eyes and fulsome smile. To Jay's relief she appeared far more relaxed than the last time they'd spoken, and was apparently ready, at least on the face of it, to answer whatever questions Jay put her way.

They started with the virtual statement she'd given to the police before leaving London the day before. 'More hurried than it should have been,' Sheri confessed, 'but they insisted and so I gave them the spare ten minutes I had. Not that I could tell them much. Yes, Nessa used my flat from time to time; yes, she always got in touch first

148

to make sure it was all right, and no, I didn't receive a call or text about her needing to use it last Monday.'

After noting it down, Jay decided to come back to it and said, 'When we spoke the day before yesterday, you said that what you had to tell me wouldn't help Edward . . .'

'Yes, I remember what I said, and I realized after that I probably didn't phrase it well. I wasn't trying to imply that he might have done this, only that what I do know won't help to remove him as a suspect.'

'I'd like to hear it anyway.'

Sheri took a breath, and checked a message that had apparently arrived on her phone.

Jay waited, impatiently.

Finally, Sheri said, 'I'm sure you know by now how unhappy Nessa was, and fragile. It was a relief for her to get away from Edward sometimes, to lose herself in other . . . *things*. He was a constant reminder of what they'd lost. She loved him, there was never any doubt about that, but sometimes she couldn't stand to be with him. She hated herself for it, for everything she did to hurt him, but she didn't seem able to make herself stop.'

'What sort of things did she do?'

Sheri turned from the camera as she considered the question, her exquisite profile in sharp relief against the backdrop of ocean blue silk drapes. 'I don't know if I really want to get into that,' she replied, her eyes returning to the screen. 'It seems so . . . disloyal, I guess. She trusted me – and Melissa – to keep her confessions to ourselves, and if I told you, believe me, they'd only hurt Edward more.'

Suppressing her annoyance, Jay said, 'You mean hurt him as a man, or as a defendant in a murder trial?'

Sheri didn't take long to reply. 'Both, because it could all be so easily misconstrued.'

'What could?'

'Please don't press me on this.'

Determined to do just that, Jay said, 'I'm not the police, I'm his defence lawyer . . .'

'Yes, yes, I realize that, and it's not that I don't want to help him. I do, because I truly don't think he did it. He adored Nessa, and understood her in a way most men would have a very hard time managing, considering how she was.' She laughed self-consciously. 'I'm making him sound like a saint, and he definitely wasn't that. He could give her as good as she gave him, believe you me, he has a temper too, and he was hurting just as much, but he'd never lay a finger on her, not in that way.'

'Maybe she pushed him too far?'

Sheri wrinkled her nose. 'I guess it's possible. Anything is.'

'Can you tell me who else might have killed her?'

Sheri shook her head for some time before finally saying, 'I don't know any names.'

Jay's pulse quickened. This was the first time anyone had come even close to admitting there could be another suspect, and maybe not just one. 'Did you tell the police this?' she asked carefully.

'They didn't ask. I could tell that the officer I spoke to – female – had it in her head that Edward was guilty and that I was just a formality to be got through. I was too busy to do more than run with it, thinking I'd clear it up when I spoke to you.'

'You're speaking to me now. It's possible you can help Edward, even though you're saying you can't.'

'Maybe, but I don't want all of her dirty laundry aired in public. Or mine.'

Intrigued, Jay leaned forward. 'What do you mean?'

Sheri sighed. 'It was a long time ago, but Ed and I were an item once. Actually, that might be putting it too strongly. We slept together a few times.'

'Was he married to Vanessa at the time?'

Sheri grimaced. 'No, but they were together. They'd only recently met, a few weeks before. She introduced us at a *vernissage* one night, in London, and it was like I just had to have him. He said the same about me. Fireworks like fourth of July. I couldn't get enough of him. Well, you've seen him, those eyes, that way he has with him of . . . OK, it might be different for you, as his lawyer, but I'll admit I'd have stolen him from Nessa if I could. But it didn't happen. As soon as he realized how hard he was falling for her, it was bye bye Sheri.'

Noting the slight edge of bitterness, Jay said, 'And you were upset about it?'

'Let's just say I . . . minded. Ed knew that and he was sorry, but he'd made his choice. I decided I wasn't going to fall out with Ness about it, she didn't even know, so that was it, really. I won't deny I hoped he'd change his mind at some point, but he never did.'

'Do you know if he was ever unfaithful during his marriage?'

'Not that I was aware of, but there was one time . . . It was just after the baby died. Ed was in a terrible place, they both were . . . He called me, I'm not really sure why. I think he was reaching out to anyone in any way, trying to seek some sort of escape or comfort . . . Of course, it didn't work, there's no such thing as escape or comfort for someone in that state of grief, but sex can help take your mind off things for a while. So we had sex.'

Flashing on how she'd imagined being with him only last night while making love with Tom, Jay felt irrationally irritable as she said, 'Just the once?'

Sheri's smile was wry. 'No, but we were only together for one night and part of the next day, before he got the train home. We never talked about it after. I realized he'd rather we forgot it happened. So that's what I did. He hasn't told you any of this?'

Jay shook her head.

'I guess because he doesn't think it's relevant, and it's not, is it?'

'Being unfaithful can speak to what sort of character we're dealing with.'

'OK, but take it from me, there's nothing wrong with his character. He's a man of integrity, although not without faults – how dull he'd be if he had none. He's also a man who found a woman – me – attractive before he realized he was falling in love with somebody else. And he was a man who was hurting so badly after losing his son that he probably wasn't even really aware of what he was doing.'

Accepting that for now, Jay returned them to the more crucial insinuation that Sheri had made earlier before veering off into her own involvement with Edward. 'You said just now that you didn't know any names. What does that mean exactly?'

Sheri's mouth pursed as she stared hard into the camera. 'You know,' she said, 'if Ed and Toni aren't talking about it, it wouldn't be right for me to go wading in with the very little that I know. Sorry, I realize how unhelpful that must seem to you, but I really don't know any names, and she was Ed's wife, Toni's sister-in-law, you have to get this information from them. I'm sorry, I need to go now, but please help Ed. He's been through so much, the poor man doesn't deserve this,' and with a click of the mouse she was gone.

Annoyed by the abrupt end to the connection, not to mention the cryptic comments, Jay sat staring at the blank screen for a while, considering the tantalizing threads of new information that seemed, right now, too tightly knotted to unravel. However, she could form several theories from them, and if any were right then Sheri was also right, they wouldn't help Edward one bit. On the other hand, she needed this information spelled out before the police got hold of it, so she must decide who to bring it up with first – Edward or Antonia?

CHAPTER FOURTEEN

It was the middle of Sunday afternoon by the time Jay and Tom were finally alone in the house, with Livvy having joined friends for a picnic on Brandon Hill and no one else expected to drop in for the rest of the day.

Tom was already packed for his week in London, his holdall still open on a rack in their dressing room, waiting for last-minute items to go in. Jay hadn't wanted to check if it was more than he usually took for three or four nights away, but she had, as subtly as possible, and to her relief it didn't look as though he was planning to go for any longer than he'd said.

She hated herself for being so mistrustful, and insecure, but it seemed there was nothing she could do to stop her suspicions in spite of him giving her nothing to feed them.

Apart from those chilling words, *I have something to tell you.*

What had happened to make them go away? Or were they still lurking, gathering force in the silence, and he just hadn't yet found the right way to break them free?

You can't say that to someone and then not deliver.

She couldn't go on hiding from it either, although she seemed to be doing a good job of trying.

'You're going to have a busy week,' she commented,

wandering into the bedroom where he was sorting through some papers on the bed. 'Do you think your guy's guilty?'

'Actually no,' he replied, stuffing files into his briefcase, 'but it's coming down to a case of her word against his and she presents a lot better than he does for all sorts of reasons.'

'Such as?'

'She's well spoken, he isn't; she's a smart dresser, he's not; she's young and pretty, he's also young, but overweight and no pin-up. Frankly, being the physical slob that he is, it'll be hard for any jury to believe the act was consensual.'

'So, you're expecting to lose?'

'We'll try hard not to, because I happen to think he's telling the truth.' Setting aside his briefcase, his expression became sardonic, even sad, as he looked at her standing in the doorway, hair loose, feet bare and wearing old yoga pants and T-shirt. 'You've got a busy week of your own coming up,' he remarked. 'I'm guessing your chap won't get bail.'

'Snowballs and hell come to mind.' She sighed, going to take the hand he was holding out to her. She looked down at their entwined fingers and back to his upturned face, not exactly handsome, but strong, striking, as familiar as her own and yet sometimes as impenetrable as a stranger's.

'So, what's it about?' she said softly. 'What do you have to tell me?'

Sighing heavily, he pulled her to stand between his legs. 'Please try to hear me out before you jump to conclusions,' he began.

Jumping right into one, she pulled her hand away. 'It's

her, isn't it?' she said, stepping back. 'I knew it would be. I've been trying to tell myself—'

'Jay, you need to listen. It's not what you think . . .'

'It's *not* about her?'

'Well, yes, it is, but—'

Her eyes blazed with pain and fury as she glared at him. 'I knew to my core you hadn't given her up,' she spat. 'I tried to believe you—'

'Stop it! Just stop,' he cried, trying to grab her hands again, but she snatched them away. 'Please,' he told her, getting up from the bed, 'you won't know anything unless you let me speak. I need to tell you what's happened, how shocked I am by it and worried, and yes, guilty, but I swear I didn't see it coming.'

'Oh, so you're the victim here? Is that what I'm supposed to think?'

'That's not what I'm saying. If you'd just calm down and let me tell you . . .'

'I'm calm. I'm here, but I don't want you to touch me. Not until I know what this is about.'

'You're making it very difficult.'

She turned her head away, furious, frightened, but somehow making herself breathe in and out, forcing a connection with the more adult, rational part of herself.

'So here we are,' she said tartly, 'talking about Ellen Tyler *again*, in our bedroom, and the phrase "there are three in this marriage" comes racing to mind, so I—'

To her astonishment he snatched up his briefcase and walked out of the room. 'There's no point trying to talk to you while you're being like this,' he growled, heading for the stairs.

As she listened to him going down, she tried again to

control herself, to stop allowing her dread of where this was going to prevent them from getting there. She needed to know what it was about, for only then would she be able to start dealing with it.

She found him in the kitchen pouring whisky into a tumbler, and decided she might like a drink too, so went to fill a glass with wine. Bizarrely she was thinking of the Debraynes and their summer room, their children, the demented mother, the arthritic dog, the brother in prison and the sister-in-law who was in the mortuary. Could her own situation be any worse than that?

Obviously not, but *each grief, each loss, each betrayal, is yours to hold, to suffer, to store away for the future and use for betterment or bitterness: the choice is yours.* She couldn't remember who'd said that, but she would look it up. What it told her was that her issues weren't in any way diminished by comparing them with others, they still existed and had to be confronted.

'I'm sorry,' she said, realizing the better part of herself meant it. She really didn't have to view him as an enemy, even though she was sure he was about to hurt her.

Going to the sofa she sat down and put her glass on the coffee table, suddenly not wanting the wine any more. Her throat was too dry to swallow.

He came to sit on the adjacent sofa, as close to her as he could get without being on the same seat. Staring down into his drink he said, 'She got in touch with me, last week, out of the blue.'

Jay's heart somersaulted.

'I wasn't expecting to hear from her,' he continued. 'To be honest, when I realized it was her I declined the call. I was hoping it was just one of those crazy things people do sometimes when they're feeling lonely, or slightly drunk, or maybe in need of some sort of closure. Then I saw that she'd left a message. I didn't listen to it for a couple of days, and when I did it was only by chance because it was amongst several others so it was playing back before I realized . . . She told me something.' He stopped, didn't look at her, barely even moved. 'I've kept the message so you can listen to it and understand why I had to call her back.'

Jay's mind was racing in so many directions, she wasn't entirely sure what she was thinking, apart from maybe his mistress had a terminal illness and wanted to say goodbye. She could live with that, couldn't she? 'I'm not going to listen to her,' she stated. 'Whatever it is, I want you to tell me.'

He nodded, swallowed hard, and in a voice that was quiet and strained, he said, 'There's a child. She says it's mine. Obviously I don't know if that's true, but I have to accept it's possible.'

Jay felt the breath leave her body and her head start to spin. A child? He'd fathered a child? What had happened between him and Ellen Tyler was now in life form. The most intimate part of their relationship had created an innocent child with its conception all covered in . . . deception, blame, hurt, inescapable consequences . . .

Was this really in their world now? If so, it was never going to go away, not ever.

What the hell was she going to do? What was she supposed to say?

Not quite looking at her, he said, 'I've insisted on a DNA test . . .'

She got to her feet with no idea of where she was going,

or what she wanted to do. She stared at the windows where frothy blossom was weighting a tree outside, but she saw nothing, didn't even hear the voices coming from somewhere in the street.

'Jay.'

'She wouldn't have told you about the child without being sure it's yours,' she said, keeping her back to him. 'You must know that.'

'It's a reasonable assumption,' he admitted, 'but I can't just accept what she's saying without asking for proof.'

'Has she agreed to it?'

'Yes.'

Seeing that as confirmation enough of birthright, Jay said, 'Did you see her, after the call? Or did she break the happy news on the phone?'

Stonily he said, 'I haven't seen her. She left the message while I was in Plymouth and that's where I called her from.'

'But she wants to see you this week while you're in London?'

He nodded.

Feeling suddenly violent inside, crazed even, she was almost shocked to hear herself say in a bizarrely normal voice, 'Is she going to bring the child?'

'I don't know. She didn't say.'

'Do want her to? I mean, you must want to meet your youngest . . . Is it a boy or a girl?'

'A boy. His name's Aiden.'

Her throat constricted; words were piling up but couldn't order themselves into a meaningful coherence. She was stuck on a small boy who must be at least two and a half years old, who might look like Tom, who was tying his parents together as irrevocably as Charlie and Livvy tied them.

He said, 'I didn't want to see her without you knowing about it, and I need you to believe me when I say that there's no affair now. It's over, I'm glad it's over, and I'm sorrier than you can ever imagine for the hurt it caused you.'

Still not turning around, she said, 'It's clever of you to put the hurt in the past tense, but it's very present again now. It's right here in our home, in our lives, and this time it's not going away. You have a child with another woman, that makes you part of another family . . .'

'Jay, you, Charlie and Livvy are my family . . .'

'But you can't turn your back on a little boy that's yours, pretend he doesn't exist . . .'

'She says she's not asking me to play a role in his life if I don't want to.'

Jay turned to him incredulously. Did her sensible, intelligent husband really just say something so stupid? 'If that's true, Tom, then why did she call you? Why even tell you about him?'

Without much of a hesitation he said, 'Apparently her husband said he would if she didn't.'

Jay took a breath and let it go shakily. 'So, he knows it's not his and . . . And what? Why does he want you to know?'

'I've no idea, I can only tell you what she told me.'

'Is she still with him?'

'I didn't ask. I guess I'll find out when I see her.'

Jay started to pace, hands going to her head, to her sides and back again. She couldn't find a proper place for this, a way for it not to change everything, to tear them apart no matter how hard they might try to hold on.

Facing him suddenly, she said, 'You've already discussed this with Perry?'

He didn't deny it.

Did she mind about that? It would save her from having to explain why she wasn't functioning as well as she should at the office – except she'd be damned before she would allow this to affect her work. She had commitments, loyalties, people who depended on her, colleagues, clients, friends who she'd never let down, and certainly not in the way her husband was managing to do so spectacularly with her.

'When I found out,' he said, 'my first instinct was to tell you right away. I called, but when you answered I realized it wasn't something I could do over the phone. You weren't around later that evening. I went to Perry and Gretchen's and after she'd gone to bed . . . He knew something was up, and I thought I should try to get my head straight before I spoke to you. Given he's a family lawyer, you can imagine what he said, that I had to get a test done before it went any further, and I thought about waiting until I had the results before telling you . . . But, like you, I can't believe she'd say the child is mine without being certain.'

'Unless she just wants to fuck up your marriage.'

He didn't respond to that, simply shook his head as if saying he had no idea what the motive had been. 'I thought,' he said, 'of asking you to come and see her with me, so you could hear what she has to say, and realize that there is nothing between us now.'

'But there is something,' she cried incredulously. 'A child who has your genes, your blood . . .'

'You know what I'm saying.'

'Yes, I do, and it's not as simple as you having an affair or not, is it? It's a lot bigger than that, so much bigger I can hardly believe you're not seeing it.'

'I am seeing it, but if she doesn't want me to play a role in his life . . .'

Stunned that this was the man she knew speaking, she said, 'Is that what you want? To know you have a son out there growing up without you, knowing nothing about him, whether he needs you or is like you? Are you seriously saying you're ready to turn your back on him without even meeting him?'

He fell silent, which told her that he hadn't thought it through, probably didn't even know how to, when there were so many ways this could play out, half of them probably not even guessed at yet.

'I don't want to see her,' she stated decisively. 'Whatever she has to say, whatever she wants from you – and there's something, you can be sure of that – I want no part of it.'

'How can you not be a part of it when you're my wife?'

She scoffed a laugh. 'Is that what you thought when you were screwing her, that I was a part of it?'

'Jay—'

Cutting him off she said, 'I'm not going to London with you. I have a lot to deal with here, not least of all a murder case, and I don't see that hearing what she has to say is going to change anything at all. The lies, the deception, betrayal have all happened, there's no going back on them. What *you* need to do is sort out how you want to go forward. And I'll do the same, because whatever you might be telling yourself, Tom, nothing can be the same after this, just nothing.'

He was about to respond, when the front door slammed.

'Hey you guys,' Livvy said, coming in from the hall. 'I'm so glad you're here, Mum. Everyone's talking about it – Nat has only got back with her, probably because he followed my advice, and now he keeps posting on Instagram and—'

'Then don't look at it,' Tom interrupted shortly. 'Unfriend him, you won't have to see it then.'

'But it's not the answer, is it?' she cried. 'I'll still know they're together. Mum, you know about relationships, you have to tell me what to do or I'll go mad.'

As she started to cry, Jay folded her into an embrace and buried her face in her hair. 'I'm not sure I'm the best one to ask,' she said, fighting back her own tears. 'Your . . . Your generation see things differently.' What a stupid thing to say; heartache was the same at any age, it hurt like bloody hell and there was no cure that she knew of.

Surprising her, Tom said, 'Why don't you think about the advice you'd give if one of your friends came to you with this?'

Livvy lifted her tear-stained face and Jay saw right away that her father had hit a right note.

Running with it, Jay said, 'You're very good at helping others, so why don't you try turning this around as if it's happening to someone else? What would you tell them to do?'

Livvy was clearly giving this some serious thought. 'You're right,' she said, 'it's what I should do. I just need to think about it and . . . Oh God, Mum, Dad, you're amazing, did I ever tell you that?' and after hugging them both in a frenzy of excitement, she ran up to her room to get started.

Left alone with apparently no words of advice for one another, Jay picked up her wine and took it back to the kitchen.

'Jay,' he said, following her.

'I have work to do for tomorrow,' she interrupted, emptying the glass down the sink. 'I think it's best if one of us sleeps in the guest room tonight.'

'But we can't—'

'I don't want to discuss this any more,' she said tightly. 'You do what you have to do, and while you're away I'll . . . consider my options.'

CHAPTER FIFTEEN

The next morning, right after the bail hearing, still wearing her higher advocate's gown, Jay headed straight down to the cells to speak to Blake before he was returned to the prison. As expected the application had been refused, but that wasn't the reason she was so keen to see him. He'd known how unlikely it was he'd be going home today, and though he'd clearly be disappointed, she needed to focus him on her Skype call with Sheri Razak.

As he was brought into the interview room, she noticed in a way she hadn't in court the expensive cut of his charcoal grey suit, and pristine whiteness of his shirt, a wholesomeness and elegance that seemed almost touchingly at odds with the anguished look on his face. He was a man trying to appear at his best while feeling pretty close to his worst.

God, how she could sympathize with that given her own inner turmoil.

'Come and sit down,' she said. 'Are you OK?'

His eyebrows rose in an attempt at irony. 'You always hope, don't you,' he said, pulling out the chair, 'that things will go your way even when the odds are stacked against it.'

'I know,' she said softly, 'and I'm sorry it didn't—'

'Don't be. It's not your fault. You did what you could,

and thanks for making me sound like a trustworthy, upstanding member of the community as opposed to a raving sociopath who should be kept away from civilized people.'

Still slightly aggrieved by the way the prosecution had laboured their points, she said, 'I don't think anyone thought you were that, it's just that bail is almost never granted in a murder case.'

'I know, and I'm sure you have better things to do than deal with my self-pity. Actually, I don't have much time for it myself, so shall we discuss what happens next?'

Appreciating his resilience and even feeling slightly strengthened by it where Tom was concerned, she said, 'Around six weeks from now we'll be back in court for a Plea and Trial Preparation Hearing. This is when both sides have to disclose a list of the witnesses we intend to call and, based on that, and the general outlines of the case, the judge will set a date for the trial. A junior barrister will represent you for the PTPH, and I have a Queen's Counsel in mind for later – if it comes to that. She's someone I have a lot of confidence in.'

He nodded his understanding, seeming both to absorb her words and yet to be distracted in some way.

'What are you thinking?' she asked.

His eyes came to hers. 'I'm just trying to get a handle on it all, convince myself that it's really happening, as if prison isn't already doing that for me.' Suddenly he added, 'Do you know where Nessa is now?'

Realizing she should have expected the question, she said, 'She might still be at the morgue, unless the pathologist has released her body. I'll find out for you.'

'Thank you. It shouldn't be falling to Toni to sort out

the funeral . . .' He frowned deeply, as though a sharp pain had dug in behind his eyes. 'Will they allow me to go?' he asked.

Wishing she could say otherwise, she said, 'It's highly unlikely, I'm afraid.'

'But aren't I innocent until proven guilty? And I'm her husband. I should be there. I *want* to be there.'

Understanding his frustration and sadness, she said, 'I'll put in a request, but you must be prepared for it to be turned down.'

He nodded dolefully, and needing to move things along, she said,

'I spoke to Sheri Razak at the weekend. She intimated that your wife wasn't always faithful and if that's true—'

'She shouldn't have told you that,' he broke in heatedly. 'She had no right to.'

'Edward, why would you cover up your wife's—'

'She wasn't unfaithful,' he told her, 'not in the sense you're meaning it. She . . . I . . . It's not what you're thinking.'

The pain in his face made him look so vulnerable that she had to steel herself.

'Then what was it? Sheri talked about not knowing *names*. Do *you* know them?'

His head went down, his knuckles whitened as he closed a fist. 'You have to understand,' he said, 'that she was grieving, and any one of us is capable of acting out of character when we're in the depths of so much despair. Did Sheri tell you I slept with her right after Lucas died?'

'Yes, she did.'

'It didn't mean anything. I hardly knew what I was doing . . . I needed someone, something to distract me . . .'

'Edward, what you did with Sheri isn't the issue here. It's whether your wife did the same sort of thing, and if so, who with?'

They both looked up as a guard put his head round the door. 'Transport's here,' he announced.

'My client will be right out,' Jay assured him. To Blake, she said, 'You could be going home in a matter of days if you'd just tell me who your wife was sleeping with. It could, if we can find out who was with her that day, cast enough doubt on the charge to make it unsafe as it stands.'

His eyes came to hers, penetrating them deeply as if trying to assess how far he should trust her. 'There isn't time now,' he replied quietly.

'Just give me a name.'

'I can't. I don't know who it was.'

'But there was someone.'

He was still staring into her eyes, and though she was unsettled by the blueness of his gaze, she also felt that on some level she was reaching him. 'You need to talk to Toni,' he told her. 'Tell her I said it's OK.'

Torn between frustration and relief, she got to her feet as he did. 'Please try to bear in mind that my only purpose here is to help you. You have no reason to distrust me, and surely every reason to help yourself.'

He continued to look at her, his gaze finally softening as he said, 'I know,' and turning to the door he walked out ahead of her to get into the prison van.

CHAPTER SIXTEEN

Jay spent the rest of the day going from one meeting to the next while dealing with a backlog of phone calls, and breaking off only to grab a sandwich and latte from Sean's terrace coffee stall at the market. Although it was good to get some air, even there she wasn't able to focus her thoughts in a single direction, for she inevitably bumped into people she knew, and her mobile was constantly claiming her attention.

Now she was back at her desk, but about to go and meet John and Antonia Debrayne, who she'd have spoken to this morning after the bail hearing if there had been time.

'Do you need me to stay on?' Vikki asked, appearing in the doorway.

Jay glanced up from her computer screen, head still full of what she'd just been reading, until her secretary's question registered. 'Oh, no, thanks,' she said. 'I'll be leaving any minute. Actually, any news from Joe? I was hoping he might have some info on Vanessa Blake's stepmother by now.'

'He rang about half an hour ago, but you were on the phone. He said he'd call again in the morning. Are you OK? It's been a manic day and you don't quite seem . . . well, yourself?'

Knowing she wouldn't feel herself at all if she took a moment to think about it, Jay said, 'I'm fine. Thanks. Did you set up a time for me to go to the prison?'

'You mean to see Edward Blake? Or Stella Cooper?'

Oh Christ, she'd forgotten all about poor Stella, who was on remand at Eastwood Park for attacking her abusive husband with an electric drill. 'Both,' she said, glancing at her mobile as yet another text came through.

'You're seeing Stella on Wednesday at eleven. I'm waiting for confirmation re. Blake for next Tuesday. Does that work? Do you want to change anything?'

'Not for the moment.' Should she already have passed Stella's case over to Ash or Sallyanne? She was such a sweet girl and so terrified of being punished for defending herself and her two-year-old son from the monster they lived with that Jay would feel utterly disloyal if she did. On the other hand, if she and Sallyanne went to the prison together and explained to Stella why—

'Hello! Are you still with me?'

Jay refocused on Vikki. 'Sorry, uh, you're right, it's been a crazy day, but there's no reason for you to stay. Are the Debraynes still here?'

'They went over to the Hotel du Vin, and asked if you could meet them there. I think they got fed up waiting in our less than lovely conference room.' She turned as the firm's other senior partner came to stand in the doorway beside her.

As Jay's eyes went to Perry's, clocking the way he was looking at her, she felt a sudden rush of emotion threaten to engulf her. Hurriedly pushing it back, she said, 'Still here?'

'Still here,' he confirmed. He glanced at Vikki, her cue to leave, and came further into the room.

'I'm in a rush,' Jay apologized, starting to gather up her things.

'I won't delay you, but I'm guessing Tom's told you his news. So, I just want you to know I'm here if you need to chat.'

Swallowing, she said, 'Thanks, but I'm not sure there's anything to say. Have you told Gretchen?'

'No, it's not my place to without your permission. Tom's in London this week, right?'

'He is, and apparently might meet his new son at some point.' Her ludicrous attempt to sound breezy fooled no one, least of all Perry.

'Have you heard from him today?'

'No. Yes! He's called and texted, but I haven't had time to . . . I don't want to deal with it now, Perry. I really do need to go. I'm already late for Edward Blake's sister.'

'OK. I just wanted to remind you how much you guys mean to me and Gretchen, so if there's anything . . .'

'Thanks. I promise I'll let you know if there is.'

Minutes later she was heading through the arch in the old city wall, and turning left towards the sugar warehouse now transformed into a luxury hotel. She hoped she hadn't been too abrupt with Perry, but she really hadn't wanted to discuss anything tonight, any more than she wanted to listen to Tom's messages or read his texts. The only one she'd actually seen, by fleeting mistake, said, *I'm sorry, I love you. Please call me.* It had been sent early this afternoon, but there had been no time to get back to him, even if she had known what to say, and she didn't.

By now, knowing him, his patience would be running thin, so there was a good chance his later messages would be less conciliatory.

171

It didn't matter. She had no intention of engaging with them now; she had too much else to be dealing with.

Finding Antonia and John Debrayne in the hotel's main bar, she apologized for keeping them so long and joined them in the more-or-less private niche of a sofa and two comfy chairs.

'Can I get you a drink?' John asked, raising an arm to beckon a waiter.

'A gin and tonic would be wonderful,' she replied with feeling, 'but I have to drive, so just the tonic.' As he dealt with the order, she turned to Antonia and felt a fleeting sense of solidarity as she saw how shattered the woman looked. Even if Jay didn't appear as torn apart herself, she was close to feeling it. 'I know this is tough,' she said kindly, wishing she could come straight to the point while understanding that this chat was going to need more careful handling than a rush to the omissions, perhaps even lies, that had played a part in most of their conversations before.

'I just wish I didn't have to wait so long to see him,' Antonia complained. 'How was he when you spoke to him earlier?'

Jay considered this, wanting to be truthful but tactful. 'Stoic, frustrated, grieving – all the things you'd expect. He told me—'

'He hasn't rung yet. I thought he would have by now. Are they allowed to call mobile numbers?'

'Yes, and I'm sure he'll be in touch. Sometimes there are queues for the phones.'

Antonia blanched slightly, clearly disturbed by the picture this created. 'Guy and Camille are at home waiting,' she said, 'just in case he calls there.'

172

Jay thanked the waiter as he brought her drink and set out more bowls of nuts and olives. 'I guess Melissa's returned to London?' she asked, after raising her glass in a silent toast.

'She went right after she spoke to the police,' Antonia replied. 'I don't think there was much she could tell them, or she said there wasn't. Have you caught up with Sheri yet?'

With a glance at John, Jay said, 'I have, and I've discussed what she told me with Edward. As a result of that, he's asked me to tell you it's OK to talk to me.'

As Antonia stiffened, John deflected with, 'About what in particular?'

'I think you know,' Jay replied, 'but if you'd like me to spell it out. Sheri implied, so did Edward, that Vanessa might have been involved with someone, perhaps more than one person . . .' She let it hang, hoping they'd pick it up from there, and eventually John did.

'Are you sure Ed is OK with this? If we could speak to him . . .'

'I can assure you I wouldn't lie to you, Mr Debrayne. There wasn't time for him to tell me anything himself this morning, which is why he wants you to explain what's missing, and we all know that something – or someone – is.' She thought briefly of Maguire, feeling certain he knew, or at least had an idea of who it was, but there was nothing to be gained from mentioning him right now.

'He won't want it getting out,' Antonia cautioned hastily. 'We've worked so hard to keep it from the press and the police. You see, we're very private people, not at all the sort who seek fame, much less notoriety, and our intention

173

has always been to try and protect Vanessa. That hasn't stopped with her death.'

Knowing she'd never cease to be amazed by how misguided, even boneheaded some people could be, Jay said, patiently, 'As your brother's lawyer I am bound to confidence, but you must know that whatever it is you're hiding, the police will almost certainly uncover it sooner or later. So please, let's try to get ahead of it. Was Vanessa having an affair – or affairs? As I said, I'm led to believe there was more than one.'

Glancing uncertainly at her husband, Antonia said, 'Yes, I'm afraid there was more than one, probably more than we know. Well, we didn't *know* any of them, did we?' she said to John.

He shook his head gravely. 'We're not even sure how many might have been a fantasy, made-up stories to torment Ed with, but we're fairly certain some were real.'

'Because?' Jay prompted, feeling faintly sickened by how much betrayal there was in the world.

Swallowing, Antonia said, 'I have the phone she used to contact them. Ed slipped it to me while the police were searching the house. He didn't want them finding it and . . . He didn't want anyone thinking the worst of her and they obviously would once they found out how . . . *promiscuous* she was.'

Quietly stunned by how they'd ever thought this wouldn't come out eventually, Jay's eyes turned to John as he said, 'She wasn't always like it. It was only after Lucas. I guess it was a distraction, a way of losing herself, escaping the grief. She wasn't right afterwards, she changed . . . We could see it – not all the time, but . . . The day she met me for lunch in London?'

Jay nodded.

'She came on to me then. It was awful. I hardly knew what to say to her. She'd never behaved like it with me before . . . She cried, wanted to know what was wrong with her, and I'm not convinced she was talking about her attraction. I'm sure she knew she wasn't well, that what she was doing was . . . destructive? But she seemed unable to stop.'

'I think she was usually drunk when she picked up men,' Antonia continued, seeming relieved to be getting it out there now. 'And it mostly happened in London, I think – I mean, I don't know, but we presume, with the various photographers and artists she met.'

'Have you tried any of the numbers in the phone?' Jay asked, already itching to get hold of it.

Antonia shook her head. 'I suppose we should have, but was anyone really going to admit being with her last Monday once they knew she was dead?'

'Are there any names against the numbers?'

'Only initials, but there are photographs. You can't see any faces, other than hers, but some of the angles . . . They're quite explicit.'

Thinking of how it must have been for Blake if he'd seen them, and clearly he had, Jay could better understand now why he hadn't wanted anyone to know about his wife's 'contacts'. It wouldn't only provide a possible other suspect; it would give him the best reason in the world to have committed the crime.

Her eyes moved to John as he said sadly, 'It was like she'd lost control of herself. We don't know how often she saw other men – I don't think it happened when she was at home, amongst people we know . . .' He paused, seeming to think about that, and Jay once again alighted on Maguire and who he might have seen coming and going that he felt he had to cover for. 'Well, actually,' John continued, 'she did approach one of our friends . . . She passed a note to him at a dinner party asking him to meet her outside in his garden. Fortunately he didn't take her up on it; instead he gave the note to me and I showed it to Ed.'

'What did Edward do?'

'I think he just spoke to the man, apologized, and thanked him for not taking advantage of her. Everyone in our close circle knew she had problems, none of them would have exploited her or talked to outsiders about it. I think the police inquiries have proved that.'

Seeing how proud he was of the loyalty, how closed their ranks were, Jay felt only exasperation as she said, 'But surely you want to find out who did this to her? Holding back like this is leaving Edward completely exposed.'

'Of course we want to know who did it,' Antonia assured her earnestly, 'but you obviously realize Vanessa's . . . *behaviour* provides Ed with a perfect motive. And with the timing of it all, the evidence looking the way it does . . . He wouldn't stand a chance if any of this got out.'

Unable to deny that, Jay sat quietly considering what should be done next. 'Can I see the phone?' she asked. 'Do you have it with you?'

Antonia balked. 'It's hardly something we'd walk around with,' she whispered, as if anyone close by would know what she was talking about. 'It's in the safe at home. The children haven't seen it. They don't even know it exists. Or that she did the things she did . . . We'd rather keep it from them if we can.'

Having no problem with that as far as it went, Jay said, 'I'll ask my PA to arrange a time for me to come and pick it up. The sooner I see it the better.'

Antonia glanced at John as he nodded.

'I'd also,' Jay continued, 'like to take a look around Clover Hill Farm while I'm out that way. Would you be willing to come with me?'

Antonia nodded slowly. 'I don't see why not. We have no more to hide. That was it, and now you know . . .' Awkwardness paled her expression. 'Have you changed your opinion about Ed's innocence?'

It was a fair question, and one Jay would have preferred some time to consider, although her initial instinct was simply to feel a shared sense of wretchedness at all the duplicity and lies that had beset his marriage. 'I understand,' she said, 'why you think it's damning, and on the face of it, it is, but we need to dig deeper, find out more about her contacts and where they were on the day she died.'

'You're not going to tell the police?'

'We're under no obligation to, but I need your word that you won't dispose of the phone.'

Antonia and John exchanged looks and both promised not to. 'We're trying to get a visit arranged for ourselves,' Antonia told her. 'Are you due to see him soon?'

'Next Tuesday, by which time I hope we'll have managed to track down at least one other suspect.'

CHAPTER SEVENTEEN

By the time Jay arrived home, Tom had rung again, several times, but she still hadn't answered. She would speak to him, because she had to, just not until she felt ready, and she wasn't entirely sure yet when that would be.

As she let herself into the house, unravelling her single plait from the coil it had been in all day, she felt saddened by how easy it had been simply to think about him, to take him for granted in her life, until yesterday. Now, every thought came edged with hurt, anxiety, anger, quickly followed by a rush of dread. It was like rewinding three years to the time she'd found out about the affair, when she'd felt devastated and betrayed on an epic scale, and terrified they'd never get past it. Of course, they hadn't, not entirely, for she'd never been able to forget, and nor had she really forgiven.

At least back then she'd only been competing with another woman. How simple that seemed in retrospect, now she was up against a child whom Tom had created with said woman at a time when they'd presumably been in love. And at some point this week, Tom was quite possibly going to meet them both, and no doubt fall head over heels for his son – and where were they all going to go from there?

'Hey Mum, good day?' Livvy called out from the stairs

178

as Jay went through to the kitchen. 'I won't need any supper. Going to dance class with Giselle and might stay over. I'll text when I know.'

'OK,' Jay replied, not loud enough to be heard, but it didn't matter, Livvy had already slammed the front door.

Tugging open the fridge, she poured herself a large glass of wine and took out her phone, detesting the butterflies that assailed her insides in dread and anticipation of what messages were waiting.

On the home screen was a text from Gretchen saying: *Jenn and I at David Lloyds. Fancy a swim?*

Feeling she ought to go if only to get out of her own head, while knowing she didn't actually have the energy, she messaged back, *next time* ☺ and connected to Tom.

'So you are speaking to me,' he said, slightly irritably when he answered.

'Your tone is making me change my mind,' she told him, equally snippy. 'In fact, shall we just ring off? I've had a long day, I'm sure you have too and—'

'Before you make some unhelpful comment about me having other things to deal with, shall we at least try to speak to one another civilly?'

Sighing, she sat down on one of the kitchen bar stools and began sifting idly through the mail Livvy must have put there.

'You first,' she said.

'OK. Avoiding me, being angry with me, isn't going to help this situation. I've already told you she doesn't want me to play a role in his life—'

'Oh stop this,' she cried angrily. 'If that's true, why the hell is she in touch?'

'I've already told you, because her husband forced it.'

'And I should believe that because?'

'Because it's what she told me. Jay, you mean everything to me, nothing's *ever* going to change that . . .'

'Well, that's great for you, but if you think it's not going to change things for me . . . For God's sake, Tom, can't you see what this means for us going forward? Actually, I don't suppose you can, because you probably haven't thought any further than this week. Well, let me tell you this, you are about to meet an innocent child, who's no doubt cuter than cute, quite chatty at his age, and he's *yours*. Whether you think that means anything today, I've no idea, but believe me it will mean a lot when you see him, because one way or another he'll remind you of Charlie when he was that age. And even if you tell yourself you're not going to play a role in his life as he's toddling into your arms and giving you adorable grins, you'll be lying, because you won't be able to deal with your conscience if you don't. You'll always want to know about him, but most of all you'll want to see him. And do you know how I know this? Because I know *you*. Cold and measured as you might appear to some, even yourself, the real you, the father that loves his children, will not be able to switch off.'

There was a momentary silence before he said, 'Wow! That was quite a speech. You've obviously been giving this a lot of thought.'

'Wrong, I haven't. I don't need to in order to know what I'm saying is true.'

'Can I remind you that we're not yet certain he's mine?'

'Oh, for God's sake, let's not go there again. I thought we'd already agreed, she wouldn't be doing this, and nor would her husband, if they weren't sure of their case. But don't let that stop you getting yourself a DNA test. As a lawyer I would strongly recommend it, as your wife I couldn't care fucking less,' and she clicked off so savagely that the phone shot out of her hand.

'Oh Christ,' she groaned, dropping her head in her hands. She hadn't intended to sound off like that, or to end the call so abruptly. However, she'd meant everything she'd said and a lot more that she hadn't even found words for yet. He wouldn't be able to pretend the little boy didn't exist, and nor would she. He'd hate himself for even trying, and she'd detest herself for wanting to deprive an innocent child of a wonderful father.

Except he already had one, didn't he? If Ellen's husband had treated him as his own for the past two or more years, why on earth would he want to involve Tom now? Was the man dying? Maybe he'd met someone else and had told Ellen he wanted no more to do with the boy. How callous that would be, although in her line of work she'd come across worse.

Looking down at the phone as it rang again, she saw it was Tom, and decided to send a text rather than try to speak to him again. *I'm too tired to discuss this tonight and I still have a lot to do before I go to bed. Let's talk tomorrow.*

Minutes later he texted back: *OK, but I don't want you to go to sleep without knowing how sorry I am and how much I love you.*

Feeling tears sting her eyes, she rapidly blinked them back, refreshed her wine and made a sandwich to take through to the study. The best and only way to cope with this for now was to immerse herself in work.

It took a while for her to refocus, her mind was still

so scattered, her emotions in chaos, but eventually she was able to accept that she had no way of resolving this herself, and certainly not tonight. Like it or not, she needed to let it play out the way it had to, and meantime she would concentrate on the clients who were depending on her, mindful of the fact that some of their issues were far greater than the one she was having to face. At least she wasn't being accused of killing Tom while knowing she hadn't done it, nor had she lost her son in a tragic accident, or had to deal with a partner's destabilizing grief. Nor was she in a prison cell tonight with all the indignities, loss of liberty and fear that entailed.

With her mind fully on Edward Blake now she opened up her laptop and began emailing a list of instructions to Terry Josephs. There was a lot to be done on this case, far more now she knew that the police didn't have all the evidence, and it was possible Joe would need help with the investigation.

She stopped typing and took some time to consider the idea that was forming in her head, going through the many ramifications, complications and objections there might be to it. After consulting her diary for the next few days, she began a very different list of instructions, this one for the crime team, copied to Perry. Once it was sent, she messaged Antonia Debrayne to ask if it would be convenient for her to pick up Vanessa's mobile phone on Wednesday afternoon – the day after tomorrow. She could go straight after a prison visit with Stella Cooper, and hopefully go on from Highview Hall to Clover Hill Farm.

A reply came back ten minutes later: *That works for me. I'll see you then.*

No sooner had she read it than another text arrived from Tom. *Will I at least get a 'goodnight'?*

With a bruising clash of emotions, she pressed in the single word followed up with no x's and turned off her phone. She still had an enormous amount to get through tonight, and any more distractions from her personal life would not be welcome.

CHAPTER EIGHTEEN

'I got your email,' Perry stated as he closed Jay's office door behind him and leaned against it. 'Are you absolutely sure about this?'

Glancing up from her desk, she said, 'You mean, about getting more involved in the Edward Blake investigation? Yes, I am.'

'But why? You've got Joe, and he has others he can call on if he needs backup.'

'I'm aware of that, but I've decided to be more hands on myself, where I can.'

He stared at her searchingly, knowingly. 'I get that you're trying to drown yourself in work,' he said bluntly, 'but don't you have enough of it without adding this to the load?'

'Probably, actually definitely, but if I spread it out through the crime team . . .'

'They can cover, of course, but it's *you* your clients want to see.'

'And they shall when it's necessary. I'll always be at the end of the phone, and I'll be there for their court appearances . . . Perry, this is something I want to do, OK, and it's not as if I've never involved myself in an investigation before when a case is this . . .' She searched for the right word. 'I was going to say complex, but maybe borderline

is a better way to describe it. We don't want someone
going to prison – or staying in prison – for a crime he
didn't commit, but that's very likely what will happen if
we don't get to the root of what happened that day.'

'I hear you, but—'

She hadn't finished. 'If you've read my email, you'll
know about the phone that Blake and his sister kept back
when the property was searched. I think it could provide
us with leads the police have not yet uncovered, and with
any luck, once we have them, we'll be able to get Blake
home where he belongs.'

A moment or two passed, until apparently deciding not
to press his objection any further, he said, 'Did you talk
to Tom last night?'

She turned back to her computer as she said, 'Only
briefly.'

'Do you know when he's seeing the boy?'

The boy. She understood why Perry hadn't used his name,
if he even knew it; it would introduce a sense of familiarity
that wouldn't be welcome at this stage. 'No,' she replied,
getting to her feet, 'but I'm sure he'll tell me when we speak
later. Now, if you don't mind, I have a crime team meeting
about to start – and I'll be at Taunton Crown Court this
afternoon.' With a small smile she added, 'I hope that
persuades you I'm not shirking my duty to other clients.'

Raising his eyebrows as he watched her pack up her
files, he said, 'I know you wouldn't. I'm simply worried
that you're going into denial over this situation with the
child . . .'

'And it's where I'm going to stay until I'm forced to
come out, but thanks for your concern. I love you for it,
but I really do have to go now.'

Opening the door, he gestured for her to leave ahead of him. 'Just don't forget who your friends are,' he said quietly. 'We're here for you and we'd like to see you for supper tonight, if you can make it.'

'I'll let you know,' she replied, feeling her appetite drowned out by a surge of nervous anxiety, 'but thanks,' and shaking her head at Vikki, who was trying to attract her attention, she quickly ran upstairs to join the meeting with her team.

Two hours later, just as she was leaving to drive to Taunton, Jay received an email from Tom letting her know that he'd arranged to visit Ellen Tyler's home the following evening. He added: *Apparently her husband and son will both be there, unless I have any objection, and frankly I can't think of one that I'd be comfortable making. I'm putting this in an email now to give you the chance to think about it before we speak later. There's a dinner I need to be at by eight in Clerkenwell, but hopefully we'll have time to talk before that.*

She replied straight away: *I don't think there's anything to talk about until after you've seen them. Maybe we should wait until the weekend. Are you back on Thursday or Friday?*

He hadn't answered by the time she reached the court, probably because he still wasn't sure when his trial would end, or maybe because he was angry that she was blanking him again. Perhaps not the most adult way of dealing with this, but she really couldn't see any point in going over hypotheticals; much better to confront the whole sorry mess when there was actually something to discuss.

She was almost home that evening following a gruelling

session in front of a bellicose judge, when a No Caller ID message came up on her car's Command system. Since this was how some prison numbers displayed, she clicked on expecting it to be Stella Cooper, who she wanted to speak to before their pre-trial meeting with the barrister in the morning.

'Hello? Mrs Wells? Jay.'

'Edward,' she said, surprised, but pleased to hear him. 'How are you?'

There was a small note of irony in his tone as he said, 'You'll have to stop asking me that question, unless you want a truthful answer.'

He had a point. 'OK. So how about this? Has anyone told you yet that my visit next Tuesday has been confirmed?'

'Yes, they have. And Antonia's bringing Guy with her the following day. By then I'll be more than ready to see some friendly faces.'

Inwardly wincing at the thought of those he was regularly confronting, she said, 'Are you coping?'

'Let's just say, I try to keep myself to myself, but it doesn't always work out. Anyway, I didn't ring to lay those sorts of woes on you. I know Toni's told you about Nessa's . . . activities, and I wanted to apologize for keeping it from you. I hope you understand why I did, although I'm not sure I do myself now, when it was clearly crazy to think I could go on protecting her.'

'It certainly was,' she agreed, indicating to leave the M5. 'I'm sure you realize you might not be where you are now if you'd been honest from the start. But I understand, it's not always easy to think straight or make good decisions when you're in the throes of a crisis.'

'Thank you,' he said quietly.

She'd have asked about the phone he'd kept back next, but knew it wouldn't be a good idea to bring it up now. Apart from not knowing who might be listening at his end, it was something best discussed face to face, by which time she should have seen it herself. 'I've had no contact from the police,' she told him, 'so apparently there's nothing new for us to worry about from them at this stage.'

Managing to sound faintly dry, he said, 'Well, there's a blessing.'

She smiled and was about to speak again when he said, 'I only called to apologize, so I guess I should ring off now.'

'OK,' she said.

'I'll see you next week.'

As the line went dead she drove on towards home, trying to imagine how he must be feeling, what his greatest fears might be, attempting to put herself in his shoes. Though in truth, she acknowledged ruefully, she had plenty of issues of her own to mull over, without taking his on board as well.

To her relief there was no mention of Tom at Perry and Gretchen's place; with Livvy and Sabrina, the Forster's sixteen-year-old daughter, both at the supper table, the chat was mainly focused on the youngsters. It was entertaining, and provided a welcome break from the intensity of work and everything else that was going on in her life – although she was repeatedly assailed by it in sudden waves of nerves erupting out of nowhere.

'So you're seeing Blake's sister tomorrow?' Perry said, as he walked her to the door later.

'That's right. I'll be going straight from Eastwood Park.'

'Am I allowed to ask about Tom?'

As Livvy had walked on ahead, she said, 'He's going to see the child tomorrow after court.'

Perry nodded thoughtfully.

'Have you told Gretchen yet?' she asked.

'No.'

'Then you should. She knows something's up and I don't want there to be any secrets between you.' She almost added *we know how destructive they can be to a marriage*, but bit it back.

Hugging her he said, 'I'm going to be in Newport for most of the day, a particularly nasty divorce case, but I'll be back in the evening if you fancy a chat.'

'Thanks,' she replied, and turning away she hurried to catch up with Livvy, in need of a chat with her daughter, if only to blot out the dread that one of these days Perry would be acting for her.

CHAPTER NINETEEN

The following day Jay arrived at Highview Hall in bright sunshine to find Antonia eager to lead her straight to the library. 'I've already opened the safe,' she said, indicating the most obvious hiding place in the world, behind a hinged painting. 'The children are in the stables, so if I can do this quickly . . .'

As she took the phone out, handling it as gingerly as if it were a gun, a voice behind them said, 'What are you doing?'

Antonia started and Jay turned to find Guy, the Debrayne's eighteen-year-old son, watching from the doorway.

'Darling, I thought you were saddling up with Camille,' Antonia said, leaving the phone in Jay's hand and the safe door open as she went to him.

'What's that?' he asked Jay, his young face flooding with colour, his whole demeanour one of hostility and suspicion.

'It's just a phone,' his mother told him. 'It belonged to . . . it's Edward's.'

'So why is it here? I thought the police had taken everything.'

Antonia said, 'They did, but—'

'They missed this,' Jay explained, 'so I'm taking it.'

'I don't recognize it,' he told her stiffly. 'Ed had an iPhone. That's . . . It's not an iPhone.'

'It's an old Samsung,' Antonia said. 'I don't expect it has anything much on it . . .'

The boy's eyes were still on Jay. 'Nessa had a Samsung,' he told her. 'Is it hers? What are you going to do with it?'

Speaking steadily, kindly, she said, 'First, I'll find out what's on it, and once we know that, we'll either hand it over to the police, or I guess we'll return it to the safe.'

'Darling, what's the matter?' Antonia fussed. 'It's just an old phone.'

His head went down, and pulling him to her, Antonia pressed a kiss to his hair. 'Aren't you and Camille going for a ride?' she reminded him.

'I came back to find Dad. He's supposed to be joining us.'

'I'm here,' Debrayne announced, appearing from the hallway behind his son. 'I was just getting changed. Are the horses ready? Mrs Wells, forgive me, I didn't realize you were here.' Coming forward he held out a hand to shake.

'Please call me Jay,' she reminded him. 'I'm afraid I arrived a little early.'

'It's not a problem,' he assured her. 'We'd have missed you if you'd come any later.'

Realizing that had been the intention, a bracing ride through the countryside to get the children out of the way while Antonia handed over the phone, Jay could have kicked herself for ruining the plan.

'Is there any news?' Debrayne asked, glancing at his son, as though to warn her that if there was and it was bad it would be best not to share it right now.

Since there actually was none of any consequence, she

said, 'My investigator, Terry Josephs, has spoken to Edward's friends in Devon, the Burnses? They confirmed what happened during the time Edward and Vanessa were staying with them.'

Guy's head came up. 'You mean when Nessa tried to hang herself?' he spat angrily.

'Guy!' his mother admonished.

'Stop,' he growled, shrugging her off. 'You know that's what happened, and she only did it to try and get Ed into trouble—'

'But it didn't work,' his father interrupted, 'and we don't *know* that was her intention. Now, let's go and find Camille. She'll only be cross if we keep her waiting.'

A few minutes later, Jay was turning out of the gates of Highview Hall with Antonia in the passenger seat, en route to Clover Hill Farm.

'If you stay on this road for the next two miles,' Antonia said, 'you'll come to a sign for the Beaufort Polo Club. We need to take a right there, and wind through the lanes . . . I'll direct you again once we get there.'

Keeping to the speed limit, Jay drove in silence for a while, gathering her thoughts about where they were going and why she felt it was important to see the crime scene. Though she wasn't sure it would change anything, she hoped it might provide a deeper insight into Edward and Vanessa Blake's relationship, or give her something unimaginable right now that would help her to help him.

Antonia said, 'I'm sure you realized that Guy's taking this very hard. Actually, so is Camille, but she has a different way of dealing with things. She's a more . . .

resourceful sort of character, whereas Guy is quite sensitive. He's always been very close to Ed.'

'When I spoke to your brother yesterday,' Jay said, 'he told me you're taking Guy to see him next week.'

'Yes, I am. He's got it into his head that he's going to keep Ed's projects going until Ed can take over again – and Ed being Ed is keen to make sure his contractors are paid. So I'm sure that's what we'll spend most of our time discussing.'

'Will Guy be able to run things on his own?'

'No, not at all, but John and I will help. Guy will kind of be in charge though, because he's familiar with the various builds and conversions, and he knows some of the clients. Actually, the difficulty we're having now is persuading him not to give up uni in order to work full time for Ed. I'm sure Ed will try to talk him out of it. He's as keen as we are for Guy to complete his education.'

Slowing up behind a tractor, Jay gave it a few moments before asking about the funeral arrangements.

Sighing, Antonia turned to stare out of the passenger window. 'They haven't released the body yet. I'm not sure when they will. Ed wants to be there when it happens, but he doesn't think it'll be allowed. Will it?' she asked, looking at Jay.

'My secretary's put in a request,' Jay assured her. 'It'll be up to the prison governor.'

'It'll seem so cruel if they refuse.'

Agreeing that it would, Jay said, 'Is her stepmother involved in the arrangements?'

Antonia gave an incredulous laugh. 'Not at all, and nor would Ed or Vanessa want her to be. Have you met her yet?'

193

'No, but my investigator has spoken to her on the phone.'

'And how did that go?'

Reaching the Beaufort Polo Club sign, Jay tried not to groan as the tractor took a right turn too. 'I haven't discussed it with him yet, but his email notes didn't give the impression that he'd got very far with her.'

'Now why doesn't that surprise me? She's a truly dreadful woman in just about every respect. I've no idea what Nessa's father saw in her, I really haven't.'

Which kind of chimed with what Joe had written about her, albeit in more colourful terms. 'Have you found out yet who's going to inherit the house, now that Vanessa can't?'

'No, we don't consider it a priority while there's so much else going on, but John says it should probably go to Ed as Nessa's next of kin. Of course, Ed being where he is complicates things, and if he ends up being found guilty . . .' She took a breath and started again, 'I don't want to think about that. It can't happen. There would be no justice in this world.'

Silently agreeing with her, Jay said, 'Does the stepmother have children?'

'Yes, two. They came with her into the marriage, so not Figgy's . . . He's Nessa's father. Fergus, but we always called him Figgy.'

'Were he and Vanessa close?'

'Yes, very. It was a terrible blow for her when he died. I don't think she ever stopped missing him. He was her rock, her best friend in many ways. I guess Ed kind of took the role over; it might help you to understand why he's always been so protective of her.'

Jay guessed it did in a way, and felt glad for Vanessa that she'd found someone to care for her at such a terrible time. It mattered to have someone to lean on when the world seemed to be falling apart, the way she'd leaned on Tom when her father had passed.

There was no leaning on Tom now. She'd have to get through this particular devastation on her own, and for one awful, destabilizing moment, she wasn't sure that she could.

'How did Vanessa's father die?' she asked, mentally shaking herself.

'He had cancer, and it's quite probable that the dreadful Daphne helped him on his way at the end – which might have been an act of mercy, actually. He was in a lot of pain . . . You need to take the left fork ahead and go to the top of the hill. We're almost there. Another mile or so.'

Following instructions, Jay braked to allow a couple of hikers to cross into a wood off to the left. 'So Daphne's children are what age?' she asked, accelerating to start the steep climb.

'Jeremy must be around forty by now, and Freya's a year or two older. They're not a bad pair, although I can't say I know them terribly well. Nessa didn't have much contact with them after her father died.'

'Are they married?'

'Yes. Jeremy and his wife, Cassandra, live in London during the week, back to Mummy most weekends, or so I'm told. Freya and her husband are also London based, and have a very nice place in the village close to Sayley House. She's there quite a lot. Apparently she keeps her horses in Sayley's stables. To be honest, I can see why they feel they should inherit the place, ghastly old ruin that it is, or at least have a share in it. They lived there for most of their lives and they spent many more years with Figgy as a stepfather than they did with their real father. He's still going strong somewhere, I believe, but I've no idea where.'

'So why did Vanessa's father leave the place solely to her?'

Antonia sighed. 'I think to try and make up for how sad Vanessa was as a child. He always felt he'd married too soon after his first wife died. Vanessa was barely five when it happened, and he was worried about her growing up without a mother. By the time he realized Daphne was never going to treat Vanessa as one of her own, he'd already established a relationship with his stepchildren and didn't want to break up the home. He was a good man, but I'm afraid he could also be weak, especially where Daphne was concerned. I know he saw her coldness – some would call it cruelty – towards Nessa because he told me himself. He felt terrible about it, but there's something about the wretched woman that made him afraid, or unwilling to tackle her, much less leave her.'

Jay's tone was dry as she said, 'Well, if I wasn't seeing Cruella de Vil in my head before, I certainly am now.'

'It's a good description, believe me, but if you meet her you'll probably find her to be all sweetness and charm, provided she wants to impress you, that is. If she doesn't, you might get an idea of how incredibly rude and even poisonous she can be.'

'Mm, I can hardly wait,' Jay muttered. 'Is this it?' she asked as they reached the brink of the hill and spotted police cones at the side of the road ahead.

196

'Yes. That's where you turn into Clover Hill.'

Waved on by a single security guard who recognized Antonia, Jay steered the car carefully over an old hump-back bridge clung with lichen and ivy, and dipped down into a wide grassy glade where a single-track lane ran alongside a bubbling stream. On the stream's far bank was a wood dappled in sunlight, to the right was a wonderful buttercup field surrounded by beech hedges.

'That's where Frank Maguire and his wife live,' Antonia said, pointing to an old Cotswold stone barn as they approached it. 'Ed and Nessa camped out there for a few months while they were finishing off the house.'

'It's lovely,' Jay remarked, admiring the dovecote in the eaves, double-height windows that had presumably once been cart doors, and the several sets of French windows opening onto a patio and ornamental garden.

She'd decided not to mention anything about her meeting with Maguire until they could be sure that he really was holding back, and if so whether it was to do with the family, or someone else. So she was happy to have her attention drawn away from the barn as Antonia said,

'Over there, across the old wooden footbridge, is the place the Dutch people rent.'

Jay peered through the trees to a sunlit clearing where a quaint, whitewashed cottage with a grey slate roof and rose-covered porch looked about as picture book as any cottage could.

'I'm beginning to see the appeal of this place,' she murmured, still moving slowly forward and beginning silently to name the glorious wild flowers springing out of the banks either side of them – yellow ox-eye, Spanish bluebells, columbines, mountain bluets, cowslips . . . There were so many. She and Livvy would be in their element going through them all, the way they often did when walking in Leigh Woods.

'And here's the main residence,' Antonia announced as they approached two tall stone pillars at the end of the track with tamarisk trees either side of them and cropped laurel hedges marking the property boundary. The iron gates were open, so Jay drove past the security guard who nodded to Antonia, and into the gravel courtyard where an old wishing well provided a central turning point and copious more wild flowers filled the beds in front of a large thatched house. The windows were small, the front door settled inside a quaint stone porch, and the walls were mostly hidden by climbing jasmine and roses.

'The traditional frontage is lovely, but doesn't do it justice,' Antonia said, as they pulled up in front of the garage. 'It's all at the back, and inside. You'll see.'

As they got out of the car, Jay inhaled the tangy, fresh air of their rural surroundings and turned to look back down the lane. Would this small haven appear so enchanting if the weather was dull or raining, she wondered. She imagined it would, considering how tranquil and colourful it was.

Taking out her keys, Antonia led the way through the polished oak door into a high and spacious hallway, where Jay paused for a moment to take in a rustic console table set below an ornately framed mirror, a coat rack with a hard hat hanging over a high-vis jacket and a bright pink woollen scarf draped over a lady's navy blue Barbour. The shoe rack was full of walking boots and trainers, male and female, an elegant pair of riding boots stood beside an umbrella stand, and next to that was an open cupboard door where the alarm was presumably housed.

Spotting an empty drink bowl at the foot of the stairs, Jay said, 'Did you take the dog back with you after the police arrested Edward?'

Antonia seemed thrown for a moment. 'Oh, no,' she said, catching up. 'He was already with us. Ed leaves him with John's mother sometimes, they've struck up a bond.'

Jay smiled at the memory of the two old-timers at Highview Hall, and followed Antonia through a set of double doors into an enormous, exquisitely vaulted room with ten-feet-high windows forming the entire back wall. A fully modern kitchen was to her right, with a stripped oak table to seat twelve in the middle of the space and a large, yet cosy sitting area grouped around a Georgian-style fireplace at the opposite end. Almost everything was white, or ivory, or cream, from the overhead beams, to the porcelain flooring, to the furniture and silk drapes framing the windows. However, lively splashes of colour were provided by abstract paintings, scatter pillows and a faux animal rug in front of the hearth. It was impossible not to be impressed by such a beautiful and welcoming room, but what really caught Jay's attention was the magnificent view of fields, copses, hedgerows, and endless blue sky that flowed and dipped out to a far horizon.

'The Cotswolds,' Antonia announced wryly. 'Stunning, isn't it? Mesmeric, Nessa used to say. She loved to sit out there on the terrace just gazing at nature, spotting birds and wildlife, watching the weather change and even sometimes staying out in the rain. There's a kitchen garden around the side where she grows all kinds of veg and fruit, some I'd never even heard of until she introduced me to them. Kai-lan; Blauhilde beans; strawberry spinach.'

Jay looked around the room again, trying to get a sense of Edward designing and creating it, restoring old features and matching them with the new. She pictured him and Vanessa in the kitchen, or slouched in armchairs by the fire, or at the table entertaining friends. They were all poignantly romantic images of a couple in love. Noticing a large pastel portrait half-filling the wall behind the door, she went towards it. There was no mistaking who it was – the Blakes sitting on a lawn, her between his legs, back resting against his chest, his right hand in her hair, his left holding hers. Both were looking at the artist, and both seemed on the brink of laughter. She moved in even closer, as if its gentle power was inviting her to do so.

'Beautiful, isn't it?' Antonia said, coming to stand beside her. 'It was done just after they found out they were pregnant, which will be why she looks so radiant. After they lost Lucas she kept taking it down, but Ed always put it up again. He was afraid she might try to destroy it, but thankfully she never did.'

Jay was starting to feel   or maybe wish – that she was in some sort of dream where the people she was looking at had simply stepped out for a moment, and nothing bad had happened at all.

She turned to the fireplace and began looking through photographs displayed on the mantelshelf. The most touching of them all was of a dishevelled-looking Vanessa nursing her newborn. There was another of Edward holding his tiny son, his hands seeming impossibly large, while his pride and emotion were almost masked by what looked to be a sudden burst of mirth. He looked so different here, younger of course, although not by much, but carefree, confident, glad to be alive.

There were other shots of Lucas as he grew, blond curls, his father's blue eyes, two teeth, then four, his first pedal car; a ride on Daddy's shoulders; a cuddle with Mummy. It was almost too much to bear. 'I thought they'd have taken them down after they lost him,' Jay said quietly.

'They did for a while, then Nessa decided she wanted to see them again.'

Glancing to a door beside the kitchen, Jay said, 'What's through there?'

Going to open it, Antonia said, 'A larder, wine store, downstairs loo, and the door at the back leads into Nessa's garden room.'

Hearing a catch in her voice, Jay went to put a hand on her arm. 'I'm sorry,' she said softly. 'This must be difficult for you. I shouldn't have asked you to come.'

'It's OK, I've been a few times since . . . Once they'd finished, they allowed me to clean up a bit.' She forced a smile. 'I'm sure you want to see upstairs. If you don't mind I won't come with you. There are four bedrooms, the master suite is to the left and occupies the whole of that side of the house, the guest wing is to the right, the first room is where it happened.'

Mounting the stairs alone, Jay took in the photographs that lined the walls, recognizing Antonia and John in some, their children in others, but most were of strangers, at least to her, though they appeared to be close friends, or perhaps extended family members.

Deciding to inspect the crime scene first, she pushed open the door and saw nothing unusual, apart from a bed with no linens – presumably they'd been taken by the forensic team – and the grey residue of fingerprint powder on the posts, along with faint, purplish ninhydrin stains. Her eyes closed as an image of Vanessa lying there, dead and exposed, flashed in her mind. She wondered how long she'd been tied up before she was killed, if she'd pleaded with the attacker to spare her. She couldn't imagine how horrific it must have been for her, helpless to fight, struggling for air.

Her eyes continued to travel the room, taking in the silk panelled wallpaper, curtained windows, Queen Anne dressing table and matching stool. She tried to picture Edward in here, beside the bed, holding a pillow over his wife's face, and felt a chill go through her.

Then she imagined his shock at finding her; the horror of realizing she was dead, his desperate attempt to save her when it was already too late.

So much had happened in this room that was as silent and inscrutable now as death itself.

After dropping Antonia home, Jay drove for a mile or two before pulling over to a layby. She needed some time to think, to try to understand why the visit to Clover Hill seemed to be affecting her so much. What exactly had happened to make her feel so connected – was that the right word? – to Vanessa Blake? Edward too, but mostly to his wife, the victim, the woman who was unable to speak for herself. During the time she'd spent in the master bedroom, Vanessa had seemed to come into focus in a way that she hadn't until now. Seeing her perfumes, jewellery, nightgown and the photograph of Edward on her bedside table had brought her presence into the room as hauntingly as if she might be watching. Jay had found it easy to picture her moving about, dressing, lying with Edward, feeling the sunlight flooding in through the windows, closing the drapes at night.

On Edward's side of the bed the duvet was still flipped back, the imprint of his head remained on the pillow. Exactly as it had been, she presumed, after he'd got up last Tuesday morning. On his nightstand was a photograph of Vanessa with Max, the dog, and a handful of architectural magazines. In the bathroom she'd imagined them standing at each basin, brushing their teeth in the mirror, stepping in or out of the shower, using the monogrammed towels, V and E. Her robe was hanging on the back of the door beneath his, waiting to be taken down and worn again.

From there Jay had visited the specially designed studio wing where his desk occupied one end of the long room, and hers the other with easels and drawing boards set up in the space between. Hundreds upon hundreds of books lined the back wall, and floor-to-ceiling French windows looked back at the terrace and house one way and to the slopes of the view the other. There were no computers and many drawers were empty; she presumed most of the contents had been removed by the search team. She noticed that the dog had a bed and a bowl beside Edward's desk, and on the wall behind was a huge black-and-white blow-up of the Lab in earlier years.

Had being there unsettled her, Jay asked herself now, because the glimpse she'd just had into the Blakes' lives was making her think of her and Tom? On the outside, the perfect couple, fulfilled, happy, in love, while behind the public façade was a different truth altogether. Each time she'd looked at photos of Vanessa, she'd searched for a sign of vulnerability, of fragility even, and in some it had been there, almost masked by the radiance of her smile, but not quite. In several shots Edward had seemed protective of her, though not overly so, just a man being attentive and appreciative of his beautiful wife. But those images were flash moments in time, no more a full story of who they were and what they meant to one another, than her and Tom's albums were of them.

Tom. Where was he now? What was he doing? Was he thinking of her, missing her as she was him? Most likely he had other things on his mind.

She turned on her phone, knowing already there would be plenty of messages, and probably more than a few growls of frustration at being unable to get hold of her for so long. However, as she went through voicemails, emails and texts, she decided there was nothing that couldn't wait, not even Tom's text saying: *FYI I'm feeling quite anxious about later, I could do with your support, to know we're in this together.*

Annoyed with him for trying to guilt-trip her into caring how he felt, when he didn't seem to be sparing much thought for how this was impacting her, she resumed her journey home and felt her heart twist as she wondered if he was at the Tylers' yet. Was he even, right now this minute, sitting on a sofa somewhere with his little son on his lap, trying to make him laugh, or at least doing his best not to scare him? How was he feeling about it? Awkward, guilty, ashamed, confused? Probably all of the above, and maybe defensive too, if the Tylers were asking something of him that they'd failed to mention so far.

What the hell was this really about? Why had they waited so long to tell him? It didn't make any sense to her, and she supposed it probably wouldn't until Tom came home and explained.

Eventually, joining the M4, she sped down the fast lane towards Bristol, and allowed her thoughts to return to Clover Hill; it was easier than trying to sort out her emotions where her own life was concerned. Or it might have been, if this glimpse into the Blakes' world wasn't continuing to unsettle her. A dead child; a murdered woman; a couple who'd had everything until suddenly one day they had nothing at all. It could happen so easily, so quickly and irrevocably. She felt desperate for Vanessa, how could she not, the unchecked grief that had damaged her so profoundly, the pain she'd inflicted on her husband . . . Jay wondered how she would feel if she were accused of killing Tom and all the evidence was against her? What would she do if she had no way of convincing the police she was innocent; or of getting herself out of prison; or of stopping her future moving down the wrong path with no way of rescuing it?

By the time she arrived home, she wasn't sure whether she was doubting herself more as a lawyer, a wife or a mother, given that Livvy had rung a few minutes ago and – rather than deal with any more teenage angst right now – she'd ignored the call. There was actually only one person she really wanted to talk to at this moment, and that was Edward Blake. Focusing on him and his wife, the case and what she'd absorbed about their lives today would be far more productive than driving herself mad with what Tom might be doing now.

'Are you awake?' Tom asked.

'I am now,' Jay replied, glancing at the time. 'Why are

you calling so late? It's almost one o'clock.' Then, remembering where he'd been, where they were in their lives, a rush of adrenalin kicked in bringing her fully awake. 'Are you sober?' she asked, sitting up.

His mirthless laugh told her he wasn't.

'Where are you?'

'At my usual hotel. It wasn't . . . Well, it wasn't what I expected.'

Alarmed, she said, 'What does that mean?'

'I don't know. I . . .'

'Did you see him?'

'Yes. His name's Aiden, by the way. I think I already told you that.'

He had. 'Did you like him?' What a ridiculous question. How do you not like a child, especially your own son?

'Yes, he's cute.'

'And?'

'And I don't know, Jay. It wasn't what I expected . . .'

'You've already said that. *What* wasn't? What do they want from you?'

'To be who I really am, and right now I don't actually know who that person is.'

'Oh God, you really are drunk. Do I need to remind you that you're in court tomorrow? Someone's liberty, reputation, is depending on you?'

'No, you don't, but maybe it's a good thing that you did.'

It was a long time since she'd heard him like this; the last was when he'd broken up with Ellen Tyler and she'd assumed the alcohol was to try and drown the pain. Had seeing her again, with their son, brought everything back for him? How could it not have?

'Let's talk about this at the weekend,' she said, and abruptly ended the call, as if the disconnection could somehow still the portentous thudding in her heart, and racing images in her mind, which of course, it couldn't. Nothing could do that now, nothing at all.

CHAPTER TWENTY

Jay didn't hear from Tom again over the next two days, nor did she try to contact him. Anything – everything – they had to say could wait until Saturday, although there were long, uncomfortable moments when the silence between them seemed to have an ominous voice of its own.

There was every chance this was going to break their marriage.

How could it not if he decided to accept the child into his life?

But what did 'accepting' actually mean? Would she have to play the role of stepmother to a living reminder of his betrayal? What about Charlie and Livvy? She'd protected her husband once from their censure and disappointment; this time around they'd have to know – and he would have to live with how it could change their respect for him.

Until they fell in love with their half-brother, who was in no way to blame for this.

Round and round it kept going, always bringing up more questions than answers, and she couldn't seem to make it stop. She didn't imagine it was any different for Tom. Even if he had decided this was the beginning of the end for them – *could that really be true?* – she knew he wouldn't be able to do it with a guilt-free conscience.

Take a breath, Jay.

Most likely he hadn't come to any decisions at all yet, so she really needed to centre herself, stop creating scenarios that were probably never going to paint themselves into reality and focus on what was actually going on in her world.

Right now she was on her way back from a plea hearing at Gloucester Crown Court and clicked to answer as Joe's name appeared on the car's Command system. 'Hey, how are things?' she asked, relieved to hear how normal, even engaged she sounded. 'Did you pick up the phone I brought back from Antonia Debrayne's?'

'It's in my hot little hand as we speak,' he told her, 'and lucky for us it was easy to unlock – Edward Blake's date of birth, would you believe?' He gave a sigh with a strange sort of wheeze threaded through it. 'I'd be lying if I didn't say some of what's on it is having a destabilizing effect on this widowed old guy. She is – or was – a very attractive woman, and some of those shots don't leave much to the imagination.'

Getting the picture, and saddened by the instability that had driven Vanessa to take the shots – or have them taken – she said, 'Can you tell if she sent them to anyone?'

'Oh sure, she shared them all right, but first up, the account's only a couple of months old, so it's not giving us a long history of her clandestine life. This is presuming it's been going on a while, and we don't actually know that, but it's definitely been going on.'

'I'm still listening.'

'OK, most of the selfies were sent to a contact listed as M—'

'Maguire?' she jumped in, feeling strange even for

suggesting it, but off the top of her head it was the only M they had on their list.

He chuckled. 'I get the impression this M is an artist specializing in nudes, which could account for so many of them going to him/her. You'll see what I mean when you read the back and forth. They called each other too, maybe arranging to meet up, or to talk dirty down the phone, who knows?'

'What about the other contacts?'

'Well, there's a P, a J, a J2, a D1 and D2. I haven't tried any of the numbers yet, awaiting instructions from you.'

'Sure. Any texts or calls on the day she didn't catch the train?'

'There are, and it seems pretty clear she was expecting to see J the next day – i.e., Tuesday. We know she didn't make it, but I'm asking myself if it was brought forward a day? Nothing to say it was. Interestingly, there are no follow-ups after the death trying to find out why she didn't show.'

'So whoever it was saw it on the news?'

'Possibly. Or he's our guy.'

She wasn't getting a positive vibe from this, but there was so little to go on, why would she? 'OK, anything else?' she asked.

'There's a text sent by her on Sunday the twenty-eighth, i.e., the day before she died, to D2, saying she couldn't wait to see him. And he/she messaged back to say, *Can't wait to see you. I'll be there as promised.*'

Jay frowned thoughtfully. 'So does that mean they were meeting on Monday?'

'Your guess is as good as mine. There's no mention of a day or time. However, J asked about two weeks before the fateful day if he could see her on that very date – the twenty-ninth – and she asked if he could make it any sooner. Not in those words, exactly, but it would make me blush to read the actual ones out loud.'

Dryly, Jay said, 'I'm sure you've heard a lot worse in your time, but apparently her messages are quite . . . descriptive?'

'They're that all right. In fact, it seems like a game for her, teasing, titillating, controlling and apparently delivering. Anyway, no idea at this stage if she met up with D2 or J Monday the twenty-ninth so, moving on from that, I'm going to guess that P is into cars, in that I think he sold her one, but no mention of what it was so I can't be sure at this point if it's the BMW convertible we know was hers.'

'That should be easy enough to find out. What about the others?'

'J seems to be someone she only recently met – I quote *Thinking about you and what we did is still blowing my mind. Please say we can do it again.* It's dated the week before she died.'

'Did she respond?'

'She sent a topless selfie.'

Easing her way across three lanes of traffic to join the M32, Jay said, 'Is there any mention of Edward anywhere in the messages or contacts?'

'His number's there, but no record of her having used it, or receiving anything from it. He's listed as E with a heart next to it. There's also a number for someone listed as Ed – no heart, several calls back and forth over the last few weeks, but no texts.'

Frowning, Jay said, 'So does that mean Blake has another number?'

'Who knows? Maybe, but we won't have an answer to that until we check.'

'OK. Arrange to have the texts and contact list transcribed ready for when we can get to this. The way my diary's looking, it probably won't be until after I've seen Blake next Tuesday, but he might be able to throw some light on who these people are, which could help when we start making calls. I have to go now, Ash is trying to get hold of me, but great work so far. This might well lead to the breakthrough we're looking for.'

CHAPTER TWENTY-ONE

Although Tom returned from London on Friday afternoon and texted Jay to let her know he was going straight home, she didn't actually see him until much later in the evening at Ollie and Jenn's. It was a long-standing arrangement for Ollie's birthday, so a dozen or more friends were gathered for dinner, and in keeping with tradition no couple was seated together.

They walked home with Freddy and Carina, and because Freddy's writer's mind was constantly searching for material from the world of crime, they allowed themselves to be drawn into his quest.

'It's my guess,' Tom said, when he finally let them in through the front door, 'that everyone realized you were avoiding me this evening. Was that your intention?'

Stifling her annoyance, she went ahead of him into the sitting room and through to the kitchen. 'My only intention,' she retorted when he followed her, 'was to stop any pretence of normalcy or affection you might have been planning to subject me to.'

'Well, you certainly succeeded in that.'

Jay turned to him. 'I hope you don't want to talk now. It's been a long day, we've both had a lot of wine . . .'

'Should I make an appointment? When can you fit me in?'

'Don't be childish.'

'And that's not how you're behaving with your avoidance tactics and head in the sand? I suppose next you're going to tell me to sleep in the guest room again.'

'I think that would be a good idea. I've got yoga with Jenn at nine in the morning, I should be back by eleven. If you're around and Livvy's not, we can talk then.'

His face darkened with the anger he was trying to suppress. 'Where is she now?' he barked, as if she might be the cause of his temper.

'At a concert in Bath. I'm going up.' Moving past him she made for the door.

'There's actually nothing to discuss,' he called after her. 'Not until the DNA results come through.'

Pausing with her hand on the doorknob, she turned back as she said, 'Wouldn't it have made more sense for you to meet the child *after* the test?'

'Probably, but it didn't happen that way.'

Why was he sounding so defensive? Why weren't they handling this better? Given who they were, what they did for a living, they should know what to do, not only for themselves, but for each other. 'So, you went to their home,' she said, 'met their son – or your son . . . What's he like?'

He shrugged as he picked up his mail, as though in some bizarre universe it might actually be more important. 'He's . . . cute, I guess.'

'Does he look like you?'

Frowning, he said, 'No! I don't know, it's hard to tell.'

'Well, is he dark or fair . . .'

'He's dark.'

'Did you play with him?'

214

He nodded.

That threw her, more than it should have, but she'd had to ask. 'And how did that feel? And why aren't you looking at me?'

Bringing his eyes to hers, he said, 'This isn't getting us anywhere . . .'

'Do you want to see him again?'

His eyes closed in exasperation. 'Jay, for God's sake, can you at least try to be reasonable? I don't—'

'How am I not being reasonable? I'm asking what happened, you're telling me, but now apparently you don't want to tell me any more.' She was in the right here, wasn't she? She was trying to find out what was happening, how he felt, what their next steps should be, but he was blocking her – wasn't he?

Why was this all so difficult to get straight?

'Maybe you're right,' he said, 'we shouldn't discuss this now, when we've had a drink.'

'So it'll be easier to tell me in the morning that you want to leave?' she snapped in a way she hated herself for.

His eyes closed as he said, 'Please don't do this. That's not what I want and you know it. So, let's do as you say, sleep separately tonight, and tomorrow I hope we can talk about things in a way that we clearly can't right now.'

Early the next morning, even before she was up, Jay received a text from Tom saying: *There's been a fire at Charlie's house in Exeter. They're all fine. I've gone to help sort things out. Will call later when there's more news. X*

A second message, sent immediately after, read: *Hope*

you managed to get some sleep. Sorry for everything. I love you. Tx

Putting aside her phone she lay back on the pillows, tears burning her eyes and so many misgivings in her heart she was finding it hard to sort one from another. *Sorry* was good, so was *I love you*, but they didn't even come close to making things better. They were just words, no matter how deeply – or not – they were meant. Nothing he said was ever going to change the fact that there was a child and his mother, nor would regret prevent all the complications, reminders and split loyalties that were bound to come with them.

She didn't want to let go of her marriage, she really didn't, but how was she going to hold it together when the fractures were already evident – and unstoppable? Surely he could see that. He had to know, in his heart, that everything had changed, and there was nothing either of them could do to change it back again.

Hearing her phone buzz with another text, she saw it was from Charlie and clicked on to read. *I know Dad's already told you what happened. Not too much damage, but landlord's not happy. Sorry if I've spoiled your weekend. Will find a way to make it up to you. Cxxx*

She messaged back to tell him nothing was spoiled, all that mattered was that he was safe, and Dad would find a way to calm the landlord.

Tom always fixed things. He was that kind of husband and father. They relied on him in ways they probably weren't even aware of, took him for granted even, but she knew he wouldn't have it any other way.

It seemed Ellen Tyler was about to discover these qualities for herself and her son. He'd be there for them, there was no doubt about that, and in time he could very well want to be with them permanently, to watch his young son grow up and maybe turn his mistress into his wife.

The thought of him being happy with someone else, maybe leaving Bristol and moving to London, tore through her with a devastating dread. Would he actually do that? His chambers were here, and his partnership with Ollie . . .

She needed to stop. Once again she was allowing her thoughts to run away with her, and none of it was real – at least not yet – and it might never be. Whatever decisions had to be made for the future would be taken when the need arose. There was still a lot of talking to be done, plans to make, although right now she wasn't in a frame of mind to be rational and understanding about anything. She was more inclined to remind herself that his cheating had brought them to this; that she had every right to be furious and unforgiving. She wasn't his doormat, or his enabler, or his mother . . . Oh God, his mother! What was Moira going to say when she found out? She'd support him, of course, she always did, but Jay couldn't blame her for that; most mothers supported their children through mistakes and screw-ups. Apart from hers, of course, but that was a different story, and now really wasn't a good time to be thinking about that. Or about her wonderful father, who she still missed all the time and would give anything in the world to be able to talk to now.

OK, stop with the self-pity and get out of bed – now!

An hour later she called Tom to ask him to bring Charlie home for the night. It wasn't that she was trying to avoid talking to him – well, maybe she was – but she hadn't seen her son in a while and she felt no harm could be done by them going out for dinner as a family this evening. It might be a good idea for Tom to be reminded of how close they were and what he'd be giving up if he left them.

Except Charlie had already flown the nest, and Livvy would be going too in the summer. So the only one he'd be leaving was her.

Knowing the only way not to drive herself mad was to throw herself into some work, she made a coffee and took it through to the study. A few deep breaths and the opening of Edward Blake's file soon refocused her. She had a lot of questions for him on Tuesday, and not only about the case. She wanted more information on his background to help get a true measure of the man and who he actually was. For instance, where were his parents? No one had mentioned them, so were they still alive? Or close by and estranged? She wondered who was in touch with him, if anyone besides his sister and nephew were going to visit him. How was he passing his time in prison? Writing letters? Making phone calls? Reading books? Exercising? Had he struck up any unlikely friendships? Had he become the victim of violence simply for being posher than the normal inmate? How difficult was he finding it to grieve for his wife when shows of emotion incited abuse?

Her father's words suddenly came to her, *Considering people who are undergoing situations much worse than yours doesn't make yours any easier, but it can help to change your perspective.*

Was that working for her now?

She thought it might be, for she always seemed to respond positively to the sense of Edward Blake's inner strength, and the way he seemed to cope with the hell he was in. In fact, thinking about him could make her feel stronger, more together even, while managing to calm her in a way that thinking about Tom simply couldn't.

CHAPTER TWENTY-TWO

Their family dinner at The Clifton Sausage seemed to go well, mostly thanks to Charlie's indomitable humour and Livvy's video of herself giving an interview on local news about the benefits and dangers of social media. Her contribution was so impressive that both Jay and Tom got her to send it to them, while Charlie teased her about breaking into mainstream.

It was through the children's quizzing of their father that Jay learned the outcome of his rape trial the previous week; apparently the lad whom Tom believed had been falsely accused of rape had walked free. It was also thanks to Livvy's interest in the Edward Blake case that Tom received a brief update on Jay's investigation. Though she sensed he wanted to ask more, and actually she'd have liked to discuss it with him, this evening needed to be about them as a family, not the parents as lawyers.

When the meal was over, Charlie and Livvy took themselves off to a party somewhere on the Harbourside, leaving Tom and Jay to walk home through the moonlit streets.

For a while neither of them spoke, nor did they hold hands the way they normally would, however there wasn't as much tension between them as unease, a seeming unwillingness to be the first to speak.

In the end it was him. 'I'm going to be in Southampton next week, in case you'd forgotten.'

'No, I hadn't,' she said. 'It's the GBH case you've taken over from Ollie, isn't it?'

'That's right. It should be over by Wednesday.'

Several minutes passed as they crossed over Christchurch Road towards Clifton Park Gardens. She wasn't sure she'd really planned her next words, although it sounded as though she had as she said, 'I've been thinking that we should probably tell Jenn and Ollie what's going on with you . . .'

'Why on earth would we do that?' he protested.

'Well, it has to come out at some point, and I don't think Ollie would thank you for keeping it from him. He's your partner, after all, and if it's going to mean breaking up Brunel Chambers—'

'What?' he cried incredulously. 'Who the hell said anything . . .? What are you telling yourself, Jay? There's no way I'm intending to do that.'

'Yet,' she stated.

He was silent, and when she glanced up at him he seemed genuinely bewildered.

'You still haven't thought any of it through,' she told him bluntly, 'whereas I have and I'm afraid I can't see how—'

'Whatever you've seen is a fantasy,' he interrupted, 'something you've concocted out of nothing, because you don't know all the facts any more than I do. We still haven't had the DNA results . . .'

'Don't let's go there again.'

'OK, but please stop doing this. I want us to handle things together, the way we always do. I get that it's my responsibility and that I've hurt you deeply, for which I'm profoundly sorry, but I have no intention of leaving you, or my chambers, or this city. So maybe we should drop this now and try to enjoy what's left of the evening?'

Although she wondered how he thought that was possible, she didn't argue, simply continued to walk with him, passing all the familiar landmarks and friends' houses, until eventually they were approaching their own.

'Am I going to be banished to the guest room again tonight?' he asked as they reached the front door.

She didn't answer right away, not entirely sure what she wanted to say. In the end she turned to look at him and saw how tempted he was to pull her into his arms. A strong part of her wanted him to, but she didn't let it happen. 'I just need some time,' she told him, 'and more clarity. So, let's wait for the DNA results, in spite of already knowing what they are, and then we can sort out where we are in our relationship.'

She could tell he was unnerved, and hurt, and lost for a response that might reach her in a way he wasn't managing right now. In spite of herself she felt for him; how could she not when she loved him? But she only had to ask herself how deeply he'd considered her feelings during the times he'd been with Ellen Tyler to know that love wasn't always enough to make a difference.

CHAPTER TWENTY-THREE

Although Jay arrived at the prison on time for her meeting with Blake on Tuesday, she was kept waiting for at least fifteen minutes before he was brought in. In the various interview rooms around her, visible through the half-glass, half-plasterboard walls, she could see other lawyers waiting, some she knew, others she didn't. Most appeared to be using the time to catch up on their workload, and it was indeed something of a bonus to have this time to herself, for it was allowing her to bring Blake's case fully into focus. After this weekend's distractions with Charlie and Tom, plus a heavy day in court yesterday, she needed to review her list of questions and what had given rise to them.

By the time the door opened for Blake to come in she felt on top of things, and was touched, as she'd been before, by how pleased he seemed to see her.

'Sorry,' he apologized, realizing he'd held on to her hand for too long. 'It's just . . .' He laughed self-consciously. 'I guess I'm not living with the most . . . attractive members of the human race and the females who come and go are not . . . Well, let's say, they're not like you.' He grimaced awkwardly, clearly wishing he'd never started this, while she felt relieved that his compliment was understated. The last thing they needed was to get into anything personal, or irrelevant, or worse, embarrassing.

'How's it been?' she asked as he sat down at the small table, inwardly wincing at the bruise on his jaw and dark shadows beneath his eyes. His hair was mussed and greasy, and his pallor wasn't good, but he still managed to exude a glint of irony with a raised eyebrow.

Reading the expression she smiled. 'OK, it's obviously not a picnic, but be assured we're doing our best to make your stay as short as possible.'

'That's good to know.' He wiped a hand over his jaw and she noticed a split knuckle that looked painful and raw. 'Toni tells me you visited Clover Hill,' he said, as she began consulting her iPad.

'I did,' she replied, 'and I must say it's a beautiful home, inside and out – and you'll be pleased to hear, if you haven't already, that no damage was done during the search. Or none that I noticed.'

He seemed relieved by that, and yet also upset, and she guessed that thinking of it, picturing it, was made doubly difficult by not knowing when he might see it again.

'Before we get into the detail of the phone,' she said, needing to get things under way, 'can you tell me where you found it on the morning the police were there?' She was worried about the answer to this, since the fact he'd gone back for it, and possibly all the way to the studio, demonstrated a presence of mind, perhaps even a coolness, that she hadn't got an impression of before.

'It was where I first came across it,' he replied, 'in the cloakroom just inside the front door. I didn't know if it would be there that day, but it was, in the cabinet tucked between a box of tampons and a spare loo roll. It wasn't well hidden so I wondered if she'd meant me to find it to try and provoke a scene. She did things like that from time to time.'

'Did you ask her about it?'

'No. I knew I would eventually, especially if she carried on leaving it there, but I was no lover of those scenes. They were painful and pointless and almost always ended the same way, with her breaking down over Lucas and accusing me of not caring about her or him. She knew it wasn't true, but . . .' He shrugged stiffly. 'It's what she said.'

Deciding to run with this for a while, she said, 'Did these scenes happen often?'

He shook his head. 'That depends what you mean by often. Once a month, maybe. Sometimes we'd go for longer without any upsets. She'd seem normal, almost as if she was finally getting onto a more even keel, but I learned the hard way not to be fooled.'

'Go on.'

His eyes drifted to nowhere as he summoned the memories he'd no doubt prefer to forget. 'We'd become close again, she'd be loving and . . . And then I'd find out she'd . . .' He swallowed and lowered his head. 'The other men were mostly strangers,' he said, bringing his gaze back to her, 'men she met in London, photographers or artists whose work she was interested in. There were also local men, some of them friends of ours who she tried to seduce . . . I don't know how many she succeeded with, I only know about the ones who spoke to Toni or John, wanting to make it clear that they hadn't gone along with it.'

In spite of how hard he was clearly finding this, Jay didn't sense him withdrawing, so keeping her tone gentle, she asked, 'Was anyone ever violent with her?'

Although he shook his head, he didn't appear to have fully connected with the question.

'Did you ever see bruising on her, or any other injuries?' she pressed.

His eyes came to hers. 'No, but that's not to say . . . Sometimes she'd hide herself from me, make sure we didn't undress in the same room, or use the bathroom together. I didn't think about anyone being rough with her, but in the light of what we know now, I guess I should have.'

Still watching him closely, and experiencing an almost visceral connection to his suffering, she said, 'Did Sheri or Melissa tell you about the men in London? Is that how you know about them?'

He nodded. 'They were as worried about her as everyone else. Sheri wanted to take back her key, but didn't know how to without upsetting her.' His eyes closed and he took a moment to breathe. 'I don't know what you must think of us all,' he said, looking up again, 'trying to cover up how she was when my own life, my freedom . . . It became second nature for us. We needed to protect her, but I hope you understand it was because we cared so much for her.' He gave a distant sort of smile. 'I didn't ask the others to do it. I don't think Toni did either, it was just a safety net that we tried to keep in place for her, not always successfully . . . Well, obviously not successfully at all, given where we are . . .' He took another moment, and seemed to go inside himself as he said, 'She was always quite fragile. I knew that almost from the start. Losing her mother at such a young age, being treated so coldly by Daphne . . . Have you met her stepmother yet?'

Jay shook her head.

His expression told her little of his feelings towards the woman; his words said more. 'Nessa only stayed living at home as long as she did because of her father. She had so little confidence in herself, didn't believe she could make it on her own. Not that she didn't try, because she did, but it never ended well. People took advantage of her, stole her money, squatted in her flat and wouldn't leave . . . Her father always sorted it out and took her home again. He was very protective of her, which is I guess what she saw in me. I was someone she trusted to take care of her – and her son when he came along.'

Unable to imagine just how deep his sense of failure and grief ran, Jay kept her tone gentle as she said, 'Do you know if she was sexually promiscuous during the times she tried to make it on her own? I mean before you met.'

His eyes drifted back to the glass wall between their room and the next. Another prisoner was clearly having a heated exchange with his lawyer, but whether Edward registered it or not wasn't clear. 'All I can tell you,' he said eventually, 'is that she wasn't a virgin when we got together, and she was – how can I put it? – keen to try things.'

Jay noted this down and said, 'Did you ever tie her up?'

He shook his head. 'She never asked me to, but I'm sure I would have if she had.'

Registering his discomfort, she decided to leave that for the moment. 'You said just now that you're a protective type . . .'

He seemed genuinely amused. 'It's not how I would describe myself on a dating app,' he responded drolly, 'but yes, I guess that's true about me. You see, my mother was quite vulnerable, another of life's lost souls, thanks to early loss and parental neglect. My father did everything he could to make her feel safe, to build her confidence . . . For a long time it worked. She was a great mum. Toni and I adored her, and the feeling was definitely mutual, until we left home to go to uni. Then she started to fret that we'd never come back.' He swallowed, clearly distressed by whatever was coming next, and Jay couldn't help wondering how much she was going to fret when both her children had gone.

'We didn't take too much notice of the way she was at first,' he continued, 'she'd always been possessive and we were young, out there making our ways in the world. She'd get used to it, we told ourselves. All parents did, eventually. We didn't realize until it was too late what our independence was costing her. She wrote us both a letter to say she was sorry, please forgive her, but she'd achieved the most important thing in her life, taking care of us, and now there was no point any more.'

Jay could barely disguise her horror. What on earth must it have been like to receive such a letter? How did anyone ever get over it?

'So you could say,' he continued, seeming not to have noticed her reaction, 'that Nessa found her father in me, and in her I found a way to protect my mother.' His eyes came to Jay's. 'That's my amateur analysis, but it doesn't take much working out, does it?'

Not disagreeing, she said, 'Where's your father now?'

'He died about a year before my mother, from a heart attack. So you see, in her mind she'd lost all three of us by then.'

She'd lost all three of them. 'How old were you?' she asked.

'When my father died? I was twenty, Toni twenty-two.'

It was an awful start for them both, shattering, and hard to imagine how they'd come through it as well as they had.

Seeming to sense how deeply his words had affected her, he gave a small smile, as if appreciating her understanding. 'I guess,' he said, 'we need to talk about the phone?'

She nodded and opened the dossier in front of her. 'I have a print-out of the text messages,' she said, 'plus a list of calls and contacts.' Sliding it over, she took out a copy for herself.

As he read it she almost felt his tension increasing, saw how tightly his hands were clenching as he struggled to contain his emotions. 'Have you seen any of the texts before?' she asked.

He nodded, briefly. 'Some. I only found the phone about a week before . . .' His mouth trembled, and he gave himself a moment. 'There are . . . more recent ones,' he told her. 'Do you know who they're from?' He looked up, and the torment in his eyes was as apparent as his reluctance to know more.

'We're hoping you can help us with that.'

Studying the print-out again he said, 'It's not rocket science, is it? They're obviously initials, but whether they belong to first or surnames . . . It says here, in the notes, that P might have sold her a car.' He sighed and pressed his fingers into the sockets of his eyes. 'We bought her BMW from someone called Paul French,' he said. 'He's the manager of a dealership near Bristol. I can't remember the name of it off the top of my head, but Toni or John might. They've bought cars from there before.'

Making a note, Jay said, 'When exactly did you buy the BMW?'

'I guess, about six months ago. It was a year old and a great deal. She loved it on sight.'

'Were you in contact with Paul French at all after you bought it?'

'No, but it looks like maybe she was.' His eyes closed again as he struggled to deal with this.

After giving him a moment, Jay said, 'He seems to have called her about ten days before she died, and she rang him back a week later. They could have arranged to meet on Monday the twenty-ninth. We won't know until we speak to him, but you're not aware of them getting together?'

He shook his head.

'What about the others? M? We think he might have been an artist.'

Inhaling slowly, he looked at her, not the print-out as he said, 'It's possible he was, but I . . . I can't recall their names, the ones she told me about. Maybe talk to Melissa or Sheri; most of the artwork she brought into the gallery came from her trips to London.'

'J?' she ventured. 'We think, from the text message, that he might be someone she met quite recently. Any idea who it might be?'

He shrugged. 'I have a client called Jamie Colyer, but I also have a brother-in-law called John, a builder called Jimmy, a dentist called Jeremy, and those are just the ones I can think of. Obviously there are more, so I'm not sure where to start.'

'Try those who also knew Vanessa.'

'Well, I guess all of the above.'

'Do you know if she met any of them for the first time in the last few weeks?'

Giving this some thought, he said, 'I introduced her to Jamie about a month ago when she came out to a site with me, but I don't think he's the kind of bloke . . .' He stopped and turned his hands over, as if something somewhere was playing tricks on him. 'I was about to say I couldn't see him going behind my back, but how the hell can you know that about anyone?'

Unable to stop herself thinking of Tom and how she'd never questioned her trust in him until he'd destroyed it, she said, 'People are complicated,' and immediately wished she hadn't for how trite it sounded. Continuing quickly, she said, 'There's a J2, D1 and D2.'

He seemed at a loss.

'OK, think about it, and let me know if you come up with anything. You are also in the contacts on this phone, did you realize that?'

He nodded.

'There's also someone listed as Ed, different number, who she called a few times. Any suggestions?'

His face was starting to pale, showing the emotional strain this was putting on him. 'I'm sorry . . . I . . . Can't you just call the numbers to ask these people who they are?'

'We will. I was just hoping you might be able to give us something to work with.'

'Sorry, that's the best I can do. Will you hand the phone to the police?'

'Not yet, but if someone listed turns out to be a possible suspect, we will.'

He nodded, apparently understanding that and seeming glad to hear it.

'I have more questions,' she said. 'Are you OK to continue?'

'Sure. I . . .' Appearing uncertain of what he wanted to say, he simply stopped, so returning to her iPad, she said,

'I'm hoping to see Vanessa's stepmother later this week. Is there anything you can tell me about her that I should know in advance?'

His expression turned wry. 'Where to begin about Daphne?' he said, shaking his head as if genuinely lost. 'I guess the most important thing to know is that she'll tell you things about Vanessa, and about me—' He broke off as the door opened and a guard announced that their time was up.

Jay raised a hand requesting another minute.

'Sorry,' she was told. 'Come on, Blake. On your feet.'

Quickly pushing a pre-paid phone card across the table, Jay said, 'Use it to call me. I'll book another visit for next week.'

Taking the card, he said, 'Thanks. I'll check my schedule, but I'm sure I'll be free.'

CHAPTER TWENTY-FOUR

After a ten-minute walk back to her car, Jay carefully manoeuvred it through the tightly parked residential streets of Horfield, or was it Bishopston, she was never too sure, all the time talking to Vikki on her mobile.

'OK, got it,' Vikki replied in response to the instructions she'd been given, 'prison visit next week with EB. Find some time for you to meet with Joe . . . Aren't you seeing him today?'

'On my way to Chipping Sodbury now,' Jay confirmed, checking both ways to pull out onto the Gloucester Road, 'but we need some office time, hopefully this week, if I've got an opening. An hour should do it. Two would be better. Whatever, it needs to be before I see Edward Blake again. Any messages?'

'Loads, but nothing that can't wait till you're back.'

'OK. Before I forget, I need you to get hold of Vanessa Blake's stepmother and arrange for me to see her.'

'Will do. What's her name?'

'Daphne something or other. Joe will have it and the number. If you haven't got hold of him by the time I see him, I'll ask him to text you. Right, I need to put some directions into the sat nav or I'm going to end up lost.'

Pulling over in front of a rank of shops, she quickly entered Chipping Sodbury into the Command system, and before driving on made a brief check of her texts. One from Charlie with a link to the sports bag of his choice (his old one had been destroyed in the fire); another from Charlie wishing her a happy birthday; a third from Charlie saying sorry he'd meant to send the last to one of his mates. None from Livvy and one from Tom letting her know that his trial was overrunning so he might not be back until Thursday.

Did it matter whether or not she believed him, if in fact he'd found a way to spend the night with Ellen Tyler? The damage was done now, so what difference did it make if he was cheating again?

Maybe he'd never really stopped.

And yes, it did still matter, but she wasn't going to check up on him for the simple reason that she really didn't want to deal with it until she had to.

After taking the scenic route rather than the motorway to Chipping Sodbury, she drove slowly over the brink of a low hill to find the small town laid out before her and was surprised to discover how welcomingly quaint it was. She already knew from Wikipedia that it was a market town with medieval origins, and now here it was in all its captivating glory – plenty of modern-day sophistication all wrapped up in Olde Worlde charm.

Finding a parking space close to Hobb's House Bakery (did it have anything to do with the TV series?) she looked around for Picture This and spotted it without too much trouble, thanks to Joe waiting at the foot of a stepladder where Antonia was at the top dousing hanging baskets.

As she joined them with apologies for being late, Antonia's son, Guy, appeared from beneath the hatchback of a small white car and immediately reddened when he saw her.

Sympathizing with what a drawback this propensity for blushing must be for a lad his age, Jay gave him a friendly smile. 'I didn't realize you were joining us,' she said, shaking his hand, 'but it's good to see you.'

Sounding more confident than he looked, he said, 'I was hoping to get an overview of Ed's projects before we see him tomorrow, but the police have taken everything away. I'll just have to try doing it from memory.'

'Jay,' Antonia said warmly as she descended the ladder. 'How was he? Did you see him?'

'Yes, and he seems OK.' Jay flashed on the bruising on Blake's face and hand, but there was no reason to mention it – they'd see it for themselves when they got there. 'Hi Joe,' she said to her investigator, who was retracting the ladder. To Antonia she said, 'Can we go inside?'

Gesturing for Guy to bring the watering can, Antonia led them in through an arch next to the old stone building. 'The front door is still locked,' she explained. 'We don't want anyone wandering in while we're here, thinking we're open, so we need to go around the back.'

Following her past a handful of mews cottages, Jay looked around the small parking area Blake had mentioned, tucked away from the high street. There didn't appear to be any other way out than through the arch, so it would not be possible to drive along a service lane to join the main road elsewhere. Maybe it could be done on foot, although there was no obvious clue as to how that could be achieved either, with nothing but high walls surrounding them and no evident doorways.

Letting them in through a wooden gate, Antonia led

them across a flagstone patio where a wrought-iron table, two chairs and a collapsed parasol were soaking up the sun, and into a large, light room with three desks, a four-seater sofa, a freestanding drawing board with a half-finished design attached, and several mobile storage units.

'Can I make you some tea or coffee?' Antonia offered, heading into the corner kitchenette and filling a kettle.

Jay was picturing Edward and Vanessa working here, or entertaining clients, visitors, trades people . . . Was she getting a sense of him, maybe it was his natural scent, or more likely it was her imagination? 'Black tea for me, no sugar,' she replied, noting the dog bed and bowl in a disused fireplace. 'Whose is the third desk?' she asked, noticing how much smarter, yet more antiquated it was than the others.

'It's the one I use when I'm here,' Guy replied, his neck and cheeks firing up again. 'Nessa found it in a junk sale and Ed fixed it up for me.'

Jay pointed to an open doorway. 'I'm guessing this goes through to the shop?'

Quickly mounting two steps ahead of her, Guy led her along a narrow corridor with a cloakroom to the right, bookshelves to the left and a closed door that he opened to show her was a storeroom. The gallery itself was entered through the colourful strands of a glass bead curtain that turned out to be as musical as a wind chime when Guy pulled the shimmery strands aside.

As she stepped inside, Jay became aware of the same fragrance she'd picked up on when she'd been in the Blakes' bedroom, and remained still for a moment, almost as if waiting for a ghost to appear.

Guy said, slightly shakily, 'It still smells of her in here. Mum said it earlier and she's right.' As he swallowed, Jay deliberately didn't look at him, guessing he didn't want her noticing his emotion.

The paintings and photographs that filled the walls and display boards turned out to be an eclectic mix of architectural, figurative and oddly conceptual works that told Jay little about their collector, for the simple reason she had no expertise in such analysis.

'Were there a lot of customers?' she asked turning to Guy.

'Not really,' he admitted. 'Or not that came into the shop. Mostly Nessa went to people's houses to help them choose what might work for them, or their walls, I suppose. This place was always seen as her . . .' He shrugged. 'She kind of . . . Mum will explain it better than I can, but Ed was like . . . He kept this place going because Ness liked having it.'

Jay was leaning in to read the signatures on paintings and printed names on cards beside the photographs. Her only interest was in their initials, and finding two Js, an M, and a D right here, she used her phone to take shots of the accompanying pieces and turned back to Guy. 'We'd like you and your mother to help us with the contact list on Vanessa's phone, if you can.'

Off went his capillaries again. 'You mean the one I saw Mum giving you the other day?'

She nodded. 'The list is mostly made up of initials, some of which could correspond with the artists and photographers in here. We'll have a better idea of that once we call the numbers, which Joe and I will get around to sometime in the next few days. Right now we just want

237

to get some advance information on who these people might be.'

She followed him back to the office and was surprised when he took it upon himself to tell his mother what they were about to do, rather than leave it to her.

'Well, that's . . . That's fine,' Antonia responded, handing Jay her tea. 'We're happy to help in any way we can.'

Clocking the worried look she gave her son, Jay glanced at Joe and saw that he'd noticed it too. 'Is something the matter?' she asked.

'No, not at all,' Antonia rapidly assured her. 'I just – well . . . I hope the tea's OK. Not too strong.'

Sipping it, Jay said, 'It's fine. Thank you.' What was going on here, she wondered, because something assuredly was.

Antonia began pulling up chairs for them to sit around Blake's empty desk, and they spent the next half an hour going through each of the initials until it was clear that neither Guy nor Antonia were any more certain about their guesses than Edward had been about his. Still, at least they had a couple of names to work with now, thanks to the artworks, and Joe's next job would be to Google the artists before trying out the numbers.

'We could have done it right there,' he remarked as he walked Jay back to her car, 'but I'm guessing you have a reason for why we didn't.'

'Hang on,' she said, stopping in front of a deli. 'Is this where you said they do great food, because I'm starving.'

'Count me in,' Joe responded happily, and gestured for her to go ahead of him.

A few minutes later, with two coffees in front of them and orders for a full English breakfast/lunch underway, she said, 'Did you hear from Vikki about the stepmother? We need a number—'

'All done. Do you want me to come with you when you go?'

'Mm, yes, why not?'

'Good, just let me know when. Now answer me this, what was that look about? The one Antonia gave her son before we went through the phone numbers?'

'Your guess is as good as mine but, as we know, this isn't the first time she's held something back from us. First there was Vanessa's promiscuity, now there's . . . Whatever this is.'

He shook his head in bafflement. 'Question I'm asking myself,' he said ponderously, 'is whether it could be the same thing Maguire's holding back about, but if you're going to ask if I have any theories, then I've got to say, right now, not a one.'

CHAPTER TWENTY-FIVE

Over the next few days, although Edward Blake's case was often on her mind, Jay had little time to spend on it, for there were other meetings and hearings that needed to take priority. Most importantly for now, at least until she could speak to Antonia Debrayne and Frank Maguire again, was the fact that she remained convinced the police were not yet able to prove their case in court. She just hoped that when she did manage to get to the bottom of what was going on with the family and neighbour, it wouldn't add to the incriminating evidence that Blake already had stacked up against him.

Grasping at straws was a game she was often forced to play, and sometimes, once in a blue moon, she won, although this time she really wasn't hopeful. After all, if Antonia knew something that would help her brother, she would have surely come forward with it by now. As would Maguire, who'd stated right up front that he wanted to help Edward.

As if that wasn't causing her enough mental somersaults and frustration, on Friday evening, when Tom came home, the angst got worse. He seemed tense, almost nervous, which in turn made her feel the same way. They didn't embrace or even exchange much of a look as he went to fix himself a drink, although she was sure something would have been said, probably by her, were Livvy not all over the dining table with her revision.

Dropping a kiss on their daughter's head, he pulled up a chair to sit next to her. 'Ollie and Jenn have invited us to join them at Côte brasserie for dinner,' he announced, presumably for Jay's benefit too. 'Fancy it?'

'Too right, I'm starving,' Livvy replied with feeling. 'Can you just help me with this debate paper first? It won't take long, or it shouldn't, not for you.'

'OK, I'll just text Ollie and say we'll meet them at – seven?' he suggested, turning to Jay.

Shrugging and nodding, Jay poured herself a drink and disappeared into the study to make some calls. At least spending the next couple of hours with friends would mean they didn't have to speak to one another, which wasn't great, but maybe preferable to trying to avoid a row.

Later, on their way back from the restaurant, Livvy said, 'Whatever you two have fallen out over, please can you make up, because your weirdness is starting to do my head in.'

'We haven't fallen out,' Tom told her, his tone belying his words.

'Oh, so you've just stopped speaking?'

'We have a few things to sort out,' Jay declared more honestly, 'nothing for you to worry about.' *Yet*, she added mentally.

Once home, Livvy bid a hasty goodnight to her parents and dashed straight upstairs to her room, no doubt to update her friends on Jenn's revelation that Nat would be home for a few days the following week.

Aware of Tom watching her as she went to fill a glass with water, Jay was about to speak when he said, 'So, is this how it's going to be? Nothing to say to one another, no communication at all?'

Deciding not to remind him that he was the one who'd virtually ignored her when he'd come home, she turned to face him, and said, 'Were you with her last night?'

He frowned, clearly thrown. Then said, 'You know where I was – except you've obviously convinced yourself I was somewhere else. Why would you do that? All you had to do was call the hotel to check if I was there . . .'

'It wouldn't tell me if she was too.'

Anger flashed in his eyes. 'Well she wasn't, so let's stop this here.'

Matching his tone, she said, 'Do you have the DNA results yet?'

'Of course not. You know it doesn't happen that fast.'

'Did you send the swab, or did she?'

'She did, but I told her which labs to use.'

'So, have you been in touch with her since last week?'

Holding her gaze, seemingly defiant, he said, 'She called a couple of days ago.'

'To say what?'

'Nothing really. Just to thank me for going and to ask how I was feeling about things.'

For some reason she felt enraged by that, and almost wanted to hit him. 'And what did you say?' she asked tartly.

'That it wasn't a convenient time to talk. Look, Jay, I understand how hard this is for you—'

'*Hard?*' she echoed scornfully.

'OK, an understatement, but I'm sorry, I really am. I wish it wasn't happening, that she'd never told me about the child, but we can't let it come between us like this.'

'And how do you suggest we stop it?'

'By not doing this,' he retorted.

'Well, I'm afraid there's no escaping it, because here's what I don't get: why is her husband so keen for you to be a part of their lives? Is he planning to leave her?'

'I've already told you, I don't know what his motives are. We didn't discuss it. It didn't seem appropriate while I was there and—'

'You could have asked since. You've had plenty of opportunities to pick up the phone, she's even called you, so why didn't you ask then? Or did you, and you don't want to tell me what her answer was? You see, Tom, I've no idea what to believe any more. You're not the person I thought you were, the man I married, who I've shared my life with. You're a stranger to me now—'

'Stop overdramatizing this,' he cut in angrily. 'I know you're hurt, that you feel betrayed, and I'm totally responsible for it, but I haven't changed. I love you, everything we have together matters more to me than anything else.'

'Except when you're off making babies with someone else.'

'Oh, for God's sake! You know it wasn't intended . . .'

'But it's happened and now here we are waiting for results that we already know are going to prove you're the father. And if they do, *you* will have to decide what kind of role you're going to play in his life, if you're willing to dance to whatever tune they're about to play . . .'

'Whatever happens, I'm not going to let it break us up. We love each other, we have a good life together.'

'We did, until you found someone else.'

'I haven't—'

'I tried to forgive you when I first found out, I really did, but now, with this . . . I'm not . . . Oh hell,' she seethed as she started to cry.

Drawing her to him, he held her close, and closer still when she didn't resist. She wanted to push him away, she really did but, furious as she was with him, and herself for breaking down, she realized she actually needed this closeness. Except his arms no longer provided a place where only she and the children belonged; there were others now and she didn't want to share him.

Pulling back to look at her, he cupped her face in his hands as he said, 'If you don't want me to see him again, it's what will happen.'

Sighing, she dropped her head to his chest, knowing they'd probably continue going around in circles like this until the results were back and he knew for certain what was wanted of him.

'Can I come back to our bed tonight?' he asked softly.

She nodded. Why not? But as soon as she felt the relief go through him, she wished she'd said no. He didn't deserve to be off the hook about this, not for a minute, but what was the point of making him suffer when it dragged her down too?

'I've got some work I need to finish off,' she told him. 'You go on up and I'll try not to wake you when I come in.' He'd know this meant she didn't want to make love; she just hoped he'd respect it, and feign sleep if he had to, for that kind of intimacy wasn't what she wanted at all right now. Not with him. Not with anyone.

'Jay, it's Edward Blake. Is this a bad time?'

Surprised to hear from him at this hour, she went to

close the study door as she said, 'No, not at all. Is everything OK?'

'Yes, it's fine. I should have rung before now, it's just
things . . . You can get a bit distracted in here. Anyway,
I promised to call about Daphne, Nessa's stepmother.'

'Yes, I've arranged to see her next Tuesday.'

'OK. I think you'll find her a . . . complicated character.
Not altogether trustworthy, or truthful. You'll understand
better when you meet her. Just please try not to believe
everything she tells you.' He gave a mirthless laugh. 'I
remember Vanessa saying much the same to me before
she took me home for the first time. I had no idea what
to expect, but it wasn't what I found.'

'I'm intrigued.'

Wryly, he said, 'Just go with an open mind – and if you
have time, try to talk to Toni first. She doesn't have a
problem telling you what she thinks of Mrs Drewson-
Browne.'

'OK, I will.'

A few moments passed, and Jay wondered what he was
thinking, or not saying, how lonely he was, and fearful
of what more was to come.

'I'm sorry,' he said, 'you're probably at home and I've
interrupted your evening.'

'It's not a problem. But it's late for you to be making
a call.'

'I know. There's a guard, he's . . . He knows how hard I
find it to get to the phone at times. There can be a bit of a
scrum and I've learned it's not always a good idea to win.'

Feeling for him, she said, 'I'm sorry to hear that.'

'It's fine. Thanks for picking up. I should probably go
now.'

'OK. Goodnight.'

'Goodnight,' and a moment later he was gone.

After ringing off at her end, she continued to sit at her desk, staring at the laptop screen, not reading, not even thinking really. It was as though she'd slipped into some kind of twilight world where everything in her life seemed strangely distant, as though it was happening somewhere else, or to someone else. If only she could stay here, suspended in a place of non-reality, where her husband had never cheated on her, and where Edward Blake still had his wife.

CHAPTER TWENTY-SIX

'Hope you've all had a good weekend,' Jay said, as the crime team gathered for a meeting on Monday morning. She wouldn't dwell on hers, no reason to really, but at least things were better with Tom, for now. 'There's been an interesting development in the Edward Blake case,' she announced. 'I just got off the phone with Matt Kowalski, our trusty defence scientist, and his visit to the labs on Friday has yielded some pretty crucial information that the police have not yet shared with us.'

Satisfied she had everyone's attention, she continued. 'Apparently, a YSTR DNA test has been carried out . . .'

'A what?' Vikki asked, who was taking notes.

'It's a short tandem repeat on the Y-chromosome,' Jay explained, and laughed at the way Vikki's eyes crossed. 'For our purposes,' she explained, 'it means that male DNA – apparently from saliva – was discovered on Vanessa Blake's right breast. It is not her husband's, and nor does it belong to anyone who has been swabbed so far.'

Everyone's eyes opened with interest. 'Enter our perp,' Joe muttered theatrically.

'Quite possibly,' Jay agreed, experiencing the same swell of relief and hope she'd felt when Kowalski had broken the news. At last Blake wasn't the only suspect. Someone else *had* been there. 'The question now,' she said, 'is who have we all missed? Kowalski is sending over a list of those whose DNA has been identified, which will be helpful for elimination purposes. What we need to get on with, though, is talking to the contacts on Vanessa's secret phone before we hand it over to the police. I think we need to do that sooner rather than later. So, Vikki, if you can reschedule my appointments for the rest of the day, Joe and I will make a start right away. If anyone else can spare some time, Ash? Sallyanne?'

'Sorry.' Ash grimaced. 'I'm duty solicitor today and there's someone already waiting to be interviewed at Patchway custody. I'll have to leave right after we've finished this.'

'You can go now,' Jay told him. 'Sallyanne?'

'I can give you half an hour before I'm due to see a client's family,' she replied.

'Great. Do we have the phone?'

'I'll get it.' Vikki jumped up and almost collided with Ash as they both left the room.

Minutes later she was back with the mobile, a charger, sufficient copies of the transcript of contacts and texts and Jay's notes. 'It should have enough battery for now,' she informed them, 'and I'll organize some tea for you all.'

'Don't forget the doughnuts,' Joe called after her.

'Yeah, right!'

'OK,' Jay began, handing out copies of everything, 'let's decide first on our approach, which should go something like this . . . Tell you what, I'll make the first call and we can take it from there.' Picking up the office landline she put it on speaker, selected an initial and dialled the number. 'M,' she informed the others. 'Suspected artist or photographer, recipient of explicit selfies. Two soft-focus landscape photographs hanging in the Chipping Sodbury gallery ascribed to MJ.'

After three rings, a male voice came through the speaker, abrupt, deep and cultured. 'Mason Johns.'

Bingo – sort of!

'Hello, Mr Johns, my name is Jessica Wells, I'm the solicitor for Vanessa Blake's husband, Edward Blake.' Allowing him virtually no time to take that in, she added, 'We can see from Vanessa Blake's phone that you were in contact with her before she died and I'm hoping you can tell me when was the last time you saw her?'

Not sounding quite so abrupt any more, he said, 'It's terrible what happened to her. I was distraught when I found out. She didn't deserve . . . I thought the police would have been in touch with me by now.'

'I'm sure they will be,' Jay told him. 'When did you last see her?'

'It was the week before it happened. On the Tuesday. We met at a hotel near Malmesbury. I'd booked in for the night and she joined me for, I guess it was a couple of hours, in the late afternoon.'

'Can you tell me which hotel?'

After noting it down she said, 'Can anyone there confirm that she was with you?'

'I'm afraid I've no idea.'

'OK. How did you first meet?'

'It was when I showed her my work – I'm a photographer – and she asked if I'd be interested in taking some shots of her, for her husband. I said I'd be happy to, and when I realized what kind of shots . . . Well, I expect you're already aware of the rest.'

'Why didn't you come forward when you learned what had happened to her?'

'Because I'm married and I don't want my wife to find out. I guess she will now.'

Suspecting she probably would, Jay said, 'Can you tell me where you were on Monday the twenty-ninth of April?'

Apparently he'd already checked, because there was no hesitation. 'Yes, I was in Surrey, photographing a wedding. It's what I do to earn money. I was around people right through to the end of the evening.'

Jay glanced at the others. 'OK, Mr Johns, thank you for answering my questions.' After ringing off she said, 'We'll let the detectives check his alibi, but I didn't get any uncomfortable vibes from him, did you?'

Both Joe and Sallyanne shook their heads, and since neither had anything to add, Jay began allocating the rest of the calls.

Half an hour later, P – Paul French the car dealer – had confirmed a relationship with Vanessa. He had last seen her about a month ago. His alibi for 29 April would be his boss, he'd told Sallyanne, as he was at work that day, but he hoped no one would have to contact him. He wasn't sure screwing the clients would go down well.

J1 turned out to be Jamie Colyer, the client Edward had mentioned. He admitted to having a sexual encounter with Vanessa Blake at his office in Swindon about three weeks ago, just after meeting her for the first time. On 29 April he was in Spain with his wife and children.

D1 – Darren Gibbs – admitted to being a site manager on one of Edward's renovation projects. His meetings with Vanessa Blake had mostly happened in the back of his van when they both drove to a remote spot to get together. He wasn't sure he had an alibi for 29 April, but he'd check. Anyway, 'I definitely didn't do it,' he told Joe, 'but I wouldn't blame Ed if it was him after the way she treated him.'

J2 – Jackson Moore – was a watercolour artist from Hemel Hempstead who'd painted several nudes of Vanessa, at her request, and while she was sitting for him things often became 'amorous'. Apparently, he hadn't contacted the police because it had been several weeks since he'd last seen her, but he was more than willing to help in any way he could.

Reading from her own notes at the end, Jay said, 'The number for D2 just rang out, so no idea yet who he is, but "Ed" is an interesting one. It turns out he's Edmond Berzina who, according to Google, is the director of a rather prestigious art gallery in London.'

'Did you speak to him?' Joe asked, tapping the name into a search engine.

Jay smiled. 'I used Vanessa's phone for this one and here's how it went: he clicks on, says nothing, as if he's waiting for me to speak first – this makes me think he recognizes the number, or maybe Vanessa's name came up, though obviously he knows it can't be her. Then, smooth as you like, he comes in with, "Edmond Berzina, Modernists Institute." So I explain who I am, and that I'm calling because I believe he's a friend of Vanessa Blake's – and he promptly hangs up.'

Joe said archly, 'And how helpful did he think that would be to his cause? He's got to know someone's going to call him back.'

'By which time,' Jay pointed out, 'he'll probably have got rid of the phone I just called him on, and be all lawyered up ready to go.'

Sallyanne said, 'Much good it'll do him if the saliva DNA turns out to be his.'

'Indeed,' Jay responded. 'Now, unless anyone can tell me why I shouldn't, I'm going to hand all this over to Ken Bright in the morning. Let his detectives do the chasing up and testing, we don't have the time or the budget.'

'I can see no reason not to,' Joe replied, his attention more on his laptop than what was being proposed. Satisfied he'd enlarged his findings sufficiently, he turned the screen around for the others to read it. 'Just look at who Edmond Berzina is related to,' he said, clearly waiting for them to be impressed. And they were.

'So it turns out,' Jay told Tom later over a supper cooked by him, 'that the director of the Modernists Institute is married to Vanessa Blake's half-sister, Freya.'

Tom appeared both amused and intrigued.

How good it felt to be having a normal conversation with him.

Don't overthink it, just go with it.

'So are we to assume,' he asked, topping up her wine, 'that some kind of an affair was going on between him and your victim?'

'Quite possibly.' She wondered if he'd inwardly flinched, as she had, at the word 'affair'. 'Anyway, I tried calling him back, but he didn't pick up and he hasn't responded to the message I left either.'

'What did you say?'

'Just that it would be helpful to know when he'd last seen Vanessa.'

'Does the phone tell you when he last had contact with her?'

252

Picking up her glass, she said, 'They spoke for ten minutes the day before she was killed. Obviously I've no idea what was said, but I can't help wondering if they were arranging for him to pick her up at Chippenham Station the following day.'

'Seems a reasonable assumption. Still no sightings of her getting into a car or a taxi?'

'None that can be confirmed. I'm assuming if the police were still buying into the tip-off they'd still be running with it – unless it turned out to be Berzina's car.'

'In which case they'll have been in touch with him by now.'

'Indeed. I'm hoping to find out more when I visit his mother-in-law tomorrow. Is there any more of this? It's delicious.'

Getting up from the table, he took both their plates to the kitchen, saying, 'It'll be interesting to find out if this unidentified DNA belongs to your man. If it does, and he has no alibi to fit the crucial timings, he's going to be in a lot of trouble. When are you next seeing Blake?'

'The day after tomorrow. I should have a lot to tell him by then. Thanks,' she said as he brought their plates back to the table. 'Now, how about your day? What's new in the world of Brunel Chambers?'

Appearing glad to be asked, he began updating her on an official inquiry he was involved in concerning the potentially fraudulent practices of a local authority and its very colourful councillors. As usual he was easily able to make her laugh with his gift for mimicry and droll expressions, much as he had over the weekend when they'd driven to Somerton to take his mother to her favourite restaurant for a birthday lunch.

Everything had been going swimmingly until Patricia had asked, as she always did, 'Have you heard from your mother recently, Jay?'

'Not since Christmas,' Jay had replied blandly.

'So you don't know how she's keeping? If she's still happy over there in Australia? I hope she doesn't get lonely.'

'My sister, as you know, is close by, which is why she went. And she has my stepfather.'

'Yes, of course. I keep forgetting about him.'

Jay only wished she could do the same, for she still held Robert Hawkridge – the insufferable individual her mother had left Jay's beloved father for – responsible for everything that had gone wrong in her young life.

'Why do you think your mother always has to mention mine when we see her?' she asked. 'What is it that compels her to do that?'

Blinking at the abrupt change of subject, he sighed and picked up his wine. 'Obviously you weren't listening to a word I was saying, which would be OK if you didn't ask me the same thing every time we go to Somerton. The answer is that I don't know; maybe she's just being polite, or she'd genuinely like to know how your mother is.'

'Or it makes her feel superior to know that she's a hands-on caring mother and grandmother while mine is anything but.'

Tom's eyes darkened. 'That's unfair. She's better than that and you know it.'

'Do I?'

'You should, and now perhaps you can tell me why, when the evening was going so well, you've decided to pick a fight with me?'

254

She swallowed and looked away. It was probably thinking about her father that was making her feel suddenly emotional; it often happened when she was at a low point. 'I'm sorry,' she said, starting to clear the table, 'I didn't mean to.'

'You're upset,' he stated. 'Has something happened I don't know about?'

Keeping her head turned she said, 'No, nothing. I'm fine. Livvy needs picking up at ten. Can you do it, or shall I?'

'I'll go. So, is that it now? The end of the evening that I, for one, was enjoying?'

It ought to be, as she needed to get her head together for the meeting with Daphne Drewson-Browne tomorrow, but she said, 'No, not if you don't want it to be.'

'I don't. So can we talk some more?'

Uneasily, she said, 'Because you have some news?'

'No, because it's nice sitting here with you the way we usually do in the evenings when we're both at home. It's who we really are and I don't want to give up on it yet.'

Knowing that he'd understood the double-meaning too, she gave a half-smile and reached for his hand. 'I don't want to give up on you,' she told him truthfully, 'I really don't, we just . . . I guess, I'm taking a while to come to terms with it all.'

As he nodded his understanding, he was staring down at their joined hands, and for a moment she thought he was avoiding her eyes. *Why couldn't he look at her? There was more! Something he hadn't told her yet!* But then his head came up and he was gazing at her tenderly, as he said, 'I should never have done this to you. You didn't deserve it; I just wish it could all end right here and now.'

Did that mean there was more?

No, of course not, why was she doing this to herself? To them?

Sitting down, she said, 'I wish it could too.'

With a wry smile as he picked up his drink, he said, 'I have to admit that a part of me is still hoping he won't turn out to be mine.'

Knowing that deep down she was hoping the same, in spite of how certain they'd both felt until now that he would be, she said, 'If he is, I'm going to do my best to find the right way forward for us.' Only as she spoke the words did she realize that she meant them. If he really did still love her and want their marriage to continue, then of course she did too. It might be hard, and there would almost certainly be times when she might feel differently to the way she did now, but here, tonight, she truly didn't want to give up on all that they'd built together and that they both held so dear.

CHAPTER TWENTY-SEVEN

During the drive to Cirencester the following day, Jay found herself fighting the urge to talk to Joe about her father. She knew, if she did, he'd happily chuckle through a dozen or more anecdotes, some of which he'd heard before, and he wouldn't stop until she changed the subject herself. In some small way it would be like having her father back, but what good would it do? None, was the answer.

So, instead, gazing around at fields, trees, more fields and more trees, she asked, 'Do you know this area?' They seemed to be in the middle of nowhere, if they discounted an old coaching inn they'd just passed a few minutes ago, and a handful of signposts to well-hidden places with names as quirky as they were quaint.

'Not well,' Joe replied. 'Actually, as I recall, your dad had a client who lived around here, son of a duke or earl or something, always in trouble for drugs or drunk-driving or disturbing the peace. I think the lad topped himself in the end, but don't quote me.'

Frowning, Jay said, 'Wasn't Vanessa Blake's father the distant cousin of a duke?'

'They're all related to each other around these parts,' Joe informed her knowledgeably. 'They like keeping it in the family. It's what makes them the way they are.'

Having to laugh, Jay decided not to ask him to elaborate on that and turned left into yet another narrow country road that wound through hedgerows and small dense woods, past a working farm, over a cattle grid and through a sprawling hamlet with no one around.

In five hundred yards you will reach your destination.

'Thank goodness for that,' she commented, 'I thought we were never going to get there.'

Joe said, 'Remind me what Blake told you about this woman.'

'Sounds like she can be quite tricky, my word not his; he also called her untrustworthy – said she lies a lot.'

Joe blinked. 'Well, that's helpful. Have you told him about the unidentified DNA yet?'

You have reached your destination.

'I haven't had the chance, but I'm seeing him tomorrow.'

'Well, that should make his day.'

Certain it would, Jay slowed up, searching for signs for Sayley House. Finding none, she took the only turn available into a tunnel of trees so tightly bound overhead that no sun could get through. Twenty yards on, they broke out into daylight, and ahead of them was a narrow, winding track through a magnificent flow of wild poppy meadows.

Jay followed it for at least half a mile and, as they reached the brink of a low rise in the landscape, she braked at the unexpected sight of such a splendid old house spread out like a shimmering mirage before them.

They'd come upon it so suddenly that it was a moment before she realized how ramshackle it really was, with its crumbling castellated roofs, ruin of a gothic tower and cracked stained-glass windows. In its day it might have been a property of some standing, the seat of a nobleman, perhaps the retreat of a minor royal. She found herself wishing Blake was there to talk her through the history that emanated so potently from the towering grey stone walls.

After parking next to a Land Rover, in front of a stable block, they trudged along a rugged and grassy footpath towards the massive front door.

'Do you reckon Lurch is going to answer?' Joe muttered, pulling on a rope that might or might not be connected to a bell somewhere inside the place.

'It is a bit Addams family, isn't it?' Jay murmured. 'Creepy as hell, in fact. I'm glad I asked you to come.'

'And there was me about to offer to wait outside.' He looked up at the imposing façade, trying to locate signs of life that didn't belong to birds or bats or anything worse. 'They're either broke,' he commented under his breath, 'or they've decided not to waste any money on a house that's never going to be theirs.'

'Hello!' a female voice called out.

They turned around, searching for the source, but could see no one.

'Sorry,' the voice said again, 'I'll be right there.'

Moments later, a slight, redheaded woman of around forty came out of the stables in full riding gear, including hat and crop, and strode towards them.

Jay immediately thought of stirrup straps.

'I saw you pull up,' the woman said jovially, holding out a hand to shake. 'Freya Berzina. And you must be Mrs Wells?'

'That's right. This is Terry Josephs, my investigator.'

'Ooh,' Freya Berzina commented playfully as she shook

Joe's hand, 'that sounds mightily serious. Mummy's expecting you. Sorry, the doorbell doesn't work, much like everything else around here. Come along, I'll take you to her,' and, beckoning like a tour guide for them to follow, she led them around to the back of the house, across a grand parterre complete with statues, weeds and dried-up fountain, and in through a modern glass door.

'This is where Mummy lives,' Freya explained, discarding her hat and crop on a dresser as she continued along a dimly lit corridor. 'Obviously she can't manage the whole place, so we've created a very nice apartment for her, which includes Daddy's old library and I believe that is where we'll find her.' Pushing open a solid oak door, she put her head around and declared, 'Your visitors have arrived, Mummy. Is Mary in today, or shall I make tea?'

As Jay entered the musty, book-lined room, taking in its high, wood-panelled ceiling, large, antiquated furniture and immense stained-glass windows, she looked around for Daphne, but found no sign of her. Then a hand rose above the back of a tall armchair to flick them forward.

'Come in, come in,' they were told, 'make yourselves comfortable. Mary's sorting out refreshments, darling, but do stay if you'd like to.'

'Sorry, I've arranged to meet Sophes at midday so I should probably fly,' and leaning in to drop a kiss on her mother's head, Freya gave a little wave to Jay and Joe and tootled off to her rendezvous.

'Do sit down,' Daphne instructed, her thin hand pointing towards a bulky leather sofa with carved wooden legs and threadbare arms. She looked up as Jay came into view and didn't hide her surprise. 'My goodness, no wonder Edward wanted you as his lawyer. He's always surrounded himself with the pretty ones, especially blondes, and you're rather like Vanessa now I look more closely. Older, slimmer, but . . . I suppose it's the hair.'

Jay said, stiffly, 'This is Terry Josephs, my investigator.' She didn't add anything about him not being Edward's type, but it was hard not to.

As Daphne Drewson-Browne allowed Joe to take her hand, Jay quickly assessed her and decided that – in spite of how well-preserved the woman appeared, with her sleek, dark hair, high cheekbones and large green eyes – she had to be at least mid-seventies, and might even be a regular recipient of dermal fillers. She also had a manner that was so insufferably superior it was already making Jay bristle.

'So,' Daphne began, folding her hands together in a temple of gnarled bones, 'I don't know what you think I can tell you to help Edward, or indeed why I should even if I could, but here's where I'll begin. He is not the person you no doubt think he is, charming, kind, considerate . . . Am I right? I'm sure I am. He is, in fact, a deeply unprincipled man with next to no integrity and a history of disposing of people when he has finished with them. My own daughter Freya can testify to this. He was dating her when he was introduced to Vanessa, and I'm sorry to say Freya was extremely attached to him. This meant nothing to him, of course, other people's feelings never do. So my poor girl was discarded like yesterday's garbage while he took up with her half-sister right in front of her. Of course, it was all engineered by Vanessa; most of their lives she's been stealing Freya's friends and boyfriends. It was a compulsion of hers, a need to win, to show she was best, and the rest of us couldn't stop her, no matter what she wanted to do. As much as it hurt poor Freya, I always said that Edward and Vanessa deserved each other. They were two of a kind, only ever out for themselves and to hell with the rest of the world.'

Momentarily silenced by the diatribe, Jay glanced at Joe.

'So you didn't like your stepdaughter much then?' he commented, and Jay almost laughed.

Daphne's nostrils flared. 'Believe me, I tried to when she was young. I did my very best with her, but there was never any reaching that child. She was obsessed by her mother and spoiled by her father . . . I'm afraid to say I always knew she'd come to a bad end, although this is far worse than even I could have imagined.'

'Do you think Edward is responsible?' Jay asked bluntly.

Daphne shrugged. 'Who else? He was there, from what I hear, and I believe there are no other suspects.'

Having no intention of telling her that actually there were, especially when she couldn't name the man – *yet*, Jay said, 'Why do you think he'd have done it?'

Daphne sighed as she fanned out her hands. 'I've just told you, she could be very difficult, and he probably had no more use for her. I'm surprised he put up with her for as long as he did, frankly, and after that awful business with the baby . . . I've no idea who was to blame there, but we do know that the poor little thing didn't do it to himself, how could he? You'll have spoken with Edward's sister, of course; she's another I wouldn't trust any further than I could throw her. The whole family, her husband and children included, were there when little Lucas died, so please tell me this, how do six fully functioning adults allow a tiny boy to drown in a pool right in front of them?'

'Accidents happen,' Jay reminded her.

Daphne's expression showed her scorn for that. She called out, 'Is that you, Mary?' as the door opened.

'It's me, Mrs DB,' came the reply. 'Coffee, tea and biscuits,' the plump, fluffy-haired Mary informed Joe and Jay as she set a tray on a small table in front of them. 'Help yourself. Do you want anything, Mrs DB?'

'No thank you, dear. You can go now.'

Catching Jay's eye, Mary gave a little twinkle and took herself off.

Letting Joe pour, Jay said, 'Would your son-in-law, Edmond, happen to be around today?'

Startled, Daphne said, 'What an extraordinary question. Why would he be? He works in London during the week. Tuesdays are no exception.'

Jay said, 'We've discovered, through phone records, that he spoke to Vanessa the day before she died.'

Daphne could hardly have looked more shocked, or offended.

'Did you know they were in touch with one another?' Jay prompted.

'No. I did . . .' Daphne stopped and started again. 'If it's true . . . How do you know that it is? Phone records don't prove who was actually involved in the call, only the number it came from.'

Conceding the point, Jay said, 'I tried to speak to him yesterday, but he hung up on me as soon as I mentioned Vanessa.'

Daphne's eyes hardened. 'Well, I should have expected it, of course. As I've already told you, it was what Vanessa did, steal from Freya. I'm sorry to learn about Edmond though. I thought he had more . . . *backbone* than to allow himself to be used by *her*.'

'When did *you* last see Vanessa, Mrs Drewson-Browne?' Jay asked, taking a sip of the lukewarm coffee.

The woman's head seemed to twitch as she drew it back. Whatever secure footing she'd presumed herself to be on appeared to have crumbled under her. 'I really can't remember,' she replied irritably. 'A month ago, maybe. As a matter of fact, she came to talk to me about her father's will.'

Surprised by that, Jay said, 'Can I ask what about it?'

'Yes, you can, but I'm not inclined to answer. Our family affairs are private matters—'

'We already know that she stood to inherit this house,' Jay interrupted, thinking it might be more of a curse than a blessing given its condition.

Daphne almost laughed. 'Well, she won't now, will she?'

Shocked by the spite, Jay said, 'So who does?'

'Him, I suppose, when I die. It's mine until then. Of course, if he goes to prison for life, as he should, the whole place will probably have disintegrated into a pile of dust by the time he gets his hands on it.' She appeared quite gratified by that. 'It was why he married Vanessa,' she continued, 'but I expect you've worked that out by now. He knew all this would be hers one day and someone like him, with his passion for old buildings . . .' She let the sentence hang and stared hard towards the fireplace.

'So if I understand you correctly,' Jay ventured, 'you believe that he'd had enough of her, but couldn't divorce her or he'd lose her inheritance?'

Daphne smiled. 'Precisely.'

'And there's nothing in the will to say that should Vanessa predecease *you*, then you, or her father's other children, would get the house?'

Daphne's stare was icy. 'I repeat, our family's affairs are private and I have no intention of sharing any of the details with you.'

Knowing she wouldn't have much choice when Ken Bright came to call – and he presumably hadn't yet or Daphne wouldn't have looked so surprised at the mention of her son-in-law – Jay let it go and said to Joe, 'Could you try the D2 listing on our contacts sheet?' It was the number that had just rung out when they'd tried it yesterday, and she was interested to see if the D had anything to do with Drewson-Browne.

Clearly reading her mind far better than an arch-looking Daphne possibly could, he called up the number, pressed to connect and waited as the ringtone began. Once again there was no answer, and no sound of a phone anywhere nearby.

'It was worth a try,' Joe commented when they eventually drove back through the poppy fields to head home, 'if only for the way it confused the old bat. Holy shit. What a piece of work! No one misled us about her, that's for sure.'

Jay had to smile. 'Do you know what I'm asking myself now?' she said. 'Who's really doing the lying – her, or them, or all of them?'

'Well that's a snakes and ladders I don't want to play,' he grunted. 'Speaking personally, I've got stepsister Freya in the frame now. She found out about the affair and was having no more of it.'

'How would she have got Vanessa tied to a bed?'

'With her stirrup straps. She's bound to have some by the look of her. I thought that as soon as I saw her. Didn't you?'

'Yes, but how would she have got her *to* the bed? And remember, the saliva is male.'

'I haven't worked that bit out yet.'

They drove on in silence for a while until Jay said, 'I take it you heard what Daphne said as we were leaving?'

He thought back. 'You mean about the dog and you should ask Edward about it?'

'Yes. What do you think she meant by that?'

His hands went up in surrender. 'That woman's got so many angles and edges to her I think I might be bleeding. Luckily, you'll be able to ask the man himself when you see him tomorrow.'

CHAPTER TWENTY-EIGHT

It was the first time Jay had seen Blake laugh, and it was so good to see that it was making her laugh too. What a relief it must be for him in the midst of this nightmare to be finding something amusing.

'My dog? Max?' he said, incredulously.

'I presume it's the one she was talking about.'

He shook his head, clearly still bewildered. 'I've absolutely no idea why she said that,' he assured her, 'but something like this is typical of her. Distraction tactics. She's like a magician getting you to look over here when what's important is over there. I think they call it gaslighting.'

Jay immediately thought of Edmond Berzina and the fact that Daphne could be more interested in protecting him than she was in doing anything to help Blake, so yes, the analogy worked. Before bringing up the possible affair with Berzina, she said, 'I have some potentially very good news. We've just learned about some as yet unidentified male DNA that was taken from the scene.'

His eyes were immediately serious, and showed his eagerness to hear more.

'We've no idea who it belongs to yet,' she told him.

'Was it semen?'

'Saliva.'

His expression showed surprise and distaste. 'Shall I ask where it was taken from? Can I already guess?'

'It was her right breast.'

Apparently not expecting that, he looked away, taking a moment to process it.

Pressing on, she said, 'I'll let you know as soon as I have more to tell you about that. Meantime, back to Daphne. She mentioned you were seeing Vanessa's half-sister, Freya, before you and Vanessa met.'

He sat back in his chair, appearing exasperated and even slightly angry.

'Is it true?'

'Well, I guess it is, in its way, but we were never serious. We probably only dated five or six times, and I wasn't ever under the impression it meant any more to her than it did to me.'

Was that true, or simply how he'd like to see it? 'Had you already broken up before you and Vanessa met?'

'Insofar as we were ever together. I hadn't seen her for a month or more by the time I was introduced to Vanessa.'

'Did you know that she and Freya were related?'

'No, because Freya didn't come into the conversation, there was no reason for her to. It was only later, when Nessa told me where she lived, that I realized there could be a connection.'

'Didn't their shared surname tip you off before that?'

'Nessa used Fergus, her father's first name, until we were married.'

Noting that down, Jay said, 'Daphne says Vanessa had a history of stealing boyfriends from Freya.'

His annoyance was evident as he threw up his hands helplessly. 'This is what Daphne does. She'll say anything to slight Nessa or me. It was what I was trying to tell you when we spoke on the phone. And now you have the problem of deciding who to believe, me or her. I suppose that's something you face all the time, whether or not to believe the person sitting in front of you, especially when their circumstances are as . . . opaque as mine.'

'Actually, I believe you,' she told him. 'But I'll admit this new DNA helps.'

He nodded slowly, keeping his eyes on hers as though trying to read what else might be behind her words.

Feeling the need to break their gaze before it became more than it was, she consulted her iPad. 'I mentioned last week that there was a contact in Vanessa's second phone listed as Ed?'

He became very still. 'Do you know who it is?'

'Freya's husband, Edmond Berzina.'

His eyes flew open as his face paled. 'Are you certain?' he asked, clearly finding it hard to believe.

'He answered when we rang the number, so yes, we are. We haven't spoken to him because he hung up on us. We tried calling again, but he's no longer picking up and he hasn't responded to the message I left.'

Blake got up from his chair and walked to the partition wall. There was no one in the next room; all he could see, if he was looking, was his own faint reflection. 'Are you saying Nessa was involved with him?' he asked, sounding as wretched as Jay had ever heard him.

'All I can tell you,' she replied, 'is that they spoke on the phone the day before she died. It's possible she was arranging to meet him at the station after you dropped her on the Monday morning. We have no proof of that, but my investigator is taking the phone to the police this afternoon. Obviously, they'll want to talk to Berzina, and he won't get away with hanging up on them.'

Blake turned around; his face still taut, ashen, making his eyes seem bluer and somehow more anguished than ever. 'I had no idea they were in touch,' he said. 'I didn't think she had anything to do with her family.'

Not wanting to hurt him, but having no choice, she said softly, 'Perhaps his attraction was the fact that he was Freya's husband?'

Blake frowned and shook his head. 'I can't believe that. I know what Daphne told you about Vanessa always wanting what was Freya's, but it isn't true.' He swallowed and put a hand to his head. 'Or not that I was aware of, but I suppose this . . . I can see how it throws a different light on things.'

Coming back to the table, he sat sideways on his chair and dropped his head into his hands. 'I'm sorry,' he murmured, 'this has come . . . I never imagined she'd have anything to do with him, but maybe I should have.'

'Why?'

He shrugged. 'I guess because no one was off limits. I wanted to think they were, but . . . Have you identified the others on the contact list?'

As she ran through the names, she could see them landing like blows, the sickening images, double betrayals, humiliation. With a forced, mirthless laugh he said, 'You know, I sit here worrying about her garden, whether the veg has been watered, the weeds cut back. I keep asking Toni to take care of things, to make sure everything's OK . . . It's making me feel like a fool.' His eyes didn't fully connect with hers as he said, 'Have you ever been betrayed, Jay?'

Wanting to be honest with him, she said, 'Yes, I have.'

For a moment she thought he was going to ask about it, but he didn't, only said, 'I'm sorry to hear that.' Then, 'Do you know what's worse than losing your wife? I mean, apart from losing your son. It's being in here for her murder when any one of those men, some of whom I trusted, were very probably at the house before I got home.'

Feeling wretched for him, she said, 'In most cases their alibis seem solid, but the police will check them out, obviously.'

'But really it's just Berzina you're not sure about?'

'That's right. And there's another number we still haven't been able to connect to.'

She wasn't sure he'd heard her, so she said, 'Did you know that your wife went to see her stepmother about a month ago to discuss her father's will?'

It was a moment before he seemed to register the words. 'No, I didn't.' He turned to her. 'Are you sure that's true? Daphne says things—'

'It's what she claims.'

Clearly at a loss, he said, 'Then did she tell you what was said, why Nessa even wanted to discuss it? Because I promise you, this is the first I've heard of it.'

'No, she didn't give me any details, but she seems to think that now circumstances have changed, you might inherit Sayley House when she dies – and that its architectural value is the real reason you married Vanessa.'

Blake stared at her, apparently so stunned that it was a moment before he laughed for the second time that morning. 'That house has no architectural value,' he told her. 'It's been a hodgepodge of poorly carried-out construction and design throughout most of its history. Our intention was never to keep it. Neither of us wanted it. When the time came, we'd planned to sell it to a developer to turn into a nursing home, or flats, or to rip it down and start again. And as far as I knew, if it ended up going to Daphne, she also meant to sell. It's why she's never carried out any repairs or maintenance. She doesn't see the point in throwing money at a place she doesn't even want.'

Glad she'd seen the house for herself, since it made this much easier to believe, Jay checked to see how much time they had left. 'Going back to Berzina—'

'If the DNA turns out to be his,' he cut in, 'does that change my position here? Will they let me go?'

Wishing she could tell him what he wanted to hear, she said, 'I can't promise anything at this stage, but if it is his, it will very likely make the CPS look at your charge again. We will certainly be pressing for that, and of course for your release, but I don't want us to get ahead of ourselves. We still have no evidence, apart from the exchange of phone calls, to say that there was actual contact between them . . .'

'It's him, I'm sure of it,' he declared. When he looked up, Jay could see once again how hard he was finding this, despite the certainty in his tone. 'I don't suppose detesting someone mattered to her much,' he added. 'Or maybe that's just what she told me, that she couldn't stand him, when the truth was . . . something else.'

As he stared at her across the table, Jay was reminded of Daphne's comment that she looked like Vanessa, and wondered if he thought so too. She didn't, at all, apart from the blonde hair.

He was still looking at her, and the moment seemed to

be going on for too long as his arresting eyes, curious and penetrating, made her insides flutter with . . . what? Nerves? Anticipation? She almost asked what he was thinking but wasn't entirely sure she wanted to know. Then, to her relief, the door opened and a guard informed them that time was up.

'Thanks for coming,' Blake said, getting to his feet. 'And thanks for everything you're doing.' He lifted a hand and for a moment she thought he was going to touch her, but he pulled it back and, not looking at her again, he walked on out of the room.

CHAPTER TWENTY-NINE

It was Friday afternoon when DI Ken Bright rang to let Jay know that Edmond Berzina's alibi for 29 April checked out. 'Several members of staff at the institute verified that he was there for most of the day, so he couldn't have met Vanessa Blake at Chippenham Station in the morning,' he told her.

'Did you ask where he was in the evening?' Jay ventured, knowing what a long shot it was, but it had to be taken.

'Of course, and his wife confirmed that he came home to their London flat around four thirty and they were there until he left for work again in the morning.'

'Do you trust the wife?'

'I have no reason not to, but I'm getting the feeling you don't.'

Waving Vikki in with a stack of files, she said, 'They're a complicated family, I'm sure you know that already, and to be honest, Ken, I don't know who to believe about anything. In fact, I'm starting to think that my client knows less about what happened that day than the rest of them, possibly including his own sister.' Her loyalty wasn't to Antonia, only to Edward.

'Care to elaborate?'

'Tell me first, have you established whether or not there was an affair between Vanessa and Berzina?'

'What he says is that they got together now and again, but it wasn't a regular thing.'

So, an affair. 'And why was he in touch with her the day before she died?'

'To ask when he could see her again, and she told him she'd let him know when she was next going to be in London.'

'So not the next day?'

'Apparently not.'

'If we believe him.'

'At the moment there's no reason not to.'

'OK, so we know that Vanessa Blake was a serial adulterer, and although her husband knew this, I'm starting to discover that there are things he didn't know.'

'Such as?'

Avoiding the question, she said, 'Have you discovered who the unidentified DNA belongs to yet?'

'No, I'm afraid not, but obviously we're working on it. However, I can tell you that someone has come forward to say she saw Vanessa Blake getting into a red car near the entrance of the station's back car park at the crucial time on Monday the twenty-ninth.'

Jay sat forward to grab a pen. 'And this someone is credible or you wouldn't be telling me, so who is it, and why are they only coming forward now?'

'She's an estate agent who works in Chippenham. No names at this stage, but she was going into the station at the time to catch a train to Gatwick.'

'So she's been on holiday since the sighting?'

'Sardinia, or was it Sicily, with a man who apparently is not her husband.'

'Christ, is no one faithful any more?'

Bypassing the comment, he said, 'She came back yesterday and contacted local police this morning after catching a news update last night. I went to have a chat with her early this afternoon.'

'Did she see who was driving the car?'

'She couldn't describe him, but was sure it was a man.'

'What kind of car?'

'A red one,' he deadpanned.

Jay blinked. 'Is that it?'

'It was until we showed her a few shots of red cars, and she thinks it was quite small like a Fiesta or an Opel, that sort of thing. Apparently, Vanessa Blake waved out to the driver who was in the vehicle behind our witness's as she drove into the car park, that's how she came to notice her.'

Jay sat with this for a moment, picturing the scene, while knowing that something else was niggling her. Then it came. 'Didn't your DPD driver say he saw a red car near Clover Hill Farm during the afternoon of the twenty-ninth?'

'You're right, he did, around five thirty. As you know, their journeys are timed to the minute so his information is good, even if his description of the vehicle isn't. We're waiting for him to come in and talk to us again, but you don't need me to remind you how many red cars there are on the road.'

'No, but this is the closest we have to a connection between the station and Clover Hill right now, so forgive me for being excited.'

He laughed. 'I'll let you know when we're ready to go and talk to your client to find out if he knows anyone with a red car.'

'Sure. We know that his own is black, Vanessa's is blue, and I can't say I've spotted a red car during any visits to family. What about the contacts list from her phone?'

'It's ongoing, but so far the alibis are checking out. Joe tells me that D2's number was ringing out when you had it, but that's not what we're getting now. The recording says it's temporarily disconnected, which, as you will know, means that either the bill hasn't been paid, or, if it's a pay-as-you-go, it's run out of minutes.'

'How soon will you know what kind of phone it is?'

'I expect to hear early next week.'

'OK. Well, thanks for the chat, much appreciated.'

'And very gracious of me, I'd say, given that husband of yours ran rings around me in court yesterday afternoon.'

Surprised, she said, 'Around *you*?'

'Let's just say I was not brought up to date regarding certain information before I took the stand. I ended up looking a right moron, but tell Tom I won't hold it against him.'

After ringing off with a smile, Jay quickly composed an email detailing the conversation and circulated it to the crime team, with a copy to Vikki. 'Can you arrange for me to visit Blake next week?' she asked, going through to the senior partner's reception.

Barely looking up from what she was doing, Vikki said, 'Will do. He rang while you were talking to Bright, but he didn't want to hold on.'

'Blake rang? Did he say what it was about?'

'Only that it wasn't urgent and he'll try again when he can.'

Disappointed to have missed him, Jay returned to her office. Rather than spend time considering the moments at the prison when she'd felt herself more drawn to Blake than perhaps she should, she got to work on more immediate cases. She barely looked up again before Tom rang just after five to ask if she wanted to meet him at the health club for a swim. 'My case finished early,' he explained, 'so I'm already at home. I can bring your bikini.'

She laughed. 'The black one-piece will do, thanks. I'll see you there about six thirty. Is Livvy with you? Do you know how her English exam went today?'

'She thinks OK. She's just gone over to Ollie and Jenn's – apparently Nat's home and he wants to see her.'

'Well that will have put her in a good mood, or a state of high agitation – and if I'd checked my texts,' she continued, taking her mobile from her top drawer, 'I'd know that she's been messaging me for the past hour and, shoot me now, I haven't responded. Such a bad mother.'

'The worst. I'm sure we'll hear all about it later. I'll see you at the club.'

Clicking off the line, Jay went back to the case she was studying, but her focus was no longer entirely there, having been snagged away by Tom and everything that came with him these days. However, she was determined not to get herself worked up, the way she had when she'd first found out about the child. What mattered was that she should do her best to keep the promise she'd made the other night to him, and to herself, that whatever they learned in the next week or so, she would stand by him.

Feeling disturbed by that, she switched her thinking to the unidentified DNA in Blake's case, although thoughts of Blake could be unsettling in their way too. She could handle them better though. Uppermost in her mind now was how upset he'd been when he'd learned that Vanessa had spoken to Berzina the day before she'd died. She felt a deepening sense of regret about having to confirm the next time they met, or spoke on the phone, that it really had been an affair. Although he was clearly no stranger to betrayal, it didn't mean it became any easier to bear, as she knew only too well. At least in her case she wasn't having to cope with all the added complications and heartache Blake was facing, plus she had work and friends to distract her, people to talk to who cared and wanted to lend support. Of course, Blake had his sister but, given Jay's unease about Antonia, he could be far more alone than perhaps even he realized.

'Are you developing a soft spot for this man?' Tom teased when they were at home after their swim. 'You talk about him quite fondly.'

Leaping to the defensive, she said, 'Why do you have to try and turn it into something it isn't? I'm simply saying that he trusts his sister, and if she does let him down he'll have no one. At least in my case I have friends, my job, my children . . .'

'Why are you comparing yourself with him? Your circumstances are entirely different, the fact that I'm not dead being a major case in point.'

'It's not a comparison, it's compassion. I can empathize with his situation because I know what it's like to be betrayed. I'm sorry, I know you don't want to hear that, but it's a truth that we both have to live with.'

Not arguing with that, he poured them both a drink and handed one to her.

'I take it,' she said, 'you haven't heard anything about the DNA results?'

He shook his head, staring down at his wine.

'She should have them by now. So we have to wonder if she's deliberately holding back – and the only reason she'd do that, presumably, is because she doesn't want to admit he's not yours?'

His expression showed how much he hoped she was right, but what little faith he actually had that she was.

'You need to call her,' she stated. 'Or no, why don't I? Maybe it's time she and I had a talk?'

He shook his head.

'Why not? This is affecting my life as much as it is yours, and she should be reminded of that.'

'You don't want to speak to her,' he told her, making it sound almost like a warning.

'What do you mean? I've just said I do. Or are you afraid she'll tell me something I'd rather not hear? I think we're past that stage, don't you? You've had an affair, you have a baby together, what more could there possibly be?'

He only stared at her, his expression unreadable, but she knew him too well. There *was* more, and the shock of it made her take a step back. 'What is it?' she asked shakily.

'I don't know what you're talking about.'

'Yes you do. You're keeping something from me. Do you already know the results? Is that it?'

'You know I'd tell you if I did. Look, I'll call her tomorrow, OK? And if she still hasn't heard anything, I'll chase up the labs myself.'

Though hardly satisfied with his answer, she decided that rather than get into yet another futile row that would leave them both upset and drained and no further forward, she'd accept it for now. However, she remained shaken by her suspicion that she still didn't have the full story of what was going on with Ellen Tyler. So, if he didn't have any news by the end of the week, she was going to track down the woman's number and find out for herself what was really going on.

CHAPTER THIRTY

Jay could see how upset Blake was, in spite of how hard he was attempting to hide it behind a sardonic, self-mocking sort of smile. It was an expression that was supposed to make him seem vaguely past caring, when he clearly wasn't feeling even close to it.

'I'm glad you were the one to tell me,' he said, glancing down at his hands, flat on the table. 'I can't think why it's hit me like this. It's not as if I wasn't expecting it. I mean, once you told me Berzina's number was in her phone, it was the only logical conclusion, that they were . . . involved.' He took a moment to steady his voice. 'What gets me, I suppose, is the fact that she couldn't stand him. He was too smooth, too flash for her taste, far too pleased with himself. And yet . . . Here we are.' His eyes came to hers. 'I guess it's too soon to know if the unidentified DNA belongs to him?'

'It is,' she confirmed. And added, 'But I'm afraid he has an alibi for Monday the twenty-ninth. At least for during the day, so he couldn't have met Vanessa at the station. However, someone has come forward to say they saw Vanessa getting into a red car outside the station's back car park just after you dropped her.'

His attention visibly sharpened as he took this in.

'Do you know anyone who has a red car?' she asked. 'OK, I realize hundreds of people do, but . . .'

He took a while to begin shaking his head. 'No one's coming to mind,' he said.

'What kind of car does Berzina drive?'

With no little irony, he said, 'The last I heard it was a Ferrari, and it could be red, but I don't know if it is.'

'The car the witness saw was apparently "like a Fiesta". I don't think she'd have described a Ferrari that way, even though she doesn't know anything about cars.'

With a laconic smile, he said, 'No, I don't think anyone would make that sort of mix-up.' He was regarding her more intently now, his eyes quizzical, almost assessing, though not in a critical way. It was hard to read his expression, but she felt the sense of unformed words between them – empathy, compassion, understanding – exhaling on their silent breath. She was unsettled by it and entranced. In the end he surprised her as he said, 'I'm sorry you know what betrayal feels like.'

As her heart contracted she felt her defences rise. They weren't here to talk about her, and she really didn't want to, but nor did she want to throw his kindness back in his face.

'Your husband's a barrister, isn't he?' he asked.

'Yes, he is.'

'Was it him who let you down?'

'We're – we're getting through it.'

'That's good.' Then seeming to register how tense she was, he said, 'I'm sorry, I didn't mean to pry.'

'It's fine.' She added with a smile, 'I can hardly object when you're being forced to expose so much of your life to me, but there again I am your lawyer, which makes a difference.'

He nodded agreement, but he was no longer looking at her, was simply staring to one side, seeing only he knew what in his mind's eye. 'So what's the next step?' he asked after a moment.

Glancing at her notes, she said, 'We wait for the DNA results.' How richly ironic that both her professional and personal lives were caught up in the same need for answers. 'The police are still interviewing Vanessa's family, and the contact listed as D2 has yet to be traced. It looks as though his phone – I'm presuming it's a he – has been turned off or thrown away.'

He nodded, apparently unsurprised. 'And who would do that if they didn't have something to hide?'

'Precisely.'

'D2,' he murmured. 'D2 because there's a D1? And D1 is . . . ?'

She checked her notes. 'D1 is Darren Gibbs.'

'Ah yes, one of my site managers. A nice bloke, bit rough and ready, swears a lot, but maybe she liked that and I never knew.' He sounded as dismayed with himself for not knowing as he presumably felt towards his wife for becoming the person she did. 'I wonder where it happened?' he said, once again seeming lost in his own mind.

'Do you really want to know?' she asked softly.

After a moment he shook his head. 'Probably not.' Then, 'Did you want details, when it happened to you?' Before she could reply he said, 'Sorry, I shouldn't have asked that . . .'

'No, I didn't want to know,' she told him. 'I thought it would eat me up if I did, but I've no idea if it was the right thing to do.'

His eyes came to hers. 'Did you ever meet her? Or see them together?'

She shook her head.

'How long did it go on for?'

'Quite a while.' Starting to feel uncomfortable now, she said, 'I think we should go back to talking about you.'

'Yes, of course. Sorry. The answer's no, I don't know anyone with a red car, although . . .' He stopped and started to frown.

She waited.

'Actually, there was one,' he said. 'I'm sure of it. I just can't quite . . .' His frown deepened as he delved into his memory. 'Who have I seen driving a red car who didn't normally drive one?' he asked himself.

In the end he regarded her helplessly. 'Something's there on the periphery. I'll keep thinking about it, and if I remember, I'll give you a call.'

Sliding another pre-paid phone card across the table she said, 'I'd like to hear from you, and please don't worry about the time.' She quickly added, 'I know DI Bright's coming tomorrow so . . .'

'Won't you be here?'

'My colleague Ash Baqri is going to stand in for me. There's a hearing I have to attend at the youth court.' She didn't elaborate; he knew she had other clients and she never felt it necessary to remind someone that they might not always come first.

CHAPTER THIRTY-ONE

Jay was walking back from the youth court hearing the following day when Tom rang. 'I thought you were in conference all day,' she said, easing her heavy bag on to one shoulder.

'I've just stepped out.'

'Why? Everything's all right, is it?'

'I got an email from the Tylers a few minutes ago, so I'm calling to let you know that the child is definitely mine.'

She stopped walking and found herself, ludicrously, wanting to cry, or shout, right there in the middle of Broad Street. Why was she so upset when she'd expected exactly this? She knew her hope had been delusional, so why did it feel like such a blow to have it crushed?

'Are you still there?' he asked.

Forcing a smile as a judge she knew swept past, she said, 'You could have chosen a better time to tell me.'

'Where are you?'

'What does it matter now?'

'Jay, there was never going to be a right time—'

'You could have done it at home, for God's sake. It's the middle of the working day . . .'

'I'm sorry. How about I duck out of this meeting and come to find you?'

'No! I have a full schedule and this is *not* going to get in the way of it. We can talk later, at home,' and ending the call she stuffed the phone back in her pocket and walked on.

Her head was spinning, her heart racing, as she began to realize she wasn't as ready to stand by him as she'd tried to persuade herself she was. She hated him for this, wanted to lash out and make him pay in some way that wasn't going to hurt her just as much as him. But how? What could she possibly do to make him realize just how deeply she despised him for this?

Taking a steadying breath as she neared the office, she tried reminding herself that she was only hurting herself right now, and that in fact nothing had actually changed. They were still in the same place they'd been an hour ago, albeit without the shred of uncertainty. She needed to calm down, back away from the flare of anger that was making her irrational and vengeful. She wasn't that kind of person, not deep down. She was someone who could handle this, approach it in a judicious and constructive manner, and she'd be ready to do exactly that by the time she got home this evening.

Fortunately, it wasn't so difficult to distract herself once she reached the office, for the usual stack of messages was waiting, along with updates of ongoing cases that required urgent attention. Perry needed five minutes of her time, and as soon as he'd gone Jilly, the officer manager, grabbed her chance. Before Jay knew it, Ash was at her door ready to report back on that morning's prison visit with Blake, which apparently hadn't gone the way she'd thought it would.

Eager to know more, she took the coffee Ash had

brought her and waved him to a chair. 'So what exactly bothered you about it?' she asked worriedly.

'Well, for one thing he was kind of cagey with Ken Bright,' Ash replied. 'Polite, attentive, but I could tell he was . . . I don't know if he was holding back, or just not fully engaging, but something was going on with him.'

'So what *did* he say?'

'That he thought he knew someone who drove a red car, but then he remembered they'd sold it a while ago.'

'And that's . . . odd, because?'

'I guess because of the way he said it. It was like he wasn't believing himself, or he'd only just thought of it . . . Listen, you know the guy better than I do, you might have read him better. I'm just saying something was off-kilter, so I hung back after Bright left hoping to get more, but all he said was that he needed to speak to you.'

'So is he going to ring me?'

'I believe so. Anyway, I've written it up, so you'll have a fuller picture of how the interview went.'

'OK, thanks.'

Picking up her coffee, she followed him out to the partner's reception and asked Vikki to put Blake straight through if he called. 'And book me a visit to the prison as soon as,' she added.

It was past six thirty, and everyone else had gone home for the day by the time she began preparing to leave the office herself. There had been no word from Tom, which didn't really surprise her, but there had been nothing from Blake either. Although there could be many reasons for that, she was still worried, and so decided to call Antonia to find out if she'd heard from him today.

Before she could get to the number, Antonia rang her.

'Hi, I hope this is a convenient moment,' Antonia said, sounding slightly breathless, maybe harried. 'I wasn't sure whether to call you, but John said I should. It's this business about a red car. We saw it on the news last night and I'm not going to the prison again until next Friday. Will you be there before that?'

Jay opened her calendar and found the entry Vikki had made for her next visit to Blake and said, 'I'm due to go on Tuesday. Can you tell me what about the red car?'

'Ed and I spoke yesterday and I . . . I think I misled him . . . I told him something that I probably shouldn't have . . . I mean, he already knew . . .'

'You're not making much sense, Antonia.'

'Sorry, I . . . The thing is, we got cut off and he hasn't called back, so when you see him, or if you speak to him before I do, please will you tell him that I got it wrong and I'm sorry.' She stopped as someone spoke to her at the other end. 'Yes, yes,' she said to her husband. 'I'm just about to.' To Jay she said, 'Freya drives a red car. It's an Audi hatchback.'

Sitting back in her chair, Jay said, 'Let me get this straight. Are you saying you think Vanessa met *Freya* at the station in the morning?'

'I-I don't know. She could have. Or maybe Edmond was driving her car?'

'He has an alibi for that time.'

'Oh, I see.' She turned from the phone and spoke to her husband again. 'John is asking if you can tell Ed what I've just told you, about Freya, and if you hear from him first, will you let us know?'

Jay didn't get the chance to respond before Antonia said, 'I need to ring off now, but please will you also tell

Ed that I'm sorry and I'd really appreciate it if he'd ring as soon as he can.'

After the call ended, Jay sat mulling it over for a few minutes before trying Ken Bright's number, keen to know if the DPD driver had been able to recall the make of the red car he'd seen near Clover Hill. No matter how unlikely it was to be Freya's, she wasn't going to rule it out until she knew for certain that it wasn't.

Bright's phone went to voicemail so she left a message for him to call when he could.

'Still here?' Perry said, appearing in the doorway with a gin and tonic in hand.

'It would seem so, and I could do with one of those.'

'Then come this way, fair lady.'

Following him into his office, she said, 'I've just had the strangest conversation with Edward Blake's sister.'

'You mean your guy who's up for murdering his wife?'

'Mm. There's some odd business going on in that family,' she commented, watching him drop ice cubes into a glass as she tried to fathom the possibility of Freya meeting Vanessa and . . . Berzina joining them later? It was the only scenario that worked based on what they knew right now.

'Want to talk it through?' he offered. 'I've got an hour before Gretchen turns up. We're going to the theatre, but don't ask what we're seeing, I can't remember.'

With a smile, Jay took the drink he was offering and went to sink down on his sofa. 'Actually,' she said, stretching out her legs, 'I think I'm going to park it for this evening, because there's something else I have to deal with of a more personal nature.'

'Oh?'

'Tom rang earlier. Apparently the child's definitely his.'

'Ah, I see. Not good news, but you were—'

'Expecting it, yes. I just . . . We couldn't help hoping . . . You know how it goes. Anyway, it hit me harder than I imagined it would. I guess because it's real now, and we have to decide how we're going to deal with it.'

'Which you might have a better idea of if you knew what they're expecting of him?'

She nodded and sipped her drink. 'He didn't say whether there was any mention of it in the email he received. I guess I'll find out when I get home.' She looked at Perry helplessly. 'What am I supposed to do? What's the *right* thing to do? I keep telling myself I can't let it ruin my marriage, that what Tom and I have is strong enough to cope with this, but is it, really?'

Holding her gaze, he said, 'I guess only you know the answer to that, but let me ask you a question: what has he told you about the child? Apart from his name and who his mother is?'

Feeling her insides clench with nerves, she said, 'Nothing really, but I'm certain there's something he's not telling me.'

He nodded. 'There is, and you need to make him tell you what it is.'

Trying not to be panicked by that, she said, 'Perry, you can't do this. Please . . .'

His hand went up. 'I'm sorry, it's not my place to go into it, but I will if he doesn't tell you himself. So speak to him, let him know that we've had this conversation . . .'

She put her drink down and got to her feet. 'I'll be in touch,' she told him, already heading for the door. 'And thanks. At least I know now that it wasn't my imagination.'

CHAPTER THIRTY-TWO

As Jay let herself into the house she almost collided with Livvy on her way out.

'Hey Mum! Jazz dance class, then I'm popping over to Gemma's. I told Dad not to worry about food for me, I'll grab a sandwich or something when I get back. Expecting a call from Nat later! Bye!'

Smiling at the happy sparkle in her eyes, Jay watched her go before checking to see who was calling her mobile. Her heart tripped when she saw the ID. Of all the times for him to call, this had to be the worst, and yet maybe it was the best. Certainly she'd rather be speaking to him than her husband.

Clicking on, she said, 'Jay Wells speaking.'

'It's Edward Blake. Did your colleague give you the message that I need to talk to you?'

'Yes, he did. So what's going on?'

'I think it's best if we do this in person. Do you have another visit booked?'

'For next Tuesday, but—'

'That's good. I'm sorry this is seeming so . . . screwed up. I think it is, but I need to talk it through and you're the only person I'm sure I can trust.'

'What about your sister?'

'Not her this time . . .' He broke off and started again.

'She's not coming until Friday and I'd like to delay it so I can see you first.'

'OK. She rang me about an hour ago and wants me to tell you that she got it wrong and she's sorry. Would you care to enlighten me?'

He fell silent, though she could hear him breathing, along with the sound of male voices in the background as other inmates made their calls.

In the end, she said, 'She also told me that Freya has a red Audi.'

There was a beat before he said, 'Do you know if it was her car that was seen?'

'I don't. I've left a message for DI Bright to call me. You realize, if Freya has anything to do with this . . . Do you think she has?'

'I don't know, Jay. I hardly know what to think. All I can tell you is that we need to talk. OK, OK,' he said to someone over his shoulder. Then, 'I'm sorry, I'm being hassled here, I'll have to go. I'll see you on Tuesday,' and the line went dead.

Pocketing her phone, she freed her hair from its usual band and allowed herself a few moments to put aside the call with Blake, before going through to the kitchen to face whatever the heck was coming next.

She found Tom listening to one of his albums – Chicago, she thought – while getting a meal under way. She was surprised, even slightly annoyed, that he could appear so relaxed when he surely wasn't.

'Hey,' he said, looking up as she came in, 'are you hungry? I thought I'd make this . . .'

'I'd rather have one of those,' she said, pointing to his glass of red wine.

Taking down another glass, he filled it halfway, while she went to his turntable and removed the needle from the record.

'Have you spoken to Perry in the last half an hour?' she asked, suspecting Perry might have called to give him a heads-up.

His expression told her that he hadn't, but was probably aware of why she'd asked.

'He told me, before I left the office,' she said, 'that you've been holding something back from me. I knew it, of course, I even challenged you on it, but you denied it. So now I'd like you to tell me what it is.' She was biting out the words, leaving him in no doubt that she was going to tolerate nothing less than the truth.

He stared at her hard, his expression unreadable, but she could tell he was worried. 'We should probably sit down,' he advised, gesturing to the breakfast table.

With a coolness that belied how tense, even fearful, she was, she pulled out a chair as he went to turn off whatever he had cooking.

'Damn it,' he muttered, as something spilled.

She gazed out at the garden where the last of the apple and cherry blossoms were floating gently to the ground. For some reason it made her think of Clover Hill Farm, and how the blossom was probably falling there too, all around an empty house that was in darkness and silence, witness to so much and unable to tell its secrets. This house would be like that one day. All this with Tom would be history, long forgotten, no longer mattering to those who lived here . . .

'I'm not quite sure what to start with,' he confessed, as he came to sit down. 'Perhaps the email . . . Maybe you should read it.'

'Just tell me what it says.'

Continuing to scroll to it, he said, 'It seems they – Ellen and Jed, her husband – would like me to get to know Aiden so that there is no doubt in his mind, as he grows up, who his father is.'

She said nothing, simply waited for him to continue.

'He'll carry on living with them,' he said, 'and Jed will treat him like a son, but he, Jed, is keen for me to see Aiden as often as I can, and perhaps to let him come here from time to time to spend—'

'Just a minute,' she interrupted, 'why does *Jed* get to call the shots? If he's not even the father . . . I'm sorry, I'm not following this.'

'I'm just telling you what's in the email. I haven't agreed to anything; obviously I wanted to discuss it with you first.'

'So you want to discuss how we're going to be babysitters for them when it suits them? And how all our plans to travel more once both children have gone will have to be put on hold while we play a part in bringing up *your* child, the one that I'm not even sure I really want to get to know.'

'Jay, he's—'

'Not to blame, of course he isn't, and I've been trying to get to a place where I can accept him into our family, because that's essentially what you'll be asking if you agree to go along with this. And we more or less knew they would. But have you thought about what you're going to tell Charlie and Livvy? How do you imagine they're going to feel when they find out you didn't only cheat on me, but you made your mistress pregnant and now you want to bring your new son into our lives?'

His face was pale, she could almost feel him flinching at her words. 'It's something I'll have to deal with,' he said, 'but obviously I know it's down to me to tell them.'

'Yes it is, and I'm not even sure I want to be around when you do.'

Proving he'd already thought about it, he said, 'That has to be your decision, but I think they'll find it easier if you are.'

Suspecting that was true she didn't argue, simply stared at her wine knowing she was too wound up to take a sip even if she tried. Eventually, feeling the question building like a quiet explosion, she said, 'So what are you holding back from me? We both know there's something and now I want you to tell me what it is.'

His face was taut and pale as he went back to his phone. 'Maybe, if you see a picture of him,' he said, apparently trying to find one.

She felt herself resisting so hard that every muscle hurt. Why should she look at him? What difference could it possibly make to anything . . . unless he was trying to melt her heart with shots of a cute little toddler. At any other time that might work, but he surely had to know . . . Or was there something wrong with the child? He had some kind of illness or deformity, and if he did . . . What the heck was she going to do then?

He held his mobile out to her.

Feeling ambushed, while knowing there wasn't any way in the world she could even think about rejecting a sick or disabled child, she forced herself to look at the photo.

It took a moment for her to register the image. It was so different to what she'd tried to prepare herself for that she wondered for a dizzying moment if he'd got the photos mixed up.

There was nothing wrong with this child, or not that she could see, only that he was . . .

She looked at him, turning cold to her core as the horrible realization dawned. 'He's just a baby,' she said hoarsely.

He didn't disagree. How could he when it was obvious?

'Oh my God.' She dropped the phone and pressed her hands to her cheeks. 'I assumed he was two years old or more, but he's . . . What is he? Three months?'

'Four,' he admitted.

So the betrayal hadn't only been three years ago, it had happened again, more recently, and as a result . . .

She had a sudden urge to seize everything she could lay her hands on and hurl it at him, to see it crashing against his head, making him wince and bleed and throw up his hands to protect himself. She wouldn't stop until there was nothing left to smash, until everything was ruined, irreparable, the way their marriage was now.

But this was her home, and destroying it to hurt him would only satisfy a moment. It wouldn't change anything. The child, the second betrayal, the fact that he had an attachment to the woman that had taken him back to her in spite of everything, would still be real.

She got to her feet.

He stood too. 'Jay, listen, I—'

'Don't touch me,' she seethed, snatching her hands away. 'All this time that I've been trying to forgive you, to put it behind us, to persuade myself that I must save our marriage . . . *Jesus Christ*,' she choked, clasping her hands to her head. 'What the fuck is the matter with me that I thought I should believe in you, that I should do everything I could to get us through this, that it was *my responsibility* to keep our family together? What kind of bloody idiot am I that I even stayed with you after the first time? You didn't give her up at all, did you? You've been screwing her all this time, lying to me—'

'Of course it ended after the first time. I didn't see her again . . .'

'Until *this!*' she spat, gesturing to the phone. 'You went back to her . . .'

'It happened once . . .'

'And I'm supposed to believe that? Why the hell would I ever believe anything you say again? You disgust me, do you know that? You didn't even have the courage to tell me how old he is until you couldn't avoid it.'

'If he'd turned out not to be mine there would have been no need to.'

Her lip curled in contempt. 'So you'd have carried on with the lie, never admitting that you'd seen her again . . . How did it happen? Was it you who called her?'

'No! I-I ran into her at a function. I swear I had no idea she was going to be there, it didn't even cross my mind . . .'

'But she was there, and when you saw her *what?* We know you couldn't resist her. So was it your idea to sleep with her that night?'

'It wasn't something—'

'Did it happen that night?'

He swallowed as he nodded.

'And again after?'

He hesitated and, realizing he was about to lie, she drew back a hand and slammed it into his face. It wasn't enough, she wanted to hit him again and again, to pummel her fists into him so hard that he bled, but he quickly grabbed her wrists and clutched them to his chest.

She was breathing heavily, raggedly, and so was he.

'How many times?' she growled. 'I want to know and *don't lie.*'

'OK, it was three, maybe four.'

'And who broke it off? And don't lie about that either.'

'I did.'

'Why?'

'Why do you think? I didn't *want* to cheat on you . . .'

'But you couldn't help yourself. She has something over you, something you were willing to risk your marriage for . . .'

'That's not how I saw it.'

'Well what a pity, because it's what it's costing you.'

'Jay, it wasn't important. It—'

'*Stop lying!*'

'I'm not.'

'You said just now it only happened once, but apparently it was three or four times.'

'Once is all it would have taken to make a child.'

'Jesus Christ!' she seethed, snatching her hands away. 'I can't believe you just said that. What the hell is the matter with you? You lie, you cheat, you treat me like a fool . . . You're not the man I know. I can't even look at you any more.'

'Jay, don't walk away. I know I've handled this badly . . .'

Slamming the door behind her, she ran upstairs, knowing he'd think she was going to shut herself in the bedroom. Instead she quickly packed an overnight bag and carried it and her briefcase out to the car.

'Jay!' he called from the front door. 'Where the hell are you going?'

Ignoring him she got into the car, but before she could close the door he was there.

Desperately he cried, 'Livvy will want to know where you are. Please don't do this to her tonight. You know she has an exam tomorrow.'

'Tell her to call me,' she said icily, and grabbing the door she tugged it closed as she started the engine. Right now, in this minute, she had no idea where she was going, but she'd figure it out, just as long as it got her a long way from him.

CHAPTER THIRTY-THREE

Half an hour later, Jay was parked in a layby at the side of the Downs not so very far from home. The last thing she'd wanted was to harm someone, or herself, because she couldn't keep her mind on the road, so she'd had to come to a stop. She needed to be still to think, to decide what she was going to do, not for the long term, that would come later, but for tonight.

She couldn't, wouldn't return home. Even to think of Tom worsened the conflict inside her – fury, dread, the need to hurt him and hold onto him; the love that was laced through with bitter contempt. That he'd gone back to the woman after all they'd been through three years ago felt even more shattering than knowing they had a child. Didn't it? She wasn't sure about that, couldn't think clearly enough to be sure of much. She only knew with an instinct sharper than the hurt itself that nothing would ever be the same between them again.

She desperately didn't want to unleash the sobs that were building inside her, but tears were already rolling from her eyes. She covered her face with her hands and shouted, raged into them, howling with despair for all that they were going to lose. Everything that had gone before would now be tainted by this, and so would the future. It was what betrayal did. It wasn't an injury that could heal with no scars, no memories of the pain, no fear of it coming back. It was a monster, a ghost, that never went away. And now it was back at the centre of her marriage, pushing her and Tom apart, widening the gulf between them that already felt unbridgeable.

On the seat beside her the phone rang, and rang. Each time it was him.

If it weren't for Livvy she'd have turned it off, but she was not going to stop being a mother, even if she no longer considered herself a wife.

Text messages arrived, all from him, pleading with her to answer her phone.

Ken Bright called, but she couldn't face speaking to him now either – until suddenly she could and quickly clicked on. 'Jay Wells,' she said, aware of how nasal her voice was.

'Are you OK?' he asked. 'You sound as though you're going down with something?'

'Oh, just one of those twenty-four hour things. Thanks for getting back to me.' Why had she asked him to call? She needed to think, to focus. 'I was wondering,' she said, playing for time until it came to her. Then it was there. 'Did your DPD driver remember what sort of car it was?'

'As a matter of fact he felt sure it was an Audi A1 hatchback. No recall of number plate or driver. Why? Ringing some bells for you?'

Momentarily unsure of what she should be telling him, she said, 'It might. I need to do some more digging, but I think we could have a lead.' She'd need to hand over to him for questioning once she had a clearer picture, but only when she was certain of how it was going to impact her client.

'OK. You'll have my full attention when you're ready. Take care of that cold now.'

'I will,' she promised, and rang off.

She took a breath, and another. The short conversation seemed to have grounded her a little, at least enough to make her realize she needed to decide where she was going to spend the night. There were plenty of friends who'd willingly put her up, but as desperately as she wanted to talk to Jenn or Gretchen right now, she also felt the need to be alone.

Starting the engine, she turned on the headlights and indicated to pull out onto the road. At the next junction, she swung the car around and headed back towards town while using the handsfree to check herself into the Hotel du Vin. There was another, newer one, overlooking the Avon Gorge, but the original was close to the office and was also further from home.

Twenty minutes later she was signing in, and crossing the bar to the lift – no one around to recognize her, thank goodness. Her room was on the second floor, no number, just the name Château Latour.

As she dropped her bags on a sofa, she looked across to the bed – large, dominant, with a thick mattress and set on a wooden platform – and instead of feeling the awfulness of being alone, or of the reason why she was here, she allowed herself to be reminded of the master bed at Edward Blake's house. No posts, no anything to tie a person to, just a grand sleeping platform with plain covers and large pillows propped against the wall.

For a moment she felt an insistent need to talk to him, to hear his voice deep with concern, even to feel his arms around her as he understood and shared her pain.

As if he didn't have enough to worry about, why on

303

earth would he want to help her? And it wasn't what she wanted; she just wasn't able to think straight.

Going to the fridge, she poured herself a glass of sparkling water and checked her phone as it rang, expecting it to be Tom again.

Perry.

Clicking on she said, 'Hi. I'm guessing Tom's asked you to try and find me.'

'He has. Are you OK?'

'No, but better here than with him.'

'Where's here?'

'If I tell you, I don't want . . .'

'I won't tell him. I just need to know you're safe and why you didn't come to us?'

'You were at the theatre, and actually, I think I should have some time to myself tonight. I've got a lot to try and get straight in my mind. Have you told Gretchen how old the child is?'

'I have now. She wants me to come and get you, wherever you are.'

'I'm at the Hotel du Vin, the one near the office. Please don't come. I'm fine.'

'OK, but I'll have to tell Tom I've spoken to you. He's pretty wound up, says he didn't handle it well.'

'No he didn't, but I can't imagine what the right way would be.' Her voice faltered and she closed her eyes as she tried to block a rush of tears. Why was she defending him? 'Sorry. Tired and emotional.'

'Jay . . .'

'Tell him I'm safe, and that even if he tracks my phone I still won't see him. Actually, he won't do that, he doesn't know how to.'

'Livvy will.'

Realizing that was true, and suddenly struck by the dread that he might end up blurting something out to Livvy about the child tonight, she said, 'I'll call him myself and see you tomorrow – unless you're out all day?'

'Most of it, but let's try to catch up in the evening. If you still don't feel like going home it would be great if you'd agree to come and stay. I don't like thinking of you on your own in a hotel.'

'I'm OK, really, but thanks for the offer.'

After ringing off she drained the glass of water, refilled it, and began to pace as she connected to Tom.

'Thank God,' he said as he answered. 'I've been going out of my mind. Where are you?'

'Is Livvy home yet?'

'She's just come in. Jay, I—'

'Please don't lay your guilty conscience on her tonight. She doesn't need to find out that way, especially with her exam—'

'I'm not a total fool,' he snapped. 'But she'll want to know where you are. What do you—'

'Tell her to call me.'

'OK, but when are you coming home?'

'I'm not sure yet. Not tonight, anyway,' and ending the call she sat down on the bed feeling breathless and disoriented and shaken through to her core. It was easy to picture him at home now, angry, restless, guilty, frustration spilling over – he hated not being in control. She didn't feel sorry for him, or affected in any way by his suffering. She was too wired, or maybe too exhausted to have any feelings for him at all.

When Livvy rang a few minutes later, Jay was unpacking

her toiletries and managed to sound reasonably upbeat as she said, 'Sorry, darling, I wasn't supposed to be on call tonight, but Sallyanne's had an emergency, so I've had to come and sort out an arrest.'

'Oh that's bad luck. What time will you be back?'

'I've no idea how long it's going to take, we're waiting for an interpreter at the moment.' How easy it was to reinstate a situation from a few weeks ago that had taken half the night; how wretched she felt about lying to her daughter, but it was for the best right now.

Not sounding too worried, or even very ready for a phone chat, Livvy said, 'Any idea what's wrong with Dad? He practically bit my head off when I came in just now. I suppose he's got a difficult case tomorrow, or something. Anyway, I'm in my room and I'm staying here until I leave in the morning. I won't wake you up if you're still in bed when I go.'

'Thanks.' Would she notice that her mother's car wasn't there? 'How are you feeling about your exam tomorrow?'

'OK, I think. We'll see. I'm going to ring off now, Nat's supposed to be calling in a minute. No, we're not an item yet, but he's broken up with his girlfriend, so hey, watch this space. Love you.'

'Love you too.'

Deciding it was OK to turn her phone off now, she fished a charger from her briefcase before setting up her laptop. She was still too strung out to sleep, in fact too close to the edge for very much, even food. However, rather than torment herself with trying to foresee the future and how she wanted to shape it, she decided it would be far more productive to try and lose herself in some work.

306

It kept her going for a while, in fact longer than she realized when she next looked at the time, although somewhere along the way her Internet searches had segued into a wander through Facebook. This was something she hadn't done the last time he'd betrayed her, afraid if she did she might start obsessing, even stalking the woman, but now she was there, on Ellen Tyler's page, staring at a profile picture of the woman herself.

So this was who her husband couldn't resist; who apparently meant so much to him that he'd gone back to her, despite knowing how devastating it would be for his wife if she found out. How likely it would be to destroy his marriage.

She was nothing like Jay had imagined her. In fact, she'd never have considered her Tom's type at all, for in many ways she was everything Jay wasn't – plump faced with dark curly hair, freckled complexion, small mouth, large glasses – but what stood out most of all for Jay was her age. *Twenty-nine.* Sixteen years younger than Jay; eighteen younger than Tom.

Jay continued to stare at the girl/woman, understanding now that the true reason she'd never wanted to see her was because she'd felt certain she would understand what Tom saw in her. She truly hadn't expected it to be youth – except she knew Tom, it would have to be more than that. But what more? What had made her so irresistible to him that he hadn't been able to fight it?

In other photos on the page Ellen Tyler looked lively, full of fun, someone who apparently enjoyed nights out with the girls. And food. There were lots of shots of canapés, exotic dishes, artful desserts, which made sense given her role as PR for a catering company.

There were shots of Jed Tyler too – tall, rangy, bearded, and a keen yachtsman it seemed.

No shots of the baby. Nothing about a pregnancy or a birth, but the last post had been eight months ago.

Closing down the screen she went to sit on the sofa, hugged her knees to her chest and focused her eyes on nothing as she tried to work out why a young Ellen Tyler felt so much more of a threat than a sophisticated older one. Would it make more sense if the girl/woman was beautiful? She disliked herself even for thinking it, not wanting to accept that she was so fixated on the way someone looked, so influenced by it that she evaluated their worth based on it? She'd never been aware of such a flaw in her character before, and actually it wasn't true. She only had to recall various men – and women – she'd felt drawn to over the years to know that looks had not played a part in whatever had made her like or admire them. Or even, in the case of some men, fantasize about them so explicitly she'd almost blushed the next time she saw them.

Yes, she was as capable as Tom of finding someone else attractive; it was just that, unlike him, she'd never acted on it.

So no, she didn't fear Ellen Tyler because she lacked obvious beauty, it wasn't even the fact that she was so much younger that was troubling her right now, although she was still shocked by it. It was the dawning, chilling realization that tonight really was the beginning of the end of her marriage.

CHAPTER THIRTY-FOUR

'I want you to go.'

Tom's eyes widened with disbelief as he stared back at her. 'What?' he blurted.

Jay's tone remained tight but calm as she said, 'I want you to leave this house.'

He continued to regard her almost as if she'd gone mad. 'I'm not going anywhere,' he told her tersely. 'This is my home – *our* home – and this isn't the way we're going to sort things out.'

'I'm afraid *you* don't get to decide how we sort things out.'

'OK, it's something we have to do together, but trying to force me out is just going to make things even more difficult than they already are.'

'Are you out of your mind—?'

'Jay, for God's sake . . . !'

She turned sharply away. This shouldn't be a showdown, or slanging match, it needed to happen in a reasonable way – or as reasonable as the nature of it allowed. And had she really expected him to say, *Fine, I'll go and start packing?* How would she have felt if he had? Even worse than she did now, probably, which was hard to imagine.

It was Sunday afternoon. She'd arrived a few minutes ago, having checked first that Livvy was out and that he was at home alone. Being in celebratory mood now that exams were over, Livvy had spent the last two nights partying hard and crashing out on floors around town, so wasn't aware that her mother had failed to return since Thursday. For her part, Jay, after spending a second night at the Hotel du Vin, had gone to stay with Perry and Gretchen on Saturday, wanting to talk over her decision with them before acting on it. Hearing herself say it out loud, that she wanted him to go, hard as it had been, had helped to get everything clear in her mind before she'd come to confront him.

But this was the trouble with rehearsing one side of a script, there was no knowing what the other person might say in response.

'I looked at her Facebook page,' she stated coldly. 'I hadn't realized she was so *young*.'

The colour deepened around his neck as he continued to eye her warily.

'So we're to become a cliché. Older man falls for—'

'We're not *becoming* anything,' he cut in sharply. 'I've already told you I want us to discuss this, to find a way . . .'

'To sort things out, yes you said, but you see there's nothing to sort out. At least not for me. The child's yours, not mine. I don't want him in my life, and I know that you won't be able to turn your back on him. I'd think even less of you if you could. So as far as I can see, the only decision you have to make is where you are going to live while you get used to becoming a father all over again.'

Clearly struggling with his anger, he said, 'I will be living here. As I said a moment ago, this is my home . . .'

Struggling to hold on to her temper, she said, 'You

forfeited your right to live here with me and the children the day you chose to betray us with Ellen Tyler. My only regret is not asking you to leave the first time it happened. I'm not asking now, I'm informing you that I am prepared to take action to remove you—'

'Jay, for God's sake. This is me you're talking to. We haven't even discussed this.'

'Your decision to have an affair was taken unilaterally. Mine to end our marriage has been arrived at the same way. So please start looking for alternative accommodation – there's always the flat above your chambers, if it's free. Or, if you prefer our break-up to be less conspicuous . . .'

'I am not accepting a break-up however it comes. It's not what I want, I've never—'

'I don't care what *you* want, Tom. This is *my* decision. I'm not saying you have to go now, today, but when we talk to Charlie and Livvy to tell them about your four-month old baby with another woman, I will expect you to be ready to leave.'

The words clearly hit their mark, she could see it in the way he blanched, but he was unmoving in his refusal to go. 'It's not going to happen,' he told her.

'Yes it is, so please try to get used to it.' She started to turn away, wanting to get away from him before rage got the better of her again. The fight on Thursday night had left her in pieces, she didn't want it happening again.

'And what happens meanwhile?' he called after her. 'Do we go on living under the same roof pretending everything's OK?'

Turning back, she said, 'I intend to be as civilized about this as possible, and I hope you will too. However, one or other of us will be sleeping in the guest room until you

311

leave. I don't mind which one of us it is, only that we no longer sleep in the same bed.'

As she ran up the stairs, tears were burning her eyes and her heart was pounding insufferably hard, but she was determined not to break down, especially not in front of him. If she did, he'd seize on the weakness, try to comfort her and persuade her to see things his way. She was never going to do that, so there was no point in letting him try.

She'd hardly begun to unpack when he came into the bedroom.

She didn't turn around, simply continued to go about hanging her clothes and dropping various items into the laundry bag.

In the end he said, 'I'll take the guest room. If you're sure it's what you want.'

'It is.'

'Then I suppose it's a good thing I'll be away for three nights from tomorrow. Shall I expect the locks to be changed by the time I get back?'

Determined not to turn this into a useless scoring of points, she said, 'I wouldn't do that to you.'

'Because Livvy would want to know why?'

'Partly that, but as I said just now, I want us to try and be civilized about this. It'll be difficult enough without inflicting unnecessary spiteful acts on one another.'

He fell silent, and because her back was turned she had no idea what he might be thinking, or doing. She didn't look round, simply carried her business suit to the dressing room and went on through to the bathroom with her washbag and closed the door. She leaned against it, glad to be away from him, if only for a moment. Having him near seemed to heighten her tension, as if the air between them was too full of him for her to take a breath.

She heard him come to stand the other side of the door, and wondered if he'd try to let himself in. He didn't, and they stood silently, inches apart, and yet strangely, in different worlds. As several awful minutes passed, she wasn't sure what to do or say, only knew that making him leave the house was clearly going to be the hardest, most wrenching thing she'd ever done, and it would probably only get worse after he'd left. But her mind was made up. She could no longer trust him and there was no point trying to pretend that she could.

In the end he said, 'I still love you Jay. You know that. I've always loved you.'

Her eyes closed. She couldn't respond without betraying how close she was to tears, or to delivering the kind of bitter response that would leave her feeling diminished.

'I won't ask if you still love me,' he said. 'I understand that you probably feel you don't right now, but acting this hastily . . . I know everything seems impossible when we're where we are, but we can work things out, you know that. We're strong together, we belong together. Isn't that what we've always said?'

It was, but only in the good times when they'd been so happy and seemed so invincible as a couple, as parents, as professionals who could take on the world and win.

Walking to the double vanity unit, she began to replace her toothbrush, comb and cosmetics in the cabinets and wasn't surprised when he opened the door. She met his eyes in the mirror and her heart ached, though whether with love, regret or hurt she couldn't be sure; probably all three and more. Actually, she did still love him and couldn't imagine being without him. He'd been at the centre of her world for so long that she could barely remember a time before him. He knew everything about her, had been there for her in so many ways, from the birth of their children right through to the wrenching loss of her father. He bolstered her when her confidence was low and celebrated with her when the victories came. She'd been there for him too, doing what she could to bring light to the dark times, feeling absurdly proud when she watched him in court, and loving him simply for how much he seemed to love their family and the life they were creating.

Why the hell had he felt compelled to spoil it all?

He came to fold her in his arms and said softly, 'I know sorry doesn't do it, but it's the best I have right now. I will make this up to you, Jay, I swear it. Just please don't give up on me.'

She didn't answer, didn't ask what she was supposed to do, or think, whenever he went to collect his son from his mother; how it was going to be for her as she imagined them together, wondering how long it would take for him to give in to the attraction again?

Instead she said, 'Let me tell you why I think Jed Tyler wants you in your son's life. I think he's probably a kind and honourable man who is no longer willing to put up with his wife's affair, or passion for you, or whatever it is that you two share. But he doesn't want to leave her with a small child to bring up alone. So who better to fill the role than the baby's real father who, over time, as he becomes more and more attached to his son, will want to spend more time with him? This is what I believe Jed and Ellen Tyler are hoping for.'

Tightening his embrace, he said, 'You don't know if any of that's true, and I don't either, but even if some of it is, I'm never going to stop loving you, and I'll never leave you. Never.'

Without looking up or pulling away, she said, 'You told me once that you'd never sleep with her again, but you did – three or four times, if you're to be believed. You lied to try and keep the child's age from me. So, whatever you say to me today, Tom, I realize might not be true tomorrow, and I don't want to wait around for the next lie, or excuse, or apology, or the next time you can't resist her. So, as hard as this is for me, and I know it will be for you too, I really do want you to go.'

CHAPTER THIRTY-FIVE

'Are you OK?'

Jay flicked a quick glance at Blake and continued to set out her laptop and papers on the table between them. 'I'm fine, thanks,' she replied, knowing she looked about as bad as she felt after two virtually sleepless nights.

He said no more, but she could feel him watching her and for one awkward moment she thought she was going to cry.

'I can tell this isn't a good time,' he stated. 'Shall we postpone and—'

'No, certainly not,' she interrupted. 'I told you, I'm fine, it's just been a . . . tricky few days.' She still couldn't quite bring herself to look at him, afraid if she did that he'd say something to break down her defences completely and heaven only knew what would result from that.

'Please don't tell me he's let you down again,' he said quietly.

She gave a half-laugh that twisted her mouth, and was, she realized, probably answer enough. 'We're not here to talk about me,' she reminded him.

He didn't argue, simply continued to watch her, until she had everything in order and was ready to begin. 'The red car,' she said, finally looking at him with an expression she hoped was professional enough to strike the right balance.

His eyes held to hers as he said, 'I'm sorry if I made you uncomfortable. It's—'

'You didn't. It was kind of you to ask.'

'But I was too blunt.'

'Astute,' she corrected with a smile and, swallowing before a lump could form in her throat, she said, 'Being kind to me right now isn't going to get us very far, so if you don't mind, can we talk about the red car?'

'Of course.' And doing as instructed, he said, 'It's true that Freya has – or had – a red Audi A1 hatchback. As for why she would have been meeting Nessa at the station that day . . . I'm afraid I can throw no light on that.'

'Could it be as a result of something that came up when Vanessa went to see Daphne about the will?'

'Even if it's true that she went, I'm afraid I still can't explain it.' He shook his head, clearly baffled. 'To be honest, I think it's more likely the two events are uncon-nected, especially if we're bringing Edmond into the picture.' His eyes went down, and the way his face tight-ened slightly reminded her that he was dealing with his own betrayals, the like of which went far beyond what she was going through.

She looked at his hands on the table and felt tempted to reach out for them, to squeeze in a small gesture of comfort and maybe even take some for herself, but he was talking again.

'It's still shocking to me to discover how little I knew about my wife,' he said, 'and the crazy thing is it doesn't stop me loving her, or wanting to save her from herself . . .' His eyes showed a hint of irony as they came to Jay's. 'A bit late for that now, but it seems the instincts live on.'

Not holding back this time, she wrapped her fingers

around his as she said, 'You're trying to deal with so much, and being shut up in here is making it even more difficult. So we have to do what we can to find out what really happened.'

'Yes, of course.' He didn't move his hand away from hers, but didn't show any sense of connecting with it either, until he looked down and unravelled his fingers to interlace them with hers. She felt the sense of a current passing between them, something quiet, but deep, and wondered if he could too.

Sitting back to separate them, she said, 'The red car. One was seen—'

'Freya's isn't the only one,' he interrupted softly.

Having already guessed as much from her conversation with Antonia, she waited for him to continue.

'When Toni and I last spoke,' he said, pushing his hands into his hair, 'she reminded me that Guy, my nephew, had borrowed a friend's car around that time. Same make, model and colour.'

Her heart skipped a beat. This would explain why she'd felt Antonia was once again holding back on her. If the woman considered herself caught between her son and her brother . . . She had to protect her son, naturally, but at the expense of her brother? The ultimate rock and hard place.

It could also explain why Maguire was holding back, out of loyalty to the family. He could be waiting to take guidance from them without them even knowing it.

'To be clear,' she said carefully, 'do you think it's possible Vanessa was . . . seeing your nephew?'

Blake's face was colourless as he answered. 'I have no idea, but we obviously can't rule it out.'

No, they couldn't, and the fact that Antonia had sounded so worked up when she'd rung last week was as good as an admission in itself that she either knew, or also suspected, that something had been going on between Guy and Vanessa.

'You understand, don't you,' she said gently, 'that I have to talk to Antonia and Guy?'

He nodded awkwardly and she realized he was dangerously close to the edge. 'My nephew,' he murmured bitterly, 'who I think of as a son! Why did she have to pick on him?'

'I'm sorry,' she whispered, knowing now wasn't the time to mention that this could be viewed as a compelling motive for him to kill his wife. 'I don't know,' she went on carefully, 'if your nephew was swabbed at the same time as his parents, but even if he wasn't we can be sure his father was. This means we can also be sure that John's DNA is not a match for the unidentified sample or he'd have been called back in by now.'

Blake frowned. 'What are you saying?'

'I don't expect you to know about familial DNA, but to keep it short, if John is in the clear regarding the unidentified samples then his son will be too.'

Blake simply looked at her, clearly weighing what she'd said and seeming, oddly, as though he might be having trouble taking it in. In the end, he said, 'Guy isn't John's son.'

Thrown, Jay simply stared at him.

'Toni was married before,' Blake explained. 'They broke up when Camille was two and my sister was pregnant with Guy. John adopted them when he and Toni got together and he's brought them up as his own. He couldn't

319

be a better father, but biologically speaking he isn't . . . It wouldn't be possible for him and Guy to have a familial match.'

Jay took a breath and blew it out slowly. 'I'm glad you told me this,' she said, 'but, as a close family member, there's a good chance the police have already swabbed Guy. So we probably still don't need to worry too much about him being the owner of the unidentified sample.'

Blake's tension didn't lessen. 'When you see Toni,' he said, 'I want you to tell her I still believe it was Freya's car that was spotted at the station and leaving Clover Hill Farm.'

Understanding his reluctance to speak to his sister himself right now, or to believe in his nephew's involvement, Jay said, 'I'm going to contact DI Bright when I leave here. It's quite probable they already know that Freya drives a red car, but just in case they don't, it's time for them to take this on.'

His voice was choked as he said, 'What about Guy?'

'I won't mention anything about him yet. I'll go to see him and Antonia first, but if the questioning of Freya and Edmond comes to nothing, or proves inconclusive—'

'I don't want Guy getting mixed up in this,' he interrupted, his eyes sharp and determined. 'Even if he was sleeping with her, he wouldn't have killed her, for God's sake. He's just a boy. Can you honestly see someone like him doing something like that to anyone, let alone someone he loved?'

In truth, she couldn't, but she'd been wrong about people before and there was nothing to say it wouldn't happen again. 'I understand that you want to try and protect him,' she said, 'and his parents will feel the same, but a lot will depend on the unidentified DNA. It could be Berzina's—'

'If it's Guy's I'll confess to the murder myself,' he cut in abruptly. 'Anything, rather than see him go through any of this.'

She regarded him in disbelief. 'You can't mean that . . .'

'I do, because even if Guy did it, Vanessa would be to blame for seducing him in the first place. He should not have to pay for that.'

'Edward, you're not thinking straight. I understand how distressing all this is for you, but I won't let you go to prison for a crime you didn't commit.'

'I don't see it as your choice.'

'I can make it mine, believe me.'

He turned sideways in his chair and didn't look round as she eventually began collecting her things together. 'I'll come again next week,' she said, 'but please call me after I've spoken to Antonia on Thursday.'

'Have you already arranged it?'

'No, but I will.'

He nodded and got to his feet as she did, digging his hands into his trouser pockets. 'At least there's one thing we can be certain about,' he said, as they stood looking at one another across the table.

'What's that?' she asked.

'If there were a contest right now for whose life is the most screwed up, I'm pretty sure I'd win.'

She smiled because he did, and only wished that their time wasn't up because at least here, with him, she didn't keep thinking about Tom.

CHAPTER THIRTY-SIX

As expected, Bright and his team had already discovered that Vanessa Blake's half-sister drove a red Audi A1, and when questioned Freya had continued to insist that she'd been at home all day and night in London. Since she'd been unable to produce an alibi, apart from Berzina, she'd moved up the short list of 'persons of interest' in company with her husband.

'Once Berzina's test results are back,' Bright told Jay, 'a decision will be made on how to proceed.'

'When is that likely to be?' she asked, seeing from call-waiting that Vikki was trying to get through to her.

'I don't believe the swab was fast-tracked,' Bright replied, 'but you can check with Lacey Hamble, she's handling the science.'

Having no doubt that Hamble would have sent it to one of the slower labs to save cost, she was about to speak again when he said, 'Listen, Jay, I know what you're trying to do, you want your client released before we get to trial, but you know we can't speed things up just to suit you.'

'Not me, justice,' she corrected. 'And I know you don't really believe he did it either . . .'

'Actually, I think there's a good chance that he did, but I will accept there are anomalies that need to be addressed.'

'I'd call unidentified male DNA more than an anomaly,' she retorted. 'And wouldn't it be better to have things properly resolved before we go in front of a judge?'

'Of course, and you're being very helpful in that regard, but there's still a way to go before we get to court – and now might be a good time to tell you that I'm going to be off for the next couple of weeks, bit longer, actually, walking in the Alps with Mrs Bright.'

Thinking how much she – and Blake – would love to be taking a fortnight's break right now, she rang off, spoke to Vikki, and ended up spending the rest of the day at Patchway Police Station responding to a call from an elderly man who'd been arrested for indecent exposure. The poor soul was clearly suffering from dementia so she was eventually able to hand him over to social services and have his name expunged from police records before things got out of hand.

By the time she got home, following a late meeting at the office with the crime team, she was so tired she could have slept standing up, and yet she knew that once her head hit the pillow she'd come wide awake again. Round and round everything would go, Tom and his baby; Tom leaving the house; Tom with his lively young girlfriend. Tom turning his back on the child and its mother; Tom hating her for making him.

'Are you OK?' he asked when he rang from London at his usual time, and she realized he was the second person to ask her that today with genuine-sounding concern. She wasn't sure whether it had been easier to answer Blake or him.

She lied to Tom too. 'I'm fine. How are you?'

'Not fine. Thinking about you, trying to keep my mind on the job. Worrying about everything.'

323

Wondering if he was hoping she'd put his mind at rest, and if so exactly how he expected her to do that, she said, 'I find work helps. Where are you?'

'At the usual hotel in Clerkenwell.'

'Have you seen her?'

'No.'

'Are you intending to?'

'No.'

'So how have you left things with her?'

'I said I'd be in touch once I'd talked things over with you.'

Untying her hair and sinking into a sofa with a sigh she said, 'We've talked, Tom. You know there isn't anywhere we can go with this apart from our separate ways. I don't want another baby; you already have one, so it seems to me the decision is made.' The words made her feel light-headed, afraid, and yet also strong, ready to protect herself from any more.

'I don't understand how you can be so . . . *matter of fact* about this,' he growled. 'Have I been missing something somewhere? Do we no longer have a connection, a history, a life together that means as much to you as it does to me?'

'We had it all, Tom, until you threw it away. That's what making a baby with someone else does to a relationship.' Before he could interrupt she quickly added, 'I'm sorry, I've hardly seen Livvy since her exams finished, so I'm taking her out this evening. I need to shower and change. We'll see you on Thursday.'

'Don't do that,' he shouted. 'Stop brushing me off like you don't have time. Nothing can be more important than this . . .'

'I'm sorry, but I don't have any more to say. I haven't changed my mind about anything and I'm not going to. The child's here, he's not going away, so you need to take that in and deal with it because I don't think you are right now.'

'Don't be absurd.'

'You can't bend this to suit your will, Tom. The facts are indisputable. We're not in a court of law where you can argue your way around them, or try to bully me into saying what you want to hear. Now, don't let's fall out again. It'll only upset us both and it's hard enough already.'

As soon as she'd rung off, heart pounding, stomach wrenching, she wanted to call him back, to say she hadn't meant to be so sharp, or hurtful, but she didn't. There was no way of changing the situation, or how she felt about it, so what was the point in pretending they could?

A text arrived. *I'm not giving up on us.*

She didn't reply, simply went upstairs for a shower.

After a while she felt herself turning numb again, mercifully, bizarrely, detached from her own feelings and from his. It was a good place to be, in spite of knowing she wouldn't be there for long.

Dinner with Livvy turned out to be the very best kind of distraction, for not only was her daughter confident her exams had gone well, she was also full of some camping trip Nat wanted her to go on at the weekend.

'Just the two of you?' Jay exclaimed in surprise.

'No, others are going too. I'll have to sort out a tent, but if Nat has got two sleeping spaces, maybe I could share his?' Her eyes gleamed wickedly.

'I'm sure there are two or three in the shed,' Jay replied sardonically. 'Dad will sort one out for you.'

'Is the wrong answer,' Livvy declared, throwing out her hands. 'I want to stay in Nat's if poss, so let's pretend we don't have one, OK? At least until I've spoken to him.'

'OK. How are you going to get there?'

'Dad will take me to Temple Meads so I can get the train to Exeter where Nat will meet me and I'll go on from there in his car.'

Amused, Jay said, 'Do Dad and Nat know this yet?'

'Not exactly, but I can't see a problem with it. Dad's getting the train himself on Saturday morning. He and Charlie have tickets for the Cup Final at Wembley, remember?'

Jay did, now she'd been reminded, and it was already a relief to know that Tom wouldn't be around much at the weekend. Even as she thought it, a horrible wave of guilt swept in. She didn't want to avoid him, but she didn't want any more fights either.

'So you'll help me to pack,' Livvy was saying. 'I'm not sure what to take apart from my birth pills and condoms. Maybe I don't need anything else.'

Knowing she was being baited, Jay shot her a look and called for the bill. 'Are you coming home with me now?' she asked, as Livvy began texting.

Livvy nodded. 'I need some sleep,' she replied without looking up, 'and if you don't mind me saying, you look as though you do too.'

It wasn't until they arrived home and Jay was putting her phone on charge that she saw several missed calls and messages, most of them from Tom, so she decided to check them in the morning.

After slipping beneath the duvet, she started to wonder if any had been from Blake, but even if they were, they could wait too. She felt a warm frisson of tightness inside as her mind slipped back to the way their hands had touched earlier. He hadn't seemed to notice, or not in the way she had. It didn't matter, it had been no more than a gesture of friendship and understanding. She was sure he understood that too.

She fell asleep thinking about him, his eyes, his voice, the turbulence of their worlds, and how reflexively drawn she felt to him . . .

CHAPTER THIRTY-SEVEN

When Jay arrived at Highview House late on Thursday morning, Antonia, looking pale and close to exhaustion, led her straight through to the sunroom. John was already there with Guy and, as they got up to greet their visitor, Max – Blake's aging Labrador – struggled to his feet too. There was no sign of Debrayne's mother, or of the daughter, Camille.

'Thanks for coming,' Debrayne said, shaking her hand and looking almost as tired as his wife.

'I thought it would be easier to talk here than in my office,' Jay replied and, turning to Guy, she felt a surge of pity to see how wretched the lad looked. However, the sympathy only went so far; she needed the whole story out of him before she'd be ready to cut him any slack.

'I've made coffee,' Antonia said as Max shuffled forward to nudge Jay's leg.

She looked down into the soulful brown eyes and gently ruffled his head. If he missed Blake there was no way of telling, but in spite of never having owned a dog, she could understand why Blake missed this one; he was so gentle and adorable. 'How old is he?' she asked as he flumped down at her feet.

'Almost fourteen,' Debrayne replied. 'He's had a good

innings for his breed, but we're hoping he'll hang on for a while yet.'

Until Ed comes home, was left unsaid, but Jay heard it anyway.

After Antonia had handed around the coffees and gone to sit with her son, Debrayne settled into a chair beside them while Jay took the one opposite. Their apprehension was so intense, it was almost stifling.

Starting out gently, she spoke to Guy first, who seemed actually to be shaking. 'I want you to understand,' she said, 'that I'm under no obligation to go to the police with whatever you tell me today. I hope that will encourage you to be completely honest.'

The boy's cheeks were almost purple, his curly head seemed to jerk as he nodded his understanding.

'However,' she continued, 'if there is anything you can say to help your uncle, I would urge you to do so.' She wouldn't mention yet Blake's astonishing threat to take the rap if it turned out his nephew was the killer, but she would if it proved necessary.

Surely no one would allow that to happen.

'I want to help him,' Guy said, his voice barely above a whisper.

'We all do,' Antonia said, more firmly. 'Guy didn't do it; I hope you realize that—'

'Darling,' Debrayne interrupted, 'let Mrs Wells handle this her way.'

Antonia apologized and reached for her coffee.

'The red car,' Jay began, returning her attention to Guy. 'I understand you borrowed one from a friend and were driving it on the day your aunt disappeared from the station.'

'It belongs to one of my housemates,' he told her earnestly. 'He was away and I was between cars, so he let me use his until he got back.'

'And it was a red Audi 1 hatchback?'

He nodded miserably and let his head hang down.

'Was it you who picked your aunt up from the station that morning?'

'Yes,' he faintly managed. 'It was.'

Although she'd suspected it, Jay still felt a swell of dismay. Her eyes flicked briefly to the parents. They were staring at nothing, but their discomfort, tension, was plain to see. 'Where did you go after she got into the car?' she asked Guy.

He sobbed in a breath. 'We . . . We went to one of Ed's properties near Lacock. He . . . We'd just finished fixing it up and Ed still hadn't decided whether he was going to rent or sell.'

'So it was standing empty?'

'More or less, but I had things in the car.'

'What sort of things?'

A fresh tide of colour rushed from Guy's neck into his face; his eyes failed to meet hers. 'A foldaway table, chairs, a sleep . . . sleeping bag. Nessa told me what to bring. I took our picnic set from here, things to eat and some wine.'

'Had you ever met her in that house before?'

His fists were bunched so tightly on his knees it seemed he might start punching himself. 'Yes,' he murmured, 'a couple of times.'

'And did you go there to have sexual relations?'

The fiery redness that swamped him looked painful. He couldn't speak, and kept his head down as he nodded.

Wanting to spare him too much detail in front of his parents, she said, 'Whose idea was it for you to get together that way?'

Guy swallowed noisily, visibly. 'N-Nessa's.'

'How did she suggest it?'

'She – she gave me a phone with some photos on it of her and said if I wanted to see her any time I should give her a call.'

Understanding what kind of photos they must have been, and the kind of effect they must have had on a lad his age, Jay said, 'And so you called her?'

He shook his head. 'I was too afraid to. I've never . . . I mean I've had girlfriends, but . . .'

Realizing Guy had been a virgin until his aunt had decided to initiate him, Jay said, 'So she called you?'

He nodded.

'On the phone she'd given you?'

'Yes. I kept it with me all the time. I didn't want anyone to find it.'

'Can you remember the number of the phone?'

As he reeled it off, she wrote it down, fairly certain it was the one they'd been unable to trace. If she was right then, unlike the others in Vanessa's secret contacts, he'd been listed under the initial of his surname rather than G. 'Where's the phone now?' she asked.

'I got rid of it. Smashed it up into pieces.'

'When did you do that?'

'About a week, or a few days, after she was killed.'

Imagining what a terrible state he must have been in all this time while doing his best to hide it, she had to wonder when his parents had first suspected he was more involved than their worst nightmares would ever want to allow. As the answer wasn't relevant to this moment, she returned to the house near Lacock. 'How long were you there after you picked Vanessa up at the station?' she asked Guy.

'Um, probably a couple of hours. We – we went for a walk. There's a stream and a wood in the grounds. She wanted to see the bluebells.'

'Is the property overlooked at all?'

'No, not at the back. You can see the front from the road.'

'Do you know the address?'

'Yes, but not the postcode.'

Although she wrote it down, she suspected she'd end up leaving any visits or local inquiries to the police once she passed the information on. *If* she passed it on. 'What time, roughly, did you leave the house?' she asked.

'Um, probably around two, maybe a bit later.'

'Did you leave together?'

'Yes. I drove her home to Clover Hill.' He'd started to jerk his foot up and down, but stopped when his mother put a hand on his knee.

'Did you go in?' Jay asked.

His head went down again as he nodded.

'What time was it, roughly?'

'About three or half past, I think.'

'How long did you stay?'

'Quite a while. I'm . . . I think it might have been me someone saw driving away about half past five.'

Choosing not to ask what they were doing all that time since the answer was obvious, Jay said, 'Was Vanessa in the house alone when you left?'

'Yes.'

'Whereabouts in the house?'

'Um, the kitchen, but she came to the door with me.'

So not strapped to a bed – if he was being truthful.
'Was she expecting anyone, do you know?'

'Not that she said.'

'Did you see anyone as you drove away?'

'N-No.'

'A DPD van?'

'I-I don't think so. I don't remember. I wasn't really paying attention.'

No, she didn't suppose he was. 'Where did you go then?'

'Back to the house I share with some mates near Bath.'

'Can anyone verify what time you arrived?'

'I'm not sure. I went straight up to my room, but Jackson was in the kitchen playing video games. He might have heard me come in.'

'And that would have been what time?'

'Somewhere between six and quarter past.'

As she noted it down, she was thinking about Freya and Edmond Berzina and how this came close to ruling them out as suspects, although it wouldn't be decided until Berzina's DNA results were known. Looking at Guy again, she said, 'It's my understanding that the police took swabs from Edward's close friends and family for elimination purposes. Were you included in that?' Her fingers were crossing, desperately hoping, for his sake, that the answer was yes. For Blake's sake? She wasn't going to think about that.

'No, I wasn't,' he answered, and there was no doubt he had no idea just how difficult a position he was now in. It was quite possible his parents didn't either.

Dismayed by the police oversight, '*Lucy Hamble's in*

charge of the science,' she put away her notebook and finished her coffee. Although she was fairly convinced the lad had spoken the truth, excruciating as it had been for him, there was still a possibility that he'd returned to the house after five thirty without being noticed.

'No, I didn't go back,' he replied when she asked.

'And you're sure she didn't say anything about expecting someone else?'

'I'm sure.'

Leaving it there for the moment, she decided to seize another difficult nettle. 'Did she ever ask you to tie her up, either that day or any other?'

More flaming colour stained his cheeks. 'No. I mean, yes, once, but I didn't do it.'

'When you were at Clover Hill that day, did you make love in the bedroom, or guest room, or where?'

Tears filled his eyes as he said, 'In the bedroom.'

'You mean *her* bedroom?'

'Yes,' he sobbed, and his mother dropped her head into her hands. Her son, her brother's bed and wife . . .

Jay's heart went out to her, but Guy and his DNA were now her biggest concern. 'Would you mind,' she said to him, 'coming to my office tomorrow so we can take a swab from you?'

He looked scared as his father started to object.

'We'll have it analysed privately,' she explained to John, 'but if it turns out to be a match for the unidentified samples on record, I will be urging you to talk to the police.'

'But I didn't do it,' Guy cried, leaping to his feet. 'I didn't. I swear it.'

'Then you have nothing to worry about.'

'Oh God, oh God,' he sobbed, clasping his hands to his head as if it were about to explode. 'Does Ed know anything?' he gulped. 'Are you going to tell him?'

'He knows it's possible you were sleeping with Vanessa,' she said softly. 'He doesn't think you killed her, but if it's discovered that you did, he's saying he'll confess to it himself rather than see you go to prison.'

Horrified, Guy spun towards his mother.

'No!' Antonia cried.

'Guy, calm down,' his father interrupted. 'It isn't going to come to that. We'll make sure it doesn't.'

Hardly able to breathe through his panic, Guy began wheezing and panting. Rushing to him, Antonia grabbed his shoulders, shook him, shouted at him to stop, while Debrayne discreetly gestured to Jay to follow him out.

'This whole experience,' he said, as they walked towards her car, 'well, you saw for yourself what a traumatizing effect it's having on him, but he didn't do it, Mrs Wells. I'll stake my life on that. However, I realize Ed is your priority, and I also understand the necessity of my son being eliminated through a DNA test. So I will bring him to your office tomorrow, as requested. How long do you think we'll have to wait for the results?'

'We'll fast-track it, but I'm afraid it'll have to be compared to the DNA not yet identified. This will be done by our own scientist in order to keep it confidential, so it's not possible to put an exact time on it. I realize the wait will be difficult, but I'm afraid there is no way around it.'

He nodded acceptance and opened the car door for her to get in. 'We received a call from the coroner this morning,' he said. 'Vanessa's body is being released so we can move ahead with the funeral arrangements.'

Experiencing a rush of feeling for Blake, she said, 'Have you told Edward this yet?'

'No, he hasn't rung and, as you might already know, he's refused our visit tomorrow. Will he be allowed to attend?'

'I don't think so. We put in an application soon after he was remanded but it was turned down. I didn't tell him because it was my intention to try again when we had a date. I'll get on to it as soon as I'm back at the office.'

'Thank you. When are you next seeing him?'

'He's due to call me later, but I won't discuss much of what was said today over the phone. I'll wait until I visit him on Monday.'

'Will you tell him about what was said here today?'

'Probably. I think he's guessed most of it.'

Looking broken, Debrayne said, 'We're going to try for another visit next week, but I don't know if he'll see us.'

Not knowing either, she put a reassuring hand on his arm and said, 'I'll have my secretary call you to set up a time for tomorrow.'

It was a few minutes after six when Jay walked through the front door with the phone ringing in her hand. Guessing it was Blake, and hearing Tom talking to someone in the kitchen, she detoured into their study. 'Hi,' she said, closing the door. 'How are you?'

Sounding tired, he said, 'I wonder if I should be asking you that.'

Not sure whether he was referring to her own situation or her day with his family, she said, 'Before I tell you about Guy I have some other news. Vanessa's body is being released so your sister and brother-in-law are going ahead with funeral arrangements.'

She could only imagine how he was reacting to that, but his silence told her that he needed time to process.

'Will I be able to go?' he asked quietly.

'We've put in a request today. I'm hoping to hear back some time next week.'

'What are the chances?'

Having to be honest, she said, 'Not good, I'm afraid. The first time I requested it I received a refusal, but time has gone on, circumstances have changed a little, so I considered it worth approaching them again.'

'But I should prepare myself to be in here while she's buried?'

'It might be best if you can.'

He gave a bitter laugh, and his voice shook slightly as he said, 'OK, tell me about Guy. I guess there was an affair?'

'I'm afraid so.'

She heard his intake of breath and imagined his eyes closing against the blow he'd probably been expecting, but was a harsh one anyway. 'How was he?' he asked.

'He seemed pretty shaken up.'

'Do you think . . . ?' Apparently remembering the call was being listened to, he rephrased, 'You know what I'm asking.'

Did Guy do it? 'I don't know,' she replied. 'There's been an oversight which I'll discuss with you when I come on Monday.'

'OK.' She listened to him breathing and the mumble of other voices in the background; pictured where he was standing and imagined the frustration and helplessness he must be feeling. Not in control of his life, unable even to speak freely. 'I meant what I said,' he told her. 'He's just a boy . . .'

'Don't let's have the conversation now,' she came in softly. 'I think he, or your sister, would appreciate a call from you. They're very worried.'

'OK. I'll do it tomorrow.'

She knew she should ring off now, there was no more to say that could be chanced over the phone, but she waited and eventually he said,

'Thanks for all you're doing. Having you believe in me means a lot.'

She smiled even though he couldn't see her. 'That's good, and now I have to go, I'm afraid. I'll see you on Monday, usual time, usual place.' Before she hung up she heard him laugh, and was glad she'd heard it, for she knew that very little amused him these days.

'Who were you talking to?' Tom asked as she joined him in the kitchen.

'A client,' she replied. 'I thought someone was in here with you.'

'I was on the phone to Freddy. He and Carina have invited themselves over. I hope that's OK. He has an idea for a book he'd like to run past us.'

Going to fix herself a drink she said, 'I have no problem with it, but before they come I have to ask if you've given any thought to your future plans since the weekend.' *Why the hell had she just weighed in with that? She didn't want to pick a fight, she really didn't, but nor could she allow things to continue on as if nothing had changed.*

Tersely, he said, 'If you're talking about where I might live—'

'Hey Dad! You're back,' Livvy announced, startling them both as she bounced into the kitchen. 'I need a lift to the station on Saturday and I know you're going anyway . . .' She glanced at her phone as it rang. 'Nat,' she informed them, eyes teasing as she looked at her mother, and spinning on her heel she left.

'Where's she going?' Tom asked, emptying olives from a deli pack into a bowl.

'Camping with Nat. It seems to be working out.'

'That's good. It's what she wanted. Charlie's coming home tomorrow night, by the way, so we'll be ready to leave early on Saturday morning.'

Fleetingly she considered breaking his news while the four of them were together tomorrow, but apparently reading her mind, he said, 'It would be a very bad time to tell them anything. It'll ruin everyone's weekend and I don't think we want to do that.'

He was right, they didn't, although he surely realized it would ruin a lot more than a weekend when they did finally break it. 'So have you,' she asked, after making sure Livvy wasn't hovering anywhere nearby, 'given any thought to where you'll go from here? The children will want to know, even if you decide to go to her.'

'Jay, she's married,' he hissed, 'so why on earth would I be thinking about moving in with her? Before you answer that, I've already told you that I won't be leaving, and nor will I be giving up on us, even though you seem more than ready to.'

'Oh no,' she protested, 'you're not hanging this on me. You're the one who has all the blame here, the one who shattered what little trust I had left in you, and that's why you're the one who has to go. I'm not saying we won't sell the house eventually, we'll have to, but I will not go on living under the same roof as you while you go back and forth between me and your mistress carting the baby with you.'

Leaving him with that, she went to let their friends in the front door, astonishing even herself with how warmly she was able to greet them when inside she was falling apart.

CHAPTER THIRTY-EIGHT

On Monday morning, as Jay waited for Blake to be brought from his cell, she was finding it hard to focus on the notes she'd prepared for their meeting. Her mind was all over the place, seeming unable to settle on anything after yet another harrowing scene with Tom last night. He'd seemed to think she'd want to celebrate with him after his team won the match, that for some reason when he got home she'd be euphoric too, but she hadn't been. Football meant nothing to her, and the fact that he'd thought they could use the victory to create some sort of bridge between them had just about incensed her.

He'd even said, 'Let's imagine there's a lovely café on this bridge, overlooking a river, where we can meet for a drink and talk about all that's good about us.'

She couldn't remember now exactly what had accelerated the tussle into a full-blown fight, who had yelled first, who had thrown the first punch – actually she had and he hadn't hit her back – or who had smashed plates in the sink. She was sure that was him, but in the heat of it all, it might have been her.

By the time she'd escaped upstairs, breathless, trembling, throat sore from shouting, she was ready to walk out again. But she hadn't. It was her home; she was in the right, and one way or another she was going to make him

341

see that they couldn't carry on like this. He absolutely had to go before one of them ended up doing something they'd both bitterly regret.

Now, as the door opened and Blake came into the room, she became self-consciously aware of the extra make-up she'd applied this morning to hide the shadows under her eyes, and the lipstick she'd used to bring colour to her pale lips. Would he think she'd made a special effort for him?

If he did, he didn't remark on it, simply said, 'Sorry for being late.'

'It's OK,' she assured him.

As the door closed he went to the other side of the table and sat down heavily, fixing her with his compelling blue eyes. 'It would be polite to ask if you had a good weekend,' he said, 'but I'm not sure if you want me to.'

'It's probably best that you don't,' she admitted. 'Although, actually, I spent a lot of it thinking about you.' She'd meant professionally, of course, but could tell from the way his gaze intensified that he might have taken it another way. And of course it had happened another way too.

'I don't think I've seen you blush before,' he commented dryly.

Wishing he hadn't noticed, she said, 'Time's tight and what we have to discuss isn't going to be easy.'

'Because it concerns my nephew.' A statement, not a question, and she could see how heavily the prospect of it was weighing on him. 'Before we go there,' he said, 'do you have any news about the funeral, when it's going to happen; whether I can attend?'

'Nothing yet,' she replied, 'but I'll make sure you're told as soon as I hear anything.'

He nodded his thanks and said, 'OK, Guy – and don't worry about holding back, it can't be any worse than what I've been imagining all weekend.'

Guessing it probably wasn't, she said, 'The red car that Vanessa was seen getting into—'

'Belonged to Guy's friend, with Guy driving it. Yes, I remember it. I suppose he gave it back before anyone identified it, before he even knew that he'd been seen?'

'I believe so. He's admitted to picking her up at the station in it and taking her to one of your properties near Lacock.'

As he frowned, she sensed his mind travelling to the place, picturing it and them together, this particular betrayal undoubtedly far more wrenching than the others. 'Go on,' he said quietly.

Keeping her tone neutral, she related what she'd learned from his nephew.

When she'd finished he said, 'Do you believe him? Or do you think he went back after five thirty?'

'I'm not sure. He could have, but he swears he didn't. One of my team, Joe, is talking to the housemate today to find out if he remembers Guy coming home at the time he claimed. And his father brought him to my office on Friday so we could take a swab. If it matches the unidentified DNA, I'm afraid it really won't look good for him.'

Blake sat back in his chair, pale and agitated, but his voice was firm as he said, 'Even if it's his, I still won't believe he did it, but if there's any chance of him being arrested, never mind charged, I promise you, I will not let it happen.'

'Edward,' she said, leaning towards him, 'this is crazy. You can't take on a prison sentence to save—'

'I don't want to argue about it. I'll understand if you feel you have to resign as my lawyer. I wouldn't ask you—'

'You're right, I won't help you to plead guilty to a crime I know someone else committed,' she said, 'but we haven't got there yet, so let's try to talk things through before jumping into any rash decisions. There's always a chance the DNA won't be a match . . .'

'But you think it is.'

'It's possible. It's still just as possible that it belongs to Edmond Berzina. Or it could be someone we don't even know about yet.'

'Presumably, now the red car mystery's been cleared up, there's nothing to say Berzina or Freya were with her at all that day?'

'Not at this stage, but the police are still talking to them and I know they're not satisfied with their alibis.'

Blake turned his head away, his jaw tight as he thought. 'It's much easier to see Berzina doing it than Guy,' he stated.

Although she didn't disagree, she was too mindful of the many unlikely killers she'd come across to dismiss anything, or anyone.

At last he turned back to her and seemed slightly calmer as he said, 'When will you know the results, for both?'

'I'm hoping within a fortnight for Guy, by the time our scientist has also carried out a check. He has to gain access to the lab and the database without raising suspicion and that could take time. I'm not sure about Berzina, it's not in my hands.'

'And will they just let Berzina off the hook if there turns out to be a positive match for Guy?'

'I don't know. It'll depend if they have anything else on him. Unless they decide to share information before-hand, we won't get full disclosure until the next hearing.'

'Which is in less than four weeks?'

She nodded and didn't add that she hoped to have him out of here before that; he already knew, it wouldn't help to repeat it now. 'I'm intending to meet with Cyrus Trott next week,' she told him. 'He'll be your barrister for the plea hearing. Obviously if you end up going to trial, we'll bring in a QC. I've already spoken to Susannah Heel. She's someone I know well and have a great deal of respect for. I think you'll like her, if we get to that stage. Obviously I'm still hoping we won't.'

When he didn't respond she let the silence roll, waiting for him to think everything through until eventually he brought his eyes to hers in a way that caused a strange knotting sensation inside her. A moment or two passed that seemed longer than it was, until he said, 'Can we talk about something else for a while?'

Surprised, and slightly thrown, she was about to ask what, when he said, 'This case, the situation I'm in, is all I ever think about. It's with me twenty-four/seven and I'm afraid I'm starting to lose my mind, or at least my perspective. I need to take a step back, to focus elsewhere for a while, and apart from you there's no one to talk to.'

Touched by his honesty, and understanding how crazy it must all be driving him, she said, 'Have you contacted your family? I know they want to see you.'

'This isn't quite changing the subject,' he pointed out wryly, 'but Toni's coming on Friday. I'm not sure if John will be with her. Apparently Guy can't face me.' He smiled sadly. 'I don't suppose I can blame him for that. In his shoes I'd probably feel the same.'

'Would you want to see him?'

He gave it some thought. 'To be honest, I'm not sure. It'd be difficult under any circumstances, given what we're dealing with, but to face it in here . . .' He sighed wearily and rubbed a hand across his jaw, his expression telling her more than words how much he was hurting. 'Do you have kids?' he asked, pointedly moving the conversation away from his family.

Going with it, she said, 'Yes, two. Charlie's twenty-one and Livvy's eighteen.'

He smiled. 'I was going to say you must have had them young, but I guess you hear that all the time. Do you have any photos?'

Seeing no harm in showing him, she reached for her phone and scrolled to a few that didn't include Tom.

As he studied their faces he said, 'They're like you, apart from your son's colouring. I suppose he resembles his father in that respect?'

She nodded and took the phone back, suddenly horribly aware of the son he'd lost. She wondered if he was thinking about him now, imagining how he'd be if he'd lived. It was unbearable what he was going through, so much loss and grief that would break most people. 'Do you think about Lucas often?' she asked softly.

His eyes came briefly to hers before seeming to lose focus. 'Even if he's not at the front of my mind,' he said, 'he's never far away, and I guess that won't ever change. I'm not sure I want it to, in spite of how it makes me feel.' He looked at her again. 'Have you ever lost anyone close to you?'

'My father, which I know is nothing like losing a child.'

'It still matters, and anyway it's not a competition, is it?'

'No, it's definitely not that.'

'So you were close?'

'Very. I guess you could say I became a lawyer because of him.'

'I'm going to assume,' he said dryly, 'that means you followed in his footsteps rather than because he'd got himself into trouble.'

With a laugh, she said, 'He started the firm, Bamfield and Forster, and I took over as one of the senior partners after he died.'

'Did you always want to be a lawyer?'

'Yes, I think so. I can't remember wanting to do anything else. Was it the same for you about becoming an architect?'

He treated her to an ironic scowl. 'Just about everything in my life will end up leading us back to why we're here, and if you don't mind, I'm enjoying this break.'

Understanding, she said, 'Do you have any other visitors besides your sister?'

'This is still about me,' he objected.

'But not the case, and I'm interested to know.'

'OK. A couple of friends came last week and others have put in requests, so luckily I'm not completely abandoned.'

'That's good to hear. Do you have any other family? Cousins? Aunts? Uncles?'

'Yes, there are quite a few Blakes and Claydens (my mother's side) dotted around the place. Apparently they call Toni regularly to find out how I'm doing and I'm pretty sure they'd come to visit if I hadn't asked her to put them off.'

'Why did you do that?'

He arched an eyebrow. 'I don't want them seeing me in here. Although I'll have to rethink that if things don't go well. I'll probably want all the visitors I can get then.'

Moved by how humorous he was managing to sound, considering the enormity of what he was facing, she said, 'Do you write letters?'

He laughed. 'I do now. Actually, one of my aunts writes quite lovely letters, all about her garden. She has some impressive descriptive skills I hadn't been aware of before. Her husband, my mother's brother, always scrawls his name at the bottom with a cheery little "keep the chin up, old boy" or "we know you didn't do it so don't lose heart." Actually, he was a little more expansive in the last letter, almost half a page, would you believe, telling me he'd done his research on you and he feels sure I'm in the right hands.'

Laughing Jay said, 'I'm glad he thinks so.'

'I do too, but I'm afraid it looks as though you have to let me go now.'

She glanced over her shoulder to see a guard at the door, ready to return Blake to his cell.

'Will you come again before the DNA results are back?' he asked as they stood.

'It'll depend if anything comes up that we need to discuss, and I'm sure it will.'

'OK. And if anything happens my end, I'll call.'

As she drove away a few minutes later, she was wondering if she should have told him to call anyway if he wanted to. He was understandably lonely – how could he not be? – and it wouldn't be unusual for a client to ring for a morale boost, or simply to make contact with the outside world. She'd say it the next time they spoke, and perhaps, whether anything came up or not, she'd get Vikki to book another visit for next week.

CHAPTER THIRTY-NINE

Over the next few days, with Tom in chambers so coming home each night, he and Jay moved around one another carefully, largely silently, not wanting to say or do anything to trigger another violent scene. If they spoke at all it was only about work, the children or maybe the news, and at the end of each evening they went their separate ways to bed.

When she got home on Wednesday following a tiresome afternoon in court, it was to find him preparing a meal, and since the table was only laid for two, she presumed no one was coming over. Did it mean he wanted to talk? Had found himself somewhere to live? Or was he just trying to be friendly?

'Have you heard from Livvy today?' he asked, passing her a glass of wine.

'Only half a dozen times,' she replied with a half-smile. 'I'm beginning to wonder if she'll come home again before she goes off travelling. To quote her, she's so blissed out now that she and Nat are a thing, that she's happy to hang around at his place in Exeter until after graduation when they can all go together.'

'That's good,' he responded, glancing out at the garden. 'He and Charlie can take care of her, keep her out of trouble, and OK, I guess I'm not supposed to say things

350

like that in this post-Me-Too world, but as her father I'm allowed to worry, and tell me you don't agree.'

'I do, we just won't say it to her.'

'How about we eat outside?' he suggested. 'It's a nice evening.'

Not knowing how to refuse without provoking some sort of bite-back, she simply shrugged and went to move the place settings. She took a moment to inhale the scent of roses climbing the back wall, and another to subdue the wrenching sadness and onrush of denial that their time here together was coming to an end.

The evening passed slowly, and even fairly agreeably, as they chatted about an upcoming trial of his, and a problematic staff issue at Brunel Chambers, while she agonized over a client meeting earlier in the day that hadn't gone well. She didn't talk to him about Edward Blake's case these days, and for some reason he didn't ask.

Antonia had called earlier in the day to let her know that the funeral was set for next Friday and she'd wondered if her brother would be allowed to go.

'I'm afraid not,' Jay had replied, feeling genuinely sorry. 'I'd hoped they would change their stance, but they haven't.'

'Oh no, poor Ed. Have you told him?'

'Not yet, unless someone at the prison has.'

'He's going to be so upset. We were trying to get a visit with him for next Friday, but obviously we won't be able to go now.'

'He'll understand,' Jay assured her, 'and I'm certain he'd rather you were there for Vanessa than for him.'

'Yes, in spite of everything, I'm sure he would.'

'Will Guy go with you?'

'He – he doesn't want to. John says he has to, so we'll see. Camille will come, obviously, and the rest of the family. I'm quite overwhelmed by how many want to pay their respects. I think they see it as a gesture of solidarity with Ed. He'll be touched by that.'

Knowing Antonia was shying away from the question she most feared the answer to, Jay took them there gently.

'I'm afraid Guy's results aren't back yet,' she said. And because she had to, she added, 'His housemate is saying that he didn't know Guy was in his room that night until he went to bed himself around ten.'

Antonia gave a sob of anguish. 'It'll simply be because he didn't hear him come in,' she insisted. 'You know what youngsters are like when they get caught up in their video games. He surely can't be seen as a reliable witness.'

'Possibly not, but there's no reason to worry about it now. You have enough to get through in the next couple of weeks with the funeral. I'll be in touch as soon as I have any news.'

Actually, there had been more to tell, but Jay had decided to hold back on the fact that Berzina's DNA had not been a match for any taken from the scene; Antonia didn't need to deal with that yet.

Looking up as Tom returned to the table with more wine, she said, 'Did I hear you talking to someone in there?'

'Oh, yes. I had a call. Nothing urgent.'

Her eyebrows arched. *Not urgent, but whoever it was had rung after nine thirty at night and apparently it wasn't one of the children.* Knowing instinctively it had been Ellen Tyler, she said, 'What did she want?'

He frowned. Then, clearly realizing it was no good

trying to pretend, he said, 'The same as always, to know if you're willing to accept the . . . proposal of shared custody.'

Somehow forcing herself to stay calm, she picked up her wine and said, quietly, 'Why haven't you told her that I'm not willing?'

'Why do you think? Because I keep hoping you'll change your mind.'

She couldn't look at him, didn't want to see the anguish and uncertainty in his eyes, or the frustration and intimidation she knew was building. 'I won't,' she told him. 'I don't know how to make myself any clearer.'

'Well, I'm not going to move out, so we'll have to come to some sort of compromise.'

Getting up from the table, she took her glass inside and drank what was left of the wine. She wasn't going to have the argument again. If necessary *she'd* find a place for him to live, and even pack his bags, but the two things were non-negotiable, she informed him as he followed her in.

'I won't have the baby here, and I am not leaving.'

'Well, I guess we'll see about that,' he retorted and, apparently as keen as she was to avoid a showdown, he took himself off to the study.

The following morning, during her drive into the office, Jay connected to Terry Josephs. 'I'd like you to do something for me,' she told him, 'and it needs to stay between us.'

'No problem,' he responded. 'Just name it.'

'I'm going to email you some details about a young woman. Her name's Ellen Tyler, she's a PR executive in catering, or was at some point, and she lives in London.

I'm not sure of her address, but I think it's in the Hampstead area. Her husband is Jed Tyler; he teaches history at a local school according to his Facebook page. I'd like you to find out what you can about them and report back to me.'

'Will do. I'm guessing you don't want me to make actual contact?'

'No, not at all. I'm just interested to know whatever you manage to find out.'

By the time Blake rang at five on Thursday evening, he already knew he wouldn't be going to the funeral the following week. Apparently one of the guards had taken some pleasure in delivering the message only minutes after the decision had been made. 'So the good news is,' he told Jay dryly, 'you're not having to deal with my emotional fall-out. It's over, I'm back in control and working on how to master patience in the face of intolerable strain.'

Jay smiled, and wondered whether the fall-out had been more temper than tears, but she didn't ask. He was a proud man, or as proud as his situation allowed, and whatever the reaction it hadn't involved violence towards another or she'd have heard about it. 'I'm sorry it was refused,' she said, getting up to close her office door. 'I'd hoped for some leniency, compassion even, but unfortunately they are commodities in short supply where you are.'

'I know, but thanks for trying. I'll have to figure out my own way of saying goodbye, I guess. We're not a religious family, but there's a chaplain here, maybe I'll have a chat with him.'

Sitting back into her chair, Jay was about to speak when he said, 'Will you be going?'

Having already considered it, she said, 'It's at eleven o'clock, so I thought I'd arrange a visit to the prison at that time, unless you'd prefer the chaplain.'

She heard him take a breath, and his voice faltered slightly as he said, 'I can catch up with the chaplain another time.'

She was glad she'd made the decision to be there for him in the only way possible. It was no time for anyone to be alone.

He said, 'I guess no news about Guy's DNA or you'd have told Toni or John?'

'Not yet.'

'It's not looking good for him, is it?'

'But only we know that at the moment.'

'I truly don't believe he did it, which is partly why I wanted to go to the funeral. Don't they say the killer often turns up and mingles with the crowd?'

'It happens more on TV than in life. All the same, Joe, my investigator, will be there, and I'm hoping a detective will be too. If Bright weren't on holiday I'm sure he'd go, but maybe Hamble will. We'll see.' She glanced at the time. 'I'm afraid I have to go, but I'll see you next Friday and if you need to call before that you have the number.'

CHAPTER FORTY

It was the night before Vanessa Blake's funeral that Joe rang Jay at home to report back on what he'd discovered about Ellen Tyler. As she listened she felt herself turning hot with disbelief and rage.

Lies, lies and yet more lies.

After thanking Joe and ringing off, she gave herself a moment before going into the sitting room where she picked up the remote, killed the TV and turned to Tom.

'What the hell . . . ?' he protested. 'I was watching that.'

'Did you know,' she demanded, eyes blazing, 'that Jed Tyler is your mistress's *brother*? Not husband! Her *brother!*'

His shock appeared so genuine she almost faltered.

'It wasn't so difficult to find out, Tom,' she seethed, 'so why did you think you could hide it from me?'

'I didn't! For God's sake, I had no idea. She told me she was married—'

'And you believed her because you wanted to fuck her? I can see exactly how it went; her being married meant you weren't the only one cheating, or the only one with something to lose. Except you were. You've been set up, Tom, and—'

'Hang on! Hang on! How do you know this?'

'Because I bothered to find out, and you apparently

didn't. You were so besotted with her you were prepared to listen to anything she told you—'

'Jay, I swear—'

'No! You've done enough of that. The child could never have been his; his only role was to help her get you. And now you have a child to tie you to her for ever, so good luck with it.'

Leaping to his feet as she made for the door, he grabbed her arm and spun her back. 'Jay, I did not know about this . . .'

'It's too late now. You've been played for a fool by a woman you clearly wanted enough to betray me twice for. She's yours, Tom. Take her. Live with her, just don't ever bring her or her child into my home—'

'Our home,' he raged.

'I'm calling the children, and as soon as we can get them here *you* are going to tell them why their parents are breaking up – and where they can visit you when they come back from their travels.'

'You're being hysterical. I don't even know if any of this is true.'

'You think I'd make it up? For God's sake, get a grip on yourself. But if you need confirmation, talk to Joe. He found out for me and it didn't take him long. I just wonder why you didn't do the same? I think it's because you simply didn't care. You wanted her so badly you were ready to believe anything and you carried on believing it . . . So go to her! Now! Tonight! He's her brother. You don't have to worry about being under his roof. They've probably got everything already set up for you.'

Snatching up his car keys, he said, 'You don't get the last word on this,' and clearly deciding in the moment that he did, he slammed out of the front door.

CHAPTER FORTY-ONE

'And there's a baby,' she found herself telling Blake the following morning. 'Maybe it could all be sorted out if it weren't for that, but there's no pretending he doesn't exist, not for any of us. Even if we could, there's still the fact that Tom went back to her, I don't see how we can get past that, and with a child between them now, how long will it be before he decides it's her he wants?'

Why was she doing this? How had she even got into talking about herself when it should be all about him, especially today? Maybe if he hadn't realized as soon as she arrived that she wasn't herself, and been so insistent she tell him why, she wouldn't have given in to the need to talk. She must stop now, apologize, and turn the subject to the real reason she was here.

Gently, he said, 'Did he come back last night?'

She sighed and shook her head. 'I don't know where he went. I presume it was to her, but I don't know that for certain. I sent a text this morning to make sure he hadn't had an accident, and got one back saying he hadn't and that he'd see me this evening.' Her eyes went to Blake's and seeing his concern she said, 'You know, I really didn't mean to come here and pour it all out like this. I came to be supportive to you and now we've somehow swapped roles—'

'That's not such a bad thing,' he interrupted. 'It's clear you needed to talk to someone and, apart from me being a captive audience, I tend to be quite a good listener.'

With a smile she said, 'You're certainly both, but it's no reason for me to carry on burdening you with my affairs. It's almost eleven o'clock, the funeral service will begin soon and I thought, if you'd like to, you could spend the time telling me about Vanessa.'

The transition seemed abrupt, but with a guard waiting outside and a clock ticking too fast, she wanted to help him to honour his wife in the only way he could.

He sat back in his chair and sighed despondently. 'I've been trying not to think about it,' he confessed, 'but of course I can't think about anything else. The thoughts, memories, come crowding in on me and there's no order to them, only light and dark, happiness clouded by guilt and worry and grief. There's so much I regret . . .'

Coming in softly she said, 'Why don't you tell me about the first time you met?'

He sighed again and dropped his head as he began to murmur her name. It was so gentle it was like the sound of a caress.

She looked at his dark blond hair, thick, wavy, and wondered if he was trying to force back tears. The strength of him was as pervasive as his helplessness, even the essence of him seemed almost tangible. What a terrible day this was for him. Seeing him struggling with it all made it easy to put her own misery aside, to allow empathy and compassion to fill its space.

At last he looked up. His eyes were dry, but showing sorrow inside the self-mocking smile he so often attempted. 'I noticed her right away,' he began. 'She was too beautiful not to notice, too lively and engaging to ignore even if you wanted to, and I didn't. I could say it was love at first sight, but at the time it was no more, or less, than a powerful attraction. I didn't fall in love until I got to know her, and actually it didn't take long given how much time we spent together.' He smiled bleakly. 'To know her is to love her, I once told her father. She was capricious, but sweet-natured, passionate, curious, intelligent . . . She cared about people in a way that drew them to her, made them feel special simply for having her attention. I used to watch her and feel so lucky that she'd come into my life. She said it was the same for her, that she couldn't get enough of me, never wanted us to be apart.

'We got married eight months into our relationship on a beach in Thailand. It was romantic and impulsive and the happiest day of our lives. Toni and John threw a party for us when we got home and we could hardly believe how many people came. Her father made a speech, so did John, then I had to, of course, and I probably embarrassed everyone by quoting cheesy poetry and lyrics.

'We found Clover Hill Farm about a year later and threw ourselves into renovating the properties, always knowing that the big house would be ours when we'd finished. We'd already talked about having children and so we stopped the precautions, wanting it to happen and the sooner the better. The first time she got pregnant she miscarried. It was devastating for us both. We were terrified after that something might be wrong with one of us, but then she was pregnant again and Clover Hill was ready and everything was so perfect that, looking back, I probably should have been afraid. Nothing ever stays perfect for ever, does it?'

Knowing he didn't really want an answer to that, she simply continued to watch him, noticing how talking about his wife and happier times had seemed to lift him from the gloom and dread that daily encompassed his life.

'She always said she loved me,' he continued, 'and I believe she really did in the early years. Actually, I think she continued to, but everything became so tangled up and unpredictable and crazy after we lost Lucas.' He stopped, pressed his fingers to his eyes and didn't try to speak again.

In the end Jay said, 'What was she like as a mother?'

He took a breath, tried to answer and had to try again. 'She was doting, proud, amazed that he was ours,' he said hoarsely. 'She loved to watch me with him; took so many photos of us asleep, in the bath, playing, fussing Max, eating . . . He had a wonderful temperament, our boy, she always insisted he took after me in that way.' He swallowed noisily. 'She started reading to him when he was still in the womb, and after he was born he'd watch her in what looked like total fascination when she spoke to him; here was the voice he knew so well and he could hardly believe it.'

He looked down briefly, then turned to stare at the glass wall. 'Of course everything changed after we lost him,' he said roughly. 'How could it not? He was the centre of our world, the absolute heart of us, and now it was all broken, trampled with guilt, and so beyond repair I'm not sure we ever really tried to mend it. We just couldn't see how to. She stopped being the woman I knew, and I suppose I was different too. I still loved her, and I think she loved me, but she also hated me for reminding her of him. She blamed me and herself and me again. She couldn't wait to get away from me, but within a day, maybe less, she'd call and beg me to come and get her. I always went, but if she couldn't reach me for some reason, she'd call Toni or John or one of our friends. We all knew how vulnerable she was, how badly she needed protecting, so it became an unspoken pact between us that we'd always be there for her.'

Although Jay had meant for him to describe, even relive, only the good times, she didn't try to redirect him for he clearly needed to run with his thoughts and this was where they were taking him.

'I kept thinking it would get better over time,' he said, 'that she'd find a way to handle the grief, the guilt even, but she never did. Instead of trusting in a therapist she began sleeping with other men to try and blot it all out. It helped her to feel powerful, she said, to know that someone found her beautiful and would never ask about Lucas. She'd tell me these things to punish me for not loving her enough to keep her baby alive. Almost imme-diately she was sorry, but it wouldn't be long before she did it again. She wouldn't name names, but I was afraid that sometimes it was men we knew – well, that's been borne out now, hasn't it?'

Feeling for the torturous journey they'd been unable to escape, the devastating discoveries of who she'd chosen and who had betrayed him, Jay said, 'Why wouldn't she get help?'

He shook his head despairingly. 'She felt she didn't deserve it. She said it was right for her to suffer – for us both to suffer – after what we'd let happen to Lucas.'

He sat back in his chair, as though to distance himself from the memories he'd just allowed himself to voice. After a while his expression began to change; he seemed more present, in the moment, as he stared searchingly into her eyes. In the end, he said, 'You know, no one's keener than I am for you to find out who's behind what happened to my wife, unless it turns out to be Guy, but I still don't believe that he is capable of that.'

Aware that time was starting to run out, she said, 'I know the rest of today is going to be hard for you. I wish I could stay longer, but . . .'

'I do too,' he said softly, 'but there is a way you could make it easier if you're willing to?'

She wondered if he was going to ask her to hold him, to allow him just a few moments of human contact, something he must need a great deal right now, and what would she do if he did?

Even if it had been in his mind he didn't say it, only met her eyes with what seemed like an understanding of where her thoughts had gone. 'Toni and John are hosting the reception,' he said. 'If you're able to go there yourself, to look around at the faces, to see if something or someone doesn't feel quite right . . . It would mean a lot if I knew you were doing what I'd do myself if I could.'

'I'll do it,' she said, 'but tell me first is there anyone, *anyone* at all, you think I should be looking out for?'

He shook his head. 'I've racked my brains, and even gone through Toni's guest list, but there isn't.' He sat forward, bringing his hands close to hers. 'I'm sure your investigator is one of the best,' he said, 'but I don't know him. I do know you, and I trust your instincts as much as my own.'

She smiled. 'I guess I'm flattered, but you know I can't guarantee anything.'

'Of course, I just want us both to be sure that we've done everything we possibly can to find this man, and I don't think either of us is in any doubt that it is a man.'

CHAPTER FORTY-TWO

Jay had texted ahead so Joe was waiting at the front door of Highview Hall when she arrived. There were so many cars outside that some had been forced to park on the grass verges or under the trees, and the burble of voices could be heard through the open windows of the front drawing room.

'And it really had never occurred to him before that it might be his nephew?' Joe commented after Jay had repeated Blake's final words before she'd left.

'I don't know,' she answered, following him into the great hall where half a dozen uniformed caterers were coming and going with trays and bottles, 'but even if it did . . . To be honest, I think it would be like losing another son if it turned out to be him, and right now he just can't go there.'

As they entered the gathering they remained on the edge of it all, watching and listening and trying to pinpoint anyone, or anything, unusual amongst the hundred or more mourners. 'Has anyone stood out for you yet?' she asked quietly.

'I can't say they have. All the usual suspects are here, family, friends, neighbours . . . Pity the lad, Guy, didn't show up. I'd have liked to get a look at how he handled himself in the circumstances.'

'That could be why his father didn't insist on him coming?'

'Could be. Speaking of Debrayne senior, he's not looking too clever if you ask me. Not a drop of colour in him, and he was proper upset at the ceremony. If the bloke didn't have an alibi for the time it happened, I might have a closer eye on him.'

Jay surveyed the room again, and spotted Antonia in the midst of the crowd, looking tired and anxious in spite of her valiant efforts to play the gracious hostess. 'How was the service?' she asked Joe.

'Moving. Even brought a tear to my eye. Big turn-out. Well, you can see for yourself. Even the wicked step-mother's here.' He nodded in Daphne's direction and Jay caught the woman staring their way.

'Berzina and Freya?' Jay asked.

'They're around somewhere. It looks like half the county's here.'

'Who's that over there, talking to Debrayne?' She was looking in the direction of the fireplace.

'Oh, that's the Dutch neighbours. Can't remember their names off the top of my head. They're younger than I expected. Early forties, would you say?'

'Around that, and he's extremely attractive. The type Vanessa might go for?'

'I'm not sure looks came into it much with her, but you're right, he's a bit of a Romeo or whatever they say these days. The woman who's just joined them is the other neighbour from Clover Hill, Mrs Maguire. She sang at the service. Lovely voice.'

'Where's her husband?'

Joe scanned the crowd. 'Can't see him . . . Ah, over

there, talking to the woman in a lime green jacket. Oh, and look! Right next to them is the lovely Lacey Hamble, blending like a lump in the custard.' Catching DS Hamble's eye he gave her a jolly little wave and was treated to a vicious glare in return. 'Got to love her,' he murmured.

'Follow me,' Jay said, and leading the way she wound a path through the crowd towards Frank Maguire.

Appearing startled and slightly bemused until he recognized her, Maguire readily shook her hand, his own as shaky as she recalled from their first meeting. 'I'm not sure I was expecting to see you here,' he stated, his eyes darting to Joe and back again.

'Likewise,' Jay replied with a smile, 'but you made it down from Sunderland.'

'Of course. Of course. We had to be here. I think I told you Vanessa meant a lot to my wife. Actually, they both do – to both of us. Were you at the service?'

'No. Actually, I was with Edward.'

Compassion warmed Maguire's words. 'How is he? This must be so hard for him, being where he is. We pray for him, Maddie and I. Please tell him that. Am I allowed to ask if you've made any headway with his case?'

'You are,' she replied, 'and I'll be happy to tell you, but this probably isn't the right time or place?'

Clearly ashamed of having forgotten his sense of occasion, he said, 'Of course not. Forgive me.'

Treating him to a benevolent smile she said, 'My secretary will call to set up a time. However, before I let you go, can I ask one quick question? Do you remember seeing a red car coming or going from the main house that day?'

His face paled slightly as he swallowed.

It was answer enough. He'd apparently lied to try and

protect Guy Debrayne, and she almost felt sorry for the sense of loyalty he seemed to feel towards the family that probably wasn't even known about, much less returned.

Except where did that leave his loyalty to Edward?

How conflicted he must be.

Assuring him they'd be in touch, she parted company with Joe and proceeded to spend the next hour mingling with the guests and introducing herself, at Antonia's suggestion, as Edward's lawyer. No one seemed to flinch or feel any embarrassment when they heard this; to the contrary, many asked how he was and wanted her to send their best wishes the next time she saw him. Apart from one warty old chap who turned out to be the Debrayne's farm manager. 'Never know what a bloke's capable of when pushed,' he grunted. 'If he did it, then he's in the right place. If he didn't, let's hope you can get him out.'

Finally, having received no reliable alerts from her instincts, she said her goodbyes to the Debraynes, found Joe and walked with him out to her car. 'What do we know about the Dutch couple, him in particular?' she asked, aware of Mr Van der Berg watching them from the window.

'Nothing much, but I believe he was questioned by video link and had it confirmed he wasn't in the country at the time of the killing. But I'll get on to it.'

'Thanks. Oh, and thanks again for the little job you did for me.'

Turning to her, he fixed her with the avuncular stare she knew well and often tried to avoid. 'There's a baby, did you know that?' he asked bluntly.

She nodded. 'It's Tom's.'

His expression collapsed into dismay. 'I was afraid you

might say that. Stupid man. *Stupid, stupid* man. So what's he going to do?'

'I'm not sure yet, he's only just found out himself that she's not married to Jed Tyler – if you believe him, and I think I do. So, now he knows she's single—'

'He's not going to leave you,' Joe interrupted. 'Never going to happen.'

Leaning in she kissed his cheek and opened her car door. 'I'll see you on Monday for the crime team meeting,' she said and, already bracing herself for the evening ahead with Tom, she started the drive home.

CHAPTER FORTY-THREE

As Jay pulled up next to Tom's car an hour later, she was talking to Blake on the phone, so she remained in the driver's seat for a while, as reluctant to go inside as she felt to end the call. 'I can't say anyone actually stood out,' she told him, 'but there are a few things I want to bring up at the team meeting on Monday.'

'Such as?'

'Your Dutch tenant interested me, but let me run with it first. It could be nothing, and I don't have the paperwork to hand to go through it right now. Can I remind you that this call is probably being listened to?'

'I'm told no one ever bothers, and even if they do it's random. But yes, let's change the subject.' His voice was gentler as he said, 'It meant a lot to me that you came today.'

'I'm glad I did,' she replied, feeling the warmth of their connection softening her. She wanted to say more about her visit, but the words weren't there, only the sentiments behind them of caring and understanding what he was going through and the need to try and make him feel less alone.

'It was good to feel more human than criminal,' he said wryly. 'More who I am, I should probably say.'

'I know who you are,' she assured him.

'Thanks.' Then, 'Where are you now?'

'In the car, outside my house.'

'Where do you live?'

'Clifton.'

'Mm, I think I could have guessed that.'

She smiled. 'I won't ask where you are.'

He laughed. 'Is your husband back from wherever he went?'

'Yes. I haven't seen him yet though.'

'OK. Well, I guess I should probably let you go.'

Because there was no real reason to stay on the line, she said, 'I'll be in touch soon.'

Several moments passed as they remained connected, listening to the silence, letting it fill with the solace of knowing the other was there, until finally he ended the call.

As soon as Jay let herself in the front door, she could hear Tom on the phone in the study, so she slipped off her shoes and went through to the kitchen to fix herself a drink. Tired though she was, she could feel the adrenalin of anxiety and nervousness starting to kick in, momentarily confusing and blurring her thoughts as she tried to work out what to expect.

Hearing him come into the sitting room, she turned around and knew straight away that this was not going to go well. He was scowling, tense, appeared defensive even, and she didn't help by saying, 'Where did you spend last night?'

His jaw tightened as he said, 'If you're asking did I spend it with Ellie, then I did not.'

Her heart jolted on the *Ellie*, not Ellen. It made them seem more . . . of a couple, a special use of a name reserved for intimate friends. 'So where were you?' she asked tersely.

'In London. I went to talk to her in the light of what you'd told me and it turns out you're right, Jed is her brother, not her husband.' He rubbed his temples to ease the strain she could sense pounding there.

'So why did she lie to you?'

He took a breath and let it out slowly. 'For the reasons you'd already defined. She thought I'd feel . . .' He searched for the right words, 'more comfortable in our relationship if I believed she had as much to lose as I did – although she swears she never told me she was married, it was more of an assumption on my part that she didn't correct.'

Neat move, Ellen, she thought bitterly, *how would he remember if you managed to fudge it right from the start?* 'Didn't she wear a ring?'

'I guess so. I don't really remember.'

Yes, you do. 'So now you know she's free . . .'

'Don't go there,' he growled. 'Whether or not she's married has nothing to do with this. It's about the child . . .'

'Did you see him last night?'

'Of course. It was hard not to when I was at the house and she was feeding him.'

Oh another smart move, Ellen. Breastfeed the baby in front of Daddy. Guaranteed to hook him in. 'Did you hold him?' she asked, feeling the bottom dropping out of her world.

'He's my son, so why wouldn't I?'

As hurt by his tone as the image his words had created, she turned away to refill her glass. 'You still haven't told me where you spent the night,' she reminded him.

'I went to my usual hotel in Clerkenwell. You can check if—'

Spinning round, she cried, 'Why are you so angry with me? I'm not the one who's in the wrong here, in case you'd forgotten.'

'How could I forget when you won't let me? And I'm not angry with you. I'm just . . . Christ, I don't know what I am. It's all such a mess and I hardly know what to say to you. You won't even discuss how we can go forward with this.'

'I've told you what I want to happen . . .'

'And I've given you my answer.'

Frustration pulsed in her head. 'Did you tell her I've asked you to move out?'

'No, I did not.'

'So what did you tell her? She surely wants to know what I had to say about the fact that she's given birth to my husband's child.'

His eyes flashed with temper. 'You can't resist it, can you? Any chance to seize the moral high ground—'

'Seize it? It's completely mine. I'm not the one who cheated on you . . .'

'There you go again. Can't you see how unhelpful those remarks are? I'm trying to find a way through this that will work for us all, and what do you do apart from constantly remind me that I'm the one in the wrong and therefore I'm the one who should go?'

'Then what do you want me to say? Bring your baby here, let me play at being Mummy for a weekend a month or however often she wants you to have him? Oh, and won't it be fun to pick him up from school now and again, or focus our holidays around him, or help him with

373

his homework? We've done all that, Tom, and I don't want to do it again, especially not with a child that isn't mine.'

Glaring at her with furious eyes, he said, 'Are you trying to push me into her arms? Is that what's going on here?'

She scoffed a laugh. 'You don't need any pushing from me. Look at you! You've only just found out she's single and see what a state you're in. You don't know what to do, whether you can actually bring yourself to break up your marriage or not, and it's only going to get harder the more you know the boy – and the more you see her.'

'There you go again, assuming you know everything . . .'

'Then tell me I'm wrong, that you're not torn between us, that you're not even considering going to her.'

'I would if I thought you were listening, but you're not . . .'

'Oh, I'm hearing you all right, but you don't seem to realize how your tune has changed since last night. Before that you were sorry, desperate to make it up to me, ready to fight for us. Now you're not sorry at all.' She jumped as he suddenly smashed his glass in the sink.

'What I'm sorry about,' he raged, rounding on her, 'is that you're so damned impossible to talk to. I've told you I love you, that I don't want us to break up . . .'

'You think this is all about what *you* want. I don't believe you've tried to look at it from my perspective at all.'

'So what do you want?'

'God, how many times? I want you to leave – and if that means going to her, then so be it. Go play happy families with the mother of your child, because this . . . This . . . mother . . . Oh, for God's sake,' she seethed as she started to break down. 'Let's end this now. I can't talk about it any more. We keep going around in circles and I don't want to live with your guilty conscience, because that's the only reason you'll stay, and what that actually amounts to is pity and your pity is something I really don't need.'

'I give up,' he roared, as she walked away. 'I don't know what to say to convince you you're wrong, so maybe you're right, I should go. We're clearly never going to be able to work things out while you refuse to, so if you want me out, maybe that's what I'll do.'

She turned around, pain burning in her heart and clouding her eyes. 'It didn't take long for you to cave, did it?' she said acidly. 'I'll call the children and arrange a time for us to get together. Now, if you'll excuse me, I'm going to take a bath and I won't be wanting any dinner.'

CHAPTER FORTY-FOUR

Being at the office and heading up a crime team meeting had never felt as welcome as it did today. At last she was out of the house, no longer doing her best to avoid any more confrontations with Tom or convince him she was serious about telling the children. She'd called both Charlie and Livvy, and had arranged for them to come next Saturday to hear the news their father had to share. She knew they'd probably spend half the week trying to guess what it was, but she hadn't allowed herself to be drawn, hadn't even commented on whether it was good or bad news, had simply said that it would be for them to decide when they heard it.

She hated doing this to them, and knew she'd spend the week asking herself if she should be trying to prepare them.

But no, this was all on Tom. She'd be there when he told them, but she was not going to find the words for him.

Now, after spending the first hour of the team meeting discussing other cases and commitments, the subject finally got round to Edward Blake and had hardly begun when, with perfect timing, Matt Kowalski, their defence scientist rang.

Putting the call on speaker, Jay came straight to the

point. 'What news on Guy Debrayne's DNA? Is there a match?'

His voice was a slow Welsh drawl. 'Yes to random samples taken,' he replied, 'but we always knew the lad was in and out of the house. No to the unidentified. Definitely doesn't belong to him.'

Feeling conflicted about that, Jay looked at the others as she took it in. At least it meant she wouldn't be having to fight Blake over taking responsibility for something his nephew had done, but it still remained a saliva sample with no owner.

Ash sat back in his chair and tossed a pen onto the desk, another way of throwing up his hands. 'So it's not the nephew's and it's not Berzina's,' he stated in frustration. 'So who the hell does it belong to?'

Sallyanne said, 'OK, we need to go back to the beginning, sort through everyone we know who's given statements, who was and wasn't swabbed—'

Interrupting, Jay said, 'That's a great idea, but first, Matt, can you tell us if the neighbours have been eliminated? Frank Maguire and Hans Van der Berg. I know they've both given statements, but what about DNA?'

'OK, bear with me,' came the reply. 'The Van der Berg guy is Dutch, clue is in the name, but there's no . . . I can't see any results listed for him, but they might be . . . Hang on, let's go with Maguire first, his swab would have been taken on or around the twenty-ninth and . . . Well, there's a turn-up – or not – he's not here, unless it was taken later. But here's the other guy under D, not B, or V, or wherever he ought to be. His was taken by Dutch police and he's been eliminated.'

Jay's eyes were fixed on Joe as she said to Matt, 'Let

me get this straight. Maguire was not asked to provide a DNA sample, but Van der Berg was?'

'Seems that way on the face of it, but I'll dig deeper if you want me to, and get back to you.'

'OK, thanks.' After ending the call, she said to Joe, 'They have to have swabbed him.'

'Have you spoken to him at all?' Sallyanne asked, searching through the files.

Jay nodded. 'We know he saw the red car,' she said to Joe. 'It was evident in the way he practically flinched when I mentioned it.'

Joe didn't disagree.

Her mind was racing, coming up with more questions and scenarios than could even begin to make sense. 'When's Ken Bright back from his holiday?' she asked.

'I can check, but I think next week.'

'OK. We'll have to wait until then, because we know we won't get anything out of Lucy Hamble.'

Vikki murmured, 'You're due in court, Jay.'

Getting to her feet, Jay said, 'Set up a prison visit for me asap, will you?'

'You've got one on Friday, with Cyrus Trott,' Vikki reminded her, referring to the junior barrister.

'Of course, good.' It was time to start prepping for the plea hearing. 'Joe, call Antonia to tell her the good news about her son's DNA. She can pass it on to Blake, in case she speaks to him before I do. And now I'm out of here.'

Later, when Jay was back at the office unwinding over gin and tonics with Perry, Blake rang. 'Have you heard about Guy?' she asked, settling in more comfortably on the sofa as she sipped her drink.

'Yes, I have. Thanks for making it happen so they weren't kept hanging on for too long.'

'I'm glad for them it turned out that way.' *But not for you*, she didn't add. He'd have heard it anyway. 'We could cut DS Hamble some slack for not swabbing your nephew, if she didn't know he wasn't John's son,' she continued, 'although I don't see why we should. However, it seems her oversights don't stop there. At the moment our scientist is searching for a record of your neighbour's DNA.'

'You mean Van der Berg?'

'No, he checks out. I'm talking about Maguire.'

He fell silent.

'We're pretty certain,' she went on, 'that he saw the red car coming or going from the house that day. I thought he was trying to protect your nephew, keeping it to himself until he found out which way things were going to fall, and that could still turn out to be the case.'

'And if it isn't?' he said darkly.

'I don't know yet. I'm going to try and talk to DI Bright as soon as he's back. Chances are our scientist will have tracked down the missing sample by then, we'll just have to wait and see.'

'OK.'

He was silent again so she said,

'I'm sorry, maybe I shouldn't have mentioned it until I was more certain of the situation.'

'It's OK. I want to be kept in the picture, it's just . . .' He paused and said, 'It wouldn't have been him. If that's what you're thinking. It just wouldn't.'

'No one's saying it was. We just need to get this . . . anomaly cleared up.'

Not arguing with that, he said, 'Will I be seeing you this week?'

'I think I'm there on Friday.'

'That's good.'

She smiled. 'Call before that if you need to, but I should go now. I'm with someone.'

As she put the phone down, Perry looked up from his and shifted more comfortably in the armchair. 'Do you want to talk about it?' he offered.

She shook her head. 'There's nothing to say right now and anyway, I know you're much more interested to hear what's happening with Tom.'

He didn't deny it.

Sighing past the tremulous waves in her heart, she said, 'Well, it turns out the mistress is *not* married so he's free to go to her any time he likes. We're telling the children at the weekend.'

Startled, he said, 'Don't you think this is going a bit fast? Whether he's free to go to her or not doesn't mean that he will.'

'I don't want to wait around to find out. I just want him to leave in as amicable a way as possible, not only for Charlie and Livvy, but for me and him.'

Perry began to shake his head, clearly not liking this one bit. 'This shouldn't be happening,' he said gravely, 'not to you guys.'

'Well, I'm afraid it is, and it's . . . Actually, I don't know what it is, but I'm grateful to have you and Gretchen, because your support means a lot.'

'We'll always be there for you, you know that.'

She nodded, and swallowed hard. 'Tom will need a friend too,' she reminded him, 'because whatever he decides, he's not going to find it easy, so please don't cut him out because of me.'

'I have no intention of doing that, because unlike you I'm not accepting that this is the end. You're still in shock, Jay. You might not know it, but you're high on the drama of it right now. No, listen. I know what I'm talking about. I deal with break-ups every day, remember, couples who decide way too fast that *this is it!* They've had enough, he or she is never going to change, they'll never be able to live together again, when it's not what they mean at all. Or it won't be six weeks, maybe six months down the line. You and Tom have been together way too long just to walk away now. Your lives, never mind your emotions, are tied up in ways you probably haven't even thought about . . .'

'Perry, whatever history we have isn't going to change the future. You know that as well as I do, but if you do want to help you can try to persuade him to go as soon as we've told the children.'

Perry regarded her bleakly. 'I'll have a chat with him,' he said, 'but I might as well tell you now, I won't say or do anything to bring about the end of your marriage. I'm sorry, I just can't do it.'

CHAPTER FORTY-FIVE

Fortunately, when Jay took Cyrus Trott to the prison on Friday, Blake seemed to take to the jovial old barrister right away, which actually wasn't much of a surprise, since almost everyone did, including juries. It was why so many defence solicitors wanted Cyrus on side.

There wasn't much for her to do during the visit apart from listen, so she was free to observe Blake in a more objective way than usual without feeling as though she was staring, simply assessing the tone of his voice, his body language and readiness to engage. To her relief he neither said nor did anything to concern her; he was as forthcoming and receptive to Cyrus as she could wish for. Of course she still hoped they wouldn't end up needing the barrister's services, but with the plea hearing coming closer by the day, they had to prepare.

Later, as she and Cyrus left the prison, she reflected on how fortunate it was that neither man had been able to read her mind, or in any way sense the physical reactions she experienced simply to look at Blake's hands, or the muscles of his forearms, or the intensity of his eyes. Her thoughts were like the press of a finger to start music, or a quiet and powerful explosion of sensation.

How strange it was that her body could respond with such a determined will of its own when her heart was in such turmoil.

She was almost back at the office when she was distracted by a call from Joe. 'Just to let you know,' he said, 'that Ken Bright's back tomorrow and I've left a message to let him know we need to talk to him.'

'Good, thanks. Any news from Matt about Maguire's DNA?'

'Nothing yet, but he's got tied up on another case, so we probably won't hear from him until Monday.'

'OK, as long as it's before we talk to Bright. Is Maguire still around, do we know?'

'He and the wife are packing up the barn ready to move to Sunderland.'

'And you know this because?'

'I rang to ask him if he was swabbed and he says he was.'

Frowning she said, 'OK, so there wasn't an oversight?'

'Apparently not, which means the screw-up, if there turns out to be one, could be purely administrative, or somehow the actual physical sample has gone missing.'

'Interesting,' she murmured.

'Mm, I guess so, but hey, it's Friday and I'm looking forward to a nice sunny weekend off. So you have a good one and I'll catch up with you first thing Monday.'

Even before she'd rung off, Jay's insides were dipping and churning with a nervous dread. She'd give almost anything for this weekend not to be happening, at least not in the way it was set to, but she'd put it all in motion now and she wasn't going to back down. The children were due to arrive in the morning, Tom was getting ready to say his piece, and it was time now to start bracing herself for the next inevitable step in the break-up of her marriage.

CHAPTER FORTY-SIX

Jay could hear Charlie and Livvy downstairs, laughing, arguing, sparring with their father as if everything were normal in their world, while up here in the bedroom her heart and conscience were so turbulent and torn that she'd give almost anything to avoid joining them. She didn't want to spoil the moment, the fun they were sharing. She didn't want this to be happening at all, but whether she confronted it today, tomorrow or next week, there was no escaping the impact that Aiden Tyler's birth was going to have on their family.

Maybe he was already a Wells.

Somehow she had to make herself push through her misgivings and reluctance and deal with this in a way that would, in the end, make it bearable for them all.

When she got downstairs, Charlie and Livvy were slouched on the sofas, phones in hands as they waited to discover the reason for their summons, while Tom busied himself with lunchtime snacks in the kitchen. Clearly he'd done nothing to prepare them for what was to come.

'Hey Mum,' Livvy said without taking her eyes off her phone.

'Looking cool, Mum,' Charlie added, not looking up either, which made Jay smile. He was such an easy-going, lovable young man; as quirkily handsome as his father, with his unruly dark hair and Roman nose, although his sportsman's physique still had some filling out to do.

She could feel Tom watching her, and could sense how tense he was, even if his expression didn't show it. She wondered how he was going to start things off. They hadn't discussed it, although she'd offered to sit down with him last night to decide on the best way, but he'd said there was no need.

'OK,' Livvy declared, tossing her phone aside as her father put a plate of handmade pizza bites on the coffee table between her and Charlie, 'we've worked out what this is about, so no need to get yourselves in a sweat about us being grossed out or anything. We're totally cool with you having another baby at your age, even though Mum always said she wouldn't.' She put on a big smile and was about to get up and throw her arms around them when she saw their faces and clearly realized she hadn't guessed right at all.

'Oh my God,' she murmured, looking suddenly afraid as she clapped a hand to her mouth. 'Which one of you is it? Oh God, Charlie, I told you it would be this . . .'

'No you *didn't*,' he argued. 'You said it wouldn't be.'

Realizing their next guess was that one of their parents had a terminal illness, Jay said quickly, 'We're fine, honestly. No one's sick, and I'm not going to have a baby, but Dad does have something to tell you.'

Livvy turned to her father while Charlie sat forward, not to eat, but to stop looking way more comfortable than he was clearly feeling.

Jay watched Tom go to stand with his back to the fireplace and, as she perched on the arm of a chair, she was caught by a powerful conflict of emotions. On the one hand she wanted to stop him, to pretend that it was all just a ruse to get the children home for a weekend. On the other she felt the need to help him, maybe even speak for him.

'Not like you to be lost for words, Dad,' Charlie tried to joke.

Tom attempted a smile. 'I've got to be honest, son, these are particularly hard to find.'

'Just say it,' Livvy urged. 'As long as we've all got our health and we're not about to go broke. We're not, are we?'

'No,' Tom assured her.

Jay knew he was looking at her now, but she kept her head down; for the moment at least he was on his own.

'The thing is,' he began, 'you weren't exactly wrong a minute ago, Livvy, when you mentioned a baby. The problem is . . . Well, you see, it's not Mum's, but it is mine.'

As Charlie frowned, Livvy's eyes widened with immediate understanding. 'Do you mean you've got another woman pregnant?' she cried, wanting it spelled out.

Tom said, 'I-I'm afraid I have, and the baby's actually already here. It's a boy, he's nearly five months old—'

Livvy cut across him furiously. 'I don't care how bloody old he is,' she raged. 'The fact that you've clearly cheated on Mum, worse than cheated . . . Oh my God! How could you? Look at her!' She flung an arm towards Jay. 'Most men would die to have a wife like that and this is what you do to her? My mother! *Our* mother! Who's always been there for us, who's never cheated on anyone in her life.'

Glad that was true, Jay looked at Tom as he said, 'I promise it wasn't done to hurt her . . .'

'That's hardly the point is it? Fucking hell, Dad . . .'

'Who's the other woman?' Charlie demanded harshly. 'Is it someone we know?'

'No,' Tom replied, 'it isn't.'

Livvy addressed her mother. 'How long's he been seeing her? Is it someone you know?'

Jay shook her head.

'When did you find out?' Livvy wanted to know.

Before Jay could answer Tom said, 'She's someone I knew a few years ago . . .'

'What does that mean? You had an affair with her then?'

'Yes, but it ended . . .'

'Except it apparently didn't, if there's a baby who's only *four months old.*' Livvy's tone was so scathing that even Jay winced.

Tom said, 'I ran into the mother again last year and . . . Well, we saw each other . . .'

'Oh Christ,' Charlie muttered in disgust. 'I can't believe this. Please tell me it isn't happening.'

'Son, you don't know . . .'

'Are you still seeing her?' Charlie snarled.

Livvy came to stand with Jay, putting a firm hand on her mother's shoulder as if to say, don't worry, I've got this. 'Answer the question, Dad,' she commanded, 'are you still seeing this *other woman?* I guess you must be if you have a baby together. So how long have you actually been with her?'

Tom swallowed and Jay knew that no court appearance had ever been as gruelling for him as this. 'I'm not with her,' he said quietly.

'Then what's the real story here?' Livvy persisted. 'You had an affair, broke up, got back together . . . ?'

'Something like that, but it wasn't serious . . .'

'Not serious!' Livvy almost shrieked. 'I'd say this is about as serious as it gets.' She turned to Jay. 'How can you stand to stay with him?' she raged. 'He's been cheating on you for . . . how long?' she shouted at her father. 'You still haven't told us how long you've been with this woman?'

'I told you, it's over,' he said. 'It ended three years ago, but when I saw her last year . . .'

Livvy turned back to her mother, eyes flashing. 'I don't see how you can ever forgive this,' she cried.

Jay didn't respond.

Charlie's tone was harsh with contempt as he said, 'So now you want to leave us and go start a new family. How sweet is that?' He shot to his feet. 'Well fucking go!' he shouted, punching a hand towards the door. 'We don't want you here . . .'

'Charlie, stop,' Jay said, bunching his fist between her hands.

'Why?' he cried. 'We don't want him here if this is . . .'

'Sssh,' she urged.

'No! He needs to hear what a bastard he is, that all respect for him is dead and I for one will never want anything to do with him after this.'

'I won't either,' Livvy echoed. 'And I hope you don't think we want to see the kid,' she spat at her father, 'because it's so not going to happen. Or her! I don't even want to know her name. Do you know it?' she asked her mother.

Jay nodded.

'Have you met her?'

'No.'

'Where does she live?' Charlie asked.

'London,' Tom replied, 'and it's not my intention to leave you and go to her. It's the very last thing I want. I love your mother and that's never changed—'

'It didn't stop you screwing around though, did it?' Livvy ranted furiously.

'I shouldn't have done it and God knows I regret it . . .'

'I swear I'm going to change my name rather than carry on having you as a father,' Livvy informed him rashly.

'Listen,' Tom said, 'let's please try to calm this down and see it for what it really is . . .'

'You mean you not being able to keep it in your trousers,' Charlie growled. 'God you make me sick!'

Jay gathered a sobbing Livvy into her arms and a moment later Charlie was with them, holding them so tightly she had to ask him to ease up.

'What are you going to do, Mum?' Livvy asked her. 'Please don't say you're leaving. This is our home . . .'

'I'm not going anywhere,' Jay assured her, 'but I have asked Dad to find somewhere else to live.'

Livvy rounded on Tom again. 'So why are you still here?' she demanded menacingly.

Paler than ever, he said, 'This is also my home and I love you all more than I can say, and I'm sorrier than you'll ever know for what I've done.'

'But that's not good enough, is it?' Livvy challenged. 'Being sorry doesn't mean anything when you went out and did it again. So what's going to stop you the next time, and the time after that? None of us can trust you. And what are you going to do about the baby? You can't pretend it doesn't exist, or was that your plan?'

'No, I don't intend to do that. I'll obviously provide for him and I'd like to see him, but if you guys and Mum would prefer that I didn't . . .'

'What if he goes to live with her?' Charlie asked Jay, clearly suddenly horrified by the prospect.

'That'll be his decision,' Jay replied as calmly as she could.

'I'm not going to live with her,' Tom said quietly.

'Oh God, no, no, no,' Livvy cried, noticing the tears on her father's cheeks. None of them had ever seen him cry before and clearly Livvy couldn't bear it, for she was suddenly waving her hands as if it could make him stop.

'It's OK, I'm fine,' he tried to tell her. 'It's just this isn't easy . . . I never expected it to be. I . . .'

Jay knew that what he really hadn't expected was that the children would turn on him quite so aggressively. In truth it had surprised her too, and though she loved them for their loyalty, she couldn't bear to see them hurting their father when she knew how much they loved him really.

'I think Dad's right,' she said, taking over, 'we need to try and calm this down. Tom, I – we – we appreciate you being honest with us, and we're glad to know that you still love us. There's no doubt we love you, as angry as we are with you right now, and there's probably a long way to go before we're in a place where we can stop feeling let down by you. But for the moment I think we must at least try to be kind to one another and understand that mistakes can be made without intention of causing hurt even if they do.'

Addressing his father, Charlie said, 'I am so not close to forgiving you. I'm sorry, but what you've done to Mum, to our family . . . You showed no respect. You behaved like you were the only one that mattered, and I swear none of us deserves that, least of all Mum.'

Tom said, 'There's nothing you can say that will make me feel worse than I already do, so—'

'Believe me,' Charlie cut in, 'I haven't even started.'

'Charlie, no!' Jay protested. 'I love you for defending me, really I do, but when you hurt Dad you also hurt me.'

'Are you serious?' he cried, clearly unable to credit it.

'You don't just stop loving someone because they've—'

'Proved that they don't love you enough,' Livvy cut in savagely. 'I get that, but I wish we could. I can't stop loving you either, Dad,' she informed him, 'but right now I totally hate you, so I think you should do what Mum wants and leave. This cannot be where you live any longer, because you've betrayed us all.'

Tom didn't answer, only looked from one to the other of them, as if bewildered by the discovery of being a stranger, an outcast even, in his own home. 'Maybe I should go for a walk,' he said, 'it'll give us all a chance to think about what's been said, to take it in. We can talk again later.'

After he'd gone, Jay decided to let the children have some time to talk with neither parent in the room, so she took herself upstairs. She didn't quite understand how she was managing to remain so calm. On some strange level it was as if she were functioning outside of herself, watching her children's heartbreak, feeling it of course, while on the surface she was holding together in a way she hadn't expected to be able to.

She wondered what they were saying to each other, and knew they'd tell her if she went down there, but they needed to get past this rage against their father on their own. If she was with them they'd feel they had to keep defending her, and while she loved them for it, she understood things would change once they'd calmed down.

She looked at her phone and felt the need to call someone, to connect with a lifeline outside the house, to pour out everything she was feeling to an understanding ear. Maybe it would help to sort out what she really wanted. Perry was always a great listener, so was Gretchen, but for some reason it didn't feel right to bring anyone else into this right now. Maybe later, after everything had been said that needed to be said at this stage, when tempers weren't quite so frayed and the shock wasn't still quite so raw.

She checked her emails and texts in the hope they might provide a distraction, but they didn't. Her mind, her heart, were too caught up in the clashing emotions of wanting to keep her family together while she was tearing them apart.

Sinking onto the edge of the bed, she sobbed quietly into her hands. It would be so easy to tell him she was prepared to forgive him, that she didn't want him to go and somehow they'd work things out. All she had to do was go downstairs and tell the children that she'd decided to stand by their father; that somehow, between them all, they'd work out how to include the new baby in their family, make him feel a part of what they shared, and as special as he was, because why wouldn't he be? He was an innocent baby. Whether or not his mother had deliberately trapped his father into creating him had little relevance now; he was here and could never be blamed for his parents' actions.

So why didn't she do it? It would be a rocky road at first, and she'd almost certainly have to meet Ellen Tyler, as well as the child, but surely she had it in her to do that. Maybe it would feel more possible if her own children weren't on the verge of flying the nest. Charlie had already gone, and as soon as he graduated in a few weeks, he'd be off to Australia with Nat and Livvy. Or that was the latest plan. It could change, it often did. Months and months would go by before she saw them again, their only contact would be through FaceTime or email, unless she and Tom flew to where they were for a holiday.

They'd talked about doing that while gap year travel plans were being discussed, but it couldn't happen now, any more than she and Tom could really stay together. She couldn't forgive him, and if he stayed she just knew that it wouldn't be long before she started to despise him, and herself, for not having been strong enough to break away from him when she should have.

He didn't stay out for long. It would have been hard for him to when they knew so many people in the area, neighbours wanting to stop and chat, friends urging him to go for a drink.

Maybe he should have gone for a drive.

After he returned she stayed upstairs listening to the murmur of his chat with the children, tensing herself in readiness for more raised voices or tears or doors slamming, but as time ticked on, all seemed to remain calm.

She was about to go and join them when her phone rang. She'd have let it go to messages, but seeing Ken

Bright's name come up she clicked on. It would only be a small respite from the awful upheaval under way, but it would be a welcome one considering how eager she was to speak to him.

'I got Joe's message,' he told her.

'Have you spoken to him?'

'I have, and I want you to know that I've already got someone checking through all the DNA evidence. If something's gone missing, or a mistake has been made, I want to hear about it sooner rather than later.'

'I thought you would.'

'I'll get back to you in the next few days.'

After ringing off, her mind was fully focused on Edward Blake and his case, this possible new development and what it could mean if a mistake had been made.

The distraction didn't last long, but at least the intensity of her feelings had shifted, along with the dread of being unable to cope with losing her children as Tom began a new life with his baby son. She could and would cope, and as wretched as she felt about Charlie and Livvy going away to foreign climes, she was also glad about it. It meant they wouldn't have to be here when their father left or have to worry about her and what came next. They had their own lives to consider, and very soon, whether she wanted it or not, she'd be doing the same.

CHAPTER FORTY-SEVEN

By the time the children returned to Exeter on the Sunday evening, Tom had managed to make some sort of peace with them, if peace meant they weren't refusing to speak to him any more. They still weren't ready to accept the baby into their lives, they'd informed him, and wouldn't be until their mother was and even then Livvy wasn't sure.

Both children were calling Jay regularly, which was lovely, but time-consuming and often repetitive, as they tried to work things through. She was sorry they weren't calling Tom too, but he didn't mention it, simply carried on as only he could, feelings tightly suppressed as he came and went in his usual way, trying cases in London, Bristol and Birmingham, sometimes staying over and other times coming home. He didn't talk about Ellen Tyler or the baby, so Jay didn't know if they were in touch, but had to presume they probably were. It didn't matter, at least not for now, as she'd decided not to try to force the issue of him leaving until after Charlie's graduation.

In the middle of the week, while still waiting for news from Ken Bright, Jay and Cyrus Trott visited Blake at the prison again, continuing to prepare for the plea hearing. Although a part of her would have liked to be alone with Blake, to feel the calming pull of their connection, even to talk things over with him, she knew it wasn't a good idea to open up to him again. She was too vulnerable, and besides, it was unprofessional.

On returning from the prison via Sean's coffee stall, she asked Vikki to hold all calls while she grabbed some lunch and went through to her office. No sooner had she taken a first bite than Vikki shouted, 'Ken Bright on the line. Thought you might want to talk to him?'

'I do,' Jay confirmed, experiencing a jolt of nervousness, part hope, part dread. Putting aside her sandwich she hurriedly picked up. 'Ken!'

'Jay,' he responded. 'You may or may not be surprised to hear that we have a match for the unidentified DNA. Frank Maguire was charged an hour ago.'

Jay's eyes closed as a rush of unsteady emotion overcame her. Although she'd known there was a chance this could happen, in spite of being unable to imagine Vanessa engaging in anything at all with such a pious and unappealing individual, she still felt shocked.

'Has he confessed?' she asked.

'He has.'

Spinning with all that this meant, she said, 'Just to be clear, my client is no longer a person of interest?'

'No, he is not.'

Knowing better than to ask for more details as to how or why Maguire had done it, especially at this stage, she said, 'Who's his lawyer?'

'Julian Strange.'

Her heart sank. The long-running antipathy between her and Strange meant she'd get no information from him either. Still, what mattered now was getting Blake out of prison. So after thanking Bright for the call, she quickly rang off, aware of how fast her heart was pounding as her mind shot off in so many directions she could barely keep up with her own thoughts. She was even shaking slightly as she connected to Antonia. 'Are you expecting to hear from Edward today?' she asked.

'He might call,' came the reply. 'He doesn't usually arrange it. Why, what's happened?'

Although she desperately wanted to break the news to Blake herself, it wasn't something she could hold back from him for a minute longer than necessary. So, in case he got in touch with his sister before her, she said, 'Frank Maguire has been charged with Vanessa's murder.'

There was a stunned silence at the other end.

Jay said, 'This means your brother is free to come home.'

'Oh my God!' Antonia gulped. 'Oh my God! Jay, this is . . . When did you hear?'

'A few minutes ago. We'll talk again, but right now I need to start organizing his release. If he calls you first, please tell him to get in touch with me as soon as he can.'

As the hours passed and all the relevant documentation was put into place, Jay had to accept that she might not hear from Blake that day. Though this frustrated her, it also gave her time to consider what the end of his case was going to mean for her on a personal level. Except she couldn't go there; it simply wasn't possible for her to look at this in anything other than a professional way.

'I just heard the news, literally,' Perry announced coming into her office as he put on his coat. 'It's on the TV. So it was the neighbour what did it?'

'Apparently,' she confirmed. 'I don't have any details, other than the fact that the unmatched DNA turned out to be his and he's confessed. Where are you off to?'

'The cinema. Care to join us? We're going to see . . . Well, you know me, I never remember until we get there, but it's a Gretchen choice, so it'll probably be up your street.'

'Thanks, but I have a lot to do here. And with any luck this might be my client on the line who's about to hear the best news he's probably ever had, if he hasn't heard it already.'

Smiling, Perry gave her a wave and, as he disappeared from the reception office, Jay clicked on the line. 'Jay Wells,' she said, in spite of being certain it was him.

'It's Edward,' he told her.

'Have you spoken to Antonia?'

'Yes, a few minutes ago. I'm still trying to take it in. I . . . God, I hardly know what to say. *Maguire!*'

'I'm sorry you had to learn that he was one of her . . .' What was the word? How the hell did anyone describe that relationship?'

'Victims?' he suggested. 'No, that's too harsh. Conquests? Sounds too . . . What does it matter how it sounds? I've just got all this madness going around in my head about what actually happened, *how* it could have, when, why, and I don't think I can allow myself to believe yet that I'm really getting out of here. When will it happen?'

'There's a process to be gone through. It's not complicated, but it could take a day or two. I'm hoping to get you released directly from the prison and home by the weekend. As soon as I know when it'll be, I'll contact Antonia so she'll know when to come for you.'

'OK, thanks.' He gave a laugh and she guessed it was in part, at least, to cover a rush of heart-stopping disbelief and relief.

'I'm happy for you,' she said earnestly, 'and I'm sorry you've had to go through this. Unfortunately mistakes are made, even more since the police cutbacks, and the wrong people end up suffering.'

'One day,' he said, 'I'll find a way of thanking you.'

'I was just doing my job.'

'I know, but I like to think . . .' He broke off and said, 'I guess I should go now before I embarrass myself.'

They spoke again the following evening, by which time Jay had secured his release, and also been in touch with Antonia to let her know that she could collect her brother on Friday at midday.

'I wasn't expecting to hear from you,' she said to Blake. 'I take it you've spoken to Antonia? You know she's going to be there tomorrow?'

'Yes, I have. And she is. Except . . . I-I realize I'm in no position to ask a favour after all you've done for me already, but I wondered if you'd consider picking me up instead? If you have time. Don't worry if you haven't, Toni will come, as arranged . . . I just wanted to—'

'I'll be happy to do it,' she broke in. 'I'm glad you asked.'

There was relief in his voice as he said, 'It'll give me a chance to say thank you, although I still haven't worked out how I'm going to do that when the words are so much smaller than the way I feel. I wonder if you know how much it matters to have someone believe in you when you're going through something like this.'

With a smile she said, 'I'll be there at midday. Don't be late.'

CHAPTER FORTY-EIGHT

As Jay turned in towards the prison the following day, she found herself wanting to laugh for the sheer joy of it when she spotted Blake, standing outside the forbidding building in the middle of a residential area, looking nothing like someone who'd been on remand for the past eight weeks. He gave the appearance of someone who'd just left the gym, or stepped out of a shower after a run, with his still damp hair and heavy holdall.

He was no longer a prisoner, a fearful man with a murder charge hanging over him. He was someone who wore a leather jacket and faded blue jeans, who was an architect, a builder, a brother, uncle – and widower.

Spotting her approaching between the parked cars, he grabbed his bag and was at the kerb as she pulled up, quickly dropping his things in the back and getting into the passenger seat with an apologetic wave to the driver behind, who was already hooting impatiently for Jay to move on.

'Sorry I'm late,' she said, as he fastened his seatbelt. 'There was an accident in Stokes Croft and the road's still partially blocked.'

'Then lucky we can go in the opposite direction,' he said, and turning to look at her he waited for her to look at him too and broke into a smile that almost took her breath away.

She smiled too, captivated by the new confidence he exuded, by the dizzying reality that they were here, on the right side of freedom, together. 'How are you feeling?' she asked, hardly able to imagine how it must be after all he'd been through.

He grimaced as he said, 'Strange. Euphoric. I guess kind of dazed. It's hard to explain. I didn't sleep too well, kept thinking someone was going to come and tell me it was all a joke.'

'Well it isn't. You're really on your way home, and one day, hopefully sooner rather than later, your time in this part of Bristol will feel like nothing more than a bad dream.'

'Oh, it was that all right,' he murmured, looking around as they turned into the Gloucester Road, taking in the busy pavements, passing shops and cafés, real life going on as normal and that he hadn't seen in too long. 'Before you came,' he said, 'I was standing there watching the traffic pass and telling myself you *would* come, you really would, and you'd be driving . . . I went through a whole list of cars, and do you know what my final guess turned out to be? A black Mercedes coupé, with a cream leather interior.' Playfully he added, 'It suits you, sleek and elegant with a lot of class and extremely pleasing to look at.'

With a laugh she said, 'Thank you, it's always uplifting to be compared to a car.'

He laughed too and let his head fall back against the seat. 'It certainly beats my last form of transport,' he commented wryly.

Knowing that would have been a prison van, she threw him a glance; but he wasn't looking her way, his eyes were closed as he continued to take in this new reality. 'Nothing but the best for you from now on,' she declared. 'A

Mercedes home to where your Range Rover Sport awaits. I guess it's still there. I should have checked.'

'It's there, in the garage,' he assured her. 'Antonia told me. Apparently the police didn't take it away.' He turned to look at her again, and though she could feel his gaze she kept her eyes on the road, not wanting to overshoot a red light, or miss the signpost to the motorway.

'Thanks for doing this,' he said softly.

'I'm happy to,' she assured him. She wanted to say more but wasn't sure she had the right words to convey what she was thinking, couldn't even be certain what it was. Only, perhaps, that she might have been looking forward to this day, this journey as much as he had.

After a while he said, 'So, do you know what actually happened that night? With Maguire?'

Indicating to circle the Filton roundabout, she said, 'Are you sure you want to talk about this now?'

'Yes, please do it while you're driving. You won't have to look at me then and I won't have to see how repelled you are by it all. Maguire and my wife. I can still hardly credit it.'

'I'm not repelled,' she told him. 'It's something I wish hadn't happened, mostly for your sake, and because of what it's cost you, but obviously for your wife's as well.'

He nodded slowly. 'Thanks for that,' he murmured. Then, 'Do you always know the right thing to say?'

Smiling she pulled up at a traffic light and glanced over at him. 'Almost never in situations like this,' she replied, and if that wasn't an example of getting it wrong, she didn't know what was. However, he didn't appear to have picked up on the euphemistic nature of her words, or if he did he made no response to it.

'I don't actually have any details,' she said, as they drove on, 'the police won't discuss the case with me at this stage, apart from Ken Bright confirming that he'd confessed, and I'm not likely to get anything out of his lawyer.'

'So you don't know if it was the first time she was with Maguire? Maybe he was a regular.'

Understanding the bitterness in his tone, she said, 'I've no idea. I don't even know if he was still there when you arrived home that night. He could have been, and managed to sneak out without you hearing him.'

He inhaled sharply and turned his head away. They were on the M4 now, heading east, although their minds were inside the guest room at Clover Hill, seeing images that must be devastating for him. 'I want to know *why* he killed her,' he stated. 'I mean, what the hell made him do it?'

Having no answers, she simply shook her head, while knowing she'd try to find out more from Ken Bright when the time felt right. This was presuming Bright knew, for a confession didn't mean Maguire had to give details of motive.

'I can't imagine how difficult this must be for Maddie, his wife,' Blake said, as they exited the motorway slip road and headed north towards Tetbury and Stroud. 'Do you know where she is?'

'Joe, my investigator, tried to call her, but it seems she's left the barn. So maybe she's back in Sunderland. Your sister might know.'

He nodded and closed his eyes, fists bunched loosely on his thighs.

In as calming a voice as she could, she said, 'Why not

try to let today be about nothing more than your release and how good it feels to be going home?'

'To the house where it happened?'

Having already worried about that, she said, 'Would you rather I took you to Antonia's?'

He shook his head. 'No, it has to be faced at some point, and I don't want to put it off, or let the place become all about her death. It doesn't deserve that. And I'm pretty sure the Vanessa I married wouldn't want it either.'

Admiring his resolve, she said, 'As long as you're sure. We still have a way to go, so you can change your mind at any point.'

As he turned to her his expression was calm, but pensive. 'I've done a lot of thinking about the house since I knew I was going home,' he said. 'And before that as well, obviously, but lately I've been concentrating on the happier times, how it was when we were turning it into the place it is now; all the precious memories, with friends and family and of course with Lucas. There's been so much that was good there, I don't want to lose that.'

Wondering if she could be so brave in his shoes, she said, 'There's no reason why you should. It's a beautiful home, and it deserves to be loved.'

Seeming to appreciate her answer, he turned to watch the countryside going by, high hedgerows, woodland, villages, vast open meadows, as they continued on in silence, each with their own thoughts, until finally they crossed the quaint stone bridge into Clover Hill.

His sigh on seeing it spread out before him was as expressive as if he'd exclaimed its summer beauty in words. She could only wonder at how emotional he felt, for he didn't speak, probably because for the moment he couldn't. As she drove slowly along the track she could almost feel him taking it all in, holding it to him as if the July sunshine, sense of tranquillity and welcome were as great an elixir as the wild flowers and trees, the stream, the birds singing and flawless blue sky.

'I always said,' he murmured, 'when we came across this place, that we'd found a spot of heaven on earth, and that's certainly how it feels right now.'

Her eyes were drawn to the long barn as they passed, the shuttered windows and empty patio, and she wondered how soon it would be before he could look at it without seeing Maguire. He wasn't turned that way now, he was faced towards the cottage set back in the woods, and she could hardly blame him.

Moments later they were passing through the open gates to his home, into the courtyard, where pots of canna lilies and tumbling petunias were as vibrantly alive as the roses, oriental poppies, delphiniums and exotic daisies filling the beds outside.

'Toni never gave up hope,' he remarked ironically, but his voice was thickened by emotion. 'I think she's been coming most days, and it looks as if she got the gardener to do the same.'

'Is she meeting you here?' Jay asked, bringing the car to a stop.

'I said I'd call when I was back. Will you come in?'

Should she? She wanted to, but wasn't sure it was wise. She didn't really belong to this part of his life.

'I'd like you to,' he said gently.

Wondering if he felt apprehensive about going in alone, she got out of the car and waited at the front door while he retrieved a key Antonia had left for him from beneath a rock on the far side of the garage.

As she followed him inside she could feel the air's stuffiness suffused by the lemony scent of diffusers Antonia must have brought. There was no sign of Vanessa's coats or boots in the hall, presumably Antonia had removed them, so only his jackets and the hard hat were hanging on the hooks.

Quickly turning off the alarm, he went through to the main room and, without hesitating, made his way straight to the bifold doors, unlocking them and throwing them wide to let in the sunshine, fresh air and countryside fragrances. Beyond the terrace, the view was as spectacular as nature could create, folding and dipping, rising and spreading as far as the eye could see.

He turned back to her and she smiled to see how moved he was simply to be here.

'It's very special,' she said, 'you're right to want to stay.'

He looked around at the paintings on the walls, the one of him and Vanessa with Max, the photos of Lucas, the furniture, the rugs, the bookshelves, the log-filled fireplace. All so familiar to him, and dear. The world that had been on hold all this time awaiting his return.

'Will you have a drink?' he asked. 'I don't know what's here, but I'm sure there's something.' He was already at the fridge and laughed as he opened it. 'My wonderful sister thinks of everything,' he declared and pulled out a bottle of champagne.

'I'm sure she and John will be expecting to share it with you,' Jay protested as he held it up for her approval.

'There will be more in the wine store. I can put in another,' and tearing off the foil he popped the cork and filled two glasses that he retrieved from an overhead cupboard.

Taking one she held it up to him. 'Welcome home,' she said warmly.

'Thank you,' he said, his eyes on hers. 'If it weren't for you—'

'Ssh,' she interrupted, and taking a sip of the drink she gestured for him to do the same.

She couldn't be sure who put their glass down first, him or her, she only knew that they were no longer holding them when he pulled her into his arms and held her tightly. She didn't protest, only held him too, inhaling the now familiar scent of him, feeling the power of his relief and gratitude.

When at last he pulled back to look at her, his arms stayed around her and his eyes searched hers, as though unsure this was really happening. She gazed back at him, still holding him too, taking in the lines around his eyes, the texture of his skin, the shape of his mouth. And when he kissed her it felt the most natural and wonderful thing in the world, his lips on hers, the pressure and taste of him, the warmth of his breath, the heady flood of feeling that engulfed her. She wondered how long it had been since she'd first started wanting this, and had it been the same for him?

He was still kissing her as he loosened the clip on her hair and she felt his hands move into it as it fell.

It was as though time was suspended. All that existed was them, this moment, this insistent need to be close. She was mystified, entranced, transported even, for as they undressed one another, everything about it felt right in a way she couldn't fathom, only feel. It should have been awkward, clumsy even, and unfamiliar, but it wasn't. It was fluid and easy and continued to feel as though it was meant to be as he entered her and they moved together, turning their shared longing, the dream of this moment into a blissful, transcending reality.

A while later they lay on the rug staring at one another, their eyes seeming locked in curiosity and awe, and she wondered when life – conscience – would steal these precious moments away. She didn't want to stop looking at him, or touching him; she needed to understand what was happening, but was almost too afraid to find out.

'Are you OK?' he whispered.

She nodded.

'No regrets?'

'No,' and it was true. Maybe there should be, and would be later, but right now, in this moment, there were none.

He raised a hand to stroke her face. 'Shall I get our glasses?'

She nodded and rolled onto her back as he stood up. He looked down at her, drinking her in as she did the same to him.

'You're beautiful,' he told her softly.

She smiled, shyly, but didn't try to hide herself, and as she watched him walk across the room, naked, she slipped on his shirt, waiting again for regret and maybe dismay to push aside the pleasure and fulfilment she felt. It didn't happen. It seemed there was no place for it; it didn't belong here, not today.

Bringing their topped-up glasses to the rug, he sat down in front of her and she pulled herself up to sit facing him.

'To freedom,' he said, touching his glass to hers, 'and to you.'

She drank with her eyes on his and felt as though everything and everyone else had ceased to exist, that there was only them and whatever it was that was pulling them together here and now, and had been almost since she'd first met him.

'I've thought about this when I shouldn't have,' he told her softly.

She smiled in a way that told him she had too. 'It feels surreal, and . . . I don't know what else, I just know that I want to be here with you, like this.'

Leaning forward, he took the glass from her hand, and as she moved to him she felt bewildered and yet happy and surprised and connected to him in ways that seemed so much more than physical.

Later, he laughed as her stomach rumbled and said, 'There must be something here. Will you stay to eat if there is?'

'Your sister will be waiting to hear from you,' she reminded him.

'I'll call her,' and getting up he went to check the freezer. Holding up a pizza he said, 'Shall we share?'

She nodded and, wearing his shirt again, she went to join him, feeling suddenly carefree, happy and even reckless. How long had it been since she'd allowed herself to let go like this, to be the woman she was inside, rather than the wife, mother and lawyer she had become?

'You're smiling,' he told her.

'So are you.'

He laughed and smoothed a hand over her hair. 'Is it too much to hope you can stay?' he asked.

She thought and said, 'That will depend for how long.'
'All night?'

Why should she rush home? What was waiting for her besides the discomfort of living with Tom, the pretence of them being together when they no longer were?

'Your husband?' he asked.

She shook her head. She didn't want to talk about him now.

Pulling her to him, he spoke softly into her hair, 'There's so much I want to say to you, but I don't know if I can or should.'

'Maybe not today,' she murmured, understanding because she had a lot to say too, but it was too soon. Trying to explain or comprehend what was happening, if anything really was, would pin it to words, and all it needed right now was them to be here like this. 'You should call Antonia,' she reminded him. 'I'll set the table outside if you show me where everything is.'

A few minutes later, as she stood on the terrace, gazing out over the lush green landscape, she was aware of him talking on the phone, but not of what he was saying. Apart from him now, she found herself able to think more clearly, but didn't ask herself what she was doing here, only if she could stay the night in a bed he'd shared with his wife. Vanessa, whom he'd loved, adored, before it had all gone wrong. He still loved her, she knew that, it had been evident every time he talked about her. Was he using Jay now as a way to help himself forget?

Was she doing the same to him to try to forget Tom?

Right now it felt deeper, stronger, better than that, at least for her.

'I feel like I'm dreaming,' she said, leaning into him

as he came to stand behind her, wrapping her in his arms.

'That makes two of us.' He pressed a kiss to her ear. 'Toni and John are on their way over.'

Startled she turned to him. 'Already? Then maybe I should go . . .'

'They know you're here. They're expecting to see you, although probably not quite like this.'

Fleetingly remembering how sexy and risqué it had made her feel the first time she'd covered herself with one of Tom's shirts, she said, 'Have you told your sister? I mean, about this?'

He smiled. 'No, but she's pretty shrewd. She might pick up on it when she gets here. Is that a problem?'

Was it? 'Only because I'm your lawyer,' she said, 'and married, and she'll think I do this sort of thing all the time. I don't, by the way.'

'I never thought you did, but it's good to hear I wasn't flattering myself.'

She had to laugh and watched her fingers move into his hair. 'I think you're like I expected you'd be without all that was hanging over you,' she said.

'And how was that?' His eyes were both playful and serious, as if her answer really mattered.

'Confident,' she told him, 'non-judgemental. There's a side to you that's more . . . light-hearted than I've seen until now.'

His eyebrows rose. 'I could say that's what freedom does to a man, but that would be to brush over the part you've played in my release, and I'm not just talking about from prison.'

As her heart caught on his words, she laughed at the

way he pulled her to him, and felt almost sorry that his sister and brother-in-law were about to arrive.

When they turned up, John was looking both harried and relieved as he pulled Edward into a bruising hug. 'My God it's good to see you,' he said, his voice thick with emotion.

'You too,' Blake told him. 'Where's Toni?'

'She'll be here soon. We came in separate cars to try and shake off the press. They were outside the gates of Highview – they must have presumed you'd come straight to us. Anyway, we guessed they'd decide Toni was the best one to follow, so we set off in different directions and I've obviously turned up first.' Turning to Jay he took her hand in both of his. 'Mrs Wells, Jay, I can't thank you enough for all you've done. I'm so glad you're here. Toni is too. We wanted to invite you to celebrate with us – it wouldn't be happening without you, so thanks for giving us the opportunity to say thanks.'

Jay laughed and blushed slightly as she glanced at Edward, who was clearly enjoying the moment.

'I'll get you a glass,' he said to John. 'We've almost finished the first bottle, but there's another in the fridge. Have you eaten? Jay and I have just shared a pizza . . .'

'I'm fine,' John assured him, 'but I should warn you, Toni's turning up with a Waitrose shop.'

'I guessed she might, and that sounds like her . . .' He turned as Antonia came running through the door and flew straight into his arms.

'Oh my God, Ed, seeing you here.' She laughed and cried, hugging him so tight he winced. 'I can't tell you how good this feels. I was so afraid it wouldn't happen . . .

Jay! How can we ever thank you?' And grabbing Jay into the hug she said, 'It was so clever of you to give the press a different time for Ed's release. At least you got away without anyone following, but they'll be here, you can count on it, if not today then tomorrow.'

Jay felt herself freeze as she realized that anyone could be out there now, amongst the trees, way off on the horizon, with a long lens . . .

Clearly reading her mind, Edward said, 'We just have to hope they're not here yet. If they are . . . We'll deal with it. Now, isn't something missing?' he asked his sister.

Antonia gasped. 'Wait right there! Don't move,' and she ran back outside.

As John filled more glasses, Edward put a hand on Jay's waist and whispered, 'I'm sorry, I should have thought about the press. I guess I'm not used to this sort of . . . attention.'

She was about to respond when a joyful, awful howling was suddenly filling the room, and Max the dog came barrelling towards his master, all wagging tail and awkward gait. Blake dropped to his knees, catching the stiff old body in a fulsome hug. 'Hello boy,' he murmured, holding him close. 'God I've missed you.' He sat back to cup the greying muzzle in his hands and his voice was shaky, his eyes bright with tears as he said, 'I've missed you so much.'

Max's front paw kept going to Edward's shoulder and slipping off, as if he were trying to return the embrace.

Edward buried his face in him again. 'Thanks for holding on,' he whispered. 'I know it's been hard—'

'Oh Ed, stop!' Antonia wailed, dabbing tears from her eyes. 'It's too much, just look at him. If a dog could smile . . .'

'What do you mean, *if*?' Edward protested. 'Come on Max, give us one of your best.' He bared his teeth and they all burst out laughing as Max did the same.

'Cute or what?' he said, looking up at Jay.

'Adorable,' she assured him, and laughed again as Max broke into a wobbly dance around his master, his arthritic legs doing their best to be puppy-like.

'Will you help me fetch the shopping?' Antonia said to John. 'I think I've got everything, but we can always go again if I haven't.'

As they disappeared outside, Edward got to his feet, and Max walked with him as he came to Jay. 'I want to kiss you,' he whispered, and then did just that. 'Will you stay?' he asked, seeming uncertain that she would. 'Can you make a call?'

'I'll send a text,' she told him, and ruffling Max's upturned face she went to find her phone.

Staying over with a friend. See you tomorrow.

They spent the evening on the terrace, the four of them, drinking wine, eating cheese and fruit, as they talked about Maguire, speculating, condemning, and wondering what had pushed him into doing what he had. After a while, Blake insisted they change the subject, saying he didn't want to think about it any more tonight, and so they did, as easily as if they'd been friends for years. Whenever Jay allowed herself to stop and reflect for a moment on where she was, and who she was with, she became aware of the strangeness of it all, the newness of her surroundings, and yet somehow it felt familiar and right. It was as if she'd found something different in herself, a sense of her own freedom perhaps, or was it something even deeper that was making her feel as comfortable here as she ever had anywhere?

Mostly she was caught up in the conversation, having no thought for time or commitment or the sadness and complexities of her life beyond Clover Hill. This was an escape, a sanctuary, and what had happened with Edward today had shown her that she was as capable of feeling strongly for another man as Tom was of loving another woman. It wasn't revenge, it was simply, and complicatedly, a chemistry that she and Blake shared – and that she was no longer going to pretend wasn't real.

Eventually, as the sun began to set, a vast crimson orb on the horizon, Antonia announced it was time for them to leave. Jay wondered what she thought when her brother's lawyer made no move to do the same, when the brother came to slip an arm across the lawyer's shoulders, as if it were something he did every day. Jay wasn't sure if she felt self-conscious or not until, with a single lift of an eyebrow, Antonia let her know that she understood and maybe even approved?

After they'd gone Edward said, 'You know, we don't have to sleep in the master room?'

'No, we should,' she said. 'We both have a past, and hiding from it won't make it go away.' She was surprised by how seriously she meant that, and how unconcerned she felt about being with him in a bed he'd shared with his wife. Would it be different if he was cheating on her? Yes, of course it would.

Pulling her to him, he said, 'I can change things, if you want me to.'

Understanding he meant in the house, she said, 'Maybe, but not tonight.'

He made to kiss her and stopped. 'Actually, there's one thing I'd like to stay the same, if you don't mind. Max sleeps in the bedroom. I have to carry him upstairs these days, but he gets lonely . . .'

'It's fine,' she assured him, reaching down to stroke Max's head. 'I understand. Love me, love my dog?'

He laughed and kissed her lightly, tenderly, and then with a passion she was more than ready to respond to.

CHAPTER FORTY-NINE

As Jay drove back to Bristol the following day, she was in the grip of so many inconsistent and intense emotions that she kept swinging between elation and euphoria one minute, to being anxious and fearful the next. And she was so stunned by herself and what had happened that she could hardly keep her mind on where she was going.

When she'd left Edward, a few minutes ago, she'd promised to return later, and she had every intention of doing so. In fact, if she weren't in need of a change of clothes and some toiletries, she might not even have gone.

She asked herself if it should feel wrong, what they were doing, but couldn't think why it should. They were hurting no one. She wondered if this was how Ellen Tyler had felt when she'd first got together with Tom. Swept off her feet, uncontrollably responsive to him, unable to think about anything else?

Presumably it had been the same for Tom.

Though the thought of that still stung, it wasn't as acutely as before. She understood it better now, how chemistry, destiny, something utterly indefinable but irresistibly powerful could come alive between two people with a force that was stronger than them both. Maybe she could even find it in herself to wish them well.

Could she do that if Blake decided he wasn't actually

ready for another relationship? His wife was so recently dead, taken from him in the most awful way, and yet she knew, and he knew, that he'd lost the woman he loved a long time ago. Of course he was still grieving, for his son too, and then there was the trauma of the experience he'd just been through. So, as relaxed and relieved as he was on the surface, and seemingly entranced by her, she understood that many darker feelings were likely to begin wearing him down in the days and weeks to come.

She would discuss this with him when the time felt right. For now all they needed to do was carry on with the wonderful discovery of each other and what was happening between them.

Real life, outside influences, would come calling soon enough.

'So where were you?' Tom asked as she walked in the door.

Feeling herself turn hot inside, she put down her keys and dropped her bag on a sofa. 'I told you in my text,' she replied, not looking at him, 'I stayed with a friend.'

'Which friend?'

Irritated, she said, 'Why does it matter? We're not answerable to one another any more.'

He appeared shocked by that, and more hurt than she'd expected him to. 'You're still my wife,' he reminded her.

'In name only, and I've asked you to leave. If you had, you wouldn't even know that I didn't come home last night.'

His eyes narrowed suspiciously as she headed for the kitchen. 'Who were you with?' he demanded. 'Something's going on, I can tell.'

419

Forcing down her temper, she said, 'Is there any coffee made?' Finding there was she poured herself a mug and took a sip.

'Jay?'

How little time it had taken him to work things out; perhaps it was shining out of her. She felt as though it was. Except it was starting to feel wrong now she was with Tom, and she resented him for that. Why was it all right for him and not for her?

Quickly she switched her mind to Edward, Clover Hill, Max, Antonia and John – how easy it all was, how much more she wanted of it. She really did. All the tightness inside her seemed to unravel when she thought of being with them. Being with him.

'Who is it?' Tom asked darkly.

As she looked at him she didn't allow herself to see the husband she'd loved for so long, the father of her children, the life-partner she'd always felt so lucky to have. She saw only the man who'd had a child with another woman, who'd let her down so badly, had lied and lied to her, and ultimately destroyed all the trust she had in him.

'I don't owe you the truth,' she replied, 'but I'll tell you anyway. I spent the night with Edward Blake at his home in the Cotswolds.'

His mouth fell open as his eyes widened in disbelief. 'You can't be serious,' he growled. 'Tell me you're joking.'

She turned away to refresh her mug.

'Jay! What the hell . . .'

'Don't dare to lecture me,' she seethed, turning back. 'I will see and do whatever I please, and if we're going to continue to share this house, you will need to get used to it.'

'He's a fucking murderer, for Christ's sake.'

She saw red. 'How dare you? I can't believe that *you* of all people, would say something like that . . . You should be ashamed of yourself. You're talking like the gutter press . . .'

'OK, I'm sorry. I shouldn't have said that. I know he's been released, that they've found who did it, but Jay, please tell me it was just a moment of . . . madness? Celebration? *Revenge?*'

'Oh that's right, let's make it about you, shall we?'

'That's not what I meant.'

Fixing him with a cold stare, she said, 'I don't have to explain myself to you. I know you might find that difficult to accept, but it will be easier in the long run if you start to try.'

He was flushed with confusion and temper. 'That sounds as though you're intending to see him again,' he said. 'And I don't mean as his lawyer.'

'I am.'

He threw out his hands in frustration. 'What the hell are you thinking? The press are bound to get hold of it. Have you considered that? What it'll do to your reputation? To mine? To the children once it reaches them?'

Aware that she hadn't given any of it enough consideration, for there simply hadn't been time, she said, 'I've no idea how the relationship is going to develop, but I can tell you this: he is a decent, loyal man who did everything he could to protect his wife from herself. He supported her through things most men would have run from, and never once did he *cheat* on her. Nor did he have a child with another woman, so if you want to start talking about reputations, maybe you should look to your own before you start worrying about mine.'

Scathingly he said, 'Well, that had to come out, didn't it? You say you don't want to make it about me, but that sounds very like it is. So, OK, let's make it my fault . . .'

'Actually, let's make it no one's and stop this now. Things happen, Tom. People meet and connect. You had it with Ellen Tyler, so you know what it's like—'

'What are you going to tell the children?' he cut in savagely. 'You need to answer that.'

'Perhaps I'll start with the truth, which is more than you ever did for us.'

'Oh, how very sanctimonious of you. At least I never slept with a client.'

'You think it makes what you did better because she wasn't a client? Grow up, Tom.'

He glared at her, simmering with impotent rage. 'How long?' he asked derisively. 'I'm presuming nothing happened during your prison visits . . . Oh Christ, please don't say there were fumblings under the table—'

'I've had enough of this,' she broke in angrily, and pushed past him, needing to leave. 'If that's the kind of thing you think I'd do then you obviously don't know me.'

'Well it clearly hasn't taken you long since his release. Did you already have it planned?'

'As a matter of fact, no, but – and here's a truth for you – a part of me did hope it might happen. I was already attracted to him, and I think I knew he felt the same way. Like I said, he's a good man. I know you find that hard to believe, because you're allowing all sorts of prejudices to influence you – considering who you are and what you do, I find that very disappointing.'

'Where are you going?' he snapped as she made for the door.

'Actually, I'm going to call the children, because you're right about the press. They're going to get hold of it, so I'd rather Charlie and Livvy heard it from me than from them. I'd ask you to be with me, the way I was there for you, but I know already that you'll find that too hard.'

'You're talking about a one-night stand,' he raged, 'in my case there's a child—'

'Quit while you're ahead, Tom, if you even are,' and, shaking with anger, she left him and ran upstairs.

Allowing herself almost no time to think, she sat on the edge of the bed and FaceTimed Charlie. He didn't pick up so she tried Livvy, and within seconds up came her beautiful, sleepy face.

'Hey Mum. Everything OK? Was I supposed to call?'

'No, I don't think so . . .'

Livvy's eyes suddenly shot open. 'Oh God, has Dad left?' She sat up, and next to her Nat said, 'Should I go?'

Livvy nodded and turned back to her mother. 'He's gone to her, hasn't he? Oh fuck! He can't—'

'Livvy, stop! It's not that. There's something I have to tell you. It's unrelated . . . Well, it's about me, not Dad. You see, I-I've met someone.'

Livvy stared at her in shock. 'Already?' she finally managed.

'I've known him a while . . .'

'So Dad's not the only one who was cheating?'

'I never cheated on Dad, and now, given where we are in our marriage, I'm not sure it counts.'

Livvy blinked, trying to take it in. 'You're on the rebound,' she suddenly decided. 'I'm not saying that's bad, but—'

'I don't think it's rebound,' Jay interrupted. 'It's . . . Something else, but anyway, I need to tell you about it because it's likely to end up in the press and I don't want you—'

'Oh my God! Who is it? Is he famous? Shit, don't tell me it's Freddy.'

'It's not Freddy. It's the man I've been representing for the past couple of months, the one who's just been released from prison for *not* murdering his wife.'

Livvy was dumbfounded.

Jay waited.

'So how long's it being going on?' Livvy demanded. 'Does Charlie know? You didn't say anything when we were at home.'

'Nothing had actually happened then. He was still on remand, but he was released yesterday and . . . Darling, I'd rather not go into details if you don't mind. I just want you to be aware that at some point it's likely to hit the press.'

'You mean that my mother's shagging a killer? Fantastic! Great! Bring it on.'

Biting back an angry retort, Jay said, 'He was released because he did *not* kill her, but that sort of short-sighted prejudice is what we – you – will probably have to deal with. So perhaps you could start by getting the story straight.'

'OK, he didn't do it, but *Mum!* Really? What are you thinking?'

'You don't know anything about him,' Jay said defensively. 'If you met him you'd realize that he doesn't deserve to be defined by what someone did to his wife. He's already suffered enough because of it, and I don't expect you or Charlie to make it worse. Have some compassion, some understanding. These qualities have never failed you before; I've always been proud of how supportive you are to friends, even strangers, who are finding life difficult. Well, I'd like your support now, if you can bear it.'

'Oh God,' Livvy wailed. 'I've always got your back, you know that. I love you more than anything, I just don't want you getting into something with the wrong man because of what Dad's done.'

'I don't see the two as being related, but who knows, maybe they are. Just please don't judge me or Edward based on misinformation or lies.'

Livvy was scrolling through her phone and finding what she was looking for, said, 'There's a story here about him being let out yesterday. There's no mention of you. Oh Mum! He's on Sky, now! Talking to reporters. I guess he's outside his house. Is that his house?'

'I'll call you back,' Jay said, and hastily switching to the broadcast on her own phone, she tensed all over as she saw him standing with Max at his front gates looking calm and friendly in the early afternoon sunshine as he confirmed that it was good to be home. No, he wasn't planning to pursue a case for wrongful arrest at this time. No, he didn't want to discuss his neighbour. Yes, he would be staying at the house, at least for the time being. He thanked them for their concern, and wanted to thank his legal team too for all they'd done to help clear his name. He stooped to ruffle Max and laughed as someone shouted something that Jay didn't catch. He ended by saying he hoped they would respect his privacy as he set about getting his life back together, and with a good-natured salute he led Max back inside.

Jay looked up as Tom came into the bedroom.

'You saw it?' he asked.

She nodded. 'Please don't say anything unpleasant . . .'

'I was going to say that he handled himself well. And thankfully they don't seem to know about you yet, but they'll find out if you persist in seeing him. You have to realize that.'

'Of course I do, and I'm sorry for the embarrassment it might cause you. It's not . . .' She turned away, suddenly on the verge of tears.

'Jay,' he said softly, coming to sit with her. 'You don't have to do it. I'm not leaving. I don't want . . .'

'I've told you already, it's not about you. It's about me and him and whatever happens next between us, and I don't know yet what will. But please stop trying to diminish it by turning it into a scenario that suits your ego, or your need to control me.'

He didn't respond, and she avoided looking at him as they continued to sit side by side on the bed. She wanted to call Edward, to tell him how well he'd done with his brief statements, but she wouldn't while Tom was there. She wondered why Blake hadn't let her know he was going to talk to the press. Presumably they'd just turned up and he'd seized the opportunity to meet them head on rather than hide out and have them stalk him.

'Don't go back there,' Tom said quietly.

She got to her feet and went into the bathroom to start collecting up what she needed to take with her.

'I'm asking you not to go,' he repeated as she returned to the bedroom and took out a small suitcase.

'I'm not going to say you brought us to this,' she responded, 'because I truly don't know if I'd have stayed with him last night if things weren't the way they are

426

between you and me. But I can tell you that, feeling the way I do, it's quite possible I would have.'

As she drove away from the house half an hour later, the road ahead was blurred by tears, not because she was sorry to leave, but because she didn't want to hurt Tom. Maybe if she'd been able to tell him when she'd be back, he wouldn't have got so angry and ended up telling her she could go to hell as far as he was concerned.

'You're making fools of us both,' he'd shouted at her as she carried her bag downstairs. 'It's only a matter of time before everyone will be talking about us, our friends, colleagues, clients. You won't be able to hold your head up. Wherever you go people will point at you, whisper, laugh, sneer . . . "That's the one who's screwing the bloke she got off a murder charge," they'll say. The shame of it all will rain down on you in ways you haven't even begun to think about. And let me tell you this, if you're expecting me to pick up the pieces when it all goes wrong, you can think again. I'm not carrying this with you. You're on your own with it.'

She hadn't argued back, there had been no point. She was upset enough already, and he was clever enough with words to wound even more deeply than he already had. So she'd continued out to the car, got in and driven away, having no idea if he was watching, or even of how much he truly cared.

What she began to realize, however, as she put more distance between them, was that she didn't have to take anything he'd said with her. She could leave the bad feelings behind, cut them loose, cast them out as if dropping them from the window of the car.

She pressed on the accelerator and felt her heart starting to lift as she sped towards Clover Hill. She wanted to call and let Blake know she was on her way, and would have done if she'd had a number for him. How odd it seemed not to have it, and yet why would she when she'd never had to call him? It didn't matter, she'd be there soon, and she was already curious – and nervous – to find out how she'd feel when she saw him. How he'd feel when he saw her.

Eventually she was driving carefully over the bridge and along the track, keeping a look-out as she went for a lingering reporter or hidden lens, but everything was quiet and still. As she reached the house she saw that the garage was open and only his car was inside. Vanessa's had gone – presumably taken months ago by the police – and she wondered if he meant her to park in the empty space so he could close the doors and no one would know she was there.

Driving in, she switched off the engine and took her bag out of the car. She turned around and he was there, coming towards her, his relief that she'd come back as plain to see as Max at his heel.

'You read my mind,' he said, taking her bag. 'The press have caught up with me so it's best you keep the car in here.' He gazed searchingly into her eyes and she knew he wanted to kiss her. She wanted it too, but it was safer to wait until they were inside.

No sooner had he closed the door than she was in his arms, returning the urgency of his embrace, matching his need, and knowing that her reservations, nerves, had been for nothing. She wanted to be here, with him, looking at him, listening to him, feeling him. There was no darkness here, only light, no anger or deception, only truth and an overpowering sense of everything being right.

It was a while later, as they sat together on a swinging hammock seat outside on the terrace, cocktails on the table in front of them and Max stretched out nearby, that he said, 'Do you want to tell me how it was at home today?'

She didn't, but at the same time, holding it in would feel evasive, dishonest even, so she said, 'It wasn't easy. He said some cruel things, but I guess it was only to be expected.'

'Do you still want him to leave?'

'Yes, but he refuses to.' She gazed out at the dreamlike landscape and knew what he was going to say even before he said it.

'Stay here,' he whispered.

She wanted to, could even imagine it, but it was too soon to make such a commitment.

'I've made some changes already,' he told her. 'They needed to be done, so please don't think I'm taking anything for granted.'

'What sort of changes?' she asked, surprised, for she'd noticed nothing different when she'd come in.

'Well, to begin, I've taken down the portrait.'

'Do you mean the one of you, Vanessa and Max? But it's so beautiful, and I have no problem with it being there. She was a big part of your life, still is, and I thought we agreed that we shouldn't hide from the past.'

'You're right, but we don't need to have it staring us in the face. And to be truthful, I've found it difficult to look at for a while. It doesn't feel honest any more, more as though I'm trying to delude myself into believing everything's the same as it was before.'

Understanding that, she said, 'So where is it?'

'Upstairs, under a dust sheet. I've decided to draw up some plans to reconfigure the guest wing so that none of the rooms as they exist now will be the same after. I think it's the only way to deal with it if I'm going to stay here.'

'Good idea.'

Leaning forward to pick up his drink, he said, 'And I've moved her things out of the bedroom. They're in the main guest room until I decide what to do with them.'

Main guest room. Murder scene, but of course they'd never call it that. It wasn't necessary to be brutally explicit. The mind would do that, no need to reinforce it with words.

'And I thought,' he was saying, 'that I'd get right back to work on Monday. Toni and John – Guy too, of course – have done a fantastic job of keeping things going, but it's time for me to take over again. And I'm going to end the lease on the gallery so I'll be basing myself here from now on.'

'What about Guy?' she asked gently.

'I'll talk to him as soon as I can. I don't want what's happened to come between us. There's no reason for it to, and I know how much it'll mean to him if we can carry on working together.'

Touched by his generosity, and love for his nephew, she said, 'It sounds as though you did a lot of thinking while I was gone.'

'And most of it was about you, us, and how much I want us to see if this is . . . If it's what we both want.'

Reaching for his free hand, she said, 'I'd like that.'

With a smile of relief, he entwined their fingers and, as she looked at them – his so large and strong, hers slender and feminine – she was reminded of the first time they'd done this – across a table inside a prison. Had she imagined then that the next time they linked their hands it would be in such an openly intimate way? 'Do you think we need to discuss things?' he asked uncertainly.

She shook her head. 'No, not yet. We don't really know what this is yet, apart from wonderful, so I'm not sure we'd be able to find the right words. However, I have told my daughter. I felt I had to, because if we do keep seeing one another it's bound to get into the press.'

He nodded as he mulled the truth of that. 'You're right, it will,' he conceded. 'I don't mind so much for me, but . . . How are you going to deal with it?'

'I'll be fine. Uncomfortable at times, I'm sure, but fine.'

'And your daughter? How did she take it?'

Jay considered the best way to answer that. 'She was surprised, obviously, and thinks I'm probably on the rebound.'

His eyebrows rose. 'I guess she could be right about that.'

'She could, but I don't think she is.'

For several tender moments he gazed into her eyes, allowing his feelings to show in the deep sensuousness of his own. 'Best not to overthink things?' he said softly.

She nodded and smiled and clinked her glass to his as if to seal the decision.

Later, as they prepared a meal together, he said, 'We've been invited to Highview tomorrow. We don't have to go, but it might be awkward if I don't, because most of my extended family, all the aunts, uncles and cousins, will be there. I'll understand if you feel it's too much for you.'

Did she? Maybe.

'As my lawyer, it wouldn't seem unusual for you to want to toast my return,' he pointed out.

Deciding it would be fine if that was how they played it, she let her eyes close with a sigh of contentment. True, there was guilt stored away behind it, along with worry, even dread of how she was going to break this to her colleagues, but right now all she wanted to think about was being here with him.

The following day, Highview Hall's summer room and garden was so crowded with family and friends that Jay could hardly credit it as she walked in. Out of respect to Vanessa, and because they really weren't ready to go public with their relationship if they could help it, Edward had come ahead in his car, leaving her to follow half an hour later. He was presumably here somewhere, and would spot her at some point, but in the meantime she was happy to accept a glass of champagne from Camille and a warm embrace from Antonia.

'It's quite a turn-out,' Antonia grimaced, though she was obviously pleased. 'Even our London and Edinburgh contingent have made it, although the Scots were already staying with family in the area so not far to travel. I can introduce you to everyone if you like, but maybe it'll be less overwhelming if I let them find their way to you.'

Many did as Jay roamed the gathering, eager to thank her for everything she'd done for Ed, and to express how tragic it was that his wife had met such a sad end. Some asked about Maguire, but as she had no answers or explanations to offer, they let it go. Others mentioned Lucas and how 'dear Nessa' had never been the same after that terrible tragedy, while a couple of aunts wanted to share how glad they were that Ed's parents hadn't lived to see him go through this additional and undeserved nightmare. Affection for the couple was like another guest, one that followed Jay around like a ghost, but it didn't make her uncomfortable, only sad that Ed still had so much healing to do. The only difficult moment came when she spotted him at the far end of the knot garden talking with Sheri, his ex-lover, the high-flying financier who was almost never in the country, or available to talk to anyone, apart from today, apparently.

She saw Sheri nod in her direction and, as he turned, Jay wanted to laugh at his expression, for it gave everything away. He'd have reached her more quickly if he hadn't been stopped by aging uncles and boisterous cousins, but eventually he was there and saying,

'I thought you weren't going to come. Can I kiss you? I really want to kiss you.'

'Maybe the cheek?' she suggested, holding it up and noticing Sheri still watching them.

'Is it too much?' he whispered. 'All these people. I had no idea there would be so many.'

She wanted to mention Sheri, but didn't for fear of sounding petty, or jealous, or worried. She wasn't actually sure what she felt, but was aware that a dead rival she could cope with, one that was living and here today and who looked like Sheri Razak . . .

'Mrs Wells!'

Jay turned around and found herself being embraced like an old friend by . . . Melissa? Yes, it was a very tipsy Melissa, Vanessa's other close friend, who'd clearly also made it today for Ed.

'I saw you at the wake,' Melissa said, keeping her

voice low. 'I don't think you spotted me. It was awful, wasn't it?'

Jay glanced at Ed, wondering how Melissa could have said something so thoughtless in his hearing. 'I'm sorry I didn't see you,' she said, 'but it's good that you're here today.'

'A triumph for justice,' Melissa declared, discreetly punching a fist. 'Thank God they found out who really did it. How well did you know him, Ed? He's quite old, isn't he? And why the hell . . . ?'

Edward said, 'Would you mind if I had a quick word with Jay?' and before Melissa could respond he was gently steering Jay to the edge of the gathering. 'What is it?' he asked quietly. 'You look . . . worried?'

'I'm not,' she assured him.

His eyes stayed on hers. 'I know that's not true. We can leave if you want to.'

She smiled incredulously. 'After everyone's come so far, and gone to so much trouble? I don't think that would be a good idea.'

'Then tell me what's upset you.'

Amazed, she said, 'How do you do that? Know that something's wrong when actually it isn't?'

His eyes twinkled. 'Well, apart from you just contradicting yourself, I'm sensing a distance between us that wasn't there this morning. I realize that could be because of where we are, and if it is, I understand, but if it's anything else . . . Have you spoken to your husband since I left, or one of your children?'

'No,' she replied, feeling a pang simply to have them mentioned. Then she found herself relaxing as she remembered how new they were and why wouldn't he feel insecure too?

434

'Everything's fine,' she assured him. Then, 'Have you been asked about Maguire a lot today?'

'A few times. I admit it would be good to have some answers, but even if I did, today is hardly the right time to discuss it.' He looked searchingly into her eyes. 'Do you think you'll be able to find out more, at some point? I know it won't make a difference in that it won't bring her back, but it just feels so unfinished not actually knowing what happened.'

'I understand,' she murmured, 'and I promise, I'll do my best.'

He leaned in closer as though to whisper in her ear, but was suddenly swept away by a lively cousin. As he threw an apologetic look her way, she saluted him with her glass. Everything was wonderful at Clover Hill when it was just the two of them, but other aspects of their lives were always going to encroach so they needed to get used it.

'Are you OK?'

Jay turned around to find Antonia there, but before she could respond, Antonia said,

'I told him not to invite you today. If you were just his lawyer it would have been fine, but we know you're not, and this is . . . The trouble is, he said he wouldn't come unless you did, and I couldn't let everyone down.'

Jay started to answer, but Antonia hadn't finished.

'He's told me what you're going through in your own life, and I understand how hard it must be for you, but please don't hurt him, Jay. He really has been through enough.'

CHAPTER FIFTY

A lot of what Tom had predicted came true. Over the days and several weeks that followed Blake's release, Jay was aware of the gossip and conjecture that followed her as she came and went from the courts, or prisons, or police stations. The tabloids also made much of her affair with a man she'd got off a murder charge, a client with whom she was now apparently living after leaving her husband of twenty-five years. Although the scandal and sensationalism didn't negatively affect her relationships with other clients and close colleagues, they were naturally fascinated by it, and she guessed she couldn't blame them for that. For her part she did her best to ride out the storm, knowing she was far from the first lawyer to fall for a client, even in this close-knit community, and she almost certainly wouldn't be the last.

Something she hadn't expected, but probably should have, was the exposé of Tom's 'love child' with a 'long-term mistress'. In a horribly bitter exchange in her office one evening, he accused her of leaking the story, but she hadn't, wouldn't even have dreamt of it. However, she'd known by then who had contacted the press, but she'd kept it to herself, for it would only have made matters worse if he thought Livvy was standing by her mother more firmly than him.

'I just didn't feel it was right for everyone to keep picking on you, as if you were the only one in the wrong,' Livvy had protested when Jay had challenged her. 'It wouldn't have happened if he hadn't had an affair first, so he deserves to share the blame and have his life splashed all over the tabloids too.'

Jay had no idea what effect the exposure had had on Tom's relationship with Ellen Tyler and their son; she didn't ask, and he never mentioned it during the times they had to speak. If they ran into one another on the street or in court they always stopped, as they had before, but by unspoken agreement they kept the encounters as brief and friendly looking as possible before moving on. She hated those moments, for they always left her feeling low and guilty and deeply sorry that they had come to this.

However, they did nothing to change her feelings towards Blake.

She was happy with him in a way that couldn't be damaged, much less destroyed by rumours and gossip, and she knew it was the same for him, in spite of how frustrated and even depressed he sometimes became over not knowing what had driven Maguire. She understood his need to know more, anyone would in his position, and now that a suitable amount of time had passed she decided to try talking to Ken Bright again.

When she called to invite the detective for a drink in a pub close to the Keynsham bypass, she took heart from the fact that he didn't turn her down in spite of surely knowing what it was going to be about.

She got there ahead of time, but soon discovered that he'd beaten her to it, although he hadn't gone into the pub, was still outside in his car.

Sliding into the passenger seat next to him, she closed the door and glanced at him cautiously. 'Thanks for coming,' she said.

He nodded briefly and kept his eyes straight ahead. 'I know I don't have to point out to you that this shouldn't be happening,' he said, 'but I'm pointing it out anyway.'

'Heard and understood,' she assured him.

Still not looking at her, he said, 'The DNA business was a screw-up on our part. An internal inquiry's underway, but the buck stops here.'

Certain he'd find a way to sort that, she said, 'So Maguire *was* swabbed and it never made it to the labs?'

'Something like that. Anyway, as you know he's confessed to the killing. Actually, he went to pieces almost as soon as we turned up to arrest him. Not an edifying sight, but he surely had to have known it was only a matter of time.'

Feeling for Maguire's wife and the terrible shock it must have been for her, Jay said, 'More likely he thought he'd got away with it.' She was thinking of how sincere the man had seemed when he'd sworn he wanted to help Blake, had said he was praying for him, could never believe he'd harm his wife. Well, at least the last part was true.

'He's claiming he didn't mean to kill her,' Bright continued. 'He says things got out of hand . . .' He stopped and started again. 'Apparently they'd had adulterous relations – his words, not mine – several times before that night. Not something he wanted, according to him. He never sought it, but he couldn't help himself. She was devilish, a temptress, a Jezebel, and he was a miserable transgressor, a debaucher, who must now pay for his sins.'

Jay's brows formed a cynical arch.

'There was a lot of sobbing and self-castigation as he told us what happened,' Bright went on, 'he could barely hold himself together, but the upshot of it is, he saw Blake's nephew leaving the house around five thirty and marched up there to confront her. I'd call it a fit of jealous rage, but he says he was doing his best for the boy. He threatened to tell Blake, or one of the family, that she was corrupting the young lad if she didn't stop. Apparently she found this amusing, invited him in and suggested he tie her up before beating her.'

Sighing, Bright pressed his fingers to his tired eyes, as though not much wanting to envisage the scene, in spite of the photographs that had left little to the imagination. 'He says he was angry, and that she deserved a good thrashing, but he's not a violent man. He didn't mind tying her up – he'd done it before when she'd asked, but he refused to use the crop. However, he was very aroused – actually he described himself as shamefully provoked – so he took his own clothes off and started to "suckle" her breasts for his own satisfaction, not hers. He didn't have sex with her because, not to put too fine a point on it, he couldn't get it up. Apparently not an unusual occurrence for him. She started mocking him, calling him names he didn't want to repeat, but I guess we can work them out for ourselves. He said he was going to leave her right where she was for Blake to find. She just laughed and asked what he was going to do when she told Blake who'd tied her up. She kept on taunting him, talking about his wife and how sorry she felt for her having such a ridiculous specimen of humanity for a husband. In the end, he got a pillow and covered her face to shut her up. He didn't mean to kill her, he says, he just lost track of how long

439

he held the pillow there. He didn't even let go when she stopped struggling in case she was trying to trick him.'

Not sure how much she believed in the accidental part of it, Jay said nothing, simply waited for Bright to continue.

'Eventually, the red mist faded, and when he realized she was no longer breathing he panicked, slapped her a few times, then set about trying to clean off the straps and bedposts using her underwear. Then he put his clothes back on and ran home to start praying.'

Jay was quiet as she took it all in, repelled by the scene, and even by the woman who'd taunted an old man so cruelly. Mostly though she was repelled by Maguire, the false friend and hypocrite who'd accepted Blake's help at the time he was scammed, but would have let Blake go to prison for a crime he'd known he hadn't committed. 'So he made up the argument he claims to have heard about nine o'clock?' she stated.

Bright nodded. 'He did.' Then, 'I don't know how much closure this will give your . . . friend, but at least it answers some questions.'

Jay agreed. 'I appreciate this, Ken, I really do.'

It was still early evening when she got back to Clover Hill to find Blake standing at the windows, staring out at the gathering clouds, hands loosely in his pockets, Max at his side. He glanced round as she came to stand with him, and tilted his head onto hers as she leaned into his shoulder.

He didn't speak as she related what Bright had told her, although he tensed once or twice, and at one point gave an audible intake of breath.

In the end several minutes passed before he finally said,

'I'm not sure what difference it makes, knowing this, but I think it's better than not knowing.'

She looked up into his eyes as he turned to her, and could see how far away he was, and yet he was right there too.

'I hope things aren't going to be difficult for you with Ken Bright going forward,' he said.

'He wouldn't have told me if he didn't want to,' she replied, 'and it's going to come out in the press anyway at some point. I'm surprised it hasn't already, but at least having heard it from Ken we know what's true and what isn't.'

He nodded and dropped his forehead to hers. 'Thank you,' he whispered.

Lifting a hand to cup his face, she said, 'Do you still want to meet John and Toni for dinner?'

After giving it a moment's thought, he said, 'Yes, let's go, but first I want to do this,' and pulling her to him he kissed her tenderly, lovingly and maybe gratefully.

CHAPTER FIFTY-ONE

As time went on, she began to feel as though a part of her, perhaps even the essence of her, had stepped through an invisible door into another world. By day she was still a lawyer, as diligent and involved as ever, but when she returned to Clover Hill in the evenings, to Blake, the woman inside her moved into his arms and his life as freely and naturally as if she'd found where she truly belonged. He was so easy to be with that there was rarely any awkwardness, and even if there was he'd somehow manage to smooth it over. She was fascinated by how interesting and undemanding he was, attentive, humorous and always loving. They talked a lot, about themselves, their pasts, their dreams, and when they laughed she wondered if she'd forgotten the real joy of it because of how fulsome and intoxicating it was.

They also comforted each other through the bleaker moments of break-up and loss, and occasionally they discussed Maguire, although not often. It was too painful a subject for Blake, and though some details of what had happened had come out in the press by now, neither he nor Jay bothered to read it.

Saturdays became the day they roamed Stroud Farmer's Market with Max in the trolley-cart Blake had made for him, choosing their fruit and veg, tasting local cheeses, wines, oils, sausages, before stopping at a pub for a late lunch on the way home. Their social life could have been hectic if they'd wanted it to be, but what really mattered to them was building their new life together and finding out if they really could make everything work. The invitations they accepted meant that for the first time in her life Jay attended a polo match to watch one of Ed's cousins play. She also picnicked at a garden opera in the grounds of an old country estate, and occasionally they threw a small dinner party themselves. On Sunday mornings they often walked around Westonbirt Arboretum with Toni and John – and Max in his trolley-cart. Unsurprisingly everyone wanted to stop and talk to Max, and being the old flirt and sociable soul he was, he lapped up every minute of the attention.

The only time they spent apart was when Jay drove to Devon with Tom for Charlie's graduation. Everything went smoothly, at least no harsh words between her and Tom, and the photos showed nothing more than the joy and jubilation of tossing caps and prideful parents. Even Tom's mother did nothing to spoil the day. However, once the celebratory dinner was over she drew the line at Jay staying over at her place, as originally planned. Jay didn't make a fuss, merely caught a train to Bath where Blake picked her up and drove her home.

It was a week or two after the graduation that he learned he was now the new owner of Sayley House. His disappointment made Jay laugh, for she couldn't imagine anyone but him being crushed by the prospect of inheriting such prime real estate, even if the house itself wasn't a jewel.

'I'm going to sign it over to Daphne,' he declared decisively. 'If I gift it to her she'll be free to move out whenever she likes and then she can do whatever the heck she wants with it.'

Jay regarded him in amazement, although she knew she shouldn't be surprised, for this sort of generosity was typical of him. He could forgive, mend fences, ignore insults and forget past hostilities like no one else she knew. The only exception was Maguire, but even then he wouldn't allow himself to become embittered or morbidly obsessed by the affair that had cost his wife her life. It would always be with him, he'd say, but he wasn't going to allow it to blight his future, or ruin what he'd been fortunate enough to find with Jay.

'So are you going to see Daphne to tell her?' Jay asked curiously.

He nodded slowly. 'I think so. One last trip to the old place, why not?'

'Would you like me to come with you?'

Surprised, he said, 'Do you want to? You know what she's like, and you can be sure she'll have something rich to say about us, especially if we're there together.'

Having no doubt of it, Jay said, 'I'll come. I want to see her face when she finds out she no longer has a reason to hate you.'

Laughing, he pulled her into his arms and pressed a kiss to her hair. 'OK, I'll set it up for Saturday, and I should probably leave Max here with Guy. He's coming over to do some project assessments and the dreadful Daphne has never been kind to my lovely dog.'

Unable to imagine why, or how, anyone could ever be cruel to dear old Max, who she was coming to adore almost as much as his master, Jay stooped to give his arthritic limbs a tender hug before rushing off in time to get to a meeting.

Commuting from Clover Hill was no hardship, she'd found, in spite of it taking an hour or more most days; she didn't even miss Clifton as much as she'd expected to. Or her friends – although Perry and Gretchen had already visited for a weekend, staying at Highview Hall thanks to the work going on in the guest wing of Clover Hill. And she'd started to meet Jenn on Wednesday evenings when she could for yoga and a drink after. She understood that Ollie continued to feel uncomfortable about meeting Edward, given his close friendship and partnership with Tom; however Jenn was dying to visit, so she was working on it.

'Are you coming to the airport to see the children off at the weekend?' Tom asked one day in early August when they ran into each other in the lobby of the Crown Court.

'Yes, of course,' she replied. 'Why would you think otherwise?'

Grimly, he said, 'I can't imagine. Will you come in my car, or will you meet us at Heathrow? You can travel with Jenn and Ollie, of course, they'll be going to see Nat off—'

'I'll meet you there,' she interrupted. 'I already have the flight times, so if you can let me know where to be . . .'

'I'll send an email. Will you bring *him*?'

'If you mean Edward, I shouldn't think so. The children have never met him so it wouldn't be appropriate.'

'Is any of it?'

Sniping back, she said, 'Have they met your girlfriend yet? Or your other son?'

He flushed darkly and said, 'I'll see you on Saturday,'

and turning away he caught up with another barrister who was walking past.

'Don't worry,' Blake said later when she explained why she couldn't go with him to Sayley House on Saturday, 'Charlie and Livvy have to be your priority, no doubt about that, but if you're really keen to see Daphne, I can always put it off for a week.'

Pressing a kiss to his mouth, she popped in an olive and said, 'Actually, I think I do want to see her, so if you don't mind delaying . . .'

'Consider it done. Now I need to make a couple of calls before we eat, so can I leave you with this risotto?'

'Of course.' She smiled, and helped herself to more wine. She'd started cooking again, something she hadn't done for years after yielding to Tom's need to control the kitchen. She and Blake often prepared meals together, although occasionally she'd have something waiting when he came home at the end of a long day, dusty, tired, and so pleased to see her that it never failed to make her laugh.

Needing to make a couple of calls of her own, she lowered the heat under a simmering pan and took out her phone. She was going to try a three-way FaceTime with Charlie and Livvy – and if she could get through it without having to dab away tears at the end, she'd be accomplishing more than she had this past week as their departure drew closer. It wasn't so much that she was going to miss them, of course she would, it was more about how different this time was to the way they'd expected it to be when the travel plans had first been made. Not that she hadn't been involved in helping them to shop and pack and make sure they had the right bank cards and medication, and visas where needed. She'd even taken several days off a couple of weeks ago while Tom was in London, wanting to be at home for them while they prepared for their big adventure. She thought they'd appreciated it, they'd seemed to. On the other hand, they'd been so full of their own excitement and fears and last-minute panics that she wasn't sure they fully recognized that she had any feelings about them going at all.

That was good. They needed to feel free of the problems at home, unencumbered by concerns for either of their parents. No doubt they were telling one another they were better off out of it, and if so, she didn't blame them, because they were. Nevertheless, she desperately wanted to introduce them to Blake before they went, and she would have done, were it not for how Tom was likely to react. They really didn't need to go away on that sort of note so, like it or not, they'd just have to get to know him over FaceTime from the other side of the world.

CHAPTER FIFTY-TWO

Ten days later, with the children safely in Sydney and raving about how close their hostel was to Bondi Beach, and gasping with amazement and excitement when Blake offered to introduce them to an old uni friend who ran a surf school down that way, Jay and the children's new best friend were on their way to see Daphne. Although neither of them was particularly looking forward to it, they were as intrigued as one another to find out how she'd respond to her gift.

'I'm not expecting gratitude,' Blake confessed, as they turned into the tunnel of trees at the start of the drive, 'but I might get something along the lines of, "Well done for realizing it's the right thing to do."'

Jay rolled her eyes. 'Is anyone else going to be there, do you know?'

'I asked her not to invite Berzina, which means she probably has, although I doubt he'll have the nerve to face me. It's possible her son Jeremy will turn up to lend some moral support.'

'Because they think you're coming to give her her marching orders?'

'I have done nothing to disabuse them of that,' he responded mischievously, making her laugh. 'Although I don't think the terms of the will allow me to do that.'

After parking alongside a sleek black Jaguar in front of the stables, he waited for Jay to jump out of the Range Rover and took her hand as they started around to the back of the house.

'Who does the other car belong to?' she asked.

'Probably Jeremy,' he replied. 'Or a lawyer. She could be preparing to contest the will.'

'I almost hope she is, just to take the wind out of her sails.'

A tall, slender man in his late thirties with short, dark hair, round specs and a pleasant enough smile opened the back door before they reached it. 'Ed!' he said warmly, coming out to shake hands. 'It's good to see you looking so well, my friend. I hope you don't mind me being here. Ma asked so I thought I should do the decent. Quite understand why you wouldn't want to see Freya's other half, although it's over between them, if you didn't already know.'

'I didn't,' Blake told him tonelessly, and turned to introduce Jay.

'Very good to meet you,' Jeremy declared, flushing pink around the ears. 'May I call you Jay?'

'Please do,' she replied, trying not to wince as he crushed her hand in a manly grip.

'Lovely, lovely. Well, come along in. The old dragon's waiting. Don't tell her I called her that, but you know what they say, if the cap fits and all that.'

Not supressing a smile, Jay followed him to the library she'd visited before, Blake close behind her and a sense of trepidation starting to descend from the cobwebs.

'Is he here?' the familiar spindly voice called out as they came through the door.

'Yes, Mother, he's here, and he's brought Mrs Wells who you met before.'

'Oh, she came too, did she?'

Walking around the chair so she could be seen, Jay said, 'Yes, I came too. Nice to see you again, Mrs Drewson-Browne.'

'Really? Somehow I don't believe that, unless you've come to gloat, of course.'

'Daphne, try not to be so rude,' Blake scolded, coming to take her bony hand and giving it a faint squeeze.

'Look at you,' she snorted, staring up at him, 'flaunting your new girlfriend in my face and my stepdaughter hardly cold in her grave. I should have known it wouldn't take you long to find someone else. It never does.'

With a sigh he glanced at Jay as if to apologize, and said, 'Daphne, I'm not here to argue with you.'

'Where are her ashes?'

'They're still with the undertaker, but we're planning to scatter them once we've decided where would be most suitable.'

'Well, you won't be wanting her under your feet at Clover Hill now, will you? Or are you intending to move here once you've got rid of me?'

'That's not—'

'Where's the dog? I hope you didn't bring him. I don't like dogs.'

'Which is why he isn't with us.'

'I hope you realize,' she said to Jay, 'that Vanessa always believed he loved the dog more than his own son?'

Blake was getting annoyed now. 'It's something she said *once*—'

'Hang on,' Jeremy interrupted, putting a hand on Ed's

arm. 'Mother, stop this nonsense, please, and let Ed tell us what he plans to do with the house.'

'I'm not interested in what he's going to do with it. Why should I be when we know it's my home until I die. Perhaps he's come to murder me? Have you?'

While Jay was ready to do the deed herself, Blake refused to rise to the bait. 'Actually,' he said calmly, 'I've decided to sign the place over to you. I don't want it. I never did. So it's yours once all the relevant paperwork has been signed.'

Her eyes flew open with shock, before narrowing suspiciously. 'What kind of trick is this?' she demanded.

Turning to Jeremy, Edward said, 'Sayley House and all its land is hers to do with as she pleases. All I ask is that we don't have to see one another again, once it's done and dusted.'

'Hah! You would ask that, because you don't like hearing the truth. Well, let me tell you this—'

'Mother!'

To Jay she said, 'I expect you'd like to know why my stepdaughter came to see me a month before he killed her.'

'That's enough!' Jeremy snapped, clearly furious. 'You know that's not true.'

'By *he*, I meant the neighbour person,' she explained, contritely. 'She came to ask if she could live here again. She wanted to leave Edward, she said, because he'd never been faithful, and if he hadn't been on the phone to *some woman* the day Lucas died, her baby would still be alive.'

As Blake's head went into his hands, Jeremy said, 'I'm sorry Ed. I've no idea if that's true—'

'Of course it's not bloody true,' Edward snapped. 'I wasn't on the phone to anyone when he went into the pool. I was with her and everyone else at the table, drinking too much and not paying proper attention.'

'I'm just telling you what she told me,' Daphne put in mutinously.

Jeremy said, 'Are you sure you want to hand over this house, Ed? I know it's a monstrosity and probably more trouble than it's worth, but can you honestly say you want her to have it?'

Liking this man more by the minute, Jay looked at Daphne as she gave an unladylike grunt of annoyance.

'One more comment like the last,' Edward said, 'and everything will go to charity.'

Daphne drew breath to retort and seemed to think better of it.

Apparently at a loss for anything else to say, Jeremy rubbed his hands together and said, 'Well, shall we drink a toast to it?'

'Thanks, but we won't stay,' Edward replied. 'We only came to deliver the news.'

'What I want to know,' Daphne said shrilly, 'is why that ghastly neighbour hasn't been sentenced to life in prison yet.'

'There's a process to be gone through,' Blake told her, 'but it'll happen.'

'Will it, indeed? They're saying in the papers that it might not have been murder, more like manslaughter. If that's all they charge him with, he could be out in next to no time and where's the justice in that, I'd like to know? I might not have cared much for the girl, but she didn't deserve to die like that.'

'You shouldn't believe all you read in the papers,' Jay said coolly.

Daphne's nostrils flared, and seeming to sense she was about to become even more objectionable, were that possible, Jeremy said to Blake, 'I'll see you out.'

'No need,' Blake responded. 'We know the way. I'll contact the lawyer with my instructions about the estate, I'm sure he'll be in touch with you soon.'

They were already in the hall when Daphne shouted, 'Ask him about that Sheri person. See what he has to say about her.'

A few minutes later, as they drove back to the road in silence, Jay reached out to put a hand on his. 'Are you OK?' she asked.

'I should have known better than to come,' he replied. 'I suppose I thought finding out she was going to own the house would soften her, make her human for once, and I wanted to see it. What kind of world am I in?'

'You still don't have to give it to her. I'm not sure I would, if I were you, after that.'

'I could be having second thoughts,' he admitted, 'we'll see.'

'What about the reason Vanessa went to see her? Do you believe it was because she wanted to live there again?'

He sighed wearily. 'It could be true, but it's more likely that Nessa went just to stir things up, scare the old woman into thinking she'd have to share the place with her. She got a kick out of goading her stepmother.'

Finding herself at one with Vanessa on that, Jay sat quietly watching the countryside pass, thinking over the awful encounter and what had been said about Maguire. It was true, there was some speculation about him changing his plea to manslaughter, but she had no idea how accurate the reports were, and with the hearing having been recently rescheduled to take place in September they had to accept that they wouldn't know for certain any time soon.

They were almost halfway home, and still holding hands on the gear stick, when she finally said, 'Why did Daphne mention Sheri as we were leaving?'

Blake shook his head in bewilderment. 'Why does she do anything? To hurt people, to cause trouble, to have the last word. She's always been like it.'

Unable to stop herself, she said, 'I saw you talking to Sheri at Highview Hall after your release. Actually, I was surprised she was there.'

'Yes, you and me both. She's hardly ever in the country, but she was that day and Melissa was coming so she decided she would too.'

'So what were you talking about?'

Turning to her he gave a groan of dismay. 'Jay, please don't listen to anything Daphne says . . .'

Hating herself, she said, 'I'd still like to know.'

His eyes returned to the road, but he glanced at her again before he said, 'OK, she was making it clear that she'd be interested in something starting up between us again if I felt ready.'

Jay's insides tightened. 'And what did you say?'

'That I was flattered, but it wasn't the right time to be having that kind of conversation.'

'So you didn't turn her down?'

'What I didn't do was tell her about us, because it was too soon. She'll have found out less than a week later, thanks to the press, and as I haven't heard from her, I think she realizes it's not going to happen.' Holding more tightly to her hand, he said, 'It matters that we trust one another, Jay, and tell each other everything, so I'm sorry I didn't say anything about the conversation with Sheri. I don't expect you tell me about every conversation you have with Tom, and sometimes I worry about that. I ask myself: will he say something one day to make you want to go back to him? Or will you look at him in a court somewhere and realize you miss him and regret what's happening between us?'

'That isn't going to happen,' she assured him, bringing his hand to her cheek. 'And I'm sorry, I should have known better than to listen to Daphne.'

'Me too,' he replied, sliding a hand into her hair. 'It's who she is, I'm afraid, what she does, try to undermine people, and get them doubting themselves, or one another. It was foolish to have gone.'

With a bleak laugh, she said, 'Well, at least her son is nothing like her. I could almost forgive him for resembling Jacob Rees-Mogg.'

Blake burst out laughing. 'He does, doesn't he, although younger and I'd say better looking.'

By now they were at the house, and as he turned off the engine he stopped her from getting out of the car. 'I have something to tell you,' he said softly. 'I've been wanting to for a while, but I've never known if the time was right. I'm not even sure it is now, but I'm going to say it anyway. I love you, Jay, and if that's too much, too soon I'm sorry, but . . .' He stopped as she put her fingers over his lips.

'I love you too,' she whispered, 'and if that's too much too soon I'm sorry, but it's how—' She got no further as he pulled her to him, kissing her deeply. And now the best thing, they both seemed to decide, would be for them to go inside and celebrate this new milestone in their relationship with Guy and Max, although they didn't need to explain exactly why they were opening a bottle of champagne. They'd just say the visit to Daphne had gone well, and then celebrate in their own special way as soon as they were alone.

CHAPTER FIFTY-THREE

Life would have been settling into a steadier, more routine-driven harmony with few anxieties or outside issues to disturb them, had it not been for Frank Maguire's plea hearing now looming large in their minds. So far Blake hadn't made a decision about whether or not he wanted to be in court to hear Maguire admit to his guilt either to murder or manslaughter. One day he thought it was the right and respectful thing to do for Vanessa, possibly for him too, the next he wasn't so sure. Jay didn't try to advise him; she knew this was something he had to figure out for himself, but whatever he decided, she'd be there for him.

In the end, it was taken out of their hands, for the day before the hearing Jay received a call from Maguire's lawyer, Julian Strange, to warn her, 'as an old friend and colleague' that his client would be entering a plea of not guilty.

The world seemed to reel. She could hardly believe it. It wasn't what they'd been led to expect at all. The reverse in fact – and she was so furious with Strange and whatever tactics he was planning that she banged the phone down on him and sat fuming in her office as she tried to think what to do.

There was nothing to be done. Maguire wasn't her

client, she had no say in his case at all, but she needed more information before she broke this to Blake.

Ken Bright answered his mobile on the second ring. 'Jay,' he said, not sounding surprised to hear from her.

'I thought Maguire confessed,' she snapped, 'so what the heck's going on?'

With a sigh, Bright said, 'He's retracted his original statement. Now he's saying – or his lawyer has persuaded him to say – that it's possible Vanessa Blake was still alive when he left the house that night.'

Blake looked as though he'd been punched.

'I don't understand,' he cried. 'I thought . . . Didn't he confess?'

'Yes, but his lawyer is going to present a case for there being no actual proof Vanessa was dead before Maguire left her.'

Blake clasped a hand to his head, paced across the room and back again. 'So it's not over,' he said shakily. 'If he convinces a court that she was alive when he left, they'll come back to me.'

Unable to deny it, she said, 'There's still a way to go, a lot can happen between now and the trial, but it's highly likely you'll be called to give evidence when it comes around, so we'll need to prepare you to go into court.'

He sat down on a bar stool, pushed his hands through his hair and said again, 'It's not over. I thought it was, but it's not.'

She put her arms around him, holding him tight. 'We'll get through it, I promise. I know this has come as a horrible blow, but we won't let him get away with it.'

'But it'll be his word against mine. What am I going to do if they believe him?'

'They won't, I'm certain of it. But let's take first things first. I don't think you should be there tomorrow.'

He didn't argue; however, neither of them went to work the following day as they waited with Toni and John for news from the court.

Ash rang just after three and Jay put the call on speaker.

'Not guilty,' Ash told them, confirming the plea, and as Toni buried her face in her hands, Jay could see how hard Blake was taking it, in spite of having tried so hard to prepare himself.

'When's the trial set for?' she asked.

'Feb seventeenth.'

She watched Blake stoop to press his face into Max and felt such an ache in her heart she almost couldn't bear it. He'd been through so much, why did there have to be more?

'I don't understand,' Toni said, after Jay rang off, 'how Maguire thinks he can get away with this.'

Going to sit on the arm of Ed's chair, Jay rubbed his back as she said, 'It's his lawyer's job to create enough doubt in the jury's minds to make them return a verdict of not guilty.'

'And if they do,' Blake said, 'and they come for me, my guess is you'll mount a similar defence. Create enough doubt to make them return a verdict of not guilty – except they won't do it twice, will they? One of us has to have killed her, and if they've already decided it wasn't him . . . Jesus Christ, I can't believe this is happening.'

Gripping his shoulders to try and ease the tension, Jay watched John go to fix them all a drink.

'Whatever it takes, Jay,' Debrayne said, 'we have to make sure Ed doesn't pay for what Maguire did to Vanessa. We'll be counting on you to see justice is done . . .'

'It's not up to her,' Edward snapped. 'She won't be involved in Maguire's trial,' and getting up from the chair he called Max to follow and left the room. A moment later they heard the front door close behind him.

Understanding that he needed some time to himself, Jay accepted the drink John had made and said to Antonia,

'We're all in shock right now, Ed most of all. In a week or two it won't feel quite as bad. He'll be able to get a better perspective on it, see that there is hope . . .'

'But it'll always be there at the back of his mind until the trial comes around.'

'Of course. It'll be the same for us all, but we have to get through it the best we can, and if I know your brother, it won't be long before he's telling *us* to stop worrying and carry on with our lives.'

CHAPTER FIFTY-FOUR

'I heard about Maguire's not guilty plea,' Tom said. 'It must have come as something of a blow.'

Jay didn't deny it; she didn't want to discuss it either, at least not with him – although she knew he wasn't the type to gloat, never had been anyway. In these circumstances he might have changed.

They were sitting outside the Small Street coffee shop, both wearing coats as they sipped Americanos and absently watched the world go by. They'd agreed to meet here to catch up on issues concerning the children – both needed more money, a given, but Livvy had broken her arm and Charlie had been arrested for being drunk in public – apparently that was an offence in Australia.

'I don't think we need to fly either of them back,' Jay said. 'I'll send Charlie enough to pay his fine and if Livvy says she can cope, she won't come anyway.'

'OK. I'll send funds too to make sure they can stay in a decent place for a few nights at least.'

They fell silent again, allowing time to pass as they nodded an occasional greeting to someone they knew, aware of how the gossips would enjoy this little titbit of them taking coffee together. She glanced at him briefly and felt her heart catch on the familiarity of him, his stern looks, the dark stubble on his jaw, the aquiline nose. She

461

missed him, she realized, but not in the way she'd miss Blake if anything happened to tear them apart now. She still loved Tom too, although more as an old friend, the father of her children, and the man she'd always admired and respected until he'd betrayed her. She wondered if he was happy, if he missed her, what it was like to be at the house without her.

'How's your son?' she asked.

He didn't answer straight away – probably, she thought, because he was assessing her tone, trying to decide if it was biting or benign. 'He's fine,' he replied evenly. 'His back teeth are coming through so he's crying a lot, but that's only to be expected.'

It felt odd, unsettling even, to hear him talking like a new father about a child she didn't even know, but what did she expect? 'Do you see him often?' she asked.

'Whenever I'm in London.'

'Don't they come here, to Bristol?'

'They've been a couple of times.'

She felt a pang to hear that – remembered hurt, jealousy; maybe it was a territorial thing, another woman and child in her house with her husband? She didn't ask if they stayed there, she didn't want to know. She had no right to feel anything anyway, apart from pleased for him if it was all going well.

Draining his cup, he said, 'I guess I should be going.' As he stood he looked off down the street and she could tell he had more to say. 'I know it can't be easy for you right now,' he began, 'so you know where I am if you need to talk.'

Surprised, she said, 'About Edward? Really?'

His face was pale as he glanced at her. 'Julian Strange

is . . . Well, we all know what he is. Did you know he offered me the brief? Don't worry, I turned it down.'

Appalled even to think of Tom defending Maguire, she said, 'Thank you. God, that really would have created a spectacle.'

'Exactly. Anyway, I'll send that money to the children,' and, shouldering his heavy bag, he started off back to chambers.

Jay remained where she was for a while, feeling oddly alone as she watched him disappear into one of the narrow cobbled lanes. When he'd gone she began picturing Edward throwing himself into work back at Clover Hill. Or more likely he was out at one of the sites. She wanted to go to him, right now this minute, but she had important meetings this afternoon, and a dinner later that she wasn't able to get out of.

Deciding to call instead, she took out her phone and scrolled to his number.

'Hi,' he said after the second ring. 'Everything OK? You don't normally call during the day.'

'I was just missing you and thought I'd find out how you are.'

With a smile in his voice he said, 'You're having a harder time with this wait than I am.'

'I know, but only because I'm worried about you.'

'Well, right now I'm more worried about Max. I managed to get in to see the vet to have the lump in his neck checked out.'

Remembering how terrible she'd felt when she'd made the discovery herself last night, she said, 'Do they know what it is yet?'

'No. They have to do some tests, but given his age . . .'

It was going to break his heart to say goodbye to that dog. It would break hers to watch it, but they needed to get used to the fact that that day was going to be with them sooner rather than later.

'I wish I was there,' she whispered.

'We'll be fine. Just please give some thought to what I said last night.'

'I don't need to. The answer is no, I'm not leaving. In fact, I'm not going anywhere, so please stop trying to push me away.'

'But if this all goes wrong . . .'

'It won't. But anyway, whichever way it goes, you'll still need a lawyer, so unless you've decided to fire me, I'm going to be there for you, at home, in court and every other way possible.'

CHAPTER FIFTY-FIVE

It was a misty sort of rain, spreading and floating over the fields turning the sky and landscape all shades of dull and purplish grey. In the distance a cluster of cows was sheltering under an overhang of holm oaks, while in a field nearby a dozen or more sheep were spread out like hay bales. Jay was standing inside the steamy windows, gazing out at the landscape, reflecting on how fast the time had gone since she'd moved to Clover Hill. Five months that sometimes felt like five weeks, and at other times five years. However long, it was a curious truth that she felt every bit as at home in the wilds of the countryside, as she ever had in the city. Here, in spite of everything, she felt able to breathe, to see, to stretch and grow as a woman who wasn't only defined by what she did, or who she was to her children, to her husband, to her colleagues, but by the sense of herself that Ed, probably without even knowing it, quietly nurtured and encouraged.

Sometimes when he looked at her she could feel herself glowing inside, as though he was lighting her up, and it always made her smile. Even now, as they endured the wait for Maguire's case to come to court, he was refusing to allow the dread of it to overshadow their lives. Of course there were difficult days when the weight of it, the dread of it all going wrong, was impossible to ignore, but somehow they pushed through it and managed to focus on what they had rather than what they could lose.

Now Christmas was coming and they'd already cut down a tree, decorated it and stood it mighty and proud beside the hearth. Max, to their delight, had dragged one of his many beds over to it, so he now looked like the biggest present of all.

He would be if he could make it through to the New Year, and they remained hopeful he would in spite of his lymphoma. Because of his age, Ed had decided not to put him through chemotherapy; whatever time he had left needed to be managed in other ways, most of all as pain-free as possible, and so far the medication seemed to be working.

'Hey you,' Ed said softly, coming to stand behind her and wrapping her up in his arms.

She leaned back into him, loving the smell and feel of him, knowing she could never get enough of it, and not wanting to think about how precarious it had become. But February was still a way off, and they'd promised one another they wouldn't allow it to spoil their first Christmas together. There would be time after to prepare for the trial.

'What are you thinking about?' he asked, kissing her.

'The Seychelles,' she replied and it made him laugh. 'A safari?' she suggested.

'Yeah! Up for that,' he confirmed. 'Africa, obviously. Botswana? Tanzania? South Africa?'

'I'm thinking Botswana.'

'But don't we want to visit the Serengeti?'

She nearly melted. 'Oh God, I think we do,' she agreed. 'With a beach stay after in Zanzibar?'

This was something they'd started a few weeks ago, poring through holiday brochures and surfing the web to give themselves something to look forward to after the trial – and when they no longer had Max. It would be good for Ed to get away then, a soothing and restorative antidote to the stress of all he'd been through.

'Good news,' she said, turning in his arms. 'Perry and Gretchen would love to come for Christmas. Their children are skiing in Italy until after the New Year so they have no ties.'

'Fantastic. Have you told Toni?'

'Yes, she's expecting us all on Christmas Day. Perry and Gretchen will arrive on Christmas Eve same as Giles and Marianne – you realize our new two-bed, two-bath guest suite will be full, don't you? Anyway, I thought we could do drinks for about twenty, or thirty that evening? What do you say?'

His eyes shone with laughter. 'We'll make a list and I'll talk to Giles about supplying the wine.' Giles was a second cousin on his mother's side and an acclaimed importer of fine wines. There would be no blue moments or uneasy introspection while he and his wife Marianne were around, for they were always lively company.

They sent out forty invitations and somehow, on the night, found themselves serving champagne, mulled wine and canapés to fifty. Peter and Bjorn their new neighbours at the Long Barn, appointed themselves joint-head barmen for the occasion, while Gretchen and Marianne wandered about with trays full of salmon and cream cheese puffs, lobster stuffed mushrooms, cinnamon pear bruschetta and the inevitable mince pies. It had all been prepared and delivered by the staff at Peter and Bjorn's catering company in Bath. With so many willing hands taking over hosting duties Jay and Ed were free to mingle with old friends and new, while Max, oblivious to it all, snored away in his bed under the tree. He only stirred when an inebriated session of carol-singing began around nine, apparently keen to join in with a harmony all of his own. By the time they got to 'Silent Night', a beautiful solo performed by Marianne, he was asleep again.

The next morning, before going downstairs to tackle the mountain of clearing up, Jay and Ed lay snuggled in the warmth of the duvet gazing into one another's eyes and both looking as though they were about to laugh.

'What is it?' she asked, certain he was up to something.

'You first,' he countered.

'No you.'

Reaching behind him he produced a sprig of mistletoe and held it over their heads. 'Merry Christmas,' he whispered, and leaned in to kiss her.

'Merry Christmas to you too,' she murmured, eyes still half-closed as the effects of the kiss lingered.

'Now you,' he prompted.

She broke into a smile. 'OK, well, I know we said our present to each other will be a holiday somewhere exotic in the spring . . .'

'Don't tell me you've booked the tickets,' he cried delightedly.

'No, but I did get you something to keep you occupied until we can go.'

As his eyes widened with interest she sat up and drew a silver-wrapped box from beneath the bed.

'Shall I open it now?' he asked, clearly dying to.

She nodded, and felt ludicrously, almost childishly excited as he began to tear at the paper. 'It's what every self-respecting architect should have,' she informed him.

When he saw what it was he gave a shout of laughter. A Lego Creator Set of the Taj Mahal. 'We'll build it together,' he declared, turning to her, and his eyes softened with irony as he said, 'good choice. The iconic monument to love.'

'I thought,' she said, as he kissed her, 'when the time is right, we could go to see the real thing to find out how well we did.'

'We'll do that,' he promised, 'and now I have something for you.'

Reaching into his bedside cabinet he took out a small, feather-light package and said, 'A little something for you to take on our exotic beach holiday.'

Carefully pulling apart the tissue she held up a ruby red thong.

'A one-piece bikini,' he explained, and she fell into his arms laughing, even half-sobbing with so much happiness and love she could almost believe the lurking trepidation was nothing more than a paranoid figment of her imagination.

By the time they got downstairs their guests had made great progress with the clearing up and before they knew it Livvy and Charlie were FaceTiming from Wellington to wish them a Merry Christmas.

The call went on for over an hour and bottles of champagne were popped at each end to toast the day – now almost midnight with them.

After they'd rung off, Jay wondered if she ought to call Tom, but decided against it when Perry told her he was at his mother's. 'I don't know if Ellen and the baby are there too,' he added, 'but maybe we hope they are?'

Jay thought about it and nodded. Yes, she hoped they were if it was what Tom wanted, and she had no reason to think that he didn't.

They took Max to spend New Year with Ollie and Jenn at their weekend cottage in Devon (someone was always at home with him while the others hiked – or walking him through the village, usually in his trolley-box), and soon after that Jay and Blake returned to work. Although news bulletins were starting to fill up with reports of a deadly virus outbreak in China, it seemed so far away that they took little notice. They had other things to be worrying about. Time was running down fast now, with only a matter of weeks to go before the trial began, and their nerves were becoming increasingly hard to disguise.

'It'll be all right,' Jay kept telling him, as much to reassure herself as him. 'Ollie's going to start prepping you about ten days before, so you'll have plenty of time to go through it. His questioning will seem tough, but that's the point of it.'

'I'll be fine,' he assured her, 'promise.' But she knew very well how anxious he was in spite of how hard he tried to hide it. It showed in his loss of appetite and the way he seemed to be withdrawing into himself, almost as if he was expecting the worst. And in a way he was, for Max was weakening by the day and Jay simply didn't know how Ed was going to bring himself to accept he was ready to let his beloved dog go.

In the end he called the vet on a Friday evening and arranged for him to come to the house the following morning. He and Jay spent the night downstairs with Max sleeping between them on the floor, his breathing so shallow at times that they thought he'd slipped away. It might have been easier if he had; it would seem more peaceful if he were to go naturally, but each time Ed put a hand on his heart to check if it was still beating his eyelids fluttered.

'Easy boy,' Ed murmured, stroking his head. 'Everything's all right. I'm here.'

By the time the vet came at nine Jay knew that Ed hadn't slept at all, and if she had it would only have been for a few minutes at a time. She felt exhausted and drained and so desperately close to breaking down that she had no idea how to hold back. She stood quietly over the three of them, hands bunched to her mouth, as Ed held Max in his arms and the vet gently administered the barbiturates that took less than a minute to carry Max into his final sleep.

Jay turned away, unable to stop herself sobbing, while Ed carried his precious pet out to the vet's car. This was terrible, wretched, worse than she could ever have imagined.

When he came back, white-faced and dazed, he was holding Max's collar in his hand and she went to take him in her arms. He held her too, and she only wished she had words to comfort him, something to offer that could make this feel anything less than it was.

After a while, he said gruffly, 'I'll be back in a while,' and letting her go he picked up a key and went over to the studio.

As she heard his cry of grief she buried her face in her hands, unable to bear his pain. She'd had no idea before

471

today just how devastating it was to lose a pet, but it wasn't only Ed she was weeping for, it was also Max, because she loved him too and already she couldn't imagine the house without him. Or Ed walking into a room without the dog behind him, or wheeling him around the arboretum where he greeted the world in princely fashion.

She looked at his bed and felt its emptiness wrench at her heart, and there was his bowl full of food he hadn't been able to eat.

Understanding she needed to change things a little before Ed came back, she made herself roll up the bed and hugged it to her for a while, wondering where Max was now, if they were treating him gently and keeping his old body safe until it was time for the cremation.

Realizing she was losing it again, she tucked the bed into the back of a cupboard where it could stay until she knew what Ed wanted to do with it. She emptied the food and water bowls, washed them, but then had no idea what to do with them. There were other bowls and leads and beds all over the house, and his box-trolley in the garage. What were they going to do with them all?

'You don't have to make a decision today,' Toni said gently when she came over to lend some moral support. 'There's no rush. Ed will find a way to deal with it, he always does, you know that.'

CHAPTER FIFTY-SIX

They were two weeks away from the start of the trial, and Jay was becoming increasingly worried about how hard Ed had taken Max's death. She understood that the tangled knots of grief unravelling inside him also belonged to his other losses, his parents, his son, his wife, even his freedom for a while. There was so much for him to deal with and it wasn't as if she hadn't been expecting it all to catch up with him at some point, but it was starting to create a barrier between them that she couldn't seem to find a way past. He told her to stop worrying, that it hadn't changed anything for him, at least not in the way he felt about her. Apart from that he didn't want to talk about how he was coping. He simply wanted to be able to throw himself into the many projects he had underway and try to forget for a while.

Though she knew how helpful the distraction of a full schedule could be, she needed to focus him on what was going to happen in court.

They were at home now, and once again he'd failed to eat much of the evening meal she'd prepared. His attention seemed to be elsewhere until she waved a hand in front of his face and he attempted a smile.

'Sorry,' he said, 'miles away. Did you say something?'

'Only that you're due to meet with Ollie tomorrow at my office.'

He nodded. 'Yes, I hadn't forgotten. I just . . .'

As his head went down she covered his hand with hers and gave it a comforting squeeze. 'I know it won't be easy,' she said softly, 'but it'll all be over soon and then we can book that holiday.'

To her surprise he didn't look up; in fact he showed no sign of having heard her. 'Ed?' she whispered.

Long moments ticked by before he finally said, 'I'm sorry, Jay, I can't do this any more.'

Confused, she said, 'Can't do what? You know you have to go to court,' but there was a coldness curling from her instincts into her heart telling her that wasn't what he meant.

His eyes came to hers and were so dense and bleak that she was almost afraid for him to continue. 'I can't carry on pretending,' he said. 'I thought I could, but it just isn't possible.'

For one terrible moment she thought he was going to tell her he didn't love her, that he'd tried, given it everything he could, but after the trial their relationship would have to come to an end. She wouldn't be able to cope with that, she loved him too much, wouldn't be able to stop loving him no matter what he said.

What he said was, 'It was me, Jay. I did it.'

She felt herself stop breathing, as if it might somehow push back his words, maybe even give them a different meaning. And yet strangely, distantly, there seemed a terrible inevitability to them, as if they'd always been there, unspoken, unacknowledged even, simply waiting their time.

In case she hadn't understood, he said quietly. 'I killed her.'

She stayed sitting as she was, staring at him, unable to respond in spite of everything that was gathering inside her.

Time passed. There was only silence, no sound to the awful, shattering realization that she'd been lied to again – and again. Over and Over. Right from the beginning. Why hadn't she seen it? Why, even now, when she looked at him, could she only see the man she loved, not the one who'd deceived her? Who'd just admitted to killing his wife?

Had she known it, deep down, and refused to engage with it?

She didn't think so, but trapped in these terrible moments she hardly knew anything at all.

Her eyes moved to the fire, glowing red in the hearth, their reflections in the night black windows showed them in a ghostly, parallel world. Over there, in the darkness, they were who they'd always been, together, in love, untroubled by the world in here. At this table, in reality, they were . . . Who were they now? How were they going to deal with this? What could be done to turn everything around to make it into something else?

He spoke again, his voice seeming to come from somewhere very deep inside him. 'I found her, strapped to the bed,' he said, 'with a pillow over her face. I didn't know who'd tied her up or tried to suffocate her, I only knew she was . . . I knew she was alive when I took the pillow away. I felt for a pulse and it was . . . it was there.'

His hands tightened into fists and released again. 'I sat staring at her, waiting for her to wake up, to turn it into another terrible joke, and at the same time I was thinking of how much simpler it would be for her – and yes, for me – if whoever had left her like this had succeeded in ending it for her. I didn't think about him; I didn't even care who it was, at least not then. I just wanted it all to stop. It was all that kept going through my mind. Make it stop, make it stop. So I put the pillow back over her face and held it there until . . . Until I knew she wasn't breathing any more.'

Jay could only stare at him. All this time he'd been holding his guilt to himself, somehow living his life as if he were an innocent man. A man she'd believed in, defended, loved with all her heart.

'I'm sorry,' he croaked. 'I know I should have . . .'

'She must have fought back,' she heard herself say.

He shook his head. 'She didn't. I thought she would. I even thought, when I finally took the pillow away, that the pulse would still be there. That it would never go away and actually by then I didn't want it to go. I wanted it back, so I could think more clearly, get rid of all the madness that was clouding my mind, but it was already too late.' As his eyes went down a tear dropped onto his hand. 'It's also the truth,' he said, 'that I'd had enough. I didn't want to watch her carry on the way she was any more, being someone I couldn't love the way I once had, or help, or even feel safe with. Actually, maybe I could have, I don't know. All I can tell you is that it wasn't the men that got to me in the end, or the things she said about Lucas, it was what she did to Max.'

Jay stilled again, feeling as though she was losing a sense of what he was telling her. 'What did she do to Max?' she asked hoarsely.

476

He swallowed and pushed away another tear. 'The Friday before it happened she took him to the vet without me knowing and tried to have him put down.' He allowed no time for the shock of that to sink in, simply kept on talking. 'She wanted to kill him because she knew how much he meant to me – and she'd have succeeded if the vet hadn't rung me to check it was what I wanted.'

'Oh God,' Jay murmured. 'Oh God, oh God.'

'It's why,' he continued, 'Max wasn't here when I came home that night. I'd already taken him to Toni and John to keep him safe. I just didn't know what she might do next.' His hands tightened and loosened again as if he were powering himself to go on. 'I went through that weekend pretending everything was normal, the way I always did, and maybe I'd have ended up getting over it, managed to put it down to her disturbances, who knows? But then I came home on that Monday evening and when I found her the way she was something inside me . . .' He took a gulp of air and pressed a hand to his head. 'It was only later, when I came downstairs to call the police that I realized whoever had left her like that could as easily be blamed for killing her as I could. They quite possibly even thought she was dead when they left. So I waited, tried to think what to do. I could see that if I called and confessed to what had happened no one would ever know, or care, who'd been with her before I came home, that someone else had tried to kill her. They'd have a confession and for them it would all be over.

'I sat on the stairs for most of the night, or I paced this room, driving myself crazy with doubt and guilt and rage. I wanted to know who'd been here, who'd done that to her. I couldn't bear the thought of him getting away with it, of him watching from out there somewhere as I was arrested and charged, probably believing he'd done it but it was OK to watch me pay.

'So that's why I didn't admit to it; why I lied to you and everyone else, I needed to know who'd been here that night, who'd tried to kill her. When I thought it was Guy . . . I couldn't let him go to prison in my place, I'd never have done that, but then it wasn't him . . .' His voice faltered, but he pushed himself on. 'I can't let Maguire go to prison for something I know he didn't do.'

Jay could feel the terrible agonizing inside him, could see everything he'd described of that night almost as if she'd been there, watching him tearing himself to pieces as he tried to decide what to do. She thought about the times they'd talked in custody suites and prison interview rooms when he'd kept the truth from her, not wanting her to believe he was a killer. But even if he was, it wasn't all that defined him. There was so much more to him, he had so many qualities that were good and honourable and that mattered so much to her that she couldn't bear to lose any part of him in spite of what she now knew.

And yet deep down she was furious, enraged, although more with herself than with him. How was it possible for her to carry on loving someone who'd lied the way he had? To still want him with all her heart? She had no answers, only knew that she'd give anything in the world for him never to have told her, to have carried on protecting them both from what it was going to mean. For one insane moment she even wondered if they could keep it between them, continue as they always had, in love, happy, and with so much to look forward to once the trial was over.

As if reading her thoughts, he said, 'Maguire's not a bad man, he doesn't deserve to pay for something he didn't do, even if it was his intention.'

She didn't argue, because she couldn't.

'Before I knew it was him,' he said, 'it was just an anonymous person, someone who might never be found, and it was possible I wouldn't be blamed provided everyone could be convinced that someone else had been there that night. There would be enough doubt . . .' His eyes closed as a frown deepened between them. 'Hearing myself speak it aloud,' he said, 'it sounds so . . . cold, so detached from what I was really feeling, because inside I was horrified by what I'd done. It felt like a nightmare, something totally unreal and separate from me. Even now it's still hard to make myself believe any of it happened the way it did. But it did, and I've punished Maguire for long enough. He shouldn't have left her like that, he shouldn't have been with her at all. He might have been praying for her but he obviously took advantage of her too.'

Jay's mouth was dry; her heart was beating so hard it was painful, yet in some distant, dreamlike sort of way, she knew she wasn't engaging properly with her feelings. The sense of betrayal and horror was real, she knew that, and would probably get a whole lot worse in the days and weeks to come, but all that mattered in this moment was that she should listen as he talked and try not to interrupt.

'What I did,' he said quietly, 'is unforgivable. She didn't deserve to die like that . . . What am I saying, she didn't deserve to die at all. I should have ended our marriage the proper way, with separation and divorce, but I didn't know what would happen to her if I did. She had no one else, nowhere to go. She was broken and defenceless with no family to care for her, or real friends who might take her in. I was all she had and I think, I *know*, she resented me for that. Nothing I did could make things right for her, and God knows I tried. I wanted us to find a way of being as close as we'd been before Lucas, more than anything I wanted us to try for another child, but even she admitted she wasn't in a fit state to take on motherhood again. And as for me being a father, she scorned the very idea . . . And then she'd cry and beg me to forgive her for the awful things she said. It was all so crazy and mixed up and unpredictable. I never knew how she was going to react to anything, what she might do next to try and punish me for our loss. When she took Max to the vet . . . She'd threatened it before, but I never thought she'd do it. I felt sick when I found out, and . . . I don't know what else I felt, apart from relieved the vet had called me. She wouldn't apologize when I confronted her, just told me he was old and it wasn't healthy the way I loved him more than I'd loved my own son.' His voice was faltering, and his breath was laboured as the terrible memories seemed to fracture him inside.

'None of this excuses what I did,' he said, 'nothing can ever do that.'

Jay still didn't know what to say, how to comfort him, how to help him at all.

'The only good to come out of it,' he said hoarsely, 'is this time I've had with you. I know you probably don't want to hear that, and maybe it isn't the right thing to say, but it's the truth. I didn't know it was going to happen the way it did between us, how could I, but it did and it's meant more to me than I can ever put into words. I'm not sure exactly when I fell in love with you, but fall I did, and hard. I tried to hide it when I was still in prison, and then I didn't have to any more.

'You could say I stole this time. I didn't deserve it, but I can't regret it, because I'll never be able to regret loving you, only how much I'm hurting you now.'

She started to speak, but her voice just wasn't there.

'I'm sorry,' he said raggedly. 'I know that doesn't even begin to fix it. Nothing will. Nothing ever can, but I am sorry.'

Jay could barely see, her eyes were so hot with tears, but he was right, nothing could fix it. It simply wasn't possible, and yet even as she looked at him, heard him, understood everything he was saying – that he'd killed his wife and lied to her – she continued to see the man she loved, the man she couldn't bear to let go.

'I know you'll have some calls to make now,' he said, 'and I guess I should start shutting up the house.'

'Oh God,' she sobbed, and pushing away from the table she turned her back, her face buried in her hands. She needed some air, some way of making herself accept this so she could find the courage to take the next steps.

He came to her and clenching her fists she banged them into him, hating him and loving him, needing him to make this right while knowing he never could. He didn't try to defend himself, simply took the blows, letting her vent her rage and frustration until finally she was in his arms, and clinging to him so hard it was as if she could crush the truth away.

If only it were possible, she'd give almost anything for

it to be, but now it had found its way into words it would always be there.

Minutes ticked by and still neither of them let go. It felt strange and beautiful and even frightening as all the forces that had drawn them together in the early days, fate, circumstance, chemistry, love, seemed to exert their combined influence to try to keep them together now.

But even the alchemy of such power couldn't circumvent the law.

'I'm sorry,' he whispered over and over. 'I wish to God it hadn't happened this way, that we could have met another way. I'll never forgive myself for the pain I'm causing you, for the lies and deception . . .'

'That might have worked,' she broke in wretchedly, 'if I hadn't taken on the investigation. We could probably have got you off if it had gone to trial.'

'But you wouldn't have wanted to be with me if you'd known the truth.'

She shook her head as she gazed deeply into his eyes. 'You're wrong,' she told him, 'I would have, and I still do.' She was shocked by the truth of that, the force of feeling that made it the truth, and right now she only wanted to protect it, hold it between them as if it was everything they'd ever need to keep them together.

His smile was the saddest she'd ever seen as he cupped her face in his hands. 'We both know what you have to do now,' he whispered.

She wanted to protest, to tell him that they would find a way through this, but in her heart she knew they couldn't.

'You can drive me to the police station, if you will,' he said, 'but after that, we need to let each other go. I'll find another lawyer . . .'

'No!'

'Yes,' he said firmly. 'Maybe Ash from your office. This is going to be hard enough on you without us putting you through any more.'

'Ed, I have to be there for you.'

'No, listen to me. You're not thinking straight at the moment, but I've been thinking about nothing else for weeks. When the dust settles, and it will eventually, you'll probably come to hate me . . .'

'That is never going to happen.'

'For your sake, I hope it does. It'll be easier than continuing to love me after what I've done to you. And I'm going to prison, we both know that, probably for quite a long time. So after tonight, it must be over between us.'

'No! I can't – I can't,' she sobbed. 'Ed. Please . . .'

He drew her back into his arms and because there was no more they could do they cried together. They had no idea what more to say that would make this any easier, would even make them start doing what needed to be done. She understood that time, circumstance, other people's condemnation and prejudice would find a way to warp and influence her days without him. Maybe anger and resentment would sully the beauty of what they'd known, but she wasn't going to let it happen now.

Finally, gently easing himself from her embrace, he went to pick up her phone and handed it to her. 'Call Ash,' he said, 'and ask him to meet us at Keynsham Police Station.'

An hour and a half later, the house was locked up and most of her belongings were in the car. She had to take them now for she wasn't sure she'd find the heart to come back again. She didn't want to be here without him; she didn't want him to go.

The wrenching sense of loss as they drove away from Clover Hill was as bad as anything else she'd felt that night. Maybe it was worse. Everything seemed to be getting worse.

She tried to navigate the road but was distracted by crazy thoughts of turning in the opposite direction, of fleeing to France, or Ireland, anywhere they could start a new life and stay together.

Somehow she kept going, knowing she had to, that he wouldn't allow her to do otherwise. She wondered how he was able to stay so strong, so determined, while inside he must be falling apart. He just wouldn't show it to her. How good he was at hiding the truth of his feelings, the truth of his guilt, so good that even now she hardly knew what she was and wasn't believing.

Their hands were linked on the gear stick as he talked to Ash on the mobile, but she could hardly take in what he was saying. She realized, on some other level, that Ash would almost certainly call Perry and Perry would call Tom, but as fleetingly as the thought came it went again. None of it mattered now, all that did was him.

As they reached the end of the ring road he was finishing his call to Ash, but instead of ringing off he held out the phone and said, 'He wants to speak to you.'

She shook her head. 'No. Not now. Just tell me, is he already at the police station?'

'Yes, he is. He says Ken Bright is too.'

Her heart somersaulted. How was Bright going to handle this? What was he already thinking? 'What about

Hamble?' she asked, sickened by the thought of how triumphant the detective sergeant must be feeling to know that she'd been right all along. She wouldn't go easy on Blake, would see no reason to when he'd killed his wife and lied to them all.

'He didn't mention her,' he answered.

There was so much to be got through, not only the nightmare of parting, and God knew the dread of it was intensifying by the second, but for him there was the horror of being incarcerated again.

Later, for her, there would be shame and humiliation, maybe pity, and quite possibly the loss of her reputation.

Right now she couldn't imagine anything worse than what they were facing in the next few minutes.

She saw Ash and Ken Bright in front of the main doors as she pulled up in the street outside the custody centre. Turning to Blake she said, 'It isn't over for us. I want you to know that. I'll come to see you . . .'

'No,' he said gently. 'Please don't . . .'

'Ed, I have to. I can't just . . .'

'Yes you can, and you will. It'll be easier in the long run, I promise,' and pulling her to him he pressed his lips hard to her forehead. 'I'm sorry,' he whispered, 'sorrier than you'll ever know.'

She touched her fingers to his mouth, and tried to kiss him but he wouldn't let her.

The night was dark and bitterly cold, an icy drizzle was in the air, but she didn't feel it as they walked with their arms linked towards the dazzling lights of the station; to where Ash and Ken Bright were watching them approach. She didn't allow herself to imagine what they were thinking, how they must view her or Blake now. It

485

was of no importance tonight. All that was for another day.

Turning before they reached them, Blake pulled her into his arms, held her close, hard, and after pressing a last kiss to her hair he let go and walked on without her.

As she watched him disappear through the sliding doors she clasped her hands to her mouth, unable to stifle the desperate sobs. This was all wrong, horribly wrong, so how could it be right?

She tried to move, but couldn't, just continued to stand there, rain merging with her tears, as if he might, by some miracle come out again.

The doors remained closed. No one came or went, the night was still, deserted, until a voice behind her said, 'Jay?'

She didn't look round, she couldn't, simply stood stiffly where she was as Tom put an arm around her.

'Come on,' he said gently, and keeping her close he turned her away.

As they reached his car, she looked at her own.

'Perry's here,' he said. 'He'll drive it back.'

Suddenly it felt worse than ever. She wanted to scream and run, rant against the monstrous fates that had brought them to this. If only it was possible to break down doors, push away walls, forget the law . . .

She continued to walk, because she had to.

How could it be fair that she had people who cared for her, were here for her, tonight of all nights, when he had no one? Tom had come, he was taking her home and whatever had gone before, or whatever was in the future, she knew he would try to help her go on with her life.

Who was going to be there for Ed?

I Have Something to Tell You

She waited until they were in the car and driving away before taking out her phone to make the only call she'd be able to manage tonight. 'Hello,' she said, when Antonia answered, 'it's Jay. I have something to tell you.'

ACKNOWLEDGEMENTS

The world's biggest thank you to Nick Kelcey, defence lawyer, who oversaw each stage of this book, correcting my misunderstandings and preconceptions, and offering invaluable insights into procedure and process. It really would not have been possible to do it without so much expert guidance and Nick's swift responses kept things moving in a way that is rare when so much research is involved. If there are any errors then they are all mine.

Another enormous thank you to Claire Morse BSc. Hons, Senior Forensic Scientist for advising on the case and for sharing her expert knowledge of evidential process and diagnosis. Once again, if something isn't clear or is incorrect, it will be totally down to me.

Thank you to Ian Kelcey and Gill Hall who shared the idea for this book that allowed me to produce a fictionalized account of a true story. Much has been changed to protect real identities. Also I want to thank Linda Tiley for sharing the office routine of a legal firm with me.

Last but by no means least, a huge thank you to my wonderful husband, James Garrett, for walking me around the historic parts of Bristol and helping me to bring it to life within the book.

Read on for a sneak peek at
Susan's next captivating novel

Who's Lying Now?

Coming Spring 2022 . . .

MONDAY 18TH JANUARY 2021

'Cara, we have a bit of a mystery on our hands here that I'd like you to take a look at.'

Investigator Cara Jakes, still officially a trainee, composed her naturally sunny features into an expression of interest and sat a little straighter in her chair. It was at the bottom end of the huge conference table they were using for this meeting, in a room adjacent to the Chief Superintendent's, someone she'd never spoken to and who was, thankfully, nowhere to be seen.

Cara wasn't only eager to find out more of what this was about, she was proud to be included in whatever the mystery might be. At just twenty-four, she knew she was lucky to have this job. The competition had been fierce, but for some fabulous reason she'd been chosen to work alongside Kesterley's CID detectives, a backup when they required extra assistance with their cases. From day one she'd been determined to excel in every way possible and this, if she was reading it correctly, could be her big chance, for it seemed Detective Sergeant Natalie Rundle was coming to her first with an issue.

'A woman has disappeared,' DS Rundle continued, her smooth brow puckering in a frown, while her piercing black eyes moved between Cara and the notes in her hand. She was a frightening woman in some ways, fierce, demanding, critical – and quite beautiful in others. Cara could think of nothing she'd rather do more than impress her.

There was a third woman in the room seated opposite Cara and making up the loose, socially distanced triangle they'd formed at this end of the table. Exactly what she was doing here Cara had yet to learn. She hadn't even been introduced yet, however Cara knew very well who she was. Her name was Andee Lawrence and she'd once been a detective here in Kesterley-on-Sea. She was also a favourite of DCI Gould's; a good friend of DS Rundle's, and was much beloved by the community at large. Added to all that, she was even more strikingly lovely in person than she was on the news or in the papers. Tall, slender, a gorgeous tumble of shoulder-length curly hair, stunning aquamarine eyes and the kind of poise that Cara, at five two, could only dream about.

DS Rundle was speaking again. 'The woman's name is Jeannie Symonds. She's fifty-one, married, no children, high-powered career, and she usually lives in London. After the first lockdown ended she decided to base herself here, at Westleigh Heights, where she has a second home. As you're local you might know the place – Howarth Hall; it's the large house up on the western headland that you can see from the bay.'

Oh, Cara knew it all right, or at least she'd seen it a thousand times from down on Westleigh beach where she used to go foraging as a kid with her sister and dad. Look up and there was this amazing mansion at the top of the cliffs, all windows and towers that was a bit of a fairy tale castle in her opinion, with acres of woodland behind it and a dreamy sort of look when the light was right. She'd never been there, as far as she knew it wasn't open to the public, but she'd driven past the gates plenty of times on the way to the moor. 'This is Andee Lawrence,' DS Rundle continued. 'She's going to fill you in on what she knows and why she's decided to bring the matter to us.'

Dazzled by Andee's smile, Cara produced one of her own with dimples and said, 'Would it be all right to take notes?'

'Of course,' Andee replied.

'And I'll give you what I have when we're done,' the DS added.

Doing her best to remain calm in the face of so much trust, Cara created a new document on her laptop and made ready to type. First up came basic background info on Jeannie and her husband Guy, aged forty-five. Apparently he was a neurosurgeon working out of St George's hospital in London, and she was a senior executive at a major publishing house based in South Kensington. They'd been married for seven years and their main home was in Wimbledon, which was where they'd stayed for the first lockdown. After that, Jeannie had moved to the dream pad on Westleigh Heights while he'd carried on working in London, but he always joined her at weekends.

'On Friday January the eighth,' Andee said, reading from her own laptop, 'Guy Symonds got home to the Hall at around five o'clock to find no sign of Jeannie. He tried ringing her, but her phone was either turned off or had run out of battery. He then discovered that her car had gone, which he found concerning for two reasons, the first because she hadn't left a note to say where she was going or when she'd be back; the second because apparently she takes the lockdown rules quite seriously. So she wouldn't go anywhere unless it was essential.'

Cara was typing furiously, picturing it all in her mind as best she could, and not asking any questions yet as she felt sure most of the answers were coming.

'Over the weekend, Guy contacted everyone he could think of who might know where Jeannie was: her colleagues, friends, family, the neighbours both in London as well as those up around Westleigh Heights. By then he'd discovered that her handbag and wallet had gone, but her passport was still in her desk at the Hall. Her computer is also still there, along with her work files and calendar of upcoming video meetings. Apparently she hasn't made one of them since early in the morning of January the sixth when she spoke with her sales team about issues that had come up in Ireland due to Brexit. There were no meetings scheduled for the rest of that day, but she spoke to her assistant, Maurice Bissett, around one o'clock and we're pretty certain the call was made from the Hall, because she was seen by her landscaper at around that time. Apparently she was in her study and when she waved out to him he could see she was on the phone, and he had no reason to think she was on the point of leaving to go anywhere, nor did she seem in any way agitated.'

How close was he to the window to know that? Cara wondered.

Andee said, 'No one has seen her since then, or not that Guy, or Jeannie's assistant, Maurice Bisset, have been able to find.'

496

Cara glanced at DS Rundle, wanting to be sure it was OK to ask a question. Receiving a nod, she said, 'So she could have left any time between one o'clock-ish on January sixth and five pm on January eighth?'

'As things currently stand, that's correct,' Andee confirmed.

Cara wrinkled her nose. 'It's January eighteenth now,' she pointed out, not adding, *so what's taken so long*, in case it sounded rude.

Apparently picking up on the unasked question, Andee said, 'Guy contacted the police on January the eleventh, but he was told there was nothing anyone could do when there were no reports of an accident or any signs of foul play. Jeannie is an adult with no physical or mental health problems. If she chooses to absent herself from the family home, that's her business and no one else's.'

Seeing the point, Cara said, 'Has she ever gone off without telling anyone before?'

'Good question,' DS Rundle commented approvingly.

'Indeed,' Andee agreed, 'and actually, yes she has, but apparently she's usually back within a few days.'

'Do you know where she goes?'

'Kind of, but I'll let Guy tell you about it.' She checked the time on her phone, 'He should be here any minute.'

Cara's heart gave a flip of nervous excitement.

'I have a list of people he's already spoken to,' Andee told her, 'locally and elsewhere. I'll email it as soon as we've finished here along with all the notes I've made.'

'Thank you,' Cara responded, feeling ludicrously honoured to be included in something of Andee Lawrence's. 'Do you mind if I ask whether or not you are a friend of the Symonds's?'

Andee smiled. 'I've never met Jeannie, and the first time I came across Guy was when Fliss from the Seafront Café called me to ask if I could help with the search.'

'And when was that?' Cara asked.

'On January the twelfth, the day after the police had told him there was nothing they could do. He wasn't ready to let it go, so he asked Fliss if she'd mind putting up a photograph of Jeannie in the café in case anyone had seen her. Fliss did so and then she rang me.'

Neat move, Cara was thinking. She'd want Andee onside too if any of her loved ones did a 404.

'I met with him that same day,' Andee continued, 'and since then I've been following up on all the calls he's made to try and find his wife. In every case, I've received the same response he did. No one knows where she is, she's never mentioned anything about leaving her husband or her job, quite the reverse in fact. She seems perfectly wedded to both. So no one has stood out for me as being someone who needs further questioning, but I know Natalie here will tell you that you should satisfy yourself of that and I would urge the same.'

Cara was already working out in her mind how she was going to introduce herself when she made the calls. *Hello, I'm Cara Jakes of Kesterly CID* seemed to do it, at least it made her sound like a detective even if she officially wasn't.

Andee was speaking again. 'I've also been pulling together a general picture of what Jeannie is like as a woman, a wife, a boss and I would say family member if I'd managed to speak to her brother. He lives in New Zealand and according to Guy they're not close.'

'No other family?'

Andee shook her head. 'But feel free to double-check that with Guy when you talk to him.'

DS Rundle said, 'Did you get the impression she had enemies or business rivals with a grudge, someone from the past who might want to cause her harm?'

Andee looked thoughtful as she said, 'I think publishing can be a bit of a cut-throat business at times, and at her level she'd be dealing with some super-charged egos, and quite probably had one herself. So I think it's likely she's upset or offended any number of people at one point or another. Nothing specific was mentioned, but several colleagues referred to her as having a fiery temper – not someone you wanted to be on the wrong side of. According to one of her senior editors, her moods can change at lightning speed, and sometimes she has a way of staring at people that comes over as quite intimidating.'

'Sounds like me,' DS Rundle quipped.

Cara dutifully laughed, while thinking the DS wasn't wrong there.

'So no concrete reason to think any harm has come to her,' the DS said, 'apart from how long she's been gone?'

'Which you have to admit is concerning,' Andee said. 'I understand why you're reluctant to launch an official investigation when there's no suggestion of a crime being committed, but I'd really appreciate some help in tracking her down.'

'And that's where you come in, Cara,' DS Rundle announced grandly. 'You'll have all our resources at your disposal, which is what Andee needs to further the search, so you'll work closely with her from hereon. I can't think of anyone better for you to learn from.'

Thinking exactly the same, Cara felt warmth in her

cheeks as Andee smiled in her direction. It didn't appear she minded having Cara on board; if anything, she seemed quite pleased.

DS Rundle was saying, '. . . so you'll start by duplicating much of what Andee's already done, speaking to all the main players to see if you get the same answers she did. You'd be amazed how many little nuggets of vital information manage to find their way to the light the second and third time of asking. And how many people that were unknown, or seemed unimportant before can suddenly take centre stage when all the obfuscation and lies start to fall apart. There could be a lot of ground to cover, Andee will guide you, and you know where to find me if anything interesting turns up, such as the woman herself.'

Cara felt terrible for hoping that didn't happen, it hardly made her a good citizen to wish someone dead, which, for all anyone knew, was where this was heading. It was such a great opportunity for her as a newbie investigator; it would be a disaster if it got solved before she even got started.

'Is there anything else you'd like to ask before we go on?' Andee prompted gently.

There was, so Cara said, 'The landscaper who saw her on the phone on January sixth. I guess you've spoken to him yourself?'

'I have. His name's Neil Roberts and I know he'll be more than happy to talk to you when you call.'

'Do you know how close he was to the window when he saw her?'

Andee's eyebrows rose. 'It'll be a good question to ask when you speak to him.'

Pleased by the response, Cara said, 'Is there anyone else who works at the Hall?'

'Yes, they have a regular housekeeper, Magda Kaminska, but she was self-isolating around the time Jeannie disappeared so she hasn't been able to throw much light on things. You'll find her number, and Neil's in my notes.' She checked her phone as it pinged and broke into a smile.

'Great! Fliss from the café is here,' she declared. 'I asked her to bring coffee and pastries if she could and I don't know about you, but I say better late than never.'

'Absolutely,' DS Rundle agreed. 'I was about to leave you to it, but I'm not passing up on Fliss's elevenses.'

'Shall I go and get her?' Cara offered, her mouth already watering at the prospect of an almond croissant.

'Someone's bringing her,' Andee replied. 'And Guy should be here by now. I'll quickly text to make sure he hasn't been held up.'

'Where's he coming from?' DS Rundle asked.

'London. He still has surgeries, consultations. . .'

'But it's Monday. Has he been working all weekend?'

'I don't know if he's been at the hospital, but he has been trying to find Jeannie. She might have been at Howarth Hall on January the sixth, but she could be anywhere by now.'

They all looked up as the door banged open and Fliss, carrying an enormous tray of flasks, covered dishes and cardboard mugs, eased her way in helped by a uniformed PC.

Cara immediately lit up inside, not only because she could happily scoff the lot, but because Fliss always had that sort of effect on people, especially when her face had a great big smile on the front of it. She was just lovely, always chatty and kind and interested in anything anyone had to say. Cara's mum always said that if she could be anyone it would be Fliss, and not just because she was so pretty and slim and friendly, but because she had the sweetest soul. On the other hand, Cara's crabby old nan used to say, "don't be deceived, everyone has a dark side, even that Fliss and I know what I'm talking about". Well, crabby-nan would know all about dark sides given it was where she'd spent most of her sorry little life. Even her own son, Cara's dad, used to say that about her.

'Sorry I'm late,' Fliss declared, hurrying to the table before her arms gave out. 'It's been hectic this morning, people queuing right along the Promenade, all thanks to the sun showing its face for half an hour.'

Knowing that she could only allow one customer at a time into her brand-new-American-diner-style café – the alterations had happened just prior to the first lockdown and then she'd been unable to open up – Cara wanted to ask how things really were for her, but didn't quite have the nerve. It wasn't as if she actually knew Fliss, she just felt as though she did, which was probably the same for everyone in town.

'Cara, how do you take your coffee?' Fliss asked, getting ready to pour, while massaging the bottom of her back. Cara was so thrilled to realise Fliss knew her name that she almost said, *however you take yours*. Luckily she said, 'White, no sugar, thanks.'

'Help yourself to something wicked,' Fliss encouraged, as she passed the coffee over. 'That's right, Natalie, don't hold back. I'm not taking them home with me.'

Andee was pouring her own coffee. 'Did you happen

to see Guy outside?' she asked, taking a moment to select a pastry.

'Yes, he was just parking up,' Fliss replied. To Natalie she said, 'I'm so glad you've decided to give Andee some help with this. It's been a terrible couple of weeks for Guy '

'It's not an official search,' Natalie warned, 'and it won't be unless I'm convinced some harm has come to her. As yet, no one's been able to say that it has. So for now, you have my best investigator on it who will be reporting to Andee and obviously to me.'

Cara blushed to the roots of her hair as Fliss turned to her and said, 'Ever since I heard you'd got the job here I've been waiting for you to come into the café so I could give you a cupcake and coffee to say well done. Your mum must be thrilled. You will say hi to her when you get home, won't you?'

'Oh, of course and she says hi too. Or she will when I tell her, you know my mum, she's always got something to say, and now I'll stop or I'll just go on embarrassing myself, but first this coffee is the best I've ever had!'

As everyone laughed, the door opened again and Cara nearly choked on her almond croissant as the same PC showed in a tall, dark-haired bloke who had to be Guy Symonds, but who looked, to her mind, more like a rock-star than a surgeon. Not that she knew any surgeons – she just hadn't imagined them to look anything like Zayn Malik, only older. Her mum would be having hot flushes for a week if she ever saw him; she might even put off the menopause altogether.

'Guy, I'm glad you made it,' Andee said warmly, keeping her distance, because everyone had to. Fliss did a Namaste and Cara couldn't help noticing the way he kept his eyes on her a moment longer than seemed necessary. He liked her, Cara decided, and from the way Fliss reacted she reckoned the feeling was mutual. Well, who wouldn't like Fliss? And who wouldn't like him, too?

'This is Natalie Rundle,' Andee said, directing him to the DS, 'and this is Cara Jakes whom I've already told you about.'

'I'm grateful to you for giving this some time,' he said. 'To be honest, I'm not sure what else to do. I've tried everything and everyone I can think of.'

'Cara will organise a check on the phone and credit cards,' the DS assured him, 'and there are ways of tracking the car.'

'Would you like some coffee?' Fliss offered.

'I'd love some, thanks,' he said, and Cara picked up on the warmth between them again. She knew Fliss wasn't married – in fact come to think of it she'd never seen her with a bloke – however, Guy Symonds was definitely not single, unless he was and didn't know it yet. Realising her brain was shooting off in too many directions at once, she deliberately shut it down and watched him take the chair the DS was pointing him to – distant, but not so far along the table that he'd have to shout to be heard.

'I should leave you to it,' Fliss said, checking the time. 'I'll come back later for the tray.'

Guy Symonds rose to his feet. 'Thanks for coming,' he said. 'Thanks for everything.'

'We'll find her,' Fliss assured him softly, and after saluting everyone in a merry way, she left the room.

'Jeannie and I don't know many people around here,' he said as he sat down again, 'so I'm not sure what I'd have done without Fliss, and now Andee.'

'And now Cara,' Rundle added, seeming to like saying it. 'I'm sorry the police weren't able to help when you came to us before, but. . .'

'It's OK, I understand. No crime has been committed, as far as we know, and she's definitely of sound mind. So I'm guessing you think she was having an affair and has decided to run off with whoever it is?'

Since it was exactly what she was thinking, Cara was keen to know the answer.

'If she was involved with anyone else,' he said, 'I knew nothing about it, and presuming her friends and colleagues are being truthful nor did they. Actually, if anyone knows her secrets it would be Maurice, her assistant, but he swears there wasn't anyone and right now I'm inclined to believe him.'

DS Rundle nodded slowly as she took this in. 'So do you have any theories at all?' she prompted.

'I wish I did. I'm completely at a loss. . .'

'Did you argue before she disappeared? You say you last spoke to her on . . .'

'January the fifth,' Cara provided.

'Was anything said then that might have prompted her to leave?'

'Nothing at all. We didn't argue, there was no disagreement about anything. Actually, we didn't speak for long. I'd just finished a Gamma Knife procedure and I wanted to discuss it with my team, so I said I'd call again later.'

Gamma Knife. What the heck was that? Sounded dangerous, whatever.

'And did you?' Rundle prompted.

'Yes, but she texted to say she was tied up in a meeting

with her American colleagues that was likely to drag on, so she'd call me back the next day.'

'But she didn't?'

'No. And before you ask, yes I checked to find out if the meeting was real and it was. It ended at ten forty-five in the evening, UK time, and there were eight of them on screen.'

Rundle nodded thoughtfully. 'It's a mystery indeed,' she sighed.

'Excuse me,' Guy Symonds said as his mobile rang. 'It's my registrar with some information I need for a patient.' As he clicked on he drew a notebook out of an inside pocket and began to jot down whatever he was being told. At the end he said, 'Thanks for this, Ed. Yes, it will be a craniotomy, but I'm in a meeting right now. I'll call him as soon as I'm free.'

As he rang off, he apologized and put his phone and notebook on the table in front of him.

'The world keeps turning,' DS Rundle commented by way of understanding and, turning to Cara, said, 'It might be a good idea for you to review everything Andee's sending your way before you and Mr Symonds have a chat. Does that work for you?' she asked Symonds.

'I'm happy to play it any way that works for you,' he assured her.

'OK, is there anything you'd like to ask now, Cara, before we break this up?'

Swallowing, Cara said, 'Yes, just a couple of things and I expect Andee's already covered them, but first of all, can you tell if any of her clothes are missing?'

Symonds frowned as he shook his head. 'She has so many I wouldn't really know, but I can tell you that no suitcases or holdalls have gone from the Hall.'

'Which isn't to say she didn't order something online that you knew nothing about,' Andee put in.

Symonds inclined his head in agreement.

Cara asked, 'Have you contacted her doctor?' From the corner of her eye she saw that Andee was impressed.

'Yes, I have,' he replied. 'She hasn't seen him for over a year, so no undisclosed health issues that we know of.'

Setting aside the theory for now, Cara said, 'My last question is about the landscaper. I know you and Andee have talked to him, so did you ask how close he was to the window that day, if he can say if she didn't seem upset or agitated.'

Appearing puzzled, Symonds said, 'No, I didn't ask that.'

Andee was shaking her head, letting it be known that she hadn't either.

'Does it make a difference how close he was?' Symonds asked. 'I think it was just a passing observation of Neil's, that he saw her and nothing seemed out of the ordinary.'

Not sure if it did make a difference, Cara said, 'Did he say if he noticed anyone else at the Hall that day? Was there another car, maybe, that he hadn't seen before?'

'Actually, I asked that,' Andee told her, 'and apparently he was only there himself for about half an hour but he was pretty certain there were no strange vehicles, and he didn't spot anyone else coming or going in that time.'

'So what was he doing there?' Cara asked.

Symonds said, 'He was dropping off some vegetable plants and while he was there he replaced a couple of fleeces that had been torn off by the wind.'

'Fleeces?' Rundle queried.

'It's what he wraps around the large plant pots to help protect the roots from the frost.'

Nodding, she turned to Cara, 'Is that it for now?' she asked.

'I think so, but it shouldn't take me long to go through Andee's notes. Can we speak again later today?'

'Of course,' he replied and he might have smiled, but she didn't know for sure. 'I have quite a lot of administrative work to catch up on,' he said, 'so I'll go to Howarth Hall. Let me know when you're ready and perhaps we could connect by video link?'

'That sounds like a good idea.' Rundle started getting to her feet. 'Thanks for coming in, Mr Symonds, it helps a lot to meet someone in person before enquiries get underway. And, of course, if you hear anything at all, you'll get in touch with us right away?'

'Of course,' he confirmed. He was on his feet too and checking his phone as it rang again. 'I'm sorry,' he said, 'It's another call I have to take. As you said, the world keeps turning, even if you wish it wouldn't.'